Secret Diary of a
Demented Housewife

Secret Diary of a Demented Housewife

NIAMH GREENE

PENGUIN
IRELAND

PENGUIN IRELAND

Published by the Penguin Group
Penguin Books Ltd, 80 Strand, London WC2R ORL, England
Penguin Group (USA) Inc., 375 Hudson Street, New York, New York 10014, USA
Penguin Group (Canada), 90 Eglinton Avenue East, Suite 700, Toronto, Ontario, Canada M4P 2Y3
(a division of Pearson Penguin Canada Inc.)
Penguin Ireland, 25 St Stephen's Green, Dublin 2, Ireland
(a division of Penguin Books Ltd)
Penguin Group (Australia), 250 Camberwell Road, Camberwell, Victoria 3124, Australia
(a division of Pearson Australia Group Pty Ltd)
Penguin Books India Pvt Ltd, 11 Community Centre, Panchsheel Park, New Delhi – 110 017, India
Penguin Group (NZ), 67 Apollo Drive, Rosedale, North Shore 0632, New Zealand
(a division of Pearson New Zealand Ltd)
Penguin Books (South Africa) (Pty) Ltd, 24 Sturdee Avenue, Rosebank, Johannesburg 2196, South Africa

Penguin Books Ltd, Registered Offices: 80 Strand, London WC2R ORL, England

www.penguin.com

First published 2007

2

Set in 13.5/16 pt Monotype Garamond
Typeset by Rowland Phototypesetting Ltd, Bury St Edmunds, Suffolk
Printed in Great Britain by Clays Ltd, St Ives plc

A CIP catalogue record for this book is available from the British Library

HARDBACK ISBN: 978-1-844-88135-2
TRADE PAPERBACK ISBN: 978-1-844-88144-4

www.greenpenguin.co.uk

5 September

Have decided that summer is seriously overrated (unless you own a top-notch villa in the South of France and have a Swedish au pair on red alert 24/7).

After eight weeks, two days and three hours alone with Katie and Jack, I am practically a shadow of my former self. Well, not a shadow of my former self exactly. In cruel twist of cosmic irony, have actually put on six pounds due to excessive strawberry Cornetto consumption, but am definitely suffering from that serious celebrity affliction – mental exhaustion. In fact, feel very strongly that I may need to check myself into the Priory at any minute.

Luckily, Katie goes back to playschool (and to bona-fide child-care professionals who actually know what they are doing) tomorrow. I will now have lots of vital bonding time alone with Jack (crucial for second children so that they don't grow up to be axe-wielding mass murderers who slay all their co-workers in one fell swoop). Will also have lots of free time to pursue fulfilling hobbies, like Pilates (how hard can it be to move so slowly?) or knitting (hot new celebrity pastime).

Vow to resist temptation to devour *Heat* in one sitting, even if I am dying to read all about Britney and Kevin.

Also vow to spend endless carefree hours (well, at least an hour and a half while Jack is napping) doing quality, life-affirming things to reclaim my spirit *à la* Oprah Winfrey. Will not resort to dawdling round shops in the Centre to fill in the time, like last year.

<u>List of Things to Do to Reclaim Spirit and Find True Inner Self</u>

• Resist temptation to lounge in new Starbucks in the Centre, drinking caramel lattes and eating muffins. Engage in productive, soul-enhancing activity instead. (Productive, soul-enhancing activity To Be Advised.)

• Resist temptation to trail round shops, buying unsuitable clothes I cannot afford. Engage in productive, soul-enhancing activity instead. (See above.)

• Ditto shoe shopping.

• Start reading quality literary fiction recommended in *Sunday Times*, instead of *Heat*, to improve intellect.

• Read Trinny and Susannah's *What Not to Wear* to focus on positive body image. Try not to be scared by pictures of them glaring out of pages at well-washed trackie bottoms and greasy hair.

• Buy Dr. Phil's *Relationship Rescue* to reconnect with Joe on a spiritual and sexual level. (Absolutely crucial to recapture romance ASAP – Joe has been picking his nose in front of me quite a lot lately. Who knows what lies ahead?)

• Investigate life-enhancing volunteer opportunities (something with elderly/poor/sick).

- Try to lose interest in Posh and Becks.

- Ditto Britney and Kevin.

- Accept, once and for all, that am no longer important public-relations assistant (with direct responsibility for ad-hoc administrative duties) but stay-at-home mother and honest-to-goodness housewife.

- Try to remember that being a stay-at-home mother and housewife is a noble profession, not a thankless job. (NB under no circumstances spend long periods of time staring vacantly into space and wondering if the selfless decision to leave the workplace after Jack was born was such a good idea. Also avoid engaging in selective-memory exercises, such as remembering what fun work lunches were or how talking to real adults was so fulfilling. Instead focus on recalling heartbreak of leaving child at crèche. Use of further memory aids such as electric-shock therapy, nettle vest, etc., may be necessary.)

6 September

Very draining day. May well need a bit of celebrity cupping like Gwyneth in order to cope.

Joe's mother rang at the crack of dawn. 'I'm just in the door from six o'clock Mass,' she wheezed (rather alarmingly). 'Poor Father John needs all the support he can get after all those scurrilous rumours about him.' Quickly decided the crack of dawn was way too early to hear sordid tales of fallen priests and loose women so kept quiet. 'Anyway, I'm just calling to wish Katie luck, dear,' she continued, sounding a bit put out that I hadn't begged her for juicy details. 'Has she had her breakfast yet? A bowl of porridge would be just the trick – I always gave it to my Joe when he was going to school.'

Made fatal error of admitting that

(a) We were all still in bed. Yes, even at 6.45 a.m.;

(b) Katie wouldn't touch porridge even if Barbie personally endorsed it and it came in a neon-pink box; and

(c) Joe now prefers Coco Pops.

'Not up yet?' she shrieked in alarm. 'You'd want to get a move on, Susie – the day will be half over. You don't want the child late on her first day back.'

The thought of it sent her into another fit of panicked wheezing. Took opportunity to stumble into Katie's room and thrust the phone at her head. 'Your granny wants to speak to you,' I mumbled, trying to wipe the grit from my eyes. (NB Must purchase lavender-dipped eye mask with soothing chamomile extract advertised on Lifestyle TV ASAP.)

Katie scowled and promptly burrowed back under her Dora the Explorer duvet.

'Not very excited, is she, dear?' Mrs H tutted, as I stumbled back on to the landing and heard Jack screaming for his bottle. 'I do hope she's not going to find it difficult to settle back in. My Joe was so brave: he used to run in like a little trooper. Not even a backward glance. Katie is probably more like *your* side of the family.'

Pretended Jack had fallen down the stairs so I could hang up.

Spent ages fiddling about making extra-special toast with smiley faces made of sugar and honey to give Katie a proper send-off in case she was feeling nervous. Getting the sugar/honey smile to look happy and not downright creepy was tricky, but persevered. Crucial to let Katie know that am here for her in case she has deep-seated issues of abandonment or rejection about the return to playschool. That sort of emotional scarring can take years of therapy (and quite possibly cupping) to get over.

Confided my fears to Joe as he gulped his Coco Pops while simultaneously trying to do his tie.

'She'll be fine, Susie,' he mumbled, chocolate milk dripping down his chin. 'She's a tough little nut.'

Was aghast that

(a) Katie's own father seems to have very little insight into her very sensitive character, and

(b) He thinks his daughter is some sort of Lil' Kim gangsta type

but was unable to pursue matter as conversation was cut short by bloodcurdling screams from upstairs.

Katie, on a mission to find the perfect back-to-school ensemble, had attacked Jack with Malibu Barbie for using her favourite pink T-shirt to wipe his snotty nose.

Had reassuring chat with Katie on way to school.

'It's OK if you feel a bit sad to be leaving Mummy and Jack,' I ventured, feeling a little wobbly. 'You'll soon get used to playschool again, and remember that Mummy will pick you up at twelve o'clock. OK?'

Caught her looking at me in the rear-view mirror as if I needed special counselling, and then she almost jumped from the car while it was still moving, she was so anxious to get away. Am a bit concerned she seems so eager to get rid of me.

7 September

Fear I may be suffering from some sort of serious attachment-adjustment disorder. Was quite sniffly and traumatized all morning, but consoled myself with two cappuccinos and a double-chocolate-chip muffin in the Centre. Katie is apparently so overjoyed at returning to playschool that she has discarded me heartlessly by the wayside. At least Jack still has some interest in me. For once, he sat quite happily in his buggy without screaming the place down to get out, but only because I let him mush some of the muffin down his pants.

PS Came home to flashing light on answerphone – dove on it in case Katie had had some serious life-threatening mishap at playschool, but it was only VBF (Very Best Friend) Louise. Afraid to call back – can't remember if she is still fighting with MOM (man of the moment) or not and don't have energy for the whole commitment-phobe discussion. Again.

8 September

Jack seems to be pining for Katie now she has gone back to school. Caught him scratching her face out of the family photo in the playroom with a Magic Marker this morning. Think it was his sweet way of expressing his confusion and sorrow.

PS Just thought – maybe I'm suffering from Seasonal Affective Disorder. May well need overseas holiday in plush Caribbean resort to restore my health and vitality. Or maybe I could dot a few UVA lamps around the living room.

9 September

Mum thinks I need to invest more time in Jack now that Katie is back at playschool. 'What sort of social activities are you involving him in?' she asked, in quite a serious tone, when I phoned to say hello.

'Em, he likes to talk to Play Along Barney in his playpen,' I said, instantly regretting calling her.

'Hmm . . . I think he may need extra mental stimulation,' she said. 'And you could do with getting out and about a bit more. Baby yoga is all the rage now – you should give it a go. I'm sure Jack would adore it.'

Am a bit annoyed. Baby yoga is obviously a blatant attempt to swindle the vulnerable out of their monthly child allowance. It's ridiculous to expect babies to contort themselves every which way at such a young age – Mum can be very unrealistic sometimes. Also, how am

I supposed to juggle a baby exercise class with my hectic schedule? *Dr. Phil* at eleven simply cannot be missed.

PS Called VBF Louise at work to relay hilarious baby-yoga conversation, but she was too busy to talk. Tried to tell Jack all about it instead, but he just eyed me with serious disinterest and waddled away in the other direction.

PPS Maybe Mum is right and I should do more activities with Jack. Am considering buying some Baby Mozart tapes to transform him into a child prodigy.

10 September

Joe in Very Good Mood.

'I really think Maurice is going to promote me, Susie,' he confided excitedly, over dinner. 'All the signs are there. This time next year I'm going to be a director and we'll be on the pig's back.' He whooped with glee, sending the dog cowering under the table with fright.

'That's great,' I said, trying desperately to chop all of Katie's spaghetti into exactly the same length and width as per her specific instructions. 'You deserve it – you work very hard.'

'Well, that's the thing, Susie,' he went on, looking a bit uncomfortable and less gleeful almost immediately. 'I'll have to put in extra hours for a while, just to guarantee the promotion. But it won't be for long, I promise.'

'How do you get on the pig's back, Daddy?' Katie piped up, her face and hair smeared with tomato sauce. 'Can you wear a cowboy hat and boots?'

PS Wonder how Joe can possibly put in extra hours

when he already commits so much time to the firm, but am keeping quiet. Must try to be supportive, loving wife.

11 September

Oprah did a very inspiring show on recycling and the environment today. It was really touching when she confided that since she visited Africa she always thinks of the poor, starving children and their dirty, insanitary water when she's having her power shower. Thought that was really kind and sensitive of her. From now on, will not run the taps for longer than necessary or use the washing-machine too much. This will teach Katie and Jack to be more environmentally conscious when they're brushing their teeth, etc. Crucial to show the next generation how to conserve the planet and so forth. Also, am sneakily quite happy to have an excuse at last to let the dirty laundry build up.

PS Rumours everywhere about Kevin sneaking out of seedy stripper joint. Lots of really good pics in *OK!* of poor Britney looking very sad. No wonder she's smoking even more than usual.

12 September

Joe wasn't home until midnight last night. Good thing I hadn't cooked him any dinner or it would have ended up in the bin.

'Is this the way it's going to be from now on?' I hissed, as he crawled into bed beside me, furious that he had disturbed a fantastic dream I was having about Brad and Jude at a crucial moment.

'Sorry, Susie,' he mumbled, then immediately fell into a deep, snore-filled sleep. Am very worried. Joe could experience serious burnout in no time if this continues. Then he will be even more useless at getting up to Jack in the middle of the night. Must remember to buy him some multivitamins.

13 September

Think Katie is being subjected to some seriously bad influences at playschool.

Mrs H was aghast when she used the S-word today. '*What* did she say?' she squeaked, spluttering her Barry's Gold Blend tea all over her perfectly ironed blouse.

'Spit?' I volunteered, glaring at Katie and vowing to have a stern conversation with her when Mrs H vacated the premises.

'No, Mummy, I said *shit*,' Katie chimed, as clear as a bell.

'Katie, that's very naughty,' I scolded, trying my best to look innocent and horrified at the same time.

'Why? You say it all the time,' she retorted, pirouetting prettily for Mrs H and smiling widely.

Mrs H looked at me through slitted eyes, obviously trying to decide whether or not to contact social services straight away.

'She must be picking it up from the other children,' I said, whipping a fresh packet of fig rolls out of the cupboard in an attempt to distract her. 'I'll have to have a word with her teachers tomorrow.'

PS Mum says all children use profanities and it's nothing to worry about. 'It's their way of exploring their boundaries and expressing themselves, darling,' she reassured me. 'Just ignore it, she'll soon get tired of it.'

Could hear Dad bellowing in the background – something about a two-finger salute.

PPS Am getting a bit sick of fig rolls – even if they are only one WeightWatcher point each. Have decided to allow myself custard creams on an ad-hoc basis.

14 September

Louise called to discuss latest developments with her MOM. 'The thing is, Susie,' she said, 'I don't have time to be playing games at my age. I need to know if we're going to get serious and I need to know it now. If I ever stand a chance of having a baby, we need to hit the ground running.'

Thought she should get to know MOM's middle name before she has a baby with him, but decided not to say anything. Louise can be a bit aggressive when she gets emotional, so mumbled something vague and supportive instead.

'You're so lucky to have met Joe when you were both young, Susie,' she went on.

'Yes, I suppose we have kind of grown up together,' I said, filled with a warm, fuzzy feeling at thought of secure and happy home life.

'Yeah, *and* you don't even have to bother trying to look good any more,' she sighed, 'he just accepts you the way you are.'

Felt a bit uncomfortable at this so tried to change the subject and talk about Katie's latest obsession with potty language and whether it reflects some sort of deep-rooted unhappiness at return to playschool.

Suddenly, Louise had to deal with some high-level emergency. Have sneaking suspicion my children may bore her, just a teeny bit.

15 September

Have decided to take up power walking and sculpt my sagging body into a lean, mean sexy machine ASAP. Just need to invest in a serious-looking three-wheel jogging-type buggy that will mow down all other pedestrians at a flick of my wrist. Also need proper walking gear – such as new trainers, breathable Lycra leggings, wraparound shades, etc.

Joe thinks it's a great idea. 'It would be good for you to get into shape again,' he said, when I told him my grand plan. 'Power walking will tone you up in no time.'

Was furious he didn't reassure me that I'm firm, fit and fabulous just the way I am. Bet Becks always says the right thing to Posh when she's feeling fat and unattractive. Or buys her a Range Rover or some such.

16 September

Have discovered that power walking is not all it's cracked up to be. Tried to push Jack at a brisk pace through the park this morning, and felt quite dizzy and disoriented.

Luckily, he insisted on stopping to look at grass, dog poo and litter every five minutes so I could catch my breath. Even luckier, new fitness survey just issued says that four minutes of intense exercise every day is enough to keep you aerobically fit and lean. Feel very smug. I am probably at my physical peak, what with all the carrying of children, lugging of vacuum cleaners, etc.

17 September

According to theperfectparent.com, Katie could be hiding any anxiety she feels about returning to school. Makes complete sense – she seems thrilled to be back, but inside she could be insecure and confused. Suspect that Mum thinks I'm right, even though she's trying not to alarm me.

'Just keep an eye on her, darling,' she breezed down the phone. 'I'm sure she's fine. Now, must dash, love. Your dad has a lunch reservation for that fabulous new Italian restaurant in town.'

Am sure I detected a note of concern in her voice, but it was hard to make out with Dad bellowing in the background – something about pesto being good for the heart.

'For God's sake, chill out.' Joe laughed when I told him how worried I was. 'Katie's delighted with herself. She loves school.'

Am very annoyed with him – who are we to argue with qualified, on-line American paediatricians? Will have to keep close eye on situation. May even have to draw up PR-type plan of action. With graphs. And pie charts.

Evil Anna, former co-worker and Official Office Gossip, called on fake pretence of general chit-chat/a.k.a. blatant mission to uncover sad details of life in the suburbs. 'How. Are. Things. Susie?' she asked slowly, in the fake-sympathy voice she reserves especially for me, and for Danny who works in the mail room and may have a few mental-health issues. 'How. Are. You. Coping?'

Panicked a bit, trying to remember what lie I had fed her last time to get her off the phone. Had quite possibly invented the fake death of close family member. 'Em, I'm fine, Anna,' I mumbled noncommittally, trying to sound sad but not overwrought in case I'd picked a *distant* relative instead.

'Really?' She sounded disappointed that I wasn't on the verge of a complete nervous breakdown.

'But you were so *down* the last time we went out for lunch.'

Could hear her tapping on her keyboard as she spoke, probably making notes for her 'Sad Housewives Dossier'.

'You said the kids were driving you *crazy*, remember? You were practically going to murder What's-his-name. So, how are things now?'

Could almost see her holding her breath expectantly, hoping for lots of juicy details about Valium-taking and secret-drinking binges she could email to everyone later.

In creepy flashback, suddenly remembered why I have been avoiding Anna even more of late. May have admitted, in drunken moment of weakness after guzzling half a bottle of Sauvignon Blanc at a work reunion lunch, that staying at home to nurture and care for children may not be bliss 100 per cent of the time. Damn that wine and its evil, tongue-loosening devil-ways.

'Really? I can't remember that,' I lied, picking some dried-in snot off my sleeve and making a mental note to try to teach Jack to wipe it on his *own* sleeves from now on. 'Things are great, never better, in fact. How are things with you?' Tried very hard to sound casual and just a tad perplexed as to why I would have painted a less than apple-pie-perfect picture of my life. Not quite sure I pulled it off.

'Reeeaaaally?' Anna didn't sound convinced. 'Oh, you know us, always busy, busy, busy. Not that you *would* know about that any more. Ha! Ha! Ha!'

She laughed in that horrible braying way that reminded me of why I had always wanted to beat her over the head with the office stapler.

'Well, they do keep me on my toes,' I countered, watching What's-his-name try to prise open the oven door and crawl in.

'Yes, we were just saying the other day,' Anna battled on, ignoring me as usual, 'what *does* Susie do with all her free time? You are *sooooo* lucky. Mind you, I couldn't do it. I need the mental stimulation of work to keep me sane. Do you know what I mean?'

'Oh, yes,' I replied, catching Jack just before he lost the use of his right hand in a horrible disfiguring oven-related accident. 'Mental stimulation is key. Absolutely.' Hung up, very annoyed with Anna and her devious mind games. It's nearly two years since I left the office.

Surely she should be getting on with forgetting that I ever existed – everyone else has.

PS Have decided to take up Sudoku to keep mentally active and challenged.

PPS On second thoughts, may start watching *Countdown* on Channel 4 instead. That annoying tick-tock music is very off-putting, but it's got quite sexed up since that nice Carol Vorderman lost the weight and started showing off her cleavage more.

19 September

Starbucks in the Centre seems to be going downhill. The waitress was quite snappy with me today when I asked if Jack could have a few empty paper cups to play with. (He loves to rip them up and chuck them about, bless him.) *And* I'm sure the caramel lattes used to be frothier.

PS Got a text message from Louise. Her and MOM are going on a loved-up mid-week break to Prague. Does she *never* get bored with rampant sex in five-star luxury surroundings?

20 September

Katie is being bullied at school! I *knew* something was bothering her. Nearly rear-ended a granny in an Opel Astra when she told me on the way home in the car. Joe said it's probably all a storm in a teacup, but I'm taking it very seriously. The *Sunday Independent* had a special supplement on bullying last week. It's a serious epidemic and it can have long-lasting, detrimental effects on children. Some of the most notorious serial murderers in history were bullied as kids.

Joe fell about the place when I told him. 'They probably had a fight over a doll or something.' He snorted. Well, he can snigger all he likes, but it will be his fault if our little princess ends up in Mountjoy Prison or some other ghastly correctional facility in twenty years' time. I watch *Bad Girls* – I know what goes on in those women's lock-ups. She could end up with badly bleached hair, a prison warder as a lesbian lover and a harrowing crack addiction. As a parent you have to be vigilant about these things. I'm going in to Little Angels Playschool to kick ass tomorrow.

21 September

Reconnaissance mission has been completed.

Bully's name: Zoe.

Age: Three and a half.

Height: Three feet two inches.

Address: Unknown.

The head teacher's watered-down version of events is that new-girl Zoe is muscling in on Katie and her VBF – Amy. Meanwhile Amy, the little turncoat, has dropped my darling daughter for the new kid on the block and poor Katie is friendless.

Am racked with guilt. The whole situation is quite obviously due to bad cosmic karma from that time in playschool when I told Jenny Kelly that I didn't want to be her best friend any more. Keep getting horrible flashbacks to poor Jenny crying brokenheartedly into the sandbox.

Joe reckons Katie will tough it out and make new friends in no time, but it's all I can do to stop myself slapping the two little monsters. And their mothers.

Have taken an instant dislike to Zoe's mother – a hippie type in baggy trousers who's always smiling in a superior way. No one can be that happy all the time. Especially not a stay-at-home mother. (Unless she owns a 4×4 and has a Filipina nanny on standby.) Eco-mother walks to and from playschool every day, pushing a freakishly smiling baby in a pram, and spends ages at the school gates trying to convert other mothers to using sunflower oil instead of petrol. All highly suspicious behaviour.

Told the head teacher, in no uncertain terms, that I wanted the situation monitored. I will not have my child victimized.

PS Have just thought – Zoe's mother could be on drugs. All those eco-warrior types are into pot and happy pills. That could be why she looks so damn cheery all the time. My God, now Katie will be exposed to drugs as well as harassment.

22 September

VBF Louise called for a pre-romantic-break pow-wow.

'What type of underwear do you think I should bring, Susie?' she mused, in a very serious voice (i.e., she was not being ironic).

'Em, matching?' I ventured, unsure where this was headed.

'Well, of course matching.' She guffawed. 'What other kind is there? No, what I mean is, should I go for the demure look with ruffles and cotton or the more vampy look with silk and leather? I don't want to scare him off, but I do want to impress him, if you know what I mean.' She laughed coyly.

Didn't want to admit that had no idea what she meant and that any kind of underwear featuring leather sounded vaguely obscene. And extremely uncomfortable. 'You don't wear matching undies all the time, do you, Lou?' I asked, peering down my T-shirt to see what I'd pulled on that morning.

'Of course I do! Don't you remember the golden rule of underwear?' She sounded genuinely shocked.

'Em, wear some?'

'No, Susie, always wear underwear that you wouldn't be embarrassed to be seen in if the man of your dreams suddenly wanted to sweep you off your feet and have mad, passionate sex with you. So, what will I go for?'

'Demure cotton, I think,' I said, aghast that if Brad suddenly wanted to roll in the hay with me he would be revolted by my grey maternity bra that sags at the nipples (boobs sadly deflated from being quite perky pre-pregnancy to saggy and droopy post-birth) and pinkish (verging on tie-dyed) pants that most definitely did not match, unless you were extremely short-sighted and quite possibly colour-blind. Which I don't think Brad is. Although he did wear those very sexy glasses in *Ocean's Eleven*.

'Yes,' I went on, 'cotton is probably best. Save the

crotchless knickers for next time.' Laughed at my own little joke, but it seemed to go over her head a bit.

'Oh, crotchless are so last year, Susie.' She tutted. 'It's all about the Virgin Look this year. Anyway, must go. I have a bloody board meeting in ten minutes.'

Hung up, resolving to bin all under-par smalls and only wear sexy matching sets from now on. Hope G-strings have gone out of fashion with the crotchless type. Brad might be even more revolted by my droopy cellulite bum hanging out than anything else.

PS Sense Louise and I are growing apart a bit. Very worrying.

23 September

Have discovered that I do not possess one single set of matching, sexy underwear. Not even an emergency, in-case-of-surprise-five-star-hotel-weekend-away pair. Am quite shaken by the revelation that I no longer value myself enough to invest in something other than well-washed mammy pants. Also, have ominous feeling this reflects very badly on the state of my marriage. Am afraid to look it up on drphil.com in case he says Joe and I have passed the point of no return and may as well proceed straight to Judge Judy's divorce court.

Asked Joe if he was concerned that I was still wearing a sagging grey maternity bra eighteen months after giving birth.

'I never really think about it, Susie,' he said, munching a second bowl of Coco Pops and looking completely unconcerned that our marriage may be on the rocks.

'But don't you remember, when we first started going out together,' I said, 'you used to buy me lots of sexy stuff in Marks & Spencer?' (Back in the nineties, when Kylie and Elle hadn't even thought of making teeny tiny pants held together by minuscule pieces of ribbon and Marks & Spencer was the height of sophistication.)

'That was years ago, Susie.' Joe laughed, apparently not the least bit worried that we could be headed for a bitter divorce any day now. 'Anyway, from what I remember, they were no sooner on you than I had them off.'

'Yes, but you *never* buy sexy underwear for me any more,' I said, trying to remember the last time he'd ripped anything off me, bar the TV remote control. 'Doesn't that worry you?'

'Why would it worry me?' he answered, looking surprised. 'Sure everyone grows out of that lovey-dovey stuff.'

Have decided not to confide all this to Louise. It's bad enough that she probably thinks I'm a sad, frumpy housewife – no need to confirm it for her.

24 September

Katie shook me awake this morning to remind me that I had promised this day last year to buy her a bikini for swimming lessons. How she remembers this stuff is beyond me. Cannot remember what I did yesterday (washing, changing nappies and vacuuming probably), let alone a conversation from this time last year. Should seriously consider getting her IQ tested – she might be gifted. Or have a photographic memory at the very least.

'I don't know, darling,' I muttered, trying to hide under the pillow and grab another five minutes' sleep. 'I don't think you're old enough for a bikini just yet.'

There was a deathly five-second silence, followed by a roar loud enough to rival the Lion King on acid. 'You promiiiiised,' she sobbed. 'You *said* I could get a bikini this year. I'm the Only One who doesn't have a bikini now.' Cue more uncontrollable shaking and sobbing.

The 'Only One' comment clinched it. Cannot have her feeling polarized from her peers. Bad enough that she's the victim of institutionalized bullying in play-school. 'OK, OK.' I caved. 'We'll go look for one this morning, all right?'

'OK.' She sniffed suspiciously. 'A pink one.'

'All right.'

'With love hearts.'

'OK.'

'Nice parenting,' Joe said, laughing, under the duvet, as Katie marched off to watch *The Little Mermaid* for inspiration. 'Very impressive the way you stuck to your guns.'

No point trying to explain the critical importance of fitting in with peer group, so I just poked him in the back with Jack's Action Man instead.

Spent entire morning battling through vicious crowds at the Centre, half of them seemingly intent on buying a girl's pink bikini. Had to undergo several to-the-death stare-downs with other frazzled mothers but eventually found one that met all the criteria:

• Pink, but not shiny pink (i.e., a ruling on the perfect colour will rest with Katie and Katie alone. The judge's decision is final).

- No 'lumpy' bits (i.e., no embroidery or logos of any kind – unless Barbie-related).

- No 'boy' pants (i.e., only totally inappropriate skimpy, pole-dancing-type bottoms considered).

Exhausted after all the searching, we skidded up to the swimming-pool in the nick of time and bolted into the dressing rooms – where all the little girls were sporting this year's new look: miniature wet-suits and goggles.

25 September

Louise back from romantic break with MOM. 'It was fab, Susie,' she gushed down the phone. 'You and Joe really should go.'

'Yeah,' I agreed, watching Joe pick his ear and wipe the wax on the Sunday supplement.

'The food was amazing, and the hotel was just *divine*. We got on so well – it's like we've known each other for ever. I really think this could be going somewhere.'

'That's great, Lou,' I agreed, trying to loosen Jack's grip on my leg while motioning to Katie that pouring Fairy Liquid on the TV to 'clean it' would not be appropriate. Didn't like to break it to Louise that knowing someone for ever is not all it's cracked up to be. Wonder if Posh has this problem? Can't imagine Becks would ever fart under the duvet or trim his nose hair in the living room, but you never know.

Joe's mother popped round at 9.30 a.m., waving a jumbo pack of acid-green dishcloths: 'It was buy one, get one free in Lidl,' she crowed triumphantly, 'so I said to myself, "Who do I know who could do with a few extra dishcloths?" And *then* I thought, Susie, of course! You can never have enough dishcloths – isn't that right, dear?'

'Absolutely,' I agreed forlornly, trailing after her as she marched into the kitchen, where the remains of breakfast (and, OK, last night's dinner) were strewn all over the place.

'What's that smell, Susie?' she asked, stopping in her tracks and sniffing the air in disgust.

'Toast?' I ventured, cursing myself for having a second cup of instant coffee instead of changing Jack's stinky nappy straight away.

'*Poo-Poo!*' Jack roared, appearing out of nowhere and flinging himself on Mrs H's legs like a mini Sumo wrestler.

'You poor little mite,' Mrs H crooned, scooping him up and sniffing his bottom suspiciously. 'Did Mummy let you sit in a stinky nappy? Bad Mummy. Doesn't she know you could get a nasty infection on your poor bum-bum?'

Jack smiled at me over her shoulder as she marched him off to inspect his bottom for any signs of maltreatment. 'Bum-bum!' he lisped, an evil glint in his eye.

Once she had gone, called Joe to put him straight. Am not doormat that she can just trample all over and wear down with her overbearing opinions. She's lucky she brings those homemade scones with her every time she drops by or I wouldn't even let her set foot inside the house. 'She has to learn that she must call before she pops in, Joe,' I grumbled. 'I could have had something on this morning. I could have been up to my eyes. I can't abandon my entire daily schedule at the drop of a hat to suit her, you know.'

'Did you have anything else on this morning, Susie?' Joe asked, sounding amused.

'That's hardly the point,' I snapped. 'I might have been busy.'

'Yes, but you weren't,' he went on. 'Give her a break. She's lonely since Dad died.'

Hung up in annoyance. Was almost tempted to remind Joe that his father has been dead for ten years and that his mother had had very little time for him when he was alive. Seemed a bit disrespectful to bring that up, though. Wonder how Joe would like it if his mother arrived at his office unannounced. Have a good mind to take up Pilates to spite them both.

27 September

Katie is acting up terribly and I'm worried sick. She's hyper all the time and is constantly baiting Jack with her toys and reducing him to tears. Last night she ran round the kitchen in her Sleeping Beauty pants, laughing like a hyena and roaring at the top of her voice. I was quite scared. Definitely think it's a reaction to the situation at school. She's obviously traumatized because her

friend has deserted her and she's 'acting out' as a consequence. Tried to get advice from theperfectparent.com,
but bloody computer on the blink. Meanwhile Jack has
started whacking the furniture, his head and anything
that moves with his favourite red truck. Am at wit's
end – nails chewed to quick.

PS Called Louise for advice but only got her voicemail.
No doubt at some high-powered, high-level meeting
wearing Armani and too busy to talk to boring, frumpy
housewife friend.

28 September

Joe sent Katie to bed with no story tonight. He also
threw all the Smarties and Monster Munch crisps in the
bin. I pleaded with him not to be so harsh (I love those
Monster Munch – they are so addictive), but he said he
had to take a stand. 'She's just being a brat, and she has
to learn that she can't get away with it,' he huffed, as he
dragged the black bin-liner packed with goodies out to
the gate and started stuffing them manically into the
wheelie-bin, a funny don't-mess-with-me glint in his
eye. (Quite sexy, actually.)

He has no time for my acting-out theory. As far as
he's concerned, she's just being naughty and eating too
many sugary snacks. For once, suspect he may be right
because Katie cried for twenty minutes in her bed, then
crept downstairs to say sorry for tying Jack to the
kitchen table with her skipping-rope. Tucked her back
in, then snuck outside to rescue some of the Monster
Munch and smuggle them in under cover of darkness.

Spent rest of night sneaking out to kitchen to have one at a time so Joe wouldn't see. Thrill of imminent discovery, coupled with pickled-onion flavour, gave me a bit of a rush, actually.

PS Louise called, but I had to let it go to voicemail – *Portland Babies* was just about to start. Screaming women in the throes of labour is addictive viewing.

29 September

Mrs H wants me to go to her bingo morning with her. 'It's great fun, Susie,' she said gleefully, as she settled herself (unannounced) at the kitchen table for another quick coffee.

Mumbled something noncommittal. Going to bingo with Jack and Mrs H is not my idea of a hot morning's entertainment. In fact, it rates just above ironing and scrubbing the toilet.

'It's very important to keep active in the community,' she went on, managing to devour all the biscuits I was saving for my date with Oprah *and* make a sly dig at my lack of involvement in any community-related events in one go. 'And, you can make a few euro as well. Oh, yes, it can be quite the little earner.' She nodded knowingly, clasping her PVC handbag a bit tighter to her chest as if one of her blue-rinse bingo cronies was about to leap through the open window and wrestle her winnings from her hands.

'Really?' I pushed another biscuit across the table, intrigued by this unexpected revelation. Could definitely do with a bit of black-market cash to invest in certain consumer items, which, strictly speaking, may not be absolute necessities but which add a little sunshine to my day, such as

(a) *Heat*

(b) *OK!*

(c) *Hello!* (especially if am in the mood for the carryings-on of Danish royal family)

'Oh, yes,' she went on, and leaned in to confide in a low whisper, 'I won two euro today.'

Wasn't sure I had heard her properly – the biscuits stuck to her dentures were making her lisp a bit. 'Did you say twenty euro, Mrs H?' I asked, quite excited that I could indulge my secret trashy-mag addiction without Joe being any the wiser.

'Twenty euro, Susie?' she gasped, looking scandalized. 'We only play for twenty cents at a time. If you're looking for the big-time you'd better take yourself off to that heathen Las Vegas. Twenty euro, indeed.'

PS Hot off the presses. Amy has dumped Zoe and wants to be Katie's VBF again. I advised Katie to play it cool for a while and be emotionally unavailable. But Katie has no pride and immediately started sorting out her favourite play dresses to bring into school – one for her and one for her turncoat buddy.

Mum called to say she has decided to replant the garden. 'According to the *feng-shui* principles of gardening, you can improve your luck by creating a balanced and har- monious outdoor space. Isn't that fascinating, darling?' she said, and explained how she was going to cut down all the climbing roses round the door and massacre the oak tree in the front garden to let the energy flow.

'What?' I croaked, aghast that such a big decision would have been made without prior consultation with me (and, OK, my permission).

'Yes, your dad's come over all Mel Gibson. He's really enjoying that chainsaw Uncle Mike lent him. It's practically given him a new lease of life.' She sounded dead pleased with herself.

'But, Mum,' I wailed, feeling a bit tearful, 'I love those climbing roses *and* I used to spend hours playing in that oak tree when I was little.'

'Did you, darling? I don't remember that,' Mum went on, sounding vague.

'Yes, I did, it was my special secret place, I even carved my name in the trunk. Don't you remember?'

Could hear lots of hacking and sawing in the back- ground and Dad calling out about having heaps of great logs for the winter and how he needed to be rubbed down with a flannel.

'Never mind, darling. I'll press some of the roses for you – how about that? You could even make pot- pourri.'

Hung up feeling most put out that parents have

erased precious childhood memories with a chainsaw and a *feng-shui* DIY guide. You would think, as I'm their only offspring, they would be highly sentimental regarding all aspects of my childhood. And adulthood for that matter. But, worryingly, they seem to be becoming more, not less, independent with every passing day. Most disturbing.

PS Eco-mother didn't look so bloody happy today – ha! Now she knows how it feels to be an outsider. Revenge is sweet, although I did feel a little bad when I saw her struggling back up the road in the rain with the buggy and a screaming Zoe.

1 October

Another re-run of *Dr. Phil* on RTÉ this morning, so called Louise for a chat. She was quite short with me – something about crisis talks and the chief executive. Am getting quite sick of her drama-queen attitude. It was all 'Can't talk now, call you later when executive crisis abates blah blah blah.' If she had to juggle two screaming children and a demanding husband she'd know all about crisis talks. All she has to worry about is which designer suit to wear and which man to toy with next. Am not going to answer phone when she calls back. Healthy relationships involve equal parts of give and take (am practically relationship guru after watching all the *Dr. Phil* repeats again). She has to validate my feelings and recognize that she can't just turn my emotions on and off like a tap, even if I have been her VBF since primary school.

PS Will compose snotty letter to RTÉ, complaining about dearth of intelligent, stimulating day-time viewing for stay-at-home mothers. Typical of bourgeois, élitist broadcasters to think they can fob off a generation of women with inferior programming.

PPS Will suggest some *Dallas* reruns to fill the programming slump. Can never remember exactly who shot JR.

2 Fairbrook Drive
1 October

Dear Ms Goode,

I am writing to you to express my annoyance and outrage at the seemingly endless stream of reruns being broadcast by your channel. I have chosen to write to you personally as, from your photo on RTÉ's website, I can tell you are the kind of person who will understand where I am coming from. You probably long to jack in your job and stay at home with your children full time yourself. But, let me tell you, it's not all fun and games.

Anyway, my point is, I love *Dr. Phil* as much as the next person, but please do not insult my intelligence by showing repeats over and over again. Contrary to popular opinion, stay-at-home mothers (at whom such programming is clearly targeted) are not brainless twits with nothing better to do than lounge in front of the TV all morning drinking coffee and eating Rich Tea biscuits. For example, I myself had an extremely successful career in PR (with direct responsibility for ad-hoc administrative duties) before

I sacrificed it all to stay at home and take care of my children. It is, of course, an extremely rewarding job, but it receives little or no recognition from the outside world, the government, or most husbands for that matter.

I schedule my day to watch *Dr. Phil* (it can be quite difficult to get an obstinate eighteen-month-old to take a nap by exactly eleven a.m., but I do manage for the most part) and when I am confronted with yet another repeat episode it does irritate me somewhat. Especially when you show repeats of particularly boring ones, such as the one when Dr. Phil pretends to be a junior staff member for the day. (Let's face it, he's fooling no one.) Perhaps you could have a word with the relevant staff member and get them to choose more exciting episodes, like the one called 'Diary of a Divorce' (the fight scenes were pretty spectacular). I trust you will rectify the situation as a matter of urgency and get back to me as soon as possible.

Thanking you,
Susan Hunt

PS You might consider doing some kind of fly-on-the-wall documentary on stay-at-home mothers. If people find watching celebrities eating maggots fascinating viewing, they're obviously open to anything.

PPS Please excuse the jam fingerprints at the top of the page – Jack wanted to make his contribution and I do feel it's important for children to express themselves creatively.

2 October

Mum and Dad are coming to Dublin for the weekend! Hurrah! They're sure to offer to babysit so that Joe and I can indulge in a romantic, candlelit dinner in some seriously expensive restaurant in the city just like we used to. We definitely need to reconnect – caught Joe casually clipping his toenails at the kitchen table this morning.

Called Louise to get low-down on happening city hot-spots. She sounded a bit strange on phone – maybe it was a bad line. Anyway, L'Écrivain is the place to go – apparently it's romantic, classy and very expensive. Perfect! Spent ages fantasizing about holding hands across the table and lovingly feeding each other titbits in the candlelight.

PS Must remember not to fight over the last canapé or argue about whose turn it is to drive.

3 October

Oh, my God! Posh Frenchwoman called me today to confirm my reservation for this Friday night at the Four Seasons Hotel! Joe has booked us a suite for the night! Am speechless with shock. Am also overcome with guilt. Had blazing row with him last night when I suggested going to L'Écrivain for romantic candlelit dinner, and he suggested going to the local for a few pints and a bag of crisps. Obviously, he has spent ages plotting with my parents to whisk me away for the night. *That*'s why they're coming to Dublin. Have to keep up pretence I know nothing – he would be devastated if I spoiled the surprise. Cooked proper M&S roast beef in a bag (with posh roasted vegetables and accompanying gravy) for dinner. He didn't bat an eyelid at unprecedented Nigella-type transformation, but obviously he doesn't want to raise my suspicions – never knew he could be so crafty.

4 October

Called Mum to let her know that I am in on the little secret. She did an Oscar-nominated performance of acting surprised.

'It's OK, Mum,' I giggled conspiratorially, 'I know all about it. The Four Seasons called me yesterday to confirm the reservation.'

Then it sounded like Mum dropped the phone and there was a lot of whispering in the background until Dad came on: 'Susie, love, it's me who's bringing your mum to the Four Seasons for the night. It's the fortieth anniversary of the day we got engaged on Friday, and I wanted to mark the occasion by doing something special.'

Good old Dad did his best to sound convincing but it didn't fool me. 'Sure thing, Dad,' I guffawed. 'So why did they call me to confirm the booking? I'm afraid you've all been caught out.'

Cue embarrassed cough. 'Em, I wanted to surprise your mother, Susie. I gave them your phone number to confirm so she wouldn't know. I meant to tell you last week to expect a call. Sorry, love.'

Hung up to squeals of delight from my mother about going to a five-star hotel and how romantic my father is.

5 October

Am being ice-cool with Joe and he hasn't even realized. Caught him muttering something to Jack about women and times of the month. Played loud Barbie game with Katie, where the prince didn't turn up and bitter Barbie had to fend for herself in the cruel world with only a dishwasher for company. Katie didn't seem too impressed, so had loud heart-to-heart with Jack about how to treat women and keep romance alive. Am sure he understood – he's so advanced for eighteen months. He really listened intently, grunting with sympathy. At least, I thought that was what it was until I got the waft of fresh poo coming from his nappy. Handed him straight to Joe. He can be on nappy duty for a while until he figures out why I'm so upset.

PS Overheard Joe congratulating Jack on producing a 'Super Dump' and telling him what a great set of tackle he has. Will have to find other devious ways to punish him for not taking me on surprise overnight stay in a five-star hotel.

PPS Have decided to be officially cross with Mum and Dad. Spending vast amounts of money in over-priced luxury accommodation for no good reason is immature and irresponsible. And very irritating.

6 October

Louise called to see how my big night of romance had gone. Must remember to check caller ID before I answer next time. Was too embarrassed to admit I had spent the night watching *The Swan* (hasn't that Amanda Byram done well for herself?) so pretended it had been fabulous and gave mouthful-by-mouthful account of romantic meal at L'Écrivain. Am shocked (and a bit impressed, actually) by my ability to lie so effortlessly. This is all Joe's fault. Have been reduced to lying to my oldest friend about *coq au vin* and *crème brûlée* to hide crushing sense of humiliation. Luckily Louise didn't notice. She was too concerned about what to wear to go to the opening night of Il Divo's bar with MOM. 'I hate these bloody corporate events. They're so boring.' She sighed unconvincingly. 'I can't possibly wear that old Gucci thing again – I might have to go to London for the weekend and get something new. Do you fancy it?'

Pretended Jack had fallen out of his high chair so I could get off the phone. Is she for real? Like I can just swan off to London and leave kids alone with Joe for a weekend. Louise has no concept of responsibility or commitment. We are definitely drifting further and further apart. Anyway, cannot possibly miss unofficial Posh and Becks documentary on Saturday night – promises shocking new intimate revelations about their marriage. Now, *that*'s what I call quality TV.

PS Joe brought home a box of Cadbury's Roses for

me and let me have all the caramel ones. Am warming to him.

7 October

Had blissful lie-in this morning. In unprecedented act of brown-nosing following five-star hotel débâcle, Joe leaped out of bed at virtual crack of dawn and announced in a Very Important Voice that he would watch the children while I slept. Was tempted to ask if he wanted a round of applause and a medal, but resisted in case sarcasm changed his mind. Was actually quite touched by thoughtfulness of the gesture – very heart-warming, especially when he brought me tea and burned toast to eat in peace. Have decided that I do not need luxury breaks away to define me.

PS Am not speaking to Joe. Arrived downstairs after relaxing lie-in to discover Katie and Jack watching *Newlyweds* Jessica and Nick getting hot and steamy on MTV while their wayward father snored in the Queen Anne chair. Meanwhile, the dog had devoured the rest of the Cadbury's Roses (in their wrappers) and had been sick all over the stairs.

'You're never happy,' Joe grumbled, when I shook him awake in a rage. 'I'm only doing my best.'

Informed him in no uncertain terms that his best is seriously below average. In fact, have sneaking suspicion that he may have deliberately sabotaged my lie-in so I wouldn't feel comfortable making time for myself in the future and thereby become a complete doormat.

As opposed to current status of half a doormat. Must consult drphil.com to confirm.

PS Am very worried that Katie is suffering from post-traumatic *Newlyweds* exposure. 'Are my boobs cute, Mum?' she asked, hoicking her T-shirt up to her navel and pouting just like Jessica while pirouetting to see her reflection in the oven door. God knows what untold damage has been done to her delicate psyche. She may well develop body-image problems and start stuffing socks down her vest soon.

PPS Dog is hiding under the kitchen table, looking very mournful.

8 October

Katie ran out from playschool today waving a note in the air and demanding that it be read immediately.

> We would like to remind parents that Little Angels Playschool operates a strict Healthy Eating policy. Please ensure your child brings a healthy snack to school each day. Sugary and salty foods are not permitted.

'How disgusting,' Eco-mother sniffed crossly after reading the note out loud in a funny booming way most at odds with her normal unnaturally cheerful demeanour. Warmed to her slightly. It does seem a bit Hitleresque to ban all sugary foods from the kids' snackboxes. They're only children, after all. If they can't indulge now, when can they? Time enough to be worrying about love handles and cellulite when they become adults and develop serious body issues.

Felt very guilty that had judged her so harshly – she is obviously just like everyone else and throws in the odd Milky Way or bag of crisps to convince child to attend school at all.

'Imagine! Some mothers actually feed their children sugar so young,' she went on, shaking her head and looking quite pink in the face with annoyance (although that may be more of a weatherbeaten thing – which just goes to prove that denying yourself the luxury of a car in a bid to be more eco-conscious can backfire in unexpected ways). Suddenly a strange chill came over me. And over half of the other mothers there, judging by the strangled looks on their faces.

'Zoe will never have processed foods. Never. People are so badly educated about diet. No wonder so many children are obese.'

Thought she threw a knowing look in my direction before she huffed off, dragging little carrot-wielding Zoe with her.

Was dumbfounded. Did she mean that Zoe had never tasted any processed food? Ever? How can she possibly survive?

Could see other mothers shuffling about and looking uncomfortable before we all sloped off in silence to digest the news.

PS Am at a loss what to put in Katie's snackbox. Wonder do Rice Krispie bars count as healthy food. They're made from rice, after all.

9 October

Joe called to ask if his mother can come for dinner. Have to give him ten out of ten for ingenuity. Will now be forced to make pleasant public chit-chat and thereby call off icy silence.

'I've nothing to give her,' I said snootily, secretly a bit relieved we were on speaking terms again. Not talking can be very tiring. Especially when you want the TV remote and have to move to reach it, instead of getting spouse to throw it to you.

'Why don't you make your famous chicken pie?' Joe answered, evidently having thought the whole thing through. (Extra bonus points for sneakiness.) 'That's delicious.'

'I don't know.' I sniffed, playing for time. 'The house is a mess.' Suddenly remembered had forgotten to wash dog sick off stairs.

'I'll come home early and give the place a quick vacuum so you can concentrate on the *cordon-bleu* cookery. How about that?' he suggested.

Agreed instantly. Offers of a moan-free vacuuming session are few and far between. Just have to think of a way to disguise the dog-vomit stain before dinner-time.

10 October

Next time I am tempted to host impromptu dinner for mother-in-law I will remember the following:

(1) Impromptu dinner is never actually impromptu. Unknown to you, mother-in-law has been given several weeks' notice of said event by evil spouse and will arrive early, expecting fancy canapés (preferably Delia's, not Nigella's – who she considers uppity and a bit scandalous) and ironed napkins.

(2) Panicking about simple chicken dish will mean that said dish is left drying in oven for a whole hour longer than necessary while you try to rustle up Delia-type canapés and find nuts (salted, not roasted) from nowhere.

(3) Hiding piles of unironed clothes under the stairs will backfire when demon children haul them out to play dress-up.

(4) Forgetting to wash children's hands before serving dinner will result in a serious international incident and possible call to social services.

11 October

Very interesting *Oprah* today. All about reconnecting with your loved ones and building strong family ties. Lots of happy celebrities were on to give advice. Could have sworn quite a few were on their third or fourth marriages, but Oprah didn't mention that. Anyway, it probably just means they're more qualified than the average person to tell us how to achieve harmony in the home. Also, *none* of them has a nanny – they do it all on their own and still manage to be a size zero and look flawless. Felt a bit unworthy but took notes anyway and applied the Harmony Checklist to Joe's life.

- Do you work very long hours? Check.

- Are you often too exhausted to play with your children when you get home from work? Check.

- Do you actively avoid family time and instead spend hours slumped in your favourite chair watching sports and grunting? (May have embellished that one just a little, but that was the general idea.) Check.

Turns out Joe is practically the poster child for Disharmony in the Home. Called him at the office to inform him that he must start spending more one-on-one time with Jack and Katie to create strong bonds for a healthy family. 'You could play baseball with Jack in the park, for example,' I said, delighted with myself for remembering Jada Pinkett Smith's very positive suggestion.

'Susie, we live in Dublin, not California,' he groaned, 'there is no baseball.'

'That is exactly the kind of defeatist, negative attitude that Oprah says destroys families,' I told him, annoyed by his selfish, destructive behaviour. 'If you were a positive person, you'd go out and introduce baseball to Ireland. How hard can it be?'

'For God's sake, Susie,' Joe said, 'nobody plays baseball in Dublin. I'll bring him to the park and teach him how to kick a football around.'

Hung up feeling most put out that Joe will not be campaigner for baseball in Ireland. Could be very newsworthy event – in fact, might make front page of the *Irish Times*, Oprah could get to see it and we might be flown first class to Chicago and have front-row seats at her show. Am furious Joe has ruined my one chance of meeting my idol.

12 October

Only two weeks to Katie's fourth birthday. After much discussion (and some serious negotiation on my part to persuade her that a trip to Euro Disney for her and all her playschool pals was out of the question), she has decided on a princess party. The theme is pink, with glitter.

Mum has promised to lend a hand (if the golfing trip to Portugal falls through, that is), but have decided I may need extra help with the preparations. Luckily, I had the foresight to keep the *Gazette* special supplement on children's entertainers. Well, it was more of an exposé, really, but I'm sure they can't *all* be rip-off merchants who 'promise the earth and fail to deliver' (feel the journalist may have been a teeny bit biased – one bad experience with a bouncy castle seems to have made him very bitter). *And* there were some useful contact details. So, if I do actually need the Fraud Squad I have the number to hand.

Am very excited at the prospect of hosting cute, old-fashioned kids' party – with professionals on full standby to organize all the details. Have flatly denied Joe's allegations that am trying to outdo other playschool mothers with lavish, over-the-top display.

'Why can't you make a few fairy cakes and play hide and seek, for God's sake?' he asked, when I showed him my special party folder with colour-co-ordination chart. 'Kids that age much prefer something simple.'

Which just goes to show that what I've feared all along is true. Joe has no idea who his daughter is. In her book simple and low key are marks of the devil.

13 October

Have called all the children's entertainers in Dublin. They cost at least a hundred and fifty euros for an hour and a half. (And that doesn't include a gourmet finger-food buffet.) One woman I phoned, called Fairy Fay, wanted two hundred to turn up in a fairy costume and look pretty.

'What do you do with the kids, exactly?' I asked, pen in hand, ready to jot it all down in my special party folder.

'Well,' she whispered, in a fake little-girl voice, 'I dress as a fairy and read the kids a story. But before I put the dress on, I tell them that it's just me, Fay, in case they get scared.'

'Riiiight . . . So you explain to them that you're a normal person, and you're just pretending to be a fairy?' I said, a bit bemused.

'Yes.'

That can't be very exciting for them, I thought. 'OK, and what do you do then?'

'Well, that's about it,' she breathed. 'But the dress is really gorgeous – all the girls love it.'

'I don't think the dress will keep them happy for two hours, though.' I laughed. She had to be joking – two hundred euro for looking pretty?

'Well, I suppose I could paint their faces if you like. But a lot of the kids are afraid of their faces being touched.'

What kind of children was she talking about? Alien children, perhaps? Everyone knows children love having their faces painted – it's practically hardwired into their genes.

In a sudden flash of inspiration, decided to organize the party myself. After all, I used to help put on impressive corporate events for hundreds of hard-nosed business people. (With folders *and* nametags.) How hard can a kids' party be? Dress up like a fairy, read a story, paint a few faces and save myself two hundred euro in the process. Easy-peasy, lemon-squeezy.

PS Will rope in Joe to do impressive array of magic tricks. Hope he can still squeeze into his tuxedo.

PPS May have to invest in clipboard and some kind of mouthpiece so party can be properly project-managed. Must investigate.

14 October

Spent all last night working on invitation list with Katie. She is adamant that no boys are allowed – even boys who like pink. Jack will barely get in by the skin of his teeth, and even then he will be forced to wear a tiara. In an unexpected twist she wants her arch-enemy Zoe to come.

'Are you sure, darling?' I asked, dreading Eco-mother's disgust at vast array of processed foods that will be on offer. 'I thought you weren't really friends with Zoe.'

Katie looked me in the eye with a sorrowful (and quite judgemental) expression. 'That's not a very kind thing to say, Mummy. Sharing is caring, you know.'

Suitably shamed, agreed to invite a grand total of seven little princesses. Should be dead easy to control. In fact, it's all so simple am considering setting up my own party company – I could make a fortune! Louise thinks I might be on to something. She was really interested in hearing all about it.

PS Mrs H has got wind of birthday party (blast Jack and his above-average vocal development) and wants to 'help'. 'Will I make some jelly, dear?' she asked, sounding quite excited at the prospect. 'My Joe used to love jelly, bless him. Jelly on a plate, jelly on a plate, wibbly-wobbly, wibbly-wobbly jelly on a plate, la, la, la . . .'

'OK, Mrs H,' I said, just to stop her singing down the phone at me. 'That would be great.' Privately think no one will touch such an outdated dessert. Will slip it in the bin when she's not watching.

PPS By amazing stroke of luck, found fabulous pink netting for my fairy tutu. (Only had to try four shops so was definitely magical, meant-to-be cosmic moment.) All I have to do is wrap it round my waist, slap on a tiara and I will be transformed into Fairy Susie.

PPPS Wanted to talk Joe through magic show, but he wasn't home until nearly midnight again – something to do with another critical accounting deadline, blah, blah, blah. Am very cross at his lack of commitment.

15 October

Evil Anna, former co-worker and Official Office Gossip, called out of the blue. 'Hi, Susie,' she simpered nicely (so I knew immediately she was Up To No Good).

'Hi, Anna,' I said, disentangling myself from the pile of pass-the-parcel gifts I had been trying to wrap. (Incredibly tricky to do without tying yourself in weird, bondage-type Sellotape knots.)

'I was just wondering, Susie, can you remember where you put the Hudson file?' she asked innocently.

'Er, probably in the large filing cabinet on the second floor,' I ventured, wondering why she needed to know and how I was expected to remember where anything was filed two years after I'd left.

'Hmm . . . yes, I've looked there. Thing is, Susie, Head Office is screaming for it – apparently there are some issues with the billing . . .' She trailed off.

'But I never dealt with billing,' I said, panicked that Head Office would blame me for some serious cock-up.

'Yes, but it *was* your project,' Anna said. 'You mustn't have checked it properly before you left.'

'But you took over all my projects before I left,' I stuttered, aghast.

'Hmm? Listen, I'll get you out of it, don't worry. I'll just tell them you've dropped off the face of the earth and they'll have to bury it. That's not such a stretch of the imagination, is it? Ha! Ha!'

Hung up, furious that my name will now be muck in Head Office. Know exactly what I want to bury, and it's not the Hudson file.

16 October

In attempt to block out fear that Head Office is hiring a top-notch private eye to track me down and slap a large lawsuit on me, have thrown myself into party planning with renewed gusto. Happily, am hitting my stride – just like old days in the cut-and-thrust world of event management.

Got some great ideas for a princess party online last night. Have updated the party folder to include the following tasks:

- Hang fairy lights everywhere to create sparkly and magical atmosphere.

- Purchase craft supplies so princesses can make their own tiaras (crafting very 'now' apparently).

- Make a giant cardboard cutout of a princess castle (looked bit tricky, but will persevere).

- Distribute personalized handmade thank-you cards from Katie after party (genius move to impress all playschool mothers).

Am confident it will run like clockwork. Am ignoring Joe's accusations that I am becoming obsessive compulsive.

Party Shopping List

- Fairy lights. I wish Joe had told me the Christmas set was broken, but am sure new ones will be easy enough to find.

- Face paints.

- Eight paper tiaras (preferably pink).

- Fake jewels to stick on tiaras (preferably pink).

- Eight tubes of glitter (as above).

- Pink streamers.

- Pink tablecloth (preferably Barbie).

- Pink goodie bags (preferably Barbie).

- Things to put in goodie bags – anything pink and Barbie-related.

Seems like quite a lot of stuff, but it's bound to be easy to pull together.

17 October

Mum and Dad are definitely going to Portugal so will miss the party. 'Take lots of photos, won't you, darling?' Mum said, when she called to break the news.

'Yes, well, if you were actually *here* I wouldn't have to worry about that,' I sulked, determined she would know that I was still annoyed about the rose/tree massacre.

'*I* know!' Mum screeched with excitement, ignoring my snotty tone. 'Why don't you take some photos on your mobile phone? Then you can text them to me!'

Cannot be normal that elderly parents are so technologically able. Things like mobile phones should confuse and exasperate them, for God's sake.

Meanwhile, Katie is campaigning for a professional magician to make a guest appearance.

'Daddy's going to be the magician. Won't that be

great?' I said cheerfully, hoping she hadn't already told everyone that David Blaine would be levitating in the living room.

'But he's not a *real* magician.' Katie pouted, unhappy with this arrangement. 'He can't make a real, live rabbit come out of a hat.'

'Well, he might,' I said doubtfully.

Wonder if that particular trick is included in *The Idiot's Guide to Magic Tricks* that I bought in the Centre. Must double-check.

18 October

Shit, shit, shit. Am way behind on party schedule. Both Katie and Jack have colds, so am trapped in the house dealing with non-stop demands for Lucozade and new-release DVDs on tap.

Confided my high state of anxiety to Louise when she called to ask whether she should tell MOM that she loves him or that she simply *cares* about him. Had to let her ramble on for a bit before I could get down to the nitty-gritty and talk about my own pressing problems – which, let's face it, are far more important than hers. Didn't say that, obviously.

'Take some Bach's Rescue Remedy,' she advised, after I explained the state of emergency. 'I do when I have to present to the board – it really works wonders.'

'Is it some sort of narcotic?' I asked suspiciously, willing to abandon my anti-drug stance and try it immediately.

'No, Susie!' She laughed. 'It's a botanical remedy for

stress. I gave you some in a gift basket last year – remember?'

Spent an hour searching frantically for the gift basket. Just when I'd given up hope, I found it hidden at the bottom of the wardrobe (along with the missing knee-high boot I've been searching for since last Easter). Squirted lots of Rescue Remedy drops into my mouth just to make sure and instantly felt a little calmer.

Finally managed to get the invites done. Seven scrolls, tied with pink ribbon.

You are cordially invited to Princess Katie's 4th Birthday Party. There will be face painting, a grand ball and a banquet. 3–5 p.m. on 22 October at 2 Fairbrook Drive. Princess dress, please!

Spent ages trying to tie the scrolls with the pink ribbon. Eventually had to staple them shut and glue the ribbon across the tiny holes. For some reason, found this hilariously funny. In fact, felt a bit light-headed and giggly all evening (probably the relief of ticking one thing off the list kicking in. Or maybe it was the glue).

PS In genius move, have ordered all the crafting materials for tiara- and card-making on-line. Thanks to excellent credit card, have cut out hours of exhausting legwork.

Disaster. Spent hours dragging Jack round in his buggy looking for fairy lights. Turns out that this year, for the first time in a decade, retailers have decided to wait until *after* Hallowe'en to put the Christmas decorations on the shelves. Eventually persuaded the spotty teenage manager in Tesco to sell me a couple of 'hot' sets straight from the stockroom.

'This could be more than my job's worth,' he whispered, shoving the thirty euro I gave him into his greasy trouser pocket and nervously handing over the lights.

'It's just between you and me,' I reassured him, quickly hiding the lights under my handy all-purpose mac. 'No one else will ever know.'

Strolled casually back up aisle three, trying hard not to look guilty, had reached the baked-beans display and thought I was home free when Jack started screaming 'Lights, lights!' at the top of his voice. Had to race for the exit and almost rammed the doors with his buggy to escape the attentions of the burly security guard. Luckily he was tucking into a box of deep-fried chicken wings at the time or we would have been scuppered.

PS Did impressive performance at school gates when quizzed by other mothers about party preparations. 'I hope you're not going to too much trouble, Susie?' one asked as I handed an invite to her.

'Not at all,' I lied. 'I haven't even thought about it, actually. I'll just throw a few things together on the day.'

Absolutely vital that event looks impressively casual.

Under no circumstances must other mothers realize that am on the edge of a nervous breakdown.

20 October

Out of the blue, Joe has announced that he will no longer be performing magic tricks at Katie's party. Was temporarily blindsided by this bombshell.

'I'm not doing it, Susie,' he insisted, helping Jack to pull his Batman suit over his head. 'I can't even shuffle a pack of cards properly and those kids will slaughter me if I get anything wrong.'

'But you *must* do it,' I gasped. 'Katie has her heart set on it.'

'Well, she'll have to settle for regular party games,' he said, unmoved. 'I'll do pin-the-tail-on-the-donkey, that kind of thing.'

Proceeded to have very heated discussion about his lack of commitment to the project but he couldn't be swayed. Can only hope that the extravaganza of fun I've organized will distract Katie from the crushing disappointment of her father letting her down.

PS Am considering sticking a sharp pin into Joe's behind to bring him to his senses.

21 October

Worryingly, Internet package with craft supplies still hasn't arrived so was forced to spend nearly a full month's child allowance in the posh craft shop at the

Centre. Outrageous that a few tubes of glitter, fake diamonds and glue can cost almost a hundred euro. The shop assistant thought all her Christmases had come at once when she saw me hauling half the crêpe paper in the shop up to the till. 'Aren't you great going to so much trouble?' she sniggered, totting it all up with glee. 'Most people would just put out a few Barbie goodie bags and play a bit of music.'

Stupid cow. Was tempted to slip a comment card to the manager on the way out expressing my annoyance, but arms were full of party paraphernalia so was at serious disadvantage.

Spent three hours after kids eventually went to bed draping fairy lights in artistic manner, hanging pink crêpe paper from every surface and cutting out gold-paper stars. Scissors mysteriously missing so had to use Katie's blue plastic pair. Abandoned the idea of making the cutout castle.

PS Louise texted me to say she can't make party tomorrow – emergency board meeting in London.

PPS Mum and Dad rang from Portugal – hotel right *on* the beach apparently.

PPPS Joe home late from work again – he didn't even notice the party decorations. Felt like throttling him with the fairy lights.

PPPPS Have just realized have forgotten to get the bloody Barbie birthday cake.

22 October: Katie's Birthday Party

Katie woke in a Very Bad Mood.

'Cheer up, Katie,' Joe ordered, in the I-will-tolerate-no-nonsense way guaranteed to send her into an even blacker frame of mind. 'It's your party today.'

'Don't want a party.' Katie kicked the leg of the kitchen table and eyed Jack aggressively through slitted eyes, trying to figure out how she could best maim him.

Sent Joe off in search of Barbie cake before he lost his temper and, in effort to quell rising panic, decided to drape some more streamers around. Effort paid off as all playschool mothers were seriously impressed with the vast array of pink decorations and my Fairy-Susie outfit (not that the entire exercise was a stunt to win their validation or approval, of course).

All except Eco-mother.

'Are those made from recycled cardboard, Susan?' she asked, about thirty seconds after she'd arrived with a mournful-looking Zoe in tow. She pointed to the Barbie banners draped everywhere.

'I'm sure they are,' I answered, smiling nervously and ushering Zoe and her bag of peeled organic fruit through to the party.

'I brought some snacks for her to munch,' Eco-mother explained, craning to see what sort of devil food I had prepared.

'No problem,' I said, trying to close the door to stop her doing a full eco-audit. 'I'll keep an eye on her.'

Things improved once the party started. In fact, I was almost reduced to tears at magical sight of all the sweet, innocent little angels (and Jack) in their princess dresses. Felt like arty earth-mother type, wafting about in my pink-net tutu, painting flowers and butterflies on kids' faces and laughing fondly at their cuteness. But after painting just two faces (face paints quite fiddly to get a handle on) Joe had to take over so I could supervise the tiara-making. Suddenly, and without any prior warning, all hell broke loose.

3.15 p.m. Laura Moore starts screaming hysterically because Joe paints a bug on her face (he *says* it was meant to be a butterfly).

3.16 p.m. Fist fight breaks out when Orla Kenny 'borrows' Lucy Connor's fake diamonds, and Amy Banks and Hannah Delaney decide that pouring tubes of glitter all over their hair will save them the bother of making tiaras.

3.20 p.m. After several failed attempts to get children to discuss their differences rationally, resort to throwing a bumper bucket of Barbie chocolate treats over them to break it up. (Joe suggests cold water might work better.)

3.25 p.m. Decide to abandon the tiara-making and go straight to pass-the-parcel.

3.26 p.m. Joe is unable to locate pass-the-parcel package (later transpires that Jack – traumatized by being forced to wear a tiara – has hidden it in the cupboard under the stairs).

3.30 p.m. More screaming and wailing.

3.32 p.m. Feeling quite sweaty and peculiar. Speedily progress to birthday cake.

3.34 p.m. Grimly relight birthday candles a zillion times so everyone gets a chance to blow them out.

3.40 p.m. Cake almost disintegrates under rain of saliva.

3.45 p.m. Katie demands that she be the only one allowed to eat the iced Barbie face atop the cake

3.47 p.m. Attempt to slice Barbie's face into eight separate pieces (luckily Jack doesn't want any), making sure the birthday girl gets the right eye and some blonde hair.

3.50 p.m. Eight princesses take one bite each of the twenty-five-euro cake and abandon it.

3.55 p.m. Progress to the opening of the birthday gifts.

4.00 p.m. Fisticuffs between guests over who can help Katie rip off the gift wrap.

4.05 p.m. Near fisticuffs between Joe and me over whose turn it was to recharge the now dead camcorder battery.

4.10 p.m. Still an hour to fill.

4.11 p.m. Resort to putting *Barbie Swan Lake* on the DVD and letting children watch it while they munch their way through truckloads of crisps and chocolate buttons.

4.15 p.m. Slug G and T out of Barbie cups in the kitchen and count the minutes until parents arrive to collect the little brats.

Eco-mother was last to arrive. Unfortunately, Zoe had inexplicably disappeared. Eventually found her hiding under the stairs, her face covered with illegal chocolate confection. Eco-mother's face turned a funny shade of red before she hauled out a screaming Zoe and propelled her into the street. Was quite merry after the G and T so happily waved them off – oblivious to the implications of Zoe scoffing illicit processed food, while under my care, for the first time ever.

PS Katie has just informed me that the party was

'OK' but she really would have preferred to see the new Disney movie, followed by a Happy Meal at McDonald's. Super.

23 October

Am exhausted. Probably suffering from post-traumatic party disorder. Was dozing on the couch today while Jack had his nap when someone pounding on the door woke me up. It was the postman with the Internet craft parcel – a day too late.

'You'd want to get that bell fixed, love,' he bellowed. 'I tried to deliver this to you the other day but I couldn't get an answer.'

Felt like strangling him there and then. Stumbled back inside to hear Jack wailing upstairs. The postman's roaring had woken him up only fifteen minutes after he'd gone to sleep.

Mrs H was hot on the postman's heels. 'Did they love my jelly, Susie?' she asked, settling down for an in-depth party post-mortem.

'Sure,' I said, handing her back the enormous trifle bowl she had filled to the brim with orange-flavoured gunk. No point breaking her heart by admitting that the dog had wolfed the entire bowl in one go and has been looking decidedly sick ever since.

PS The Internet company refuse to take all the craft supplies back! Apparently, if I'd read the small print, I would have realized there were no returns or exchanges under any circumstances. I am now stuck with a hundred euro worth of pink paper, glue and assorted fake jewels. Have a good mind to contact the Fair Trading Standards Office, or whatever it's called. Consumers should have rights. It's an absolute disgrace. Am definitely going to follow this up. Definitely.

24 October

Jack found the package of Internet craft stuff where I'd dumped it under the stairs (just a temporary measure until I had time to devise a consumer-rights manifesto-type plan of action) and poured the glitter and glue all over the hall, stairs and landing while I was washing curry sauce out of Joe's best shirt. There is now a hundred euro worth of crafts crap ground into my 100 per cent Navan wool carpet.

On the phone Mum didn't offer much sympathy. 'I told you to get the blue swirly pattern, darling,' she reminded me. 'A houseful of beige carpets is hopeless with children.' I thanked her politely for another nugget of useless advice, then hung up and chased Jack round the kitchen with the wooden spoon. He laughed so hard he nearly barfed.

25 October

Katie brought home a witch on a stick she had made at school. I had blanked Hallowe'en from my mind. Does it ever end? Do not know how many more crafty-type activities I can take. In fact, feel decidedly twitchy.

Christmas will be next. Was wandering aimlessly

through Tesco this morning when I slammed straight into the spotty teenage manager erecting a Christmas tree in aisle three. Was incensed and immediately tackled him about idiocy of putting up a Christmas tree in October. *Before* Hallowe'en.

He looked a bit confused. 'Didn't you get fairy lights from me last week?' he asked, having a good look down the M&S body top that had shrunk by at least two sizes in the dryer but which I had been forced to wear as all other half-decent or wearable clothes were still in the depths of the laundry basket.

Patiently explained that that had been a one-off emergency situation, not to be confused with rampant over-commercialization of Christmas and the loss of the true meaning of the season, etc., etc.

'I agree with you, love,' a little old lady, who had stopped to see what all the commotion was about, chimed in support. 'Our Lord must be scandalized when he sees the sinful behaviour of the world today.'

Could see spotty teenager backing away in alarm as little old lady proceeded to launch into well-practised monologue on the evils and depravity of the world today, including pornography, alcohol and Sunday shopping. Had to feed Jack an extra packet of chocolate Christmas-tree decorations he had picked up on aisle four to get him to sit still in the trolley and listen. Obviously couldn't be rude and just walk away. Also, was teeny bit afraid of her. She had a funny look in her eye and looked like she could lash out with a packet of frozen fish fingers if provoked.

Whole encounter made me think. Am determined to teach Katie and Jack all about the true meaning of

Christmas and what it stands for, etc., although will have to be careful not to get into too much detail about Mary giving birth to Jesus or Katie will grill me about baby-making. Anyway, most important thing is that they realize Christmas is not all about gaudy toys and fake Christmas trees, but about loving and giving and goodwill towards men. May well give money to charity instead of Christmas gifts this year. Am sure I heard about some charity that sends goats to poor countries. Far better than an Estée Lauder gift set. Even if that new scent is really nice. Will investigate.

PS Feel bit guilty about purchasing chocolate Christmas-tree decorations, but they *were* two for the price of one.

26 October

Got text from Louise: 'Girls' night out with college gang this Friday. Bella Trattoria, 8 p.m. Casual dress.'

Shit, shit, shit. Am now faced with agonizing Going Out vs. Hiding at Home Dilemma.

Cons
(a) Hate college gang. All successful, skinny, wealthy career types with Beemers and Louis Vuitton handbags and not a child between them.
(b) Will have to fabricate intricate web of lies about interesting, fulfilled life at home with children and devoted husband while enduring pitying looks and, as night progresses, outright drunken cries of 'Aren't you going *mad* sitting at home all day, Susie?'

(c) Will suffer massive inferiority complex for weeks afterwards and will inevitably start to question entire meaning of fruitless existence.

Pros

(a) Do quite fancy an Italian meal I could eat all in one go, without keeping one eye on Houdini trying to escape from his high chair and the other on Davida Copperfield trying to hide anything remotely resembling a vegetable up her sleeve.

Have decided to sleep on it before making any rash decisions.

27 October

Had restless night trying to decide what I would wear if I went out with college gang. Decided to rope in Katie to help and divided all possible clothing options on to bed while she supervised the Hunt for the Perfect Girls' Night Out Outfit. Didn't need to encourage her to be brutally honest about my (very limited) choices.

• Stretchy white top with sleeves – shows 'wobbly belly'.

• Black, sleeveless top – shows 'wobbly arms'.

• Black wrap dress – shows all 'lumpy' bits.

Eventually decided on boho-chic look *à la* Sienna Miller: faded jeans (only pair can wedge self into) and black, bat-wing former maternity top, with belt slung casually over hips (if I can still call them that). Very pleased with my ingenuity – top definitely doesn't look like former pregnancy tent. All I need is translucent dewy skin, flowing blonde locks, and Jude Law to complete the look. Katie not thrilled with my outfit of choice. She voted for the pink T-shirt and ra-ra skirt I had hoarded from my Wham! fan days, but don't think I could carry that off – even if I had a pair of Uggs.

PS Joe is being very sweet and encouraging. 'You deserve some time to yourself,' he said, when I explained why all of my clothes were strewn about the bedroom floor. 'And it would be good for you to hook up with some of your old friends – get you out of yourself a bit more.'

Mulled over this for ages while he took an excessively long shower in blatant disregard of Oprah's wishes to conserve water. Very disturbing that he thinks I need to get out of myself more. Fear I am turning into a sad housewife with no social skills.

28 October

Have discovered that Joe has been invited to two-day corporate golf tournament next week. Now realize that sweet encouragement to attend college-reunion bash was in fact underhand attempt to gain Brownie points so he could abandon his family for two nights with a clear conscience.

Bumped into Eco-mother at the playschool gates. Tried to hide behind latest copy of *Heat* (excellent cover story on celebs without makeup) but could see her zigzagging her way purposefully towards me, pushing her pram as if it was a weapon of mass destruction.

'Susan, I'd like a word with you, please,' she said, in a scarily steely way.

'Who, me?' I said, as if I was surprised. 'Yes, sure – what's up?'

'What's up is that my Zoe seems to have developed some sort of food allergy since your daughter's party last week.' She looked me fiercely in the eye.

Felt myself go weak with fright. I was about to be hauled off by social services for poisoning a minor. 'She only had a few chocolates,' I stammered, wondering if I could make a run for it.

'Yes, but it only takes a few,' Eco-mother lectured. 'Chocolate is a serious addiction that can take a lifetime to overcome. Her bowel movements this week have been most disturbing.'

Felt even fainter. If I'd known she was going to talk bowel movements I'd have sprinted for the car.

'Anyway,' she went on, 'I wanted to give you this.' She thrust a copy of *You Are What You Eat* under my nose. 'You should read it – it's a Bible for healthy eating and I think you need some guidance, don't you?' She turned on her Birkenstock heels and took off abruptly. (Probably to pick berries from the hedgerows or some such.)

PS Have decided to hide *You Are What You Eat* under the stairs. Suspect fierce-looking Gillian McKeith would disapprove of the pasta carbonara and tiramisu I plan to devour in one sitting tonight.

30 October: Morning After Night Before

On my deathbed. Throbbing head twice normal size. Tongue stuck to roof of mouth and coated in vile, post-alcohol scum. Evil husband relishing my hell and allowing children to jump all over me.

'Serves you right for drinking too much.' Joe laughed as Jack bellowed in one ear, and Katie tried to plait my hair as I lay prone on the bed.

'Tea! Get me tea,' I croaked. (Quite pleased with husky, sex-goddess voice, actually.)

Only had a few glasses of wine, but it might as well have been a few bottles. Years of pregnancy-induced abstinence means am practically born-again alcohol-virgin, my tolerance to chilled Sauvignon Blanc is so low. Feel like I have been on a proper student binge-drinking pub-crawl instead of having civilized meal and collapsing in bed by twelve thirty p.m. (seventy-five euro poorer).

Night not totally horrendous, but couldn't contribute much to conversation as it revolved round salaries (nil), cars (embarrassing people-carrier) and designer clothes (one as yet unworn D&G fluorescent orange mini-skirt bought in TK Maxx bargain bin). Didn't even get to chat to Louise as she sat at the other end of the table. Kept very low profile and shovelled pasta carbonara down throat way too quickly – couldn't shake feeling that Jack or Katie was about to jump out from under table to sabotage leisurely pace of eating. Luckily, newly engaged Frannie was centre of attention for the night so didn't have to answer probing questions about my lifestyle choices. Snuck off early. One more all-men-are-bastards story would have sent me over the edge. They'd all been watching way too much *Sex and the City* for my liking.

PS Casual dress, my eye! They all had blow-dried poker-straight hair, plunge bras and tailored suits! Will shove Louise's GHD straightening irons somewhere unmentionable when I get my hands on her.

31 October: Hallowe'en

Spent all day persuading Katie that dressing as a Bratz Rock Angel for Hallowe'en would not be age appropriate. 'But everyone's dressing as Bratz Angels!' she pouted, kicking Jack for no apparent reason. 'I want to wear a bikini top and hot pants and look sexy.'

'Sexy! Sexy!' Jack roared.

'*And* you don't even have any good scary lights,' she went on, pointing accusingly at the half-hearted carved pumpkin on the front step. 'Zoe's mum made brilliant skeletons to hang up *and* she has a real witch's broom.'

'I'll bet she does,' I muttered, imagining Eco-mother swooping in with some homemade sugar-free fudge at any second.

Luckily Joe arrived home unexpectedly early, dressed as a vampire with fake blood dripping from his mouth.

(Cheap Hallowe'en costume picked up in Spar on the way home: surprisingly effective.) Once I had got the kids out from behind the sofa where they were cowering in fear, we spent ages happily bobbing for apples in a bucket of water and chasing monkey nuts with our noses, just like the Waltons. Was grateful to him for saving the day with some good old-fashioned fun. Wish I could have captured some of it on camcorder (Katie and Jack looked so cute in their costumes) but Joe had forgotten to charge the battery (again). Decided not to tackle him about it – just tried to treasure the heart-warming family moments (before Jack threw the bucket of water over Katie's princess dress and she whipped his Spiderman mask from his face and tried to strangle him with her bare hands, that is).

In a fit of housewifely nostalgia, was almost tempted to make traditional Hallowe'en dish, colcannon, but went to Bella Italia for pizza instead, guzzled four glasses of Pinot Grigio and hopped on Joe when the kids were asleep. Best bonk we've had in months.

PS Louise called for post-mortem on girls' night out. Too loved-up to call her back.

PPS The dog seems to be suffering from post-traumatic stress disorder after all the Hallowe'en fuss – he refuses to come out from under the stairs.

PPPS Pesky trick-or-treaters have cleared out my secret stash of Monster Munch. Must restock ASAP.

After our lovely smoochy session last night, have decided that Joe and I need a break away from the kids. Happy parents make happy kids – Dr. Phil is always saying so. Spent ages trawling through Internet sites when I should have been unloading the dishwasher and sorting the washing. Found a spa resort in Wicklow that looks amazing. Now all I have to do is persuade someone to take the children so Joe and I can escape to the country, act like love's young dream and recapture our youth. Called Louise to gloat about happy marriage and romantic-break plans. She didn't sound too enthusiastic. 'Sounds lovely, Susie.' She sighed. 'So, what do you think about Frannie getting engaged?'

'Yeah, great, I suppose.' I shrugged. I couldn't have cared less about Frannie and her vulgar two-carat rock. Who does she think she is – J.Lo? (Mind you, her bum *is* big enough.)

'I'd love to get engaged.' Louise sounded positively *depressed.*

Was quite miffed with her. I call to talk about my romantic weekend away and all she wants to do is talk about *herself.* Getting sick of this toxic selfish behaviour. Anyway, she'll have to hold on to a boyfriend for longer than two minutes if she wants to get engaged. Didn't say that out loud obviously.

PS So glad I am happily married to my soulmate and officially don't have to worry about GHDing and sexy underwear.

2 November

Had a huge row with Joe this morning. He stomped round the kitchen with a face like thunder until I asked him what was wrong.

'There are no bloody clean shirts and I have a big meeting on today,' he snapped.

I felt like telling him to ram his clean shirts up his bum. 'I am not your skivvy,' I hissed back, not wanting the kids to hear.

'Is it too much to ask that a man has a clean shirt to wear to work, for God's sake?' he said. 'What in the hell do you do all day?'

He could not have said anything worse. Gave a screech so loud I'm sure old Mrs Doyle next door heard it through the wall. 'I mind your children, that's what I do, mister,' I roared, like an inner-city extra off *Fair City*. 'And not only do I get no thanks for it but I don't get a pay-cheque either. I am exhausted all of the time – I have never worked so hard in my life! *And* I never get a minute off, just to myself. At least in an office you get a coffee break. I don't even get to go to the bloody toilet on my own.'

Ranted on and on like a thing possessed, until I noticed Katie and Jack staring up at me over their corn flakes, their little mouths open with shock.

'Well done,' Joe snarled, before storming out of the kitchen.

'Mummy, what's a skivvy?' Katie asked, beady little eyes riveted on my face.

'Nothing, darling,' I muttered, wiping away tears of frustration and rage.

There's no way I'm talking to Joe until he comes grovelling on his bended knees. And he can shove his romantic night away as well. He doesn't deserve a five-star resort, with spa, Jacuzzi, indoor heated swimming-pool and two acres of manicured gardens.

PS Had words with Mum on the phone. She had the nerve to say that a bit of ironing really wouldn't kill me! What does she think this is – the Dark Ages? Women aren't expected to do all that drudgery any more. That's why dry-cleaners were invented.

3 November

Cold War continues. At this rate, we will be Kramer vs. Kramer soon.

4 November

Mrs Kenny next door came scooting out of her house wielding a huge bouquet of pink roses as I was unloading the kids from the car. 'I saw the florist trying to deliver them to you, love,' she announced triumphantly, 'so I just popped out and said I'd take them in. Have you and Joe had a little row, pet?'

Mrs Kenny can seem like a harmless little old lady, but she's really the most vicious gossip-monger in the city. She was almost rubbing her hands with glee at having a bit of hot news to spread to all the other grannies in the neighbourhood. 'No, not at all, Mrs Kenny. It's our anniversary.' I smiled grimly, holding on to Jack as he tried to throw himself in front of an oncoming car.

'I thought you were married in May, dear?'

Fifteen–love to Mrs Kenny.

'Oh, not our wedding anniversary, Mrs Kenny,' I stuttered, furious she was still so mentally able, 'the anniversary that Joe proposed to me. Isn't he so romantic?'

'Isn't he just?' she smirked knowingly, as I hauled the children and the offending bouquet inside.

PS Joe is seriously deluded if he thinks a vulgar-looking bunch of flowers will get him back in my good books. It'll take a piece of jewellery at the very least. Or a trip to a day spa.

PPS Have just noticed card attached to the bouquet: 'Susie, I'm sorry – please forgive me.' No wonder Mrs Kenny was looking so bloody pleased with herself. Could kill Joe. He should have told the florist to put the card in a bloody envelope.

5 November

Joe brought me a solitary cup of tea in bed this morning. Apparently a slice of toast is too much to ask for.

'I'm sorry I lost my temper, Susie,' he mumbled, balancing the tea frustratingly just out of my reach. 'Things are very pressured at work and I guess I'm a bit stressed.'

I grunted sarcastically, keeping my back firmly facing

him, just so he would be sure to know I wasn't going to forgive him that easily. Also, was desperate for the tea and afraid if I turned round I would gulp it down in one go and he might think he had won.

'Anyway, you're a great mum,' he went on. 'Katie and Jack couldn't ask for better.' Before I had a chance to grunt sarcastically again, Katie burst through the door and threw herself at the bed like a heat-seeking missile, sending the tea flying across the duvet cover.

'That's just great,' I muttered. 'One more thing for me *not* to wash. Why don't you add it to the pile?'

Heard Joe sigh loudly before he ushered Katie out to her howls of protest.

6 November

Mum and Dad are back from Portugal. 'The resort spa was amazing, Susie,' Mum gushed, when she called. 'Your dad became practically addicted to those mud wraps.'

'Sounds lovely,' I said, privately a bit peeved. Wish I could visit a top-notch spa and indulge in all sorts of outlandish treatments. Nearest I can get to a mud wrap is making mud pies with Jack in the back garden. And even then I have to pick all the creepy-crawlies out first.

PS Have decided to forgive Joe. It's exhausting being in a huff all the time. Also, really need to refuel the people-carrier and cannot figure out how to open the petrol cap.

Louise called round for coffee. 'Just passing,' she sang on the doorstep, holding a bag of designer cookies aloft in one hand and clutching a cream cashmere shawl round her Armani trouser suit to ward off the chill with the other.

Wish she'd call first – was still in my crumpled pyjamas with unwashed hair and Sudocrem lathered all over my chin to combat unsightly acne outbreak. Had to fake cold-type symptoms to explain bed attire at eleven a.m., so she wouldn't be appalled at how badly I'm letting myself go.

'You poor thing,' she sympathized. 'If I'd known you had a cold I could have brought some whisky round and made you a hot toddy.'

Was appalled by her insinuation that I would engage in binge-drinking in the middle of the day while trying to care for two children. However, decided to say nothing and busied myself making tea and trying to find two clean cups in the mountain of crusty crockery in the sink. (Note: vow never again to buy ready-made supermarket lasagne sauce. Stains left on outrageously expensive pastel bakeware impossible to remove, even after days of soaking.)

'What gorgeous flowers, Susie.' Louise's mane of perfectly highlighted golden hair brushed her face as she bent gracefully to inhale the scent of Joe's bouquet, like something out of a soft-focus ad for hair conditioner. 'Did Joe send them to you because you're sick?'

Was overcome by mean-spirited, dishonest streak

and, for once, decided to give in to it. 'Oh, no.' I fake-coughed. 'No special reason. Just one of those silly, married things. Now, would you like tea or coffee?'

Could see Louise's line-free face crumple in the kettle and felt a bit guilty. But a person can only take so much.

8 November

Am at wit's end. Vile article in parenting section of the *Gazette* says that soothers are filthy, evil products of Satan, used by lazy parents who have no real interest in their child's welfare. Katie is still really attached to her binky at the age of *four*. You're supposed to wean children off them at three months! Three *months*! Was anxiety-ridden all day and ate even more custard creams than usual. Have horrible suspicion I'm creating a future drug-abuser or, *even worse*, a future smoker. Article said tough love may be needed in order to separate child from binky.

Spent all afternoon devising strategic plan of action so will not crack under pressure.

New Ground Rules for Binky Usage

• Having the binky in bed is OK.

• Having the binky when tired and emotional at home is also OK.

• Taking the binky outdoors (or generally anywhere that people who read the parenting supplement might see it and judge me and my bad parenting) is a no-no.

74

Katie is refusing to co-operate fully. In fact, she is refusing to co-operate in any way, shape or form.

'Is my binky a secret, Mummy?' she asked innocently, curling her hair round her finger and dangling the soother tantalizingly in front of me with the other hand.

In a flash of the rare, creepy 'mothering instinct' I had only ever read about in *Babytalk* magazine, I knew immediately any sign of weakness would be fatal. If she sensed my binky-related embarrassment, she would insist on leaving it in her mouth for every family photograph from here to eternity.

Tried to meet her gaze without flinching. 'Not really, darling,' I replied (quite nonchalantly, I thought). 'Mummy just likes to see your pretty face and I can't when you have a soother in your mouth.'

She considered this at length before she launched her counter-attack. 'My binky's pretty. See? It's pink!'

9 November

Am living on my nerves. Katie is insisting on having her soother in her possession 24/7. Tackled her about it when we were in Tesco this afternoon. 'Give me the binky, pet,' I said, as matter-of-factly as possible (theperfectparent.com said to be calm and measured in your approach, rather than using bribery or other forms of extortion).

'No,' she replied, just as matter-of-factly.

Jack perked up in the trolley, sensing that things might get interesting.

'I am the adult, I am the adult,' I repeated silently to

myself, praying she wouldn't have a full-scale meltdown in a packed shop on a Friday afternoon. 'You don't need it in the supermarket, Katie.'

'Yes, I do.' She eyeballed me back, confident that I would never resort to a full-on shouting match in front of members of the public. She was right.

'Why can't you give it up?' I pleaded, caving almost immediately. 'You're a big girl now.'

'Me no big girl,' she lisped in her best put-on baby voice. 'Me ickle baby.' The child operates at a higher level.

Dad was only too delighted to remind me that I am completely at fault for Katie's illicit addiction. 'You gave it to her, Susie,' he reminded me, when I called for some sympathy. 'You can't expect the child to want to give it back now, just when it suits you.'

This, quite annoyingly, makes perfect sense, but is of no help whatsover.

Mum was more of a comfort. 'Have you ever seen an adult sucking on a soother?' she said, in a wise way. 'She'll give it up in her own good time.'

Decided to forgive her for the ironing comment.

10 *November*

Called Louise to discuss the soother issue. She was blatantly uninterested. 'Does it really matter when she gives it up?' she asked, a bit irritable and distracted.

'Well, of course it does,' I replied, shocked that she didn't realize the serious implications. 'It could affect her speech, or her socialization skills, even.'

'There doesn't seem to be too much wrong with her

speech,' Louise said drily, as Katie started screaming hysterically because Jack had pulled on her ballet tutu over his Batman outfit and was pirouetting round the kitchen.

Hung up quite annoyed. Louise never really listens to my problems but she always expects me to listen to hers. Which I would do if I wasn't so busy all the time.

11 November

We're going away for a night of unadulterated passion! At last Joe has come good. He has booked a superior room in a spa resort in Wicklow (printing off their web pages and scattering them round the kitchen worktops worked a treat). He has even arranged for Mrs H to stay the night with the children. Am teeny bit disappointed that he didn't book the junior suite and that we're only staying for one night, not two, but am also thrilled with unexpected romantic gesture. Finally, we'll get a chance to spend some quality time together and remember why we got married in the first place. And who knows? We might be upgraded to the presidential suite. Must remember to remind Joe to look like we're in love and to drop hints that we're celebrating a Very Important Occasion.

All I have to do is clean the house from top to bottom before Mrs H arrives. It's one thing her popping in for coffee at the drop of a hat. It's quite another to hand the house keys over and give her full licence to snoop – you never know where she might poke her nose.

To Do List Before Night of Passion

- Empty fridge of mouldy food. Scrub with Milton. Fill with vegetables and healthy options.

- Wash down skirting-boards and outside of cupboards (remove egg stain on handle with wire brush if necessary).

- Clean and rearrange cutlery drawer so that spoons, forks and knives all face one direction.

- Wash out bin and pick bits of dried, crusty food off inside of cupboard door.

- Vacuum entire house (under things as well as around them).

- Polish entire house (see above).

- Clean oven and scrub grill pans (in fact, hide grill pans in garage).

- Hide mounds of dirty laundry in garage.

- Bring all of Joe's unironed shirts to dry-cleaner.

- Scrub toilet and remove mildew from shower doors with vinegar.

- Iron and fold all children's clothes.

- Hide pile of useless gossip magazines.

- Get hair and nails done.

- Book bikini and leg wax.

- Pack overnight case.

Am in agony. Forgot how painful getting a bikini wax is. Which is probably why I haven't had one done since my honeymoon. Obviously blocked it from my subconscious, like you do with childbirth. Will skin Louise for recommending that butcher beautician.

'It's a fab salon, Susie,' she enthused down the phone. 'It's really luxurious [code for ridiculously overpriced]. You should treat yourself for once – I go there at least twice a month.' (Code for 'You lead a sad, frumpy existence, and even if Amanda Byram chartered a private jet and flew to Ireland with a team of beauty professionals to give you a *Swan*-style makeover, it wouldn't make a blind bit of difference'.)

Had hair and nails done first, and was so overjoyed at having spent two hours reading useless gossip mags and drinking frothy cappuccino that I drifted dreamily into the backroom, where they do the waxing, like a lamb to slaughter.

The waxing girl was really nice and chatty so I whipped off my trousers and was quite at ease. She seemed a bit taken aback by the jungle that is my nether regions, and muttered something about using an extra tub of wax. Then, without warning, she started yanking at my privates, barking at me to raise my legs higher and whipping the strips off ferociously. Was so shocked I almost kneed her in the face. There was no use begging her to stop, because Sergeant Major just snapped at me to get a grip, then yanked even harder. Once the torture was over, I had to endure a five-minute homily about the importance of regular waxing. Apparently the more you wax, the finer the hair becomes, until eventually you're a hairless freak. Hobbled out of there with a false smile pasted to my face, handing over a ten-euro tip as I left.

Can barely walk, let alone vacuum. Will have to clean house tomorrow.

PS Hope bitemarks on my hand from trying to stifle the screams disappear soon.

13 November

The reality of mother-in-law staying over has hit me and I am like a thing possessed. Spent all day scrubbing every visible surface. Jack and Katie have taken to hiding under the kitchen table with the dog. Feel guilty for inflicting serious emotional trauma on offspring, but am putting it on hold – the most perfect housekeeper in Ireland is descending on me, and she will be unsupervised in my house for more than twenty-four hours. The snooping possibilities are endless. Must focus.

14 November

House is gleaming from top to bottom. I don't think it has ever been this clean. Not ever. Can finally say with confidence that Joe's mother will not be able to find fault with anything. In fact, she will literally be able to eat her dinner off the floor. May suggest she tries it.

Am stalking the kids like a madwoman to make sure

they don't undo the domestic perfection. Will have to purchase seriously OTT gifts from night away to make amends and buy back their affection. Possibly something Baby Dior.

PS Bikini area quite red and sore. Crazy waxing girl said I might be a bit sensitive for a day or so. Just hope it will be gone by tomorrow when I am lounging by the Olympic-sized indoor pool (with hot tub and steam room) in the sexy black swimming togs I bought two years ago and have yet to wear.

PPS Mum and Dad rang to ask me to say hello to the hotel manager – they still remember how nice he was when they spent a week there last year.

PPPS Just had last-minute shower and tried to clean shower door with vinegar at same time. Vinegar went everywhere – crotch on fire!

15 November

Overnight break did not start well. Joe spent entire journey to hotel fielding calls from office on his headset and using his I-Am-a-Very-Important-Executive voice instead of indulging in sexy and flirtatious behaviour with me. Luckily for him, was completely exhausted after all the marathon cleaning so had a little nap to freshen myself for all the luxurious pampering that lay ahead.

Five-course dinner was divine, even if Joe was a bit distracted by his BlackBerry vibrating every five minutes, and my throbbing nether regions put me right off the lobster. Was determined to be as romantic as possible, so rubbed Joe's foot seductively under the table for ages and couldn't understand why he continued shovelling duck pâté into his mouth unaffected. Years ago, one touch of my stiletto was enough to drive him insane with lust. Mystery was solved when I realized that I'd been fondling my fake Gucci handbag, which I'd placed carefully under the table before the hunky French waiter helped me sit down.

When we got back to the hotel room, I darted into the bathroom and spent ages trying to disguise the oozing green pustules round my crotch (may well be suffering from some kind of serious post-waxing infection) with my Clinique foundation. Eventually wafted sexily out of the en-suite bathroom to discover Joe snoring softly on the king-size bed, his laptop perched on his pot belly.

Proceeded to spend the night flicking between the dozens of channels on the massive flat-screen TV and eating the contents of the mini-bar out of spite. Cried bitterly over *Who Will Love My Children?*. Feel I may have deep-seated issues of abandonment myself. Luckily the buffet breakfast was spectacular, although thought I caught the waitress throwing funny looks in my direction when I had the full Irish swiftly followed by the continental option. Proceeded to ignore her in a lofty the-customer-is-always-right fashion. Unfortunately, it turned out that I couldn't eat everything (the midnight raid on the mini-bar might have been a bad idea) so shoved a few croissants into my bag for the journey home. Also, was unable to use spa facilities due to pulsating green pustules (probably just as well as waistline seemed to have mysteriously expanded overnight and not sure if I would have managed to wedge myself into those sexy black swimming togs I got two years ago), but Joe spent ages in the Jacuzzi, dangling his mobile phone over the side in case it got washed away in a sea of bubbles. Spent the afternoon sitting by the pool in a plush white towelling robe reading the latest copy of *Heat* and pretending I didn't want to use the Jacuzzi or the steam room. Can now understand why celebs wear white robes on movie sets – they're so comfy, with the added bonus of covering all your unflattering bits. *Heat* was excellent. Very comforting to see that even Paris Hilton may suffer from cellulite – and *she* has an army of top nutritionists, stylists and quite possibly lymph-drainage specialists on hand 24/7.

16 November

Arrived back to be met at the door by Mrs H, feather duster in one hand, vacuum-cleaner in the other. 'Just doing a little tidy, dear,' she chirped, as Jack and Katie threw themselves on my legs, whipping the chocolate bars I had brought them out of my hands at lightning speed.

'Mummy, Mummy, the binky fairy came while you were away,' Katie yelled, shoving the entire bar into her mouth in one go. 'I gave my soother to her and she left me a present under my pillow. I'm not going to use a binky any more. They're only for *babies*.'

Was speechless. All my plotting and planning and Mrs H had got the blasted soother off her overnight.

'Yes, dear,' she simpered. 'It was high time she gave

that filthy thing up. By the way, I gave Jack's high-chair a little clean when you were gone – there was quite a bit of old food under the plastic seat. We don't want the poor little pet to get food poisoning so we don't.'

17 November

Louise called for blow-by-blow account of luxury spa break. Sexed up bedroom activities quite a bit, just to make sure she doesn't think I'm a total has-been in that department. 'I was really looking forward to a good night's sleep, to be honest, but we just couldn't keep our hands off each other.' I giggled as girlishly as I could manage after another night of Jack waking every hour on the hour.

Truth is, am already even more exhausted than usual. Payback for a night of child-free bliss began at dawn when both kids mobilized forces to Make Up for Lost Time.

'We barely even saw the rest of the hotel,' I continued (in for a penny in for a pound), 'we were holed up in our room so much!' Sounded quite convincing. May have second career as international spy, just like Jamie Lee Curtis in that movie with Arnold Schwarzenegger.

'Of course, the kids missed us terribly [actually, don't think they even noticed we were off the premises], but it's very important to reconnect as a couple once in a while.' Threw that in for good measure.

'Sounds fantastic.' Louise sighed. 'I'd love a break like that.'

Why Louise thinks she needs a break is beyond me!

A break from what? Posh client lunches and glam nights out with MOM? Had to bite my tongue to hold back sarcastic remarks straining to get out.

'Work is so stressful at the moment,' she went on. 'I'd give anything to be able to stay at home all day like you do, Susie. You're so lucky to have Joe and the kids.' Could hear her twirling her perfectly blow-dried hair round her immaculately manicured fingernails as she spoke.

'Well, it's not all a barrel of laughs, you know,' I retorted, very cross that she thinks I watch TV and drink coffee all day. 'I've never worked harder in my life, actually. It's non-stop.'

'Yes, but at least it's really fulfilling. And Katie and Jack are so *cute*. If I have to listen to one more presentation about some bloody micro-chip I'll tear my hair out.'

Had to cut conversation short before I could respond – Katie had wrestled Jack to the ground and was attempting to poke his eye out with a Magic Marker.

18 November

Broke Guinness world record today. Filled and emptied dishwasher a grand total of six times. Luxurious mini-break seems a lifetime ago.

19 November

Eco-mother was looking even more pompous and self-satisfied than usual at the school gates this morning.

'Oh, yes, it's definitely the way forward,' I heard her preach loudly, as the other mothers stood round her looking sad and defeated. 'Zoe has the maths skills of a seven-year-old now and she's on track to beat all the targets before Christmas.'

'What's going on?' I whispered to another mother, out of the side of my mouth.

'Kumon maths,' she answered, sounding depressed. 'It's the latest craze. Apparently, it gives children an excellent head start in maths and English skills.'

Am outraged. Playschool is way too early to be introducing pressure of that kind. May well write to the Department of Education and demand that this kind of excessive home tutoring be banned immediately.

20 November

Researched Kumon on-line. It looks above board in a give-your-child-the-best-start-in-life way. Have sent off for info pack.

PS must remember not to admit this to Eco-mother.

21 November

Panic. Discovered horrible meningitis-type rash on Jack's tummy when I changed his nappy this morning. Tried to do tumbler test but he wouldn't stay still long enough for me to see if the dots were still visible through the glass. He didn't seem to have a temperature, but that bloody thermometer's unreliable at the best of times, especially since Katie tried to ram it up Baby Annabel's bum playing doctors-and-nurses. Called Joe at work, hyperventilating down the phone about blood transfusions and amputations. He told me to ring the meningitis hotline before I railroaded my way into the children's hospital.

Reassuring motherly nurse calmed me down. 'Is Baby hot?' she asked in a *sloooow* he-isn't-going-to-die voice. 'Is he irritable to the touch?'

No and no. In fact, Jack was happily clapping along to Barney singing on TV as I spoke on the phone. Kind-hearted nurse thought it might be a reaction to something rather than life-threatening disease. 'Have you changed your washing powder recently, dear?' she asked, before ringing off to answer some genuine life-or-death emergency.

Suddenly remembered that Jack's perfectly ironed vests had smelled a bit strange when I came back from luxury spa break. One more call and mystery was solved: Joe's mother had used a scented ironing spray to give the kids' clothes a 'touch of spring'. Never knew scented ironing sprays existed! Where does she do her shopping? The Perfect Housewife's Store? Was too relieved that Jack was not dying to tell her about mystery rash, so just thanked her politely before mumbling something about having to get the dinner on and hanging up.

'You're welcome, dear,' she said, sounding pleased with herself. 'Always happy to help.'

PS Rang meningitis hotline back to make a donation. Kindly, underfunded nurse very grateful.

Joe is alarmingly unperturbed that Jack almost died yesterday. In fact he is insisting that there was nothing wrong with him in the first place.

When I expressed outrage at his cold and unfeeling nature he laughed. 'Well, you weren't here to see how sick he was,' I countered. 'For all you knew he could have been at death's door.'

'Yes, but he wasn't,' he said, helping Katie snap the velcro shut on her trainers and looking annoyingly unruffled.

'But what if he had been seriously allergic to that ironing spray?' I said, getting angrier by the second. 'He was practically in anaphylactic shock as it was. Your mother should never have used it.'

'She was probably trying to be helpful, Susie.'

'Well, it could have been a tragedy,' I fumed, furious he was not taking my concerns seriously enough. 'I don't think Jack has been the same since.'

Unfortunately Jack chose that moment to bound into the kitchen and do his best Spiderman impression. He did jump a little less violently than usual, though – think some of his spark has been snuffed out after his brush with death.

23 November

Received two letters from RTÉ today.

Dear Ms Hunt,

Thank you for your recent letter. Your comment about my appearance was kind. I do not actually have any children, but I do admire women who choose to stay at home to devote themselves to child-rearing.

I can fully understand your frustration that repeats of your favourite show are shown on a regular basis. Unfortunately, as a sales and marketing co-ordinator, I am not in a position to influence programming schedules, but I will pass your letter on to the relevant department where I am sure they will take all of your comments on board and get back to you with a swift and appropriate response.

Yours sincerely,
Jennifer Goode

Dear Ms Hunt,

Thank you for your recent letter concerning repeats of *Dr. Phil.* We have been having difficulty acquiring new episodes of the show recently. However, we do hope to rectify the situation as soon as possible. Please continue to bear with us – we value your viewership!

Best wishes,
P. Baxter

Decided to reply immediately and express my disquiet at the obvious total disregard that our national broadcaster has for a silent, disenfranchised minority.

Dear Jennifer [feel I have already established real and deep connection with this woman so decided to eschew formalities]

I hope you are well. I was sorry to hear you have no children – you have such a kindly, maternal face.

Please find attached a letter I recently received from a P. Baxter. As you can see it is most unsatisfactory. None of the real issues have been addressed here. For example, he/she has not addressed the obvious lack of commitment to quality programming for housewives. Let's face it, anyone who has the arrogance to sign a letter using only an initial is most definitely not interested in the bigger picture. Furthermore, there have been no assurances that the boring repeats will be dropped. In fact, I strongly suspect this is yet another attempt to brush the legitimate concerns of an under-represented minority under the carpet. Of course, I should probably expect nothing else from our sexist, patriarchal society but I can guarantee you that if men stayed at home, the quality of programming would improve tenfold.

Meanwhile, the repeats are coming thick and fast. I will have to resort to watching *The Ricki Lake Show* if this is not sorted as a matter of urgency. I would be sorry to switch loyalties after such a long time, but it is reaching crisis point. I can tell you are a can-do person – can you please do something to rectify the situation?

Thank you,
Susie

PS Have you thought about my fly-on-the-wall housewives' documentary? Perhaps you could suggest it at the next board meeting. A hot new idea like that might lead to an enormous promotion and pay rise. I know how these things work. (I often reported directly to the CEO when I was in PR.)

24 November

Have just done mental calculation. Joe and I have not had nookie since well before the spa break. Nothing unusual there – we have gone for longer than that (much longer, if I'm brutally honest). But the unsettling thing is, Joe has not pestered me for nookie since then either. In fact, cannot remember when he last expressed any interest in me at all. Am very seriously concerned. My God, what if he's having an affair? Louise nearly collapsed with laughter when I texted her to call me *urgently*. (May as well have her employer pay for crisis talks – all these multinationals have endless supplies of cash.) 'Joe? Have an affair? Don't be ridiculous, Susie! He's the most unlikely person to have an affair. In the world. Ever.'

'Well, why hasn't he been pestering me for sex, then?' I pouted down the phone. 'That's never happened before. In fact, if I remember rightly, he once told me that the day he stopped looking for some action was the day he was officially dead.' Felt quite sniffly and in need of serious attention.

At the first sign of tears, Louise instantly morphed into her ball-breaking business suit and stiletto-heels-wearing persona. 'Get a grip, Susie,' she chided, in a brisk, I-will-tolerate-no-nonsense tone. 'Joe is not having an affair – he's probably exhausted from all those late nights. And before you even *think* it, no, he is not lying to you about working late at the office and really having steamy sex with his secretary across his desk. Anyway, didn't you have a sexathon when you went on your spa break?'

Forgotten that I'd exaggerated the bedroom activities just a bit to Louise in an effort not to seem like a dried-up old prune so hummed vaguely at that bit.

Anyway, have decided that Louise is probably right – I've seen Joe's secretary: she's sixty if she's a day.

PS Have decided to take the initiative and initiate some nookie. Some night soon, when I'm not too knackered.

25 November

Rubbed my toe up Joe's leg last night in half-hearted seductress attempt. He told me I need to trim my toenails! And then rolled over and went to sleep! Had horrible nightmare where Dr. Phil hauled me on stage in front of all my friends and family and lectured me in scary Southern accent about sex being the most accurate indicator of happiness in a marriage. Audience was booing and hissing, and Katie and Jack were sitting in the front row looking abused and sorrowful. This requires serious action – *Men Are From Mars, Women Are From Venus* just will not cut the mustard this time. It's time to go to the next level. I am sending off for Dr. Phil's *Relationship Rescue* tomorrow.

26 November

Joe brought a jumbo box of Jammie Dodgers home from work. 'They were left over from the team-building day, and I know they're one of your favourites,' he said, handing them to me gallantly. Was touched by his thoughtfulness. Have decided that it's these romantic little gestures that matter as a marriage matures, not working your way through the *Kama Sutra*.

27 November

Mum thinks Dad may be having prostate problems.

'Really? What are the symptoms?' I asked, panic-stricken that Dad might collapse into a semi-conscious state at any moment.

'Well, we're not as *active* as we used to be, if you know what I mean,' she whispered furtively, down the phone.

'You're the most active people I know.' I laughed. 'You went hill-climbing last week!'

'No, not that kind of active,' she said. 'In the bed-room. *You* know.'

Wish Mum wouldn't confide in me quite so much.

'Maybe he needs a little pick-me-up,' she mused. 'Ginkgo is meant to be good for virility. I think I'll brew him a special tea later on.'

Spent rest of the day trying to wipe out of my mind vivid images of parents doing it. Feel most uneasy.

28 November

Evil Anna, former co-worker and Official Office Gossip, called to 'invite' me to Christmas drinks. (Probably in spiteful effort to see how much weight I have piled on since I became a bona-fide housewife.)

'Come on, Susie, everyone's going.' She tittered drunkenly (the boozy pre-Christmas lunches must have started already). 'You *never* get out and this is the perfect excuse. *And* it's dress down so you won't even have to make an effort.'

Made superhuman effort to control myself before answering. 'Actually, I'm just back from a fantastic spa break with Joe,' I boasted, dead pleased with myself and my quick wit.

Annoyingly, Anna decided to ignore me as usual. 'Do you know what you need, Susie?' she slurred. 'You need to go out and get roaring drunk! You stay-at-home mothers are all the same – you're so *boring*.' Could hear her hiccuping quietly into the receiver. 'Why don't you live a little? The kids won't *die* if you leave them for the night, you know.'

Agreed to go just to get her off the phone. Luckily, it is ages away so have loads of time to concoct decent excuse.

29 November

Oh, my God. Have realized there is less than a month to Christmas. Feel very sick.

30 November

Much better today. Will make organized to-do list. Shouldn't take long. Kids at this age have no real concept of gifts or brands. Will probably get away with one small gift each.

1 December

Mrs H has reduced the children to gibbering wrecks. 'Only four weeks to go, only four weeks to go,' she sang loudly (and terribly out of tunc) on the doorstep at midday, waving Christmas decorations (and what looked like a bottle of eggnog) about.

Jack and Katie looked at her suspiciously, wondering where this was going and whether there would be any free chocolate involved.

'Not much Christmas spirit here, is there, Susie?' Mrs H said, narrowing her eyes and surveying the bare living room. Could see her trying to decide where she could hang a few gaudy baubles to 'brighten up the place'.

'Well, I suppose they're immune to decorations at this stage – they've been all over the city since Hallowe'en,' I said, ducking to avoid getting hit by flying tinsel.

'If you and Joe can't be bothered to create some Christmas excitement,' she went on, half staggering into the hallway, 'then I'll have to.'

Suddenly realized she might have partaken of an eggnog or two at the bingo. Katie and Jack perked up, sensing drama. 'Why don't you come into the kitchen, Mrs H?' I hissed, terrified she'd wind them up into a frenzy of Christmas excitement and they'd peak too early.

But there was no stopping her. She swayed down until she was at their level (in fairness quite graciously and only bending at the knee), a very serious look on her face. 'Christmas is only four weeks away, children. Do you know what that means?'

'Baby Jesus is coming?' answered Katie, suspecting chocolate might be on offer for a good religious answer.

'Yes, darling, that's right,' said Mrs H, whipping out a Milky Bar and tearing off the wrapper in one swift movement, 'but it also means that Santa will be here soon.'

'Thanta, Thanta!' Jack screeched.

'Sho,' she slurred, 'you need to start making your lists and checking them twice, isn't that right?'

Decided to retreat to the downstairs toilet and call Joe to consult. Funnily enough he was in a meeting and Could Not Be Disturbed Under Any Circumstances; even if his drunken mother was slowly ensuring we'd have to remortgage the house to pay our Santa bill.

Emerged to find Katie considering her options, flicking from channel to channel to watch every toy advertisement possible.

'Such special Christmas memories, Susie,' Mrs H

announced, misty-eyed, then collapsed onto the sofa for three hours.

2 December

Have made extensive Christmas gift list.
  Joe: TBA (mini-break voucher, perhaps?).
  Mum and Dad: TBA (technologically advanced gizmos to be avoided at all costs. *Joy of Sex* also off limits).
  Katie: Vast array of branded, disproportionately expensive toys.
  Jack: As above.
  Louise: TBA (something expensive and perfectly gift-wrapped).
  Mrs H: TBA (maybe some kind of bingo-related accessories).
  Oprah is right. Making a list really *does* help you regain control of a situation.

3 December

Jack and Katie are in a state of High Alert. Meanwhile, Joe has started his morose Christmas-is-overrated routine, and Mum and Dad have announced that they're escaping to Co. Clare for the holidays. For *another* luxury break. Which has really screwed up my plan of decamping to them for the duration. Have noticed that, since they hit their sixties, they have become quite selfish. Had devised detailed plan to spend all of Christmas and New Year in a rural idyll, and suddenly they decide to spend Christmas in Dromoland Castle – Dromoland bloody Castle no less. There will be no inheritance left if they keep spending like this. Was so cross I almost had a row with Mum on the phone.

'Darling, we've always wanted to stay in Dromoland, and now that Daddy's retired, we have no excuse not to,' she said.

Was sure I could hear Dad sniggering in the background.

'But, Mum,' I wailed, 'we wanted to come to you for Christmas. The kids are really looking forward to it.'

I threw that last bit in for good measure – maybe a bit of the guilts would do the trick.

But there was no shaming her. 'Well, they can come down to us in the new year, darling. Now, must go, we're going out for dinner tonight.' She was positively *dismissive*.

'What happened to the plan of my parents turning old and grey and their lives centring round their grand-children?' I fumed to Joe that night. 'This is not part of the master plan at all.'

He wasn't even listening to me. *Fear Factor* was on so he was cheering some imbecile who'd just eaten a hand-ful of maggots.

Which is precisely why we need another mini-break ourselves. We definitely need to reconnect on both a spiritual and sexual level. Instead, I now have to endure Christmas with Mrs H, a morose husband, a hyper four-year-old and a seriously deranged toddler. Think I'll start drinking the sherry now – may as well get a head start.

PS One consolation is that Mrs H will organize all the Christmas food – she's like a well-oiled Christmas juggernaut.

4 December

Louise called to say that MOM is whisking her away to Andorra for the holidays. Turns out she already has all of her Christmas gifts bought. And wrapped. In Tiffany-blue paper (this year's *in* hue). With matching ribbon. And gift tags.

'How do you do it?' I wailed, in misery, down the line. 'You're not human, you can't be.'

'It just takes a bit of organization, Susie. I jot things in my gift-ideas notebook during the year, then buy as I go.'

Was totally gob-smacked. Feel like useless, disorganized lump. Should probably already have Christmas cake baked and be making homemade decorations to trim the tree *à la* Martha Stewart (pre-prison obviously).

'I gave you a gift-ideas notebook as one of your presents last year, actually.' Louise's voice jolted me back from 'White Christmas' and fresh-cinnamon-cookies scenario. 'Didn't you use it during the year?'

Desperately tried to remember what she was talking about. 'Yes, of course I did,' I lied quickly. 'I was just kidding – I'm all set as well. Can't wait, actually.' Have vague suspicion that gift-ideas notebook is Katie's favourite scribbling pad. Must remember to hide it before Louise's next visit.

PS Mrs H has announced that she will be visiting second son David in London for the festive season. 'He's going to take me to see *Les Misérables*,' she said proudly, when we paid her a flying visit on the way back from Tesco. 'He loves the theatre, bless him.'

'Just like every other poof on the planet,' Joe muttered, under his breath. Had to kick him hard under the table to stop him saying any more. Mrs H is still unaware that David bats for the other side and thinks that moisturizing his hands every night is a sweet and hygienic habit that will make some woman very happy one day.

PPS Has just dawned on me that am now in double quandary. Not only are we going to be unable to decamp to the country for the Christmas period, we will no longer be able to rely on the impressive culinary skills of Mrs H to get us through. Will have to cook proper Christmas lunch for first time. A rite of passage I'm not sure I'm ready for.

5 December

Made big mistake of watching *Miracle on 42nd Street* on Sky Movies last night and am overwhelmed by crushing burden of responsibility to give Katie and Jack idyllic Walton-family Christmas before they succumb to complete cynical commercialization of the season (at age five approx.). Must devise cunning plan.

6 December

<u>Cunning Plan to Capture Christmas Spirit and Stamp out Scrooge-like Tendencies</u>

• Frolic in snow, building snowmen and enjoying hilarious snowball fight.

- If snow unavailable, organize idyllic family trip to park to gather holly and mistletoe wearing colourful assortment of woollen garments as in Gap ads.

- Visit convincing-looking Santa in festive department store. Preferably in New York.

- Make Christmas wreath and other festive arts and crafts with twigs and scraps of ribbon. (Buy *Prima* Christmas Special for inspiration.)

- Involve kids in hours of happy making of said decorations. Remember to have vat of mulled wine first.

- Make impressive homemade Christmas cards with brown paper and string. Bribe Katie to draw cute Christmas angel for 'aaah' factor.

- Make own Christmas cake and plum pudding. Or, at least, buy homemade versions in the overpriced deli in the Centre.

- Place scented candles (pine, cinnamon) all over house. Do not light until children are unconscious.

- Play seasonal Christmas music (such as Bing Crosby and Perry Como) for atmosphere. Hide annoying Mel 'n' Kim and Slade CDs.

- Bin fake tree. Organize idyllic family trip to Christmas-tree farm in the country.

7 December

Really enjoying capturing the Christmas spirit. It is very easy to forget all about the cynical commercialization of the season when you put your mind to it. May well spearhead a campaign to do just that some time soon.

Persuaded Joe to come home early so we could erect the Christmas tree last night (fake one, just until trip to Christmas-tree farm can be organized). Spent ages unearthing all the decorations and helping Jack and Katie arrange them on the branches. It was really magical watching their little faces aglow with excitement – in fact, before they tried to strangle each other with the tinsel, it was almost perfect. The only other scuffle was when the dog made off with the Christmas fairy, but otherwise a Hallmark-card winter's evening.

8 December

I am sick to death of bloody Christmas. In a misguided attempt to capture festive spirit, took Jack and Katie to see the *Polar Express* movie. Now they are seeing Santa *everywhere*. In the sky, outside the window, in the veg-etable aisle in Tesco. (I *just* missed him passing by the broccoli apparently.)

Am exhausted trying to feign excitement 24/7 and may well collapse into a sobbing heap anytime soon.

PS Joe grim-faced. Suspect he may regret buying the sing-along Santa for the porch.

In age-old Christmas tradition, riotous behaviour of demon children has begun. Yesterday Katie spent all afternoon goading Jack into a rage with her Christmas list. 'You can't even spell your own *name*.' She smirked as she drew intricate pictures of her preferred toys all over the embossed cream writing-paper that Joe saves for special occasions. 'So Santa won't come to you.'

Jack responded by sinking his teeth into her favourite Polly Pocket doll and shaking her into an early grave. Katie retaliated by attempting to give him permanent hearing loss by belting him round the head with her *Swan Lake* Barbie.

Mum thinks I should trick them into better behaviour. 'Tell them that Santa's watching to see if they're being good,' she said, when I called her to say I was considering turning them both out on to the street and running far, far away.

Didn't like to tell her that manipulating children into behaving better is a very old-fashioned and outdated idea, practically verging on child abuse. Theperfectparent.com suggests sitting down and talking through the implications of their misbehaviour in a quiet, calm way. Will try it tonight.

10 December

Have resorted to using ominous, doom-type voice to declare, 'Santa's watching,' to try to restore some semblance of order.

An attempt to discuss bad behaviour in calm and rational manner backfired when Jack tried to push the TV off its stand and on to Katie's head. (Admittedly she had just announced for the millionth time that Santa would be devoting an entire sleigh to her, while he would be receiving a sackful of coal.)

Surprisingly, the new ploy is working a treat so I'm now using it liberally and without restraint. In nanoseconds, Katie goes from demon to angel and Jack stops mid-howl (don't think he knows why, but it seems to strike fear into his heart, bless him). In fact, am so pleased with my clever ploy/blatant manipulation that am considering putting Bing Crosby and 'Santa Claus Is Coming To Town' on a loop on the CD-player. The lyrics are really very effective.

11 December

Louise's staff Christmas party is in the Four Seasons! A casino night with free champers and Michelin-rated food all night. *And* they can stay over! 'I don't even want to go,' she moaned. 'Steve's away so I won't have some gorgeous hunk to dangle off my arm. I'll be the only loser there on my own.'

'Who's Steve?' I asked, absentmindedly rubbing a patch of Jack's dribble off my top.

'The guy I've been dating for the last four months, Susie.' Louise's voice was like ice.

'I was just *kidding*,' I stuttered, making an Olympic bid at comebacks. 'Of *course* I know who Steve is.'

Spent rest of call making fake consoling noises into the phone (my years of training in PR came in useful), then rang Joe to interrogate him about his company do this year. They're not having one until January!

'Takings are down, Susie,' he hissed, in his do-not-disturb-me-while-I-am-saving-the-world voice. 'Lots of companies aren't having dos until the new year – it's a lot cheaper that way.'

Have good mind to write to Joe's chief executive, outlining reasons why the company should be ashamed of their evil, anti-Christmas policy. Will declare outrage at discrimination against the dozens of unappreciated corporate housewives who run said company employees' homes like clockwork, thus making it easier for said employees to devote more time to said company. Just have to work on said wording.

PS Will point out that said under-appreciated housewives should in fact receive lavish Jo Malone hampers for their behind-the-scenes contribution to company profits.

PPS Have decided to attend Christmas drinks do with Evil Anna and former work colleagues. How bad can it be?

Katie arrived home from playschool in Very Superior Mood. 'Amy said that Santa can't watch all the children all the time,' she announced, watching my face carefully. 'He doesn't have a million eyes – he only has two.'

Was appalled by this unexpected hiccup in the 'Santa's watching' scenario. Pesky kids and their natural curiosity. Surely playschool teachers should be stamping out all this gossip-mongering at source.

'OK,' I admitted hastily, deciding to try another sneaky tactic. 'Maybe Santa can't watch everybody all the time, but he does have elves to help.'

'No, Mummy,' Katie retaliated stoutly. 'The elves make the toys. They don't watch children.'

This was going to be tricky.

'Well, *some* elves make toys,' I went on, grasping at straws. 'Other elves make sure everyone's being good. In fact, I saw one of Santa's elves in our chimney last night.' (Turns out the nuns at school were right – one lie really *does* lead to another.)

'Has that elf *always* been there?' Katie demanded suspiciously, starting to look a little bit worried.

'No, he only came yesterday,' I replied guiltily. 'In fact, I saw his little hat hanging down the chimney when I was cleaning it.' (The cleaning bit may have been a bit far-fetched, granted.)

Miraculously, it worked. Both children spent all afternoon lying on the hearth trying to spot the elf up the soot-filled chimney. Was even able to watch *EastEnders* repeat in peace.

PS Am considering writing a comprehensive child-care book — am obviously more gifted at it than I'd previously thought.

13 December

How annoying. Joe caught me telling the kids that if they didn't let Mummy watch *EastEnders* instead of Nick Jr., the Christmas elf would blacklist them. Elf has been put on the back-burner.

14 December

All hell has broken loose at playschool. Apparently Katie has been involved in some sort of altercation with two others about who will play Holy Mary in the nativity this year. Now, like something out of a Nazi war movie, the head teacher has decreed that none of the three will get the part. In a very humiliating scene, I was called to one side by said head teacher to 'discuss the situation'.

'I don't like to take such a serious stance, Mrs Hunt,' she said, in a sorrowful (but surprisingly stern) voice. 'But we have a Zero Tolerance policy here at Little Angels. Hair-pulling is a serious offence.'

Am furious. I am sure Katie didn't start the argument. She's non-confrontational — just like me.

Mrs H called to inquire when it would suit to pop over and collect second-son David's Christmas gift. 'I'm packing my suitcase this evening, dear,' she said, 'so will I come round and pick it up now? We don't want to be squashing it in at the last minute, do we?'

Decided not to ask why she was packing her case a full four days before she was due to fly to London. Also decided not to reveal that had completely forgotten to buy second-son David any sort of a Christmas gift. 'Yes, I suppose that's OK,' I said, wondering if I could throw a few moisturizing creams into a bread basket and pass them off.

'And have you got your card written? David does like a nice Christmas card.'

Felt strange hot rage bubbling to the surface. 'I've been quite busy, Mrs H,' I said. 'Christmas cards haven't been at the top of my to-do list.'

'I see.' She sniffed. 'Well, if a nice card is too much to ask for, that's fine. I'll explain to David, on your behalf, that you don't have the time to be thinking about him. Even if he is all alone in a strange city, miles from home.'

Can now completely understand how Katie may have lost control momentarily, lashed out and pulled some hair. Some people deserve it.

The plot thickens. Discovered by devious, underhand sleuthing (i.e., hanging around the school gates trying to look uninterested while the other mothers gossiped) that Zoe is one of the others involved in the 'Virgin Débâcle'.

'*I* think we should have some sort of non-denominational service instead of a nativity play,' Eco-mother said loudly, as she marched up. 'Type-casting young girls into unobtainable ideals of perfection is very unhealthy.'

Zoe didn't look convinced. 'I *want* to be Mary!' she screamed, with passion. 'You wear a blue scarf *and* kiss Joseph.'

Have discovered that the third wheel in the Virgin Débâcle is Katie's VBF Amy – a sweet child, but not exactly Judy Garland. There is no way she could have carried off such a high-profile and demanding role without dissolving into snotty tears.

Katie, on the other hand, has the confidence and the poise, she is stunningly beautiful (a fact independently verified by non-blood relatives) *and* she is the best singer in class. She would have been spectacular.

Joe wasn't very supportive when I confided my distress. 'She has to learn that pulling someone's hair is not on, Susie,' he said, shovelling a spoonful of lasagne into his mouth in a most unattractive way. 'She might get the part next year.'

What Joe obviously does not realize is that Katie will be attending proper school next year. The pool of talent will be much bigger. For all he knows, there may even be professional child actors in her class – she won't stand a chance.

PS Feel that poor Katie is devastated by this knock-back to her confidence – she is feigning indifference at the moment, but who knows? It might scar her for life.

PPS Maybe I should enrol her in stage school. Will investigate.

17 December: Joe's birthday

Have discovered that I have not exactly purchased all of the gifts on my Christmas list (which I cannot locate). In decisive, kill-two-birds-with-one-stone move, made a quick trip to the local chemist for the following:

Dad: Davidoff Cool Water aftershave.

Mum: Coty White Musk body lotion.

Mrs H: as above.

Joe: Chanel Egoiste aftershave and balm (excellent two-for-price-of-one special introductory offer).

Feel very virtuous that I am shopping locally and supporting neighbourhood traders instead of increasing profits for greedy multinationals. Sulky chemist didn't look all that grateful to be getting so much trade – but maybe the stress of dealing with hordes of pensioners looking for discount on gift sets is getting to her.

PS In all the excitement, forgot to buy Joe a birthday card. Or cake. Feel a bit guilty, but am sure he's used to it by now – what else can he expect, having his birthday so close to Christmas?

PPS Feel Mrs H's over-the-top gift was deliberate

attempt to embarrass me. Am sure Joe won't even use that iPod.

18 December

Mrs H arrived at 9.35 a.m., hauling a large black sack behind her. 'Just a few Christmas presents for the children, Susie,' she panted, dragging it through the hall and into the kitchen, with some difficulty.

'You shouldn't have spent so much money, Mrs H,' I said, touched by her generosity. 'You'll spoil them.'

'Yes, well, I like to spoil them,' she said stoutly, with what looked suspiciously like a tear glinting in her eye. 'They're the only grandchildren I've got.' Then she sighed dramatically. 'Sometimes I do worry about poor David, you know, Susie.'

I held my breath, wondering if she was finally going to admit her fear that second son's obsession with Broadway shows was bordering on the unnatural.

'There's no sign of him settling down and having a family. I know his showbiz lifestyle is very glamorous, but he's not getting any younger. It does play on my mind.' She shook her head sadly.

'Well, he has plenty of time,' I said kindly, feeling a bit sorry for her. 'Charlie Chaplin had children when he was in his eighties.'

No point in revealing that

(a) Going to see *Chicago* every Saturday night does not count as a glamorous showbiz lifestyle.

(b) The only way David will have children is with the
  help of a friendly lesbian and a turkey baster.

'Did he?' She perked up at this news. 'Of course, it
is different for women. Take you, for example – you're
probably far too old to have another baby.'

'Well, I'm not sure about that,' I stuttered, aghast.

'Yes, he has plenty of time,' she continued happily.
'Better to live a little before he settles into the humdrum
and ordinary, isn't that right?'

PS Spent ages trying to decide which outfit to wear
to the Christmas drinks do. Have sneaking suspicion
that Evil Anna told me it was a casual affair so I
would arrive in stonewash jeans and a mouldy AC/DC
T-shirt. Have decided to pull out all the stops and wear
a sparkly blue number I bought for a song in TK Maxx
two years ago. It is a teeny bit tight but, luckily, thanks
to J.Lo and Beyoncé, curvy women are all the rage so
I don't have to worry about it straining over the buttock
area.

PS Katie says that if Ciara is sick tomorrow, she gets
to carry the star of Bethlehem across the stage at the
nativity. I might have imagined it, but I think she had
a funny gleam in her eye.

19 December: The Nativity Play

Scrambled into the church, hauling a screaming Jack
under my arm, ten minutes before the play was due to
start. Thought we had plenty of time, but hadn't
counted on the hordes of obsessive stage mothers jost-

ling for the best positions in the front pew, camcorders and spare glitter lip gloss at the ready.

Spent ages elbowing my way to the front (encouraged Jack to keep kicking and screaming for all he was worth: worked a treat).

Couldn't see Joe anywhere. Then, just as it was about to start and a reverential hush had fallen over the congregation, my mobile phone rang (note: must find out how to change ring tone to something other than 'The Chicken Song').

'I'm stuck in fucking traffic! Will you ever move over, you fucking *wanker*?' Joe yelled, his voice bouncing off every wall in the church.

Stuffed phone into pocket just in time to see Katie tripping out to the altar, carrying the star of Bethlehem aloft (poor little Ciara had had some mysterious fall backstage and sprained her arm).

She looked gorgeous, and she sang like an angel. In fact, she was so good that I heard a mother in front saying how her voice was practically drowning out all the other kids. Was so proud I almost wept.

Mary was played by a scared-looking Hannah Delaney. Suspect the teachers were quite disappointed with her – they had to prompt her every line. Serves them right for stunting proper child-star talent.

PS Can't believe that Joe missed such a monumental event in the life of our first child. He is to blame if she dates unsuitable men in later life.

Katie has decided that she no longer wants Santa to bring a My Little Pony Dance Mat and Castle. She now wants the Princess Alexa doll. And all her blingin' accessories.

Desperately tried to explain to her that Santa will already have packed his sack – she can't change her mind now – but she is adamant that Santa is magic and this change of heart is no problem whatsoever. Shit, shit, shit.

In no mood for drinks do but forced myself to go – cannot turn into sad old recluse with no social skills who sits at home shouting at the TV. (Actually, do this already, but only at Judge Judy and that's perfectly acceptable.)

With heavy heart, left Joe scowling at the piles of unwashed pots in the kitchen sink and a belligerent Katie rewriting her letter to Santa at the kitchen table.

In attempt to boost self-confidence, I tried to do a bit of self-hypnosis in the back of the cab on the way into the city (tips garnered on Lifestyle TV very useful). Caught taxi driver giving me very odd looks in the rear-view mirror, but was too busy visualizing myself as a confident, sexy woman to care.

Unfortunately, self-induced state of sexy confidence dissolved when I walked into the club and realized that everyone else was, in fact, dressed in jeans and sweaters and that I looked like a high-class hooker in my skin-tight sparkly blue dress and glitter eye shadow. Someone was even wearing a fleece.

'Susie!' Evil Anna screeched across the empty dance-floor, deliberately drawing more attention to me. 'You look so . . . *blue*!'

Downed three G and Ts in quick succession to get over the shock of being a laughing stock, then spent the night in a dark corner discussing the merits of *American Idol* vs. *Big Brother* and bitching about Evil Anna with Noel from accounts. Not a bad night out, actually.

21 December

Mum called to say goodbye. 'Now, darling, we ordered all your Christmas gifts on-line so they should be delivered any day now,' she said, sounding annoyingly jolly.

'On-line?' I stuttered, raging that I hadn't thought of it.

'Oh, yes, it's stress free – they even gift wrap so you don't have to worry about a thing. All you need is a credit card,' she tinkled happily. 'Now, I must fly, darling. Daddy wants to make Dromoland by two so we can use the spa this afternoon.'

Hung up feeling most put out. Mum and Dad are enjoying their retirement years far too much for my liking.

22 December

Am a nervous wreck. Have trawled through every toy shop known to man to find Princess bloody Alexa. Was laughed at by spotty teenagers all over the city.

'You haven't a hope, missus – she's been on special order since October.'

'We sold the last one this morning.'

'We sold the last one five minutes ago.'

Finally, in a last-ditch attempt, I tried the small, local toy shop. When the balding middle-aged owner said they had one, I nearly flung myself, weeping, into his arms with relief. He didn't bat an eyelid when I started hyperventilating. 'Seen it all before. Bloody Christmas makes you barmy,' he muttered, as he shoved Alexa into a paper bag.

PS Have just realized that have yet to buy Louise thoughtful, and very expensive, present (gift-wrapped to within an inch of its life). Don't know how much more of this pressure I can take. Feel I will have to resort to Mrs H's eggnog soon.

23 December

Joe has informed me that he will be working until at least six p.m. tomorrow (Christmas Eve). Meanwhile Jack has eaten most of the leaves off the poinsettia plant and crushed half the baubles on the tree, and Katie has announced that she might like Santa to bring a Barbie bike instead. I am officially having a nervous breakdown.

24 December

Was woken at crack of dawn by Christmas carollers. 'Ding dong merrily on high,' they screeched, as I wrenched open the door in a panic, desperate for them not to wake Jack. 'Is this where the mad party is?' one slurred, looking confused.

'Em, no,' I said, realizing they were not carollers but drunken college students looking for a Christmas rave.

'Em, do you want to have a party?' another ventured, looking hopeful.

Gave them a box of Tesco mince pies and sent them away, suddenly and strangely infused with a heartwarming sense of Christmas spirit. Who needs snowball fights and roasted chestnuts when you have a dozen rowdy teenagers looking for a good time?

In last-ditch attempt to make Christmas unforgettable, made dawn raid on Marks & Spencer and bought their entire Christmas range, including a boneless turkey, assorted veg and as many luscious chocolate confections as I could cram into the trolley. (Just in case there's a freak blizzard and we're all stranded indoors and forced to survive on luxurious handmade truffles for a week.) God bless twenty-four hour Christmas opening hours.

PS All the Santa presents are now stacked neatly under the tree and calm has at last descended over me. Think it may have helped that Mum and Dad's gifts were delivered and Katie's is a Barbie bike. Mrs H's eggnog may also have helped a tad.

PPS Have been shaking the pressie Joe has for me under the tree. No idea what it is . . . Very exciting!

25 December

Joe bought me a Thigh Master for Christmas. Too traumatized to write any more. Our marriage is officially in crisis.

26 December

Joe is brazening out the Thigh Master situation. 'You kept going on and on about them,' he insisted. 'How was I to know you didn't want one? I thought you'd be delighted.'

I am horrified. Obviously Joe doesn't know me at all. Yes, I may have commented on it when I saw the ad on TV, but only because I was drooling over the model's rock-like thighs and bum. I never wanted to *own* one.

Had laughed uproariously at first when I opened it. Joe was having a little joke by hiding my real present in a Thigh Master box. What a funny, thoughtful husband he was. Proceeded to rip open the box like a child, frantically looking for huge diamond earrings or the gift token for a luxury weekend away. But there was nothing. Just a device that looked like a torture contraption and screamed, 'You are fat and middle-aged!'

Am trying to put on a brave face and capture magical Christmas memories of Katie and Jack playing with their new toys (or, in Jack's case, the cardboard boxes the toys came in), but my heart isn't in it. Meanwhile Joe is oblivious to my anguish and is guzzling all the selection boxes and watching back-to-back movies on

Sky Digital. *And* he has no appreciation for the hours I spent slaving over a hot stove to produce a scrumptious, three-course Christmas dinner. It's no joke trying to be Superwoman and organize a Christmas feast while looking after two demanding young children as well. If I could bring back his Chanel Egoiste aftershave and balm I would.

27 *December*

Joe found all the empty Marks & Spencer food containers while he was recycling the Christmas gift-wrap (carefully folding the paper edge to edge first). Unfortunately I can no longer pretend that I spent hours peeling a full sack of potatoes and four different kinds of vegetables while whipping up homemade cranberry sauce and plum pudding from scratch. Thought Joe might barf he laughed so hard. 'I thought your poor hands were *raw* from all that peeling, Susie?' he gulped through tears of laughter, fishing all the incriminating evidence from the bin and swinging it over his head victoriously. 'I thought you were *exhausted* from all those hours of kneading and baking?'

The kids gathered round, sensing larks at my expense.

'Well, I didn't hear you complaining, Mr Cordon Bleu,' I retaliated, drawing round me in self-defence the garish red fleece dressing-gown that his mother had given me for Christmas. (Little does she realize it, but her warped Oedipal attempts to kill any desire that Joe may have for me by giving me the most vile nightwear available to man are pointless. *She* is probably getting more nookie than I am.) 'In fact, if memory serves me correctly, you said it was the best Christmas dinner you've ever had, bar none.'

'You're right, Susie,' he answered, mock serious. 'It was even better than my mother's. Of course, hers actually *tastes* of blood, sweat and tears!' More guffawing and riotous laughter.

Decided to cut my losses and retreat, maintaining a dignified silence.

Sat fuming in the bathroom while Katie, Jack and Joe whooped and hollered with glee in the kitchen, and the kids didn't even know *why*.

PS Hate to admit it, but garish red fleece dressing-gown (with rose appliqué on collar and cuff) is the perfect ensemble for covering extra Christmas poundage – with added bonus of being comfy and festive.

28 December

Woke up to breakfast in bed, and small blue box lined up alongside the toast (soggy, but you can't have it all). 'Here's your real present, Susie,' Joe whispered, snuggling back under the duvet. 'It had to be shipped from London, so it's a little late.'

Thought I was having some kind of chick-flick fantasy, where strong manly type showers me with ludicrously expensive gifts, until I realized I was still wearing my fleece dressing-gown and Joe had not morphed into Colin Firth so it had to be real life.

Quickly decided to forgo huffy silence for squeals of excitement. Opened box to find real Tiffany charm bracelet inside! With *Return to Tiffany* engraved on the charm and everything! (So it is definitely genuine article and not some cheap imitation available for two a penny on dodgy Internet sites.)

Am overwhelmed with guilt and remorse. Have wonderful, thoughtful husband who does not take me for granted (not all the time anyway) and who is still capable of wild, romantic gestures. Unfortunately we were unable to indulge in passionate, spontaneous nookie to celebrate renewed love as Katie and Jack came bounding in at that moment, but we exchanged lots of lovely lustful looks over the tea and toast.

PS Can't wait to tell Louise that I am in possession of actual Tiffany item, shipped specially from London by wonderful, thoughtful hubby. She will be sick! Ha!

PPS Thank goodness I trusted my inner instinct and did not divulge the Thigh Master fiasco to her via text. (Just as well my mobile-phone battery was low, or I might have been tempted.)

29 December

Bliss. Will enter *Guinness Book of Records* for Most Selection Boxes Eaten in One Sitting (five), Most Cups of Tea Drunk (six) and Most Movies Watched Back to Back (three).

Spent ages admiring my new Tiffany bracelet. Think it may make my wrist look thinner. It's eerie – my body seems to know I was destined for exclusive designer jewellery and is reacting appropriately.

Spent ages fantasizing about future surprise gifts that

may be just round the corner. A diamond eternity ring may be next. Or possibly tasteful, yet inordinately expensive, diamond stud earrings.

PS Louise texted from luxurious skiing trip in Andorra with MOM. Snow is powdery apparently – not sure if that's good or bad. Held off on revealing existence of Tiffany bracelet. Didn't want to seem boastful.

PPS Mum and Dad called to say they will be away for Christmas from now on. 'It's the only way to go, darling,' Mum said gaily. 'No more slaving over a turkey and spending hours peeling potatoes. This is *soooo* relaxing. And the food is wonderful.'

PPPS Duck is the new turkey, apparently.

30 December

This morning Katie announced that she is 'so totally over' Christmas. (Must have a word with her teacher about the disturbing teenage Americanisms creeping into her vocabulary. Cannot think where she's picking up this kind of stuff at four years of age.)

Have to agree that Christmas is done. Even selection boxes are losing their appeal. In one last-ditch attempt at slovenly festive behaviour, spent the afternoon lying on the sofa, watching another Mary-Kate and Ashley movie. (How many movies can two girls make? There must be more than two of them. Seriously.) This one was even more far-fetched than all the others. Cannot understand how movie director expects us to believe that twelve-year-old girls can cavort round Paris in designer clothes and cars on their own. It's exactly this kind of thing that sets unrealistic standards for kids of this generation. Katie kept telling me that the twins *rocked* and that their outfits were *hot*.

Explained in serious, adult manner (even sat upright to underline the gravity of my conviction) that the whole movie, was, like, *so* totally unrealistic and that real life is *so* not like that (unless you happen to break Hollywood by the time you're four and go on to earn millions of dollars off your cute, upturned noses and precocious ways).

PS Katie announced that she wants to be a TV star and earn millions of dollars so she can buy the complete Bratz doll collection.

PPS Am planning intimate, romantic New Year's Eve in with Joe. May possibly remove fleece dressing-gown especially for the occasion.

31 December: New Year's Eve

Joe has been called into the office tonight for emergency, absolutely-cannot-be-postponed teleconference with American office, blah, blah, blah . . .

What is wrong with Americans? Have they never seen *It's a Wonderful Life*? Do they not realize the importance of spending quality time in the bosom of your family at this most special time of year?

Joe tried to point out that he has had a full week off already (which apparently, according to Americans, is tantamount to taking a six-month leave of absence), but I shouted him down. New Year is a time to recommit yourself to your ideals and values (and maybe indulge in a little hanky-panky with your wife and her Tiffany bracelet in front of a roaring log fire), not pander to your employer's every whim.

Will now have to spend New Year's Eve alone, like some twenty-first-century Cinderella, watching Jonathan Ross lisp his way through some cringe-inducing spectacle.

'I'm sorry, Susie.' Joe shrugged, wrapping the new designer cashmere scarf his mother had bought him round his neck as he left. 'If I want to get a directorship, this is the kind of sacrifice I have to make.'

Not sure I want him to get a directorship if he has to put work before his wife and family. Although the money might come in handy.

Had to endure revolting New Year's Eve variety show, full of B-list celebs trying to make a career comeback. All the real celebs were busy at home, having fun with their families and entourages, so they couldn't make it. Was positively sulky all night. (Caught myself pouting in the mirror – in the firelight I looked quite like a tragic, yet sensual, Jilly Cooper heroine. Except for pus-filled boil on chin. Bloody selection boxes.)

PS Joe still not home by twelve when Katie and Jack both woke, screaming with fright because of all the drunken revelry and car horns on the street. Honestly, pensioners are the worst of all. Old Mrs Kenny next door looked totally out of it. I'm sure I spotted her taking swigs from a sherry bottle while she was letting off those fireworks (took a little peep out from behind the blinds to make sure).

PPS Louise texted me a happy-new-year photo of herself and MOM on ski slopes. Can't be sure, but thought I could make out some serious-looking diamonds in her ears.

1 January

New Year's Resolutions
Allow kids to watch just one hour of quality TV a day.
>Note: *Barney & Friends* does not count as quality TV.

Cook at least one Nigella-type nutritious meal for family every day.
>Note: spaghetti hoops do not count as nutritious food.

Restart sex life.
>Note: shave legs and defuzz bikini line more than once every six months.

Get Jack to sleep all night, every night.
>Note: reread *Secrets of the Baby Whisperer for Toddlers* (not while watching *The X Factor*).

Get hair done (by qualified professional) every six weeks.
>Note: clear bathroom cabinet of all half-empty bottles of Loving Care home tint.

Do fifty Thigh Master squeezes every day.
>Note: may as well use the bloody thing.

2 January

Crisis. Katie and Jack launched themselves screaming into our bedroom at six thirty a.m. Thought someone was dead until I deciphered their distorted gabbling and realized that the TV was on the blink. Stumbled downstairs to check it out and discovered, for once, they weren't exaggerating. We are without TV on the most boring day of the year. It is sleeting outside and the kids are already 'so totally over' their Christmas toys. No wonder so many people find January utterly depressing.

Dragged Joe downstairs kicking and screaming and he fished out the number of the satellite company so we counted the minutes until nine o'clock when we could call. Filled in hours by colouring back of empty selection boxes and playing *Shrek 2* on a loop. Luckily, the satellite company is in England so they opened at nine on the dot. The English really are so reliable and courteous.

Joe then proceeded to have heated discussion with call-centre staff member who claimed that we have not paid the bill for three months! Toffee-nosed Brit! How dare she? Anyway, this is impossible: everything is paid by direct debit! Ha! For once, Joe's alphabetized file of bills and household items will come in handy.

PS Had screaming argument with Joe who, at a glance, was able to tell me that he asked me, on 12 October at ten thirty a.m., to speak to bank about continuing direct-debit thingy. Have absolutely no recollection of said conversation, but it's there, in black and white. This is what happens when you marry an anal-retentive organizer.

PPS Will not be reconnected until 14 January! Fascists.

3 January

Could cut atmosphere with a knife. If I see *Shrek 2* one more time, I will quite possibly hurl myself and the DVD player down the stairs. Why did we have to loan all the other DVDs to Joe's mother to bring to London over Christmas? Blast second-son David and his unnatural Disney obsession.

PS Joe has gone back to work – suspect he was quite glad to escape.

4 January

Hurrah! Mum and Dad are back from their luxury break in Dromoland Castle so we are going to the country for a late family Christmas. Just have to pack.

List of Things to Pack for Country Retreat

- All of Katie's clothes.

- All of Jack's clothes.

- Wellies for long walks with family in frosted country lanes.

- Cosy knits for lounging round blazing log fire, eating mince pies and reminiscing.

- Camcorder to capture memories for generations to come.

Pity I do not possess large green Land Rover and golden retriever puppy to complete country-gentry look *à la* Madonna and Guy, but embarrassing people-carrier and collection of My Little Ponys will have to do.

PS Joe seems unnaturally happy to be getting rid of us.

5 January

Am in state of shock! Mum and Dad haven't even put up their tree! 'There was no point, darling,' Mum consoled me, over a slice of shop-bought Christmas cake. 'When we weren't here, it seemed a bit silly.'

'But what about the kids, Mum? They'd have loved to see your tree.' I sniffed into the dried-up cake, still devastated by the shrivelled oak-tree stump in the front garden.

Mum eyed Jack warily as he swung precariously from the leg of a kitchen chair, with a garland of tinsel I had found under the stairs wrapped round his neck. 'I don't think they've even noticed, pet,' she said, patting my hand.

'Did we show you the digital photos of the Christmas tree in Dromoland Castle?' Dad asked cheerily, pulling out his prized digital camera again. 'It really was quite magnificent.'

I'm in despair – no Christmas tree, plum cake that was bought in the garage down the road: what has become of us all? Before you know it, Mum and Dad will be jetting off to Florida for Christmas. It just isn't the same. Consoled myself with a full layer of Milk Tray and half a bottle of Fleurie.

PS Dad asked if I wanted to try out his new digital scales. 'They're as accurate as the ones you get in a doctor's surgery,' he said meaningfully, dangling them in front of me. 'I've lost seven pounds since we got it!'

6 January

Decided to go for long country walk in attempt to rekindle lost family-Christmas atmosphere. Was really looking forward to rambling through woodland, pausing to admire hedgerows and spot squirrels, etc., but when we got to the park Mum and Dad tore off ahead of us at about twenty m.p.h., their matching purple tracksuits and sweatbands a blur of speed.

'Got to get the heart-rate up, love,' Dad breezed, as he did his second lap round us.

We lagged behind, Katie refusing to cycle her new Barbie bike because the helmet would mess her hair, and Jack stopping every two inches or so to inspect slugs, stones and random blades of grass. Lasted all of half an hour before I snapped and reloaded them into the car. Stopped off at Blockbuster on the way back to rent a DVD – anything other than *Shrek 2*.

PS Have decided to go back to the city tomorrow – the pressure to take up power walking and stop gorging on Milk Tray is too much to take.

7 January

Must reassess my life. Definitely got lazy over Christmas and slipped into old, disorganized habits. Have reread my new-year resolutions to focus.

List of Things to Do to Get Act Together

- Do huge supermarket shop to stock up on nutritious superfoods.
    Note: buy organic, socially conscious food *à la* Nigella. Also, find out what superfoods actually are.
- Put DVD player in attic and hide remote control.
    Note: instal handy attic ladder in case of absolute emergencies.
- Find *Baby Whisperer* book.
    Note: might be with pile of junk under stairs.
- Will be reformed earth-mother in no time.

8 January

Am in serious state of shock. Have discovered that organic baked beans cost two euro a tin! A jar of Fair Trade coffee costs five euro! Am all for supporting poor Brazilian farmers, etc., etc., but will not be able to afford a packet of measly custard creams to have with the coffee at this rate.

Was so outraged had showdown with spotty teenage manager in aisle three. 'This is scandalous,' I fumed.

'Ordinary mothers can't afford this! No wonder I have to buy own-brand rubbish.'

Spotty supermarket manager looked at me blankly and shrugged.

Have vowed to write to world leaders to explain that ordinary mothers cannot be socially conscious if prices are so astronomical. On way out passed suggestion box so wrote that supermarket should consider lobbying government on this issue. Also suggested that teenage boys were not appropriate manager material. Further suggested that spotty teenage manager use Clearasil to clear up pimples – he put me right off buying any meat. There was not enough room on the minuscule piece of paper provided by supermarket (blatant attempt to discourage consumer activism) so in moment of ingenuity ripped top off detergent box to finish off.

PS Have a good mind to write to Nigella and urge her to start campaign for lower-priced, quality organic goods on our supermarket shelves. She probably has a lot more clout than any world leader. She could even rope that Charles Saatchi bloke in. Apparently he's quite big in advertising.

PPS Got home to discover that entire load of shopping painfully lugged into boot of car is now covered with Persil non-biological detergent.

9 January

Received two letters from RTÉ today.

Dear Ms Hunt,

Thank you for your recent letter and your kind remarks. I do not actually attend board meetings, but I do think your fly-on-the-wall housewives' documentary idea is most interesting. Also, I have never seen *The Ricki Lake Show* but I believe it does very well in the ratings.

I am sorry to hear you were not satisfied with the response you received from Patrick Baxter. I think he signs all of his letters that way, so I wouldn't take offence. I believe the volume of correspondence his department receives is enormous, so it is probably a logistical thing. I will pass your comments along and see if the issue can be resolved to your satisfaction.

Best wishes,
Jennifer Goode

Dear Ms Hunt,

Thank you for your feedback regarding *Dr. Phil.* We have been having difficulty accessing new episodes of the show recently, but we hope to rectify the situation as soon as possible. Also, there are plans in the pipeline for an afternoon show geared specifically towards mothers in the home – it is at the development stage at the moment, but things are looking hopeful.

In the meantime, please accept, with my compliments, audience tickets for our long-running chat show *Doyle Tonight*.

Keep watching – we value your viewership!
Patrick Baxter

Feel quiet sense of pride at phenomenal achievement. I am practically responsible for creating new afternoon programme for women! Was definitely a suffragette in a former life. Also, am really looking forward to attending *Doyle Tonight* – they sometimes have real stars on, ones who have been in *OK!*.

PS Called Louise to tell her all about my social campaigning – and invited her to go to *Doyle Tonight* with me. She was suitably impressed.

10 January

Mrs H is back from her Christmas sojourn to London. 'It was fabulous, Susie,' she gushed, presenting me with half a dozen Big Ben tea-towels and a jumbo roll of Westminster Abbey kitchen paper. 'David knows all sorts of glamorous showbiz celebrities so we got to meet lots of really interesting people.'

'Really?' I said, doubting this was true. 'Like who?'

'Well,' she went on, whispering conspiratorially, 'don't tell him I told you – he's really rather modest about it – but he's *very* friendly with an up-and-coming weatherman. Isn't that exciting?'

More exciting than you know, I thought, privately deciding not to tell Joe the great news.

'So, what's been happening here since we left? Nothing exciting, I suppose?' Mrs H laughed gaily, full of confidence after her brush with a real-life Z-list celebrity.

'Well, I got audience tickets to *Doyle Tonight*,' I said, determined to bring her down a peg or two ASAP.

'Really?' she said, faking uninterest and taking a slow sip of the tea I had made her. Could tell she was very impressed. In fact, before I knew what was happening, she was whipping her Sacred Heart calendar out of her handbag and looking at it carefully. 'Yes, just as I thought,' she said. 'I'm absolutely jam-packed over the next few weeks.'

Then it dawned on me. Mrs H had got hold of the wrong end of the stick and somehow imagined that I was inviting her to attend a recording of *Doyle Tonight* when in fact I'd just been rubbing the tickets shamelessly in her face. Thank goodness the bingo leagues are due to kick off any day and she'll be otherwise occupied – those tickets have mine and Louise's names all over them.

'I'll just have to juggle a few things to go with you,' she went on, patting my hand. 'It can be a bit intimidating meeting these sorts of people at first, and you'll need someone to show you the ropes. I do have the experience, after all.'

PS Called Louise to admit that

(a) Mrs H has used some kind of voodoo sorcery to secure the second *Doyle Tonight* ticket.

(b) She will no longer be able to examine lots of real celebrities up close and personal and decide once and for all whether Botox is brilliant or downright creepy.

Was hoping she wouldn't be desperately disappointed and/or furious but, surprisingly, she didn't seem to mind all that much.

'It's OK, Susie,' she tinkled, in a funny girlish fashion. 'I don't think Steve would like me leaving him for the night anyway. We can't bear to be apart at the moment. I really think he might be The One.'

All this love-in-a-bucket stuff is getting quite tiring. May have to tell her that soon.

11 January

Child of Our Time (fascinating social-commentary documentary) was on BBC last night. Made sure to shuttle kids to bed extra early so I could focus. Joe refused to watch it and sulked for ages because he was missing the football. Sometimes I worry that he's unconcerned about the long-term development and well-being of the children. He hadn't even *heard* of psychometric testing. Anyway, it was fascinating viewing. Felt most intellectual curled up on the sofa with my glass of Pinot Grigio and my notepad to jot down crucial parenting tips. Some of the children featured seemed practically emotionally *abused*. Like kids who watch TV all day and all night. They can't even fall asleep unless the TV is on. It nearly brought tears to my eyes. Some people are very unfortunate really. Felt extremely virtuous that Katie and Jack are so stimulated and challenged on a daily basis. They barely watch TV any more (except before breakfast and after dinner). Professor on programme says a mother's education is the best predictor of how well kids will do at school. No worries there, then – at last my useless arts degree will come in handy for something.

Took notes on high-tech scientific tests to determine how ready Katie is for school. Must ask her the following:

• Why do we have a clock?

• What happens to water when it freezes?

• How can you make a square shape with only three pieces of straw?

Am going to test her tomorrow – am sure she'll pass with flying colours.

12 *January*

Katie thinks an elf lives in the clock (may be throwback to Christmas-elf scenario). She thinks water turns into snow when it freezes (not bad) but, worst of all, it took her almost *two minutes* to make the square from the three pieces of straw! (I kept watch with the oven-timer.) There must be something seriously wrong with those tests. That old professor seems all twinkly and kind, but suspect he can't be as nice as he looks, treating children like laboratory rats. That's what's wrong with the world today – people are pigeonholed from infancy. No wonder children don't live up to their full potential when society forces them to perform like little monkeys. I've a good mind to write to the BBC.

13 January

All the playschool mothers are agog about the *Child of Our Time* tests. Apparently, after Katie's arch-enemy Zoe made the stupid straw square in a record-breaking fifteen seconds, she asked Eco-mother if she could make a circle as well.

I kept quiet. There's no way I'm admitting to Eco-mother that I'm in any way concerned about the sociological development of my child. I have already seen her eyeing Katie's plastic Barbie snackbox with distaste. Anyway, it's so vulgar to boast about your children. I'm taking the higher ground.

14 January

Woke in a panic in the middle of the night, realizing I had forgotten to give Katie a scissors to cut the straws. No wonder the poor child took so long to figure it out. In fact, she's quite possibly a genius to have figured it out at all. Let it drop at the school gates that Katie did the test in fourteen seconds – well, she would have done if I hadn't screwed it up. Zoe's mother just smirked in that really irritating, superior I'm-saving-the-world way of hers and made some comment about children being labelled so young. I almost strangled her – she was the one who started it! Condescending witch. I could shove her face down in a heap of recycled compost, except she might enjoy it.

PS Louise is going on some all-expenses-paid trip to Dubai with MOM! 'It'll be totally boring, Susie,' she lied, to console me. 'All hotels start to look the same after a while.' She was definitely just trying to make me feel better – saw promo for Dubai on Teletext Holidays and it looks like paradise (with your choice of cocktails and Tiffany jewellery on tap). My life is so utterly suburban.

PPS Jack acting up terribly. Feel he may be harbouring resentment about his exclusion from psychometric testing.

15 January

Am barely functioning am so tired. Jack woke up four times last night and, as his *pièce de résistance*, decided that five a.m. would be a reasonable hour to rise and shine. Joe, meanwhile, managed to snore his way in a very unsavoury fashion through the entire thing. Was eventually forced to take Jack into bed with us where he spent another hour pulling my hair and playing peek-a-boo under the duvet.

Was so exhausted almost tripped and fell down the stairs this afternoon. Might have been killed and my children would have grown up motherless, with their father sleeping through their screaming nightmares. I can see the headlines now 'Devoted Mother and Wife Dies in Tragic Domestic Accident – Family Grief-stricken'. For the sake of my orphaned children, the madness has got to stop and the baby whispering has got to start.

PS Told Joe that if I was killed in a tragic, domestic accident he wouldn't be able to cope. He laughed his head off and said he would hire a Brazilian nanny with the life insurance.

16 January

Found *Baby Whisperer* book shoved under our bed (along with my favourite black bra, four of Katie's hairclips, three old soothers and a half-eaten mouldy apple). Have already reread half of it. Should have done this a lot sooner. It's all common sense, really. Just have to draw on experience in implementing important PR campaigns to ensure success. (Am bit hazy on the details after years out of the loop, but am sure it will come back to me.) Operation Jack kicks off tonight.

<u>Operation Jack</u>

• Establish foolproof routine of soothing bath,
  followed by quiet bedtime story in dimly lit room.
  (NB Hide *Spiderman* DVD.)

• Comfort child when he cries by patting him
  rhythmically on back and humming. (NB Must
  practise.)

- Avert eyes if baby tries to stare you down and keep humming. (Must also practise.)

- *Never* take baby into bed with you.

- Act as a united parenting team (for once).

17 January

Operation Jack not going exactly to plan.

- *7.00 p.m.* Filled bath with half a bottle of lavender aromatherapy baby bubble bath from the Pure and Simple Store (a steal at ten euro), but instead of 'calming and soothing' (as claimed by swirly, new-age writing on the back of the bottle), it turned Jack into some sort of mini hooligan.

- *7.20 p.m.* Chased Jack round landing to dry and dress him into the comfy new fleece PJs I bought in Next for twenty euro (cherubic sleeping child on front of packet gave me false hope).

- *7.45 p.m.* Calming bedtime story turned into a wrestling match as Jack tried to eat book.

- *8.15 p.m.* Jack eventually asleep, thirty minutes later than usual.

Consulted *Baby Whisperer* book, which said it may take a while for baby to adjust to the new routine. Must persevere.

PS Katie so cross that Jack has new bubble bath and

PJs that she had a tantrum and demanded to stay up to watch *Sponge Bob, Square Pants* on Nick Jr. Finally got her to bed at nine thirty – an hour and a half later than usual.

PPS Joe arrived home at ten thirty, claiming to be exhausted from work and looking for a home-cooked meal. Refrained from beating him round the head with a blunt object.

PPPS Am returning bubble bath tomorrow. Companies must realize that if they make claims about calming and soothing they have to follow through with the product. Could well make a claim for false advertising.

18 January

Am at wit's end. Jack screamed and roared half the night demanding to get into our bed, and patting his back was bugger-all use. Yet again, Joe the hero snored his way through all the wailing and gnashing of teeth (and that was just me). So much for co-parenting and presenting a united front.

In fact, if Joe ever appeared in Jack's room in the middle of the night, the child might pass out with fright. (This could be a plan.) His contribution to the baby whispering was to wake Jack up again by flushing the toilet at three a.m. I nearly attacked him with the toilet brush I was so enraged.

'Take him into bed with us, Susie,' he grumbled, as I ranted and raved with sleep deprivation. 'We'll all get a night's sleep then.'

I was speechless with rage at this gem. What hope have I of ever resolving what the *Baby Whisperer* has identified as Jack's serious sleeping abnormalities if I get no support from my spouse? Partner engagement in the process is vital to the programme's success. Ended up throwing the book at him in a temper and spent the rest of the night balanced precariously on the edge of the bed, plotting my revenge with Jack lying on my head.

PS My arm really aches from all that rhythmic patting and am almost hoarse from humming like a bloody moron half the night.

19 January

Was bemoaning my failure as a Baby Whisperer to a rapt audience of mothers at the playschool gates, when Eco-mother butted in. She announced, in her haughty I-know-it-all voice, 'You should try *Contented Little Baby*. Both my children have slept through the night since they were six weeks old.' Cue smug, superior grin from both mother and smiling, freakishly contented baby in pram. Everyone was agog. Surely babies who sleep through the night from six weeks are only an urban myth?

Feel intense violent tendencies towards Eco-mother and her stupid, docile baby. (May well be side-effects of serious sleep deprivation.)

Luckily everyone knows that only children with lower IQs sleep through the night so early in life. Jack may not be a sleeper, but he may well be a future Mensa candidate.

PS Dad claims he spent three years walking the halls with me through the night as I screamed blue murder. 'He'll grow out of it, darling.' He giggled. 'You did – eventually.'

Mum says he's talking nonsense and that I'm to ignore him, but she didn't sound all that convinced. My God, what if it's hereditary and I have more than another year of this to endure?

PPS The Pure and Simple Store refuses to take back the bubble bath. Hippie-type, sarong-wearing shop assistant told me they cannot give a full refund once the merchandise has been more than half used. (Not my fault if the bottle's almost empty – Jack poured most of it down the toilet when I wasn't looking.) Buoyed up by recent outstanding success with RTÉ, I decided to bypass her and her greasy dreadlocks and take it to the next level – composed stern letter of complaint to CEO 'multi-millionaire-with-a-conscience' Beth Howard.

Dear Ms Howard,

I am writing to you directly, as I know you take a keen interest in the goings-on of your company, even though you are now a multi-millionairess and probably living in the lap of luxury somewhere exotic.

I recently purchased a full-size bottle of 'Sleep Tight, Little Mite' in my local Pure and Simple Store. Call me naïve, but I was taken in by the new-age swirly writing on the back of the bottle that promised to lull my baby to sleep, with extracts of blueberry and lavender. (Frankly, I thought the combination a little strange, but I am not an aromatherapy expert, so I decided to take a chance.)

However, imagine my surprise when, instead of calming and soothing my son, the product seemed to aggravate his hyperactivity. (He hasn't actually been professionally diagnosed as hyperactive, but you know what boys are like – a totally different kettle of fish from girls. My daughter never had a sleeping problem, although this may be because she had a soother until she was four.)

I don't know if you have ever had a child with a sleeping disorder (again, not professionally diagnosed, but a mother's instinct is not to be trifled with) but, trust me, if you are sleep deprived, you will do anything to get a few extra hours' rest. In fact, as you are probably aware, having worked in many impoverished countries round the world (work I truly admire, by the way), sleep deprivation is actually used as bona-fide torture in many backward Communist countries. It is right up there with electrocution and thumb-screwing and all sorts of other deplorable things. In fact, given the choice, I'm sure lots of poor tortured prisoners would choose thumb-screws over a lost night's sleep any day of the week.

Anyway, my point is, I firmly believed that your product would do what it says on the label and result in a night of relaxed bliss all round, so imagine my dismay and surprise when the opposite happened.

I may be a stay-at-home mother now, but I used to work in PR (I often had direct personal contact with the CEO, so I have experience of high-level executive decision-making).

Now, PR is not advertising, but I do have a good understanding of how these kinds of ad campaigns work. I understand that some companies feel the need to sex up their products, but I am shocked and saddened that the Pure and Simple Store would choose to do so. I would therefore expect you either to refund my money (the local store would have none of it – I do think you need to look into your recruitment procedures) or at least send me some free products for the trouble and disappointment I have suffered because of this false advertising.

I am sure you can take time out from helping saving the rainforests to answer my query quickly.

Thanking you,
Susan Hunt

PS If you do send me some free products, can you please not send anything with lily-of-the-valley? It reminds me of my maths teacher at school.

20 *January*

Parish flyer dropped through the door today and, for once, I read it. (Was a bit desperate as had already read *Heat* twice. Poor Posh looks exhausted – can sympathize: it's no joke minding two children, not to talk of three.) Anyway, it turns out there is a mother-and-toddler group in the parish hall on Thursday mornings. Should really go and mingle with other stay-at-home mums. Let's face it – Louise is fat-all use to me, living it up in Dubai. Also, according to theperfectparent.com, Jack needs to be interacting socially with children his own age – not just being bossed about by his older sister. More importantly, extra activity may tire him out and get him to sleep all night. May go. As long as it's not all holier-than-thou types singing hymns and breastfeeding, how bad can it be?

Mum is delighted with my new plan to surrender to housewife status. 'I used to have such fun at those coffee mornings, darling,' she reminisced. 'We'd swap recipes and knitting patterns. You'll pick up some great tips. And it'll be lovely to meet women more like you. Louise is lovely, but she's such a high flyer.'

Felt thoroughly depressed afterwards. Ate six fig rolls and half a packet of custard creams.

21 January

Mother-and-toddler group was roaring success! Felt really at home with all the other frumpy put-upon mothers (and one lone father), who are also being driven demented by screaming toddlers and lack of sleep. The kids were let loose in the hall and we stood on the sidelines moaning about our saggy bellies and useless husbands (except for Lone Father). It was quite empowering. Felt comforted by knowledge that am not alone in my struggle. Also, there were free scones and coffee! Bonus! There was a bit of a scuffle when Jack tried to wrestle another toddler to the floor for an Action Man, but it turned out OK. Funnily enough, it was Lone Father's son Rodney whom Jack was trying to attack so the father and I ended up having a nice chat. *And* he didn't seem to mind when Jack hit him over the head with a Bob the Builder truck.

Heartwarming to see a man who is comfortable enough with his masculinity to brave hordes of jelly-belly mummies and spend quality time with his son. He is probably a new-age house-husband or else has a really interesting job that involves shift work, like award-winning war correspondent. Didn't like to seem nosy and pry too much, even though I was dying to know, so stuck to chatting about Wendy and Muck.

All in all, a success. Will definitely go again next week.

PS Tried to tell Joe about new mother-and-toddler group, but he didn't seem all that interested. Something about an accounting error and millions of lost dollars, blah, blah, blah.

PPS Bet Lone Father could teach my husband a thing or two about sensitivity and child-rearing.

22 *January*

Only a week until Joe's Christmas party and I still have nothing to wear. Cannot possibly try to wedge myself back into blue sparkly number I wore for Christmas drinks with Evil Anna and Co. Raked through my wardrobe again, hoping for divine intervention by St Chanel, in the form of a stunning ensemble I had bought and forgotten about jumping out at me, yelling, 'Problem solved!' But it's official: every single item of clothing I possess is covered with snot or vomit stains, or both. In a fit of abnormal, superhuman energy (those probiotic yogurts may be working), decided to do huge Trinny and Susannah overhaul of self and wardrobe.

Plan to Overhaul Wardrobe and turn into Stunning Yummy Mummy

- Throw out all misguided purchases (anything short, tight or made with shiny material that you can see cellulite through).

- Remember golden rule for future impulse purchases: a bargain is not a bargain unless the item fits you and you plan to wear it. (May have to surrender fluorescent orange D&G mini-skirt bought in TK Maxx bargain bin.)

- Admit that I am not a size ten.

- Luckily size twelve is the new size ten.

- Stick to clothing styles that suit my shape.

- Decide what my shape actually is.

Worryingly, I seem to fall into more than one of Trinny and Susannah's body categories. Have biggish boobs so I should wear fitted V-neck tops with sleeves to cover saggy arms. But – have bulging tummy so shouldn't wear anything too fitted. Also possess big bottom, which is apparently OK to put on display – but only if pert. Unfortunately I possess the type of awful bottom detested by Trinny and Susannah above all others – the one that trails against the back of the knees. I should therefore wear looser fabrics to disguise it.

Very confusing. I'm sure if Trinny and Susannah

were here they would beat me over the head for being so indecisive and weak.

Decided to start overhaul by unfurling a dozen black sacks and placed each one carefully on bedroom floor. This took ages as

(a) could not find perforations to separate bags, and

(b) Jack kept mushing the bags and shoving them under the bed.

Got so carried away with the organization that completely forgot the time and was twenty minutes late picking Katie up from playschool. If this is what it takes to be a yummy mummy I'm not sure I'll make the grade.

23 January

Feel Zen-like sense of calm and new purpose from overhaul of wardrobe. Have filled four black sacks with rubbish from former life as frumpy mother and am ready to be transformed into cream, fitted-cashmere-V-neck-wearing goddess like Liz Hurley. Just have to buy a whole new wardrobe and a 4×4, lose three stone, have Botox, hire half a dozen nannies, and the transformation will be complete. Joe is slightly panicked by all the black sacks on the landing. Serves him right – it's probably his fault I've let myself go so badly. Trinny and Susannah definitely think so. My first purchase will be a fabulous new outfit for his Christmas party to wow all the boring office types and make him sit up and take notice.

PS Have just realized why Liz Hurley wears white all the time: to hide the snot and vomit stains that can ruin perfectly acceptable black outfits. The woman is a style goddess. Is it any wonder she has won Celebrity Mother of the Year award so many times?

24 January

Spent a blissful morning hunting for a stunning new ensemble to wow office nerds. Felt positively Liz-esque swanning round the Centre, trying on as many expensive cocktail dresses as I could manage in a three-hour period (the longest Joe could keep Katie and Jack under control at home).

Turns out that shopping for eveningwear can be quite physically demanding – no wonder Liz is so toned. Had to refuel with coffee and muffins quite a few times to keep my energy levels up.

Eventually decided on a gorgeous green sequined Armani dress, selling in TK Maxx for half the recommended retail price (it said so on the label).

Had stern talk with myself in the changing room to make sure I was buying dress because of suitability for occasion and not because of astonishing low price and designer bling. Am very proud that am capable of being so mature and responsible and can avoid impulse buys that turn out to be disasters. Did mental checklist just to make sure.

- Does dress suit me? Yes. Colour brings out green flecks in my eyes. Also, is not too short. Is a little tight, but purchase of new suck-it-all-in mammy pants will put paid to that. Also, hem needs slight adjustment, but can do that myself.

- Will I actually wear dress? Yes: Joe's Christmas party on day after tomorrow.

- Does dress match anything else in my wardrobe? No, but it is eveningwear and therefore question is null and void.

- Is dress in price bracket? Three hundred euro for an Armani dress? Yeah, baby!

Trinny and Susannah would be so proud.

PS May have been a tad hasty with the wardrobe overhaul. Now have no clothes to speak of (bar amazing Armani dress, which may not be appropriate for daywear) so had to rescue some (OK, all) of the frumpy outfits from the black sacks. Just until I garner enough energy to go shopping again and complete my transformation.

25 January

In freakish psychic manner, Katie has sensed we're going out tomorrow night and is Not Happy. She had a full-scale tantrum in Tesco today, flinging herself violently to the ground in the vegetable aisle, kicking and screaming with rage – exactly like those scary delinquent children on *Supernanny*.

Desperately tried to remember how Supernanny would tackle such unacceptable behaviour. (Aside from wearing old-fashioned glasses and looking stern, think she may have advised to ignore the child turning purple by the broccoli and continue shopping in calm you-can-choke-for-all-I-care manner.)

In a panic, tried reasoning, then cajoling, then full-on bribery with chocolate buttons. Finally ended up grabbing her by the arm and hauling her out of the supermarket like some kind of child-abuser. Jack was slung under the other arm and the trolley, half full with a week's shopping, was left in aisle three. Was sweating like a footballer and swearing like a sailor when I slammed straight into Lone Father from the mother-and-toddler group walking through the car park, his little angel sitting astride his muscular shoulders, like something out of a Ralph Lauren ad. Tried to make polite chit-chat through gritted smile while restraining demon children when, like a little eel, Jack wriggled out from under my arm and made a sprint for it across the car park. Stood frozen in horror as he bounded in front of a minivan when, like a super-hero, Lone Father dived across a yellow Mini Cooper and whipped Jack from the jaws of death. Was so relieved started to sob un-controllably. Said shaky thanks to Lone Father, wiping snot from my streaming nose, and shoved kids into the car as quickly as I could. Katie and Jack were both struck dumb with terror by my sobbing and, for the first time ever, sat in their car seats without bribery or argument.

PS Vow never to lose temper with the kids again. Jack could have *died* in that car park today. This brush with death has put all trivial matters into perspective. Feel quite spiritually enlightened.

PPS Lone Father must think I'm some kind of maniac. First I look like a fishwife hauling the kids out of the supermarket, and then I almost kill one. I'm lucky if he doesn't contact the authorities.

26 January: Joe's Christmas Party Night

Period arrived mid-morning. Which explains yesterday's uncontrollable sobbing and despondency. Green sequined Armani dress now definitely erring on the too-tight side of slinky as my huge stomach is bloated out of all proportion to the rest of my body. Suck-it-all-in mammy pants simply relocate blubber to under my ribcage so now look as if have pair of enormous deformed boobs. Also have huge spot on chin that no amount of Yves St Laurent Touche Éclat will cover. However, saggy, wrinkled skin from another sleepless night will probably draw attention away from that area. (Should lobby cosmetic companies to develop a product for those of us who suffer from spots *and* wrinkles. May well write to Posh and suggest multi-million-pound venture. She would make an excellent spokeswoman. And I'm sure she confessed to being prone to the odd inconvenient breakout.)

For once, Joe came home early so I spent half an hour trying to relax with glass of wine in the bath (quite tricky to balance glass in sudsy water – don't know how celebs manage it, especially with acrylic nails). Relaxing experience slightly marred by Katie knocking on the door to do a wee every five minutes but soldiered on. Spent another hour slapping on foundation and loads of blusher to conceal deathly pallor. No time to apply tan to blue-white skin, so decided to go for pale and interesting look. If it's good enough for Nicole Kidman, it's good enough for me and, anyway, fake tan is so *Footballers' Wives*.

Finally squeezed into dress and managed to zip it up with Herculean effort. Looked quite presentable, considering I had forgotten to tack the dodgy hem and had to use Sellotape instead. Was exhausted by all the preparations when Joe sailed in, jumped into his tuxedo, brushed his teeth, greased back his hair and was ready to go in five minutes flat. Descended stairs to Katie, who yelled 'Mummy looks just like Shrek!' and Joe's mother, running her fingers up the dusty banister in disgust.

Spent next ten minutes trying to ignore direct implication that I was a fat green ogre with dusting issues and searching frantically for my evening bag, Joe tapping his fingers on the hall table and his mother pretending to help by looking under the sofa (really hunting for evidence that I don't vacuum under there either).

Left house to Jack squealing, 'Shwek, Shwek!' and Mrs H muttering something about mutton dressed as lamb.

PS Had second thoughts about pale and interesting look as we took off in the car, so dashed back in and dusted loads of bronzer over arms and chest to disguise dimpled, turkey-like skin. Sometimes I think that Nicole could do with a few sun-bed sessions. It's too much of a coincidence that Tom has gone for dark-skinned sultry types ever since they broke up.

And the award for Most Boring Christmas Party in the World Ever goes to . . . Pyramid Consultants Ltd.

Was horrified to find that we had to sit at official fuddy-duddy table with ancient directors and make boring chit-chat all night. At least last year we got to sit with the managers and their wives and I could guzzle as much free plonk as I liked to blank out the mind-numbingly boring proceedings.

Joe nearly whooped with joy when he discovered we were sitting with the big-wigs. 'They *must* be considering me for promotion, Susie,' he whispered delightedly, as we sat down. 'Don't start an argument with anyone, will you?'

Have no idea what he meant but he looked so earnest and nervous I was on my best dumb-housewife behaviour all night, laughing politely at dated sexist jokes and pretending to be interested in accounting regulations.

'That Sarbannes-Oxley ruling will be the downfall of the entire profession,' the old codger beside me huffed over the starter, spraying reheated tomato soup down my bronzed cleavage. I nodded sagely in agreement, though had no idea what he was blathering on about.

Sent Joe tons of psychic rescue-me-rescue-me messages across the table, but he was too busy chatting to the chief financial officer and his dowdy wife to notice. He looked quite sexy in his tux, but he was so busy schmoozing we didn't get a chance to dance together. Instead, had to dance with seventy-year-old senior partner to Wham!'s 'Last Christmas' (in January) while he leered down my dress and told me I had magnificent bosoms.

Highlight of the evening was a sweet presentation made to Joe's ancient secretary – who is finally retiring at the age of sixty-seven. She didn't look too happy with her gift basket of Bobbi Brown makeup, but word on the dance-floor was that she felt she was being pushed out before her time. Asked Joe who his new secretary was going to be and he pointed out a blonde, doe-eyed twenty-year-old in a skin-tight, slashed-to-the-navel dress on the other side of the room.

'She's a bit young, isn't she?' I wheezed, breathless after being spun round the dance-floor by the seventy-year-old lech.

'She's meant to be very experienced,' he said, as if the fact that he was getting a Barbie lookalike as a PA was of no consequence to him.

'Yeah, I bet she is,' I muttered, under my breath, before I excused myself to go to the ladies'. Was barricaded into a cubicle, peeling off the suck-it-all-in mammy pants, which had been cutting off the circulation to the lower half of my body, when I heard giggly whispering from outside.

'You lucky cow!' one voice slurred. 'Can't believe you get to work with that ride Joe.'

'Yeah,' another voice piped up. 'He could adjust my balance any day of the week, if you know what I mean.' There was riotous laughter and much whooping before the door opened again and they were gone.

Almost flushed mammy pants down toilet with shock before I came to my senses. They can't have been talking about my husband. His days of being called a 'ride' are well and truly over.

Cornered a hassled-looking Joe at the bar and tried to ask casually how many other Joes there were in Pyramid Consultants. 'Just one,' he replied, pointing to a tanned Adonis type with highlighted hair shaking some serious (and very toned) booty to 'Lady Marmalade' on the dance-floor. 'Everyone reckons he's gay – what do you think?'

Nodded silently, feeling sick. He was a dead ringer for that guy off *Queer Eye for the Straight Guy* (an excellent gay barometer). Those girls *had* been talking about my Joe – his new secretary actually *fancies* him.

28 January

Have horrible itchy rash all over from that damned Armani dress – once I took the mammy pants off those bloody sequins were so *scratchy*. No wonder that thing was reduced to less than half-price. Will have to plant it in harm's way (i.e., under Katie's nose) to make sure it comes to a sticky end and I never have to wear it again.

PS Louise is back from Dubai today – probably laden with pots of diamonds, gold, and designer gear to beat the band.

PPS Just thought – maybe rash is psychological reaction to shock of marriage trauma/husband-being-called-a-ride scenario. Must look it up online.

29 January

Katie and Jack are covered from head to toe in little pink dots after playing *Shrek* with the toxic dress from hell. Will have to inform TK Maxx that they are stocking killer merchandise. May have a claim there.

PS Have decided was totally overreacting to potential marriage crisis. Joe and I may be in a rut of serious *Dr. Phil* proportions, but it's not like he would ever cheat on me – he wouldn't know how. It's very healthy and normal that his new Barbie secretary finds him attractive. As long as he never finds out, everything's fine.

30 January

Katie and Jack have chicken-pox! Am overwhelmed with guilt for blaming top designer dress for their rash, when really they were both suffering from horrible, debilitating childhood disease. Thesickkid.com says chicken-pox can lead to blindness, deformity and even brain damage! Am distraught that I could have killed my own children because I was not paying enough attention. Arrived unannounced at the doctor's – where I had to beg the power-crazy receptionist for an appointment.

'The doctor is very busy this morning.' She glared through her bulletproof-glass partition. 'You really should have made an appointment.' Was furious – that witch has no concept of a medical emergency – it would serve her right if someone dropped dead right under her hooked nose.

Crisis situation was not helped when Katie said, at the top of her voice, 'That lady looks just like the Wicked Witch from *The Wizard of Oz*, doesn't she, Mummy?'

Had to do extra grovelling and begging to be allowed sit for an hour in the smelly, stuffy waiting room with sick people coughing and hawking all over us. One old bag had the nerve to tell me to keep Jack under control! Is it my fault if the waiting room hasn't got one child-friendly item in it? Anyway, he didn't mean to hit her over the head with my handbag: he was aiming for Katie.

Finally got to see the doctor and he had the nerve to tell me to dose them with paracetamol and bathe them in bread soda twice a day if they're itchy! *And* he charged me fifty-five euro for the privilege! Voiced my concerns about brain damage and deformity but he laughed nervously and said it would take more than chicken-pox to damage these two.

Finally managed to get Jack to loosen his death grip on the doctor's stethoscope by bribing him with a roll of I've-been-good-at-the-doctor's-today stickers, and headed for the chemist, where I had a screaming row with a twit in a white coat who refused point-blank to sell me more than two bottles of junior paracetamol.

'My children are sick, possibly *dying*,' I hollered, in the mother of all rages, 'and you are trying to deny them pain medication? What kind of a sick pervert are you?'

'It's illegal to sell more than two bottles at a time,

madam,' she informed me primly. 'Are you asking me to break the law?'

I fixed her with my best evil squinting stare (more effective when wearing eye-liner, but still a conversation-stopper). 'I've a good mind to write to your governing body,' I declared. 'I knew the health system was in crisis, but to discriminate against helpless children – that really takes the biscuit.'

Katie and Jack started to cry, and all the grannies in the queue behind me perked up and took notice.

But Evil Chemist Woman was not backing down that easily. 'Madam, there are reasons for the regulations,' she said, glancing nervously over my shoulder at the grannies, who were unashamedly turning up the volume in their hearing aids so they could earwig properly. 'Some people may use the medication unscrupulously.'

'Are you insinuating,' I roared, pulling myself up to my full height (five foot three in heels), 'that I would harm my own *children?*'

The grannies tutted with disapproval at the very idea, and Chemist Woman shifted uncomfortably in her white Scholl sandals. A mad mother she could handle, but a group of vengeful pensioners was another matter altogether.

Crumpling under the pressure she shoved five bottles into the bag, pronto. Did victory lap round pharmacy, junior paracetamol bottles held aloft, to a little round of applause from the grannies. Erin Brockovich eat your heart out.

Am shattered from endless rounds of bread-soda baths and rubbing hysterical children with calamine lotion. Katie inconsolable that spots are all over her face and scalp. 'Will you have to cut all my hair off, Mummy? Like in *Rapunzel*?' she sobbed, looking at her reflection in the oven door for the millionth time. (Joe has banished all other mirrors in a fit of self-preservation.)

Made mistake of telling her if she scratched her spots they would leave a mark on her skin. She nearly had to be sedated she was so hysterical. 'I'll be like Quasimodo!' she shrieked, tears and snot running down her poor spotty face. 'I'll never get a boyfriend now.' (She must get this melodramatic stuff from Joe's side of the family – I'm such an easy patient to care for when I'm sick. Not that I am allowed to be sick any more.)

Felt it was wrong time to have the people-should-love-you-for what-you-are-on-the-inside-instead-of-the-outside conversation so instead I promised to bring her to the hairdresser's to get a proper grown-up cut when all this trauma is over.

PS Jack poured half a bottle of calamine lotion down the toilet and the other half over his head. Too tired to care.

PPS Louise had *Beauty and the Beast* DVD couriered over to amuse kids. Suddenly remembered how kind she can be and felt a rush of gratitude. Must call her for Dubai low-down.

PPS Katie inconsolable that she looks more like the Beast than Beauty.

Katie and Jack got get-well-soon cards from Mum and Dad today. Dad enclosed a photo of me when I was four – covered with oozing pink pustules and looking fierce.

Called him in outrage. Very worrying that he photographed distressed child (me) during a serious medical emergency.

He howled with laughter down the phone. 'You were hilarious, Susie,' he guffawed. 'All you were worried about was if Conor Dunne would love you any more. And poor old Conor couldn't stand the sight of you – with or without the spots!' Cue more uproarious laughter.

'I did *not* care what Conor Dunne thought about me, Dad,' I huffed, 'and, anyway, it was him who had the crush on me, not the other way round.'

'Riiiight . . . So is that why you packed an overnight case, brought it into playschool and announced to Conor's mother that you were moving in with them?' That did sound vaguely familiar. 'Then, when Conor said, "No way," you sulked for about two months!' More snorting laughter.

'The way I remember it, *actually*, Dad, is that Mrs Dunne invited me to play and stay overnight, but then Conor didn't feel well so I couldn't go.'

'And, you fell for that old line.' Dad could barely speak, he was laughing so hard. Could hear Mum wrestling phone from his hands before there was a click. Have sneaking suspicion that she may have rewritten some of my past errors of judgement to protect my feelings.

PS Louise called, wanting to regale me with glamorous stories of Dubai escapades – does she not realize I'm in the middle of a major medical crisis here?

PPS Just realized I missed the mother-and-toddler group yesterday. Probably better off – am still mortified about car-park/Lone Father débâcle.

2 February

Had hissing row with Joe over corn flakes after he arrived home late from work *again*. 'Susie, I'm doing my best,' he said, in a world-weary no-one-works-as-hard-as-I-do way. 'Work is crazy at the moment, and if I want to be made a director I have to be seen to be putting in the hours.'

'What's the point of you being made a director if you never get to see your own children?' I screeched. 'I may as well be a single mother for all the help you give me round here.' Launched into full-scale lecture on being unappreciated wife, mother, nurse, housekeeper, etc., etc.

'It's not just me who has to stay late,' he said, spooning some Weetabix into Jack's mouth, which he promptly spat back out. 'The whole team was there until eleven last night.'

'Including Busty Barbie, I'll bet,' I spat with real venom, just like a bitter spouse from *Wife Swap*.

'What the hell are you on about now?' Joe mopped the Weetabix off his tie with a tea-towel.

'Your new secretary,' I ranted. 'Let's face it, she's not exactly hard on the eye, is she?'

'Becky?' Joe had the grace to look outraged. 'I'm old enough to be her father, for God's sake.'

Trust her to have a butter-wouldn't-melt-in-my-mouth name like *Becky*. Most at odds with the porn-star dress she wore to the Christmas do.

'Well, maybe you like the idea of being a sugar-daddy.' I wasn't giving up yet.

'Oh, for God's sake, Susie, get a grip,' Joe grunted, rolling his eyes to heaven in that really irritating way he's had since he was nineteen and someone told him it was a sophisticated thing to do during an argument. 'To be a sugar-daddy, you have to make some money. Now, I have to go. I'll see you later.'

'Yeah, much later, I'll bet,' I yelled to his back, as he kissed the kids goodbye. (Was tempted to throw a few plates at the wall, for good measure.)

Am quite shocked by my little outburst. Obviously, somewhere deep in my subconscious, I feel threatened by Joe's new secretary, her endless legs and pert bosoms. Am also probably resentful that Joe did not administer one bread-soda bath or apply one drop of calamine lotion over the past week.

Must explore these feelings or I will be bitter and twisted before too long.

PS Made mistake of telling Mrs H that Joe has been less than useless with sick children.

'Susie, it is the *mother*'s job to look after the children,' she gasped, shocked. 'All this new-fangled nonsense that fathers should change nappies and get up in the middle of the night is ridiculous. Joe's dad never lifted a finger to help. Never.' Ironically, she looked proud at the memory. Have decided to buy her a copy of *The Female Eunuch* for her birthday.

3 February

Almost all of Katie's spots are healed over, so I decreed her well enough to go back to playschool today. Met Zoe and Eco-mother at the gate. Zoe was swinging a papier-mâché dinosaur over her head like a miniature Zulu warrior.

'It was such fun getting the chicken-pox, wasn't it?' Eco-mother said gaily. 'We had so much time to bond and do arts and crafts together!'

Zoe smiled evilly at Katie in that universally understood my-mummy's-better-than-your-mummy smirk.

'Yes,' I simpered back, praying that Katie wouldn't let me down. 'We made lots of great stuff, didn't we, Katie?'

Katie seemed to understand exactly where I was coming from and joined in enthusiastically: 'Yeah – *we* made a *much* bigger dinosaur than yours, Zoe,' she taunted with glee. 'I'm going to bring it in tomorrow! Aren't I, Mummy?' She eyeballed me in that threatening co-operate-or-I'll-sing-like-a-bird way, so I nodded mutely.

No wonder Katie was happy to play along with my pack of lies. Tried not to blanch – but am filled with dread at prospect of having to make fake dinosaur from wet toilet paper and glue.

PS Zoe's face is completely scar-free. Apparently

Eco-mother concocted some homeopathic paste from weeds and green tea and slathered it all over. Am sure this violates some health-and-safety regulation. Must investigate.

PPS Dying to tell Joe about freakish Eco-mother, but obviously can't until he apologizes for being so unreasonable the other day.

4 February

Had running battle with Katie this morning over her outfit of choice. Stupid playschool teachers told the children that spring has begun, so Katie expected to wear pedal-pushers and a crop top today. Never mind that it's about three degrees outside. Really, formal education can be quite wearing at times.

Finally persuaded Katie to wear her fleece and jeans – but only if she could wear her sunglasses on her head like some kind of Hollywood starlet. (Maybe I should consider recycling all those back issues of *Heat* magazine with Catherine Zeta-Jones pouting on the cover.)

PS Joe still holding out. Crawled into bed beside me at eleven thirty and fell straight to sleep on his back – resulting in all-night snoring. Wanted to tell him to be quiet, but couldn't as that would have meant being first to speak.

5 February

Plucked up courage to return to mother-and-toddler group after car-park débâcle. Lone Father didn't bat an eyelid when I sidled in: he just gave me a friendly, we're-all-in-the-same-boat wave. Nice to see a man who can take life's hiccups in his stride – his wife must have him well trained. *And* he doesn't have any problem with being a house-husband. Joe would rather eat a handful of maggots. He seemed to be causing a bit of a stir among the mothers, though – there was definitely more lipstick being sported this week and I spotted at least three unbuttoning their trackie tops just a little too low. Two particularly glam apparitions, Marita and Heidi, were blatantly throwing themselves at him.

I ignored all the fluttering of eyelashes in lofty I-am-above-this-type-of-behaviour fashion, and had a great one-to-one play with Jack – until he decided he'd had enough and waddled out of the door, leading to a minor security alert.

PS Felt really sorry for Lone Father today – he didn't get a minute's peace with all the desperate housewives flinging themselves at his suede loafers. As if an award-winning war correspondent was going to be interested in sad jelly-belly mummies. Some women have no self-respect.

PPS Cold War still in progress, although Joe did ask me to pass the milk this morning. Think he's coming to his senses.

6 February

Oprah was fascinating today. It was all about forgiveness and healing. She had loads of really good, tearful guests on, telling how they had to forgive their enemy before they could begin to heal themselves. Could have sworn I saw Oprah welling up. That *never* happens (sometimes I suspect she may have issues about expressing her emotions), so I took it as a sign to call Joe. Technically, am not making first move – he did speak to me at breakfast yesterday.

Poor guy sounded quite bunged up and sniffly on the phone – I think he might have been crying he was so relieved we're back on speaking terms. He promised to be home for a family dinner tonight. Feel very virtuous and spiritual. Oprah was right – taking the higher ground really *is* fulfilling. Off to Iceland to buy deep-fried Southern chicken for dinner – Oprah's favourite.

7 February

Joe is off work sick – hallelujah!

Took the opportunity to meet Louise for leisurely mid-week brunch in the city, just like when I was a PR gal-about-town and could quaff cappuccinos until the cows came home. Joe seemed a bit concerned I was leaving him alone with Jack, and upped the ante on the fake coughing and sneezing front as I was getting ready. 'I'm not sure I'm up to minding him, Susie,' he fake-wheezed. 'I feel really rough.'

'I'll pick up some Lemsip for you, love,' I called, banging the door behind me. 'Oh, and by the way, Katie needs to be collected at twelve.' Shouted last bit through letterbox in case he hadn't heard me.

Felt quite carefree and Audrey Hepburn-esque, sipping a latte in swanky city-centre restaurant, wearing my black polo-neck and best black wool trousers (special-occasion bobble-free boot-legs). Was fantasizing about being mistaken for some top-notch society lady, plotting huge charity bash for orphaned children, when Louise breezed in wearing a pale blue linen suit (annoyingly crease-free) and carrying a cream basket-bag. Realized my four-year-old fashionista had been right all along: winter clothes are *so* last season.

'Mineral water, please,' Louise called, to a smiling waiter who had appeared from thin air, tongue hanging out. 'I really have to detox, Susie,' she told me, her perfect complexion reflecting off my coffee cup and blinding me momentarily. 'My body clock is all over the place from so much travelling.'

Spent the rest of the lunch pulling at my polo-neck and downing at least four lattes. (And, if am totally honest, a cheeseburger with curly fries and cheesecake with extra cream.)

'So, Susie, what will I do about Steve?' Louise sipped her mineral water like a beautiful, delicate gazelle as I wiped the grease from my lips.

'What do you mean?' I asked cautiously. Had she already told me what was wrong and I had blanked it? Desperately tried to remember as I shoved another curly fry into my mouth.

'I don't know what it is,' she said sadly, staring into

the middle distance. 'I'm just not sure he wants the same things I do.'

Bingo! We were going to have the I-want-a-commitment conversation. Easy-peasy. Wouldn't even have to listen, just nod sympathetically in the right places. Tried to catch waiter's eye and mime 'A vat of coffee, please,' but he was too busy picking his fingernails to notice.

Hummed and hahed my way through another hour of will-I-won't-I? drone before waddling home to find Joe prone on the sofa, deathly pale and in a delirious trance, while Jack finished off using his Magic Markers to play dot-to-dot. All over Joe's face.

8 February

Joe is genuinely sick. Doctor made a house call (first time in living memory – obviously some kind of secret boys' club thing) and diagnosed real flu. 'You'll be out of action for at least a week, Joe,' he said, clasping his stethoscope to his chest and eyeing Jack nervously. 'You'll have to take it easy – no physical exercise and avoid stress.'

'Well, that's the marathon training out, then.' I chuckled.

Joe and the doctor turned their reproachful boys' club gazes on me.

Don't they know that laughter is the best medicine?

Quickly rearranged face into concerned, loving-wife expression.

'Now, remember, lots of fluids and rest,' Dr Feelgood

advised, edging out of the door as Jack sized him up. 'He'll need lots of TLC, Susie,' he instructed.

No problem there – have seen *ER* a million times. Could probably perform triple-bypass surgery, if push came to shove. Spent rest of day at Joe's beck and call, enduring sorrowful I-told-you-so looks, and trying to refrain from suffocating him with Jack's favourite Nemo pillow. Eventually sent Katie up with her doctor's kit to play Nurse Nightingale and mop his brow – desperate times call for desperate measures.

9 February

Endured severe bad-wife verbal beating from Mum today. 'I hope you're looking after Joe properly, Susie,' she lectured, down the phone. 'He needs lots of fluids and lots of rest. Flu is a serious illness, you know. It can wipe you out for weeks.'

Quite worried about last bit – don't think can endure this agony much longer. Had to cut her off when the doorbell went. It was Joe's mother, laden with chicken soup and dodgy-looking car magazines with buxom blondes draped across Porsche Boxsters. 'How is the poor boy?' she asked, brushing past me and sprinting upstairs before I had a chance to set Jack on her. Couldn't bear to witness Joe's wheeze and pained expression going into overdrive so I locked myself into the kitchen, pretending to peel vegetables for more soup.

Mummy Dearest eventually resurfaced, muttering about dust mites and flu jabs. 'You really should get a

Dyson vacuum-cleaner dear.' She cast a critical eye over the sticky work surfaces and greasy breakfast dishes. 'It's so important to keep nasty germs at bay, especially for the little ones.'

Jack eyed her suspiciously as he mashed the last of his morning Weetabix into his hair, just in case she was going to come at him with a J-cloth.

'Joe needs to be in the best of health if he's going to support you all, Susie,' she continued, unabashed. 'I mean, he's the only breadwinner now, you know.'

Tried to restrain myself from attacking her with the potato-peeler.

PS Caught Joe acting manly and in charge on the phone to work. Eavesdropped outside the bedroom door as he fired orders left, right and centre, just like the guy from the Lemsip Max ad. 'Just get those accounts over to Charles, pronto,' he ordered, in the I-will-stand-for-no-nonsense tone I thought he reserved only for when he was trying to change Jack's nappy. Not even a *hint* of a sniffle.

10 February

Gruff motorbike courier nearly banged the door down at eight a.m. with piles of top-secret documentation for Joe to examine. Am furious his employers can get away with such harassment when he is officially off sick (*with* a doctor's note). I mean, how can he be expected to mind Jack all morning, while I go to the hairdresser, *and* review files?

That's the problem with corporations today: they

have no human face. They expect employees to be heartless robots, capable of working 24/7. No wonder Lemsip Max is a bestseller – it simply feeds employers' unrealistic expectations. Have a good mind to write to RTÉ to let them know that carrying that ad may be an infringement of human rights. Will have to check Amnesty International website when I get back from the hairdresser.

PS Mrs H rang to see how her 'poor pet' was doing. Was tempted to tell her that the soft-porn mags she had given him were working a treat.

11 February

Joe limped back to work today. Don't think he was up to it yet, but he seemed eager to get back in. Have to admire his dedication to his work – even if it is misplaced. House eerily empty and silent (except for Jack head-butting the floor to Bob the Builder song). Felt a bit bereft so called Louise for a woe-is-me chat. She was in sparkling form.

'Thanks for all the advice the other day, Susie,' she gushed. 'It's working a treat. I didn't call Steve at all for the last two days and he's all over me like a bad rash.'

Cannot remember doling out any relationship-saving advice. Am obviously so spiritually in tune with others that I inspire them without even trying. So pleased with myself that treated myself to *OK!* (the exposé of celebs' freakishly lined hands was just too good to miss), a double-chocolate-chip muffin and a latte.

Louise called at eight a.m., just as I was trying to corral the kids in a corner and wrestle them out of their PJs. Almost died of fright when the phone rang – was sure someone was dead or injured or at least severely maimed in horrific, tragic accident.

She could barely speak she was crying so hard. Was finally able to decipher what she was saying. 'Steve f-f-finished with me last night,' she sobbed dramatically.

Tried to make sympathetic noises while keeping a headlock on Jack to get his sweatshirt on. 'Maybe you're better off without him,' I suggested. 'You weren't really sure how you felt about him anyway, were you?'

'I think he's been two timing me.' She ignored my question. 'When I met him last night he stank of cheap perfume.'

'Oh, no!' This was awful.

'I *know*.' She hiccuped. 'I think he's been having it off with that Debbie trollop from the office. She's the only tart I know who still wears such vile perfume.'

'Maybe they genuinely had to work late?' I pulled up Jack's combats with my teeth. I didn't think the working-late scenario would be a goer, but you have to be careful what you say in these situations. (If Jerry Springer has taught me anything, it's that feuding couples can be reunited and acting like love's young dream in no time, and it's always the truth-telling best friend who ends up as the bitch from hell, being hissed at by the trailer-trash audience.)

'Don't be ridiculous, Susie,' Louise sniffed. 'That lazy

bastard's never worked a minute's overtime in his life. The working-late excuse *always* means they're shagging someone else.'

'Not necessarily.' I interrupted, feeling a bit uncomfortable.

But she ploughed on: 'Anyway, it doesn't matter if he's been bonking someone else or not. He says he's sick of playing stupid games.'

'What does *that* mean?' I asked, thinking Steve sounded like a total loser.

'It *means*, Susie, that your stupid advice about treating him mean to keep him keen has totally backfired and I'm now on my own *again*.'

'That's a bit unfair,' I said. 'It's not my fault if he was doing the dirty.'

'Oh, *all* men do the dirty, Susan,' she spat, in a really dark, evil voice. 'Don't kid yourself.'

Was still reeling from the 'Susan' usage (last time she called me that was after I accidentally snogged her boyfriend when we were thirteen) when we were either cut off or she slammed the phone down on me. Am shocked to the very core. Why is it my fault that Steve is a commitment-phobe? Dr. Phil would definitely suggest that Louise should look at her own behaviour patterns before she plays the blame game. Maybe she's seeking out psychologically damaged men in some warped, self-destructive manner that will need years of intensive therapy to resolve. Anyway, I cannot be held accountable for advice I give when under the influence of lattes and curly fries. Louise should know that by now.

PS Haunted by her all-men-are-cheats comment. What could she have meant?

PPS May well call the café where alleged conversation took place to see if they caught it on secret CCTV footage. Louise could quite possibly have hallucinated the whole treat-him-mean-to-keep-him-keen exchange. It doesn't even sound like something I would say. All I need is the video proof.

13 February

Woke in a panic last night, heart pounding in my chest like in true-life *ER* emergency. The full-length flannel nightshirt Joe's mother bought me for Christmas to match the garish red fleecy dressing-gown (blast it, but it's so bloody *comfortable*) was pasted to me with sweat.

Had blinding epiphany. Louise thinks Joe's having an affair! That's what she meant when she said all men cheat – she was trying to send me a coded message about my own husband. Definitely should never have told her that his new secretary thinks he's a ride. Spent rest of the night tossing and turning, imagining Joe getting down and dirty with another woman (quite difficult to do through his grunting and snoring, but I managed it).

Am horrified that Louise would try to sabotage my marriage because of her own petty insecurities and (quite frankly) her inability to commit to a relationship. It really is unforgivable for her to insinuate that Joe is cheating, just because her MOM fell for the charms of a trollop.

Thought Louise was my VBF, but am not so sure now. In fact, may well have to forge unlikely life-changing friendship with another woman *à la* chick-lit novel.

PS Mum called to say that she and Dad are going to Madrid for spur-of-the-moment romantic Valentine's break. Good thing I think Valentine's Day is an over-commercialized sell-out or I might have been inconsolable.

She was horrified to discover that I'm a non-Valentine's Day believer (a fact she seems to forget from one year to the next). Don't think she would have been as shocked if I'd told her that Joe is probably shagging his secretary or that Louise and I are officially not talking. 'You *should* celebrate the day, darling,' she twittered down the phone, like a lovestruck teenager. 'Love is the most important thing in a woman's life.'

Thought I heard Dad make a lewd comment in the background, something to do with Chianti and paella.

Was on brink of confiding in Mum about horrible fight with Louise and suspicions that Joe may be playing away, but felt the time wasn't right. No point spoiling her romantic delusions just yet.

14 February: Valentine's Day

Katie made a gorgeous Valentine's Day card at play-school. There was a big red monster creature on the front, smothered with silver glitter. It was most artistic. May well enrol her in proper art classes to cultivate her talent.

'Who's that, darling?' I asked, as she dangled the card just out of reach of Jack's grubby fingers when I strapped her into her car seat.

'That's you, Mummy,' she said, with confidence. 'The silver glitter is your tears.'

'Tears? Why am I crying?' I gave a little chuckle at her active imagination.

'Cos Daddy's at work and you're sad that you're all alone. Can we go to McDonald's for Hearts' Day?'

Drove to McDonald's in a daze. Even Katie thinks there's something wrong with my marriage. Maybe Louise is right – maybe Joe *is* having an illicit affair. Had weak moment in McDonald's and ordered a double cheeseburger and fries with a Diet Coke instead of healthy-option salad. Cannot be expected to eat lettuce when under such enormous strain. Luckily, it brought me to my senses. (Who says junk food is all bad?) There's no way Joe's playing away. He's simply not the unfaithful type. Louise is deflecting all her negative, man-hating energy on to me in a classic case of toxic transference behaviour. It all makes perfect sense.

PS Just in case, I have decided to carry out a thorough and exhaustive investigation of infidelity for research purposes. Googled 'infidelity' – there were approximately four million websites! Are the world and his wife cheating? Research may take longer than I had originally anticipated.

<u>Reasons to Think Joe May Be Having an Affair</u>

- We never have sex any more (approximately six weeks since last nookie session).

- We barely talk to each other ('Pass the salt/remote control/loo roll' does not count).

- He has a gorgeous new secretary with pert thirty-six-inch breasts and a twenty-inch waist.

- His new secretary thinks he's a ride.

- He's working later and later every night.

Reasons to Think Joe Is Not Having an Affair

- He has not lost weight (in fact he may be a bit lardier than usual).

- He has not started to exercise (channel-surfing does not count).

- He has not bought sexy new aftershave (I did, however, purchase Chanel Egoiste aftershave and balm pre-Thigh Master débâcle).

- He has not started to dress inappropriately young for his age or use embarrassing henna hair-rinse in outlandish bid to look ten years younger.

- He wouldn't know how to chat anyone up (can go quite red and stammer in charming boyish manner when he tries to be sexy).

- He loves his children (even though he barely sees them).

- Note: delete last one – everyone knows men are able to blank their kids from their minds when they're shagging their secretary across a desk when they should be at home in the bosom of their family watching *Fear Factor*.

Really want to call Louise and get her advice, but I have my pride. Am truly alone in the world.

15 February

Joe arrived home last night with a huge bouquet of red tulips. 'I have to go back to the office for a late meeting, Susie,' he said, kissing me chastely on the forehead and handing me the flowers, 'but why don't you wait up for me?'

Katie almost swooned with delight at this Public Display of Affection. 'Isn't Daddy romantic, Mummy?' she said dreamily. 'You're so lucky – he's just like Prince Charming.'

Was instantly suspicious. We never, *ever* celebrate Valentine's Day. In fact, we naïvely decided before we got married that we were going to be so sickeningly romantic every day of the year that Valentine's Day would be a day just like any other. (This was back when we went supermarket shopping together, held hands across the trolley and snogged by the frozen foods.)

Consulted infidelitysucks.com, once Katie and Jack had gone to bed. (It seems to have the most comprehensive cache of bitter testimonials from dumped spouses.) Quickly concluded that beautiful (and ludicrously expensive) bouquet of exquisite red tulips was a classic guilt gift and a sign that Joe is having a torrid affair with his twenty-inch-waisted, thirty-six-inch-busted secretary of freakish Barbie proportions.

A pop-up ad for Catch That Bastard Red-handed Detective Agency flashed across the screen.

Is your husband suddenly buying you flowers for no reason? If so, he may be cheating on you! Call this toll-free number for free advice about how to Catch That Bastard Red-handed! (Terms and conditions apply.)

Had to open new tub of Ben and Jerry's chocolate-chip ice-cream I was so distraught. Racked my brains to try to remember when Joe had last bought me flowers – the time he'd accused me of watching TV all day instead of ironing his underwear sprang to mind. (Initially thought it was when he slept with my half-sister and he was so guilty he wanted to make amends. Then realized I was thinking of the serial adulterer on Dr. Phil's cheating special.)

Shoved flowers in a vase with a sick heart and went straight to bed with an even sicker stomach (Ben and Jerry's is delicious, but half a tub is probably enough for one sitting). Feigned sleep when adulterous low-life husband crept in beside me, whispering sweet nothings.

Spent sleepless night plotting my revenge. First, will hire big-shot lawyer – preferably some arrogant American who shouts and smokes cigars – and sue Joe for every penny he earns and will earn in the future. Then, will instruct animal American lawyer to apply for sole custody of the children and deny him access. Everyone knows the mother has all the rights. Then will remarry millionaire-type self-made man (possibly said lawyer, if he stops smoking cigars) with a yacht, a holiday home in the South of France and a Porsche (Joe's favourite car). Must purchase some oversized sunglasses and a headscarf to hide anguish and heartbreak. But, first,

I have to gather some evidence. Luckily my twisted fascination with *Judge Judy* will finally pay off.

16 February

Had big row with Joe over breakfast. Quite anxious that this is becoming a regular occurrence. Even *seeing* breakfast cereal makes me feel twitchy, these days.

'What the hell is wrong with you, Susie?' he muttered at me across the table, after I'd thrown him the umpteenth dagger look of the morning. 'You're so bloody moody.'

Managed, with great difficulty, to restrain myself from chucking the Coco Pops at him. 'And what are *you*, Joe?' I muttered back. 'What are *you?*' (Couldn't really think of anything concrete to retaliate with on the spot, so tried the mysterious, evasive approach to frustrate him.)

'What on earth are you talking about?' he said.

'You *know* what I'm talking about,' I responded. 'The *flowers* are what I'm talking about. Is there any particular reason that you decided to break our no-Valentine's tradition for the first time in our seven-year marriage?' Threw meaningful look at the vase of tulips wilting in the corner (forgot to put any water in last night, probably in subconscious act of sabotage).

'For Christ's sake, Susie, I thought the bloody flowers would cheer you up,' he growled. 'I know we don't usually celebrate Valentine's Day, but you've been feeling so grumpy lately I thought they might do the trick.'

'You're never around long enough to know how I *feel*, Joseph,' I retorted, in the high and mighty manner I'd perfected after years of practice.

'I can never do the right thing, that's for sure,' he said, before he stomped off to work in an unironed shirt and mismatched socks. Ha!

PS Noticed Joe didn't actually eat any cereal this morning. This might be the start of the affair overhaul. Have decided that two can play at that game. Need to start investing in myself now, before it's too late and I'm a hopeless case swigging gin in a bed-sit while Joe parades his floozy all over town in a Porsche Boxster. I may even go to the gym.

17 February

Called Mrs H to ask her to take the kids so I could spend a luxurious morning being pampered at the hairdresser's. Complete overhaul required, possibly involving something to do with tinfoil and GHDs. Louise had recommended some top salon in the city pre-MOM argument but, after the last waxing débâcle, have decided to plough my own furrow. Said a little prayer to Posh for good luck, then stuck a pin in the *Yellow Pages*.

Salon receptionist sounded quite bored on the phone when I explained I needed a whole new image, but have decided to give her the benefit of the doubt. She's probably over-worked and underpaid (rather like myself). I'm sure she'll be lots more chatty in person. Will lay out special trendy-as-I-can-manage hairdresser outfit tonight. Probably something black and form-fitting is required. Must also remember to do full make-up (including mascara and eyeshadow) to offset horrific salon lighting. Still a bit shell-shocked from last visit when I saw pores I never knew existed waving at me from the mirror. However, am quite looking forward to a nice latte and special salon biscuits. Will also be able to catch up on vital *Heat* gossip in peace.

18 February

Had to endure half-hour mother-in-law lecture on the importance of personal grooming before I could make my escape this morning. 'Off you go, dear,' Mrs H simpered at the door. 'I did notice a while back that you needed your roots doing, but I didn't like to say anything. Best not to interfere in these things.'

Don't think she was trying to be ironic, but not sure.

'I still, to this day, get my roots done every other week,' she droned on. 'And I use my Unislim belt every day. You can't let yourself go, dear.' Cue ridiculous girlie giggle that would be inappropriate in a woman half her age (and girth).

If only she knew her precious son is probably committing lecherous adultery while she tries to battle her cellulite. Have decided she may be to blame if Joe is cheating. Sprinted down the garden path to her hollering offers to 'do your colours' and let me borrow her WeightWatchers recipe book.

Was a bit embarrassed to discover everyone in salon was dressed in pristine white instead of chic black (bloody springtime) but tried to carry off my black-polo-and-bootleg look with panache. Was also mortified to discover that freakish salon super-lights showed up every fleck of dandruff round my shoulders, as well as some old vomit of Jack's that had never washed out properly. (Note: special Black Velvet Persil may be a good investment instead of useless advertising ploy.)

Luckily voluminous (and extremely unflattering) salon bib contraption covered me from head to toe – once I managed to get into it. (Definitely caught the receptionist laughing when I tried to put it on back to front, but decided not to challenge her.)

Spent ages flicking through hair magazines in the salon, deciding which celeb I most wanted to look like. Was quite tempted to try a Catherine Zeta-Jones and get glossy hair extensions, but Zandra (the stylist) per-suaded me against it: 'You need great bone structure to carry off something like that.' She raked her comb through my fuzzy locks and curled her lip with disdain (quite difficult while chewing half a packet of Wrigley's spearmint, but she managed it). 'You'd be better off going for something like this feather cut,' she dead-panned, pointing out a mannish style on an androgy-nous (i.e., unattractive) model.

Was quite disappointed to discover that Zandra thinks I look more like Michael Douglas than CZJ, but decided to take her advice. She's the expert, after all, even if she does look about twelve. Anyway, am sure I read somewhere that young virgins are shaved of their hair to make those extensions, or they have to sell it to feed their families, so made best possible socially conscious choice.

Settled in for marathon coffee-drinking, *Heat*-reading session, when Zandra (she changed it from Sandra to make a statement, apparently) decided to break the habit of a lifetime and talk to me. I got the low-down on her sister, her sister's husband, her sister's husband's sister and eventually, to much cringing (mine), a blow-by-blow account of how she caught crabs from her sister's husband's married best friend. She stopped blow-drying my hair so many times to whisper the gory details into my ear that half of it dried unevenly and looked a bit lumpy. All in all, not the CZJ glossy locks I had hoped for, but an improvement all the same. Made hurried exit from salon, pressing an extra ten-euro tip into her outstretched palm as I left.

PS Was practically assaulted in Boots when capable-looking lady in white coat almost wrestled me to the ground to inform me I definitely needed some new, natural-type makeup to go with my new, natural-looking lowlights and feathered style. Suspect that the makeup may have been slightly extravagant, impulse-type purchase, but I think she knew her stuff: her rhinestone-encrusted nails were very impressive. Anyway, if it does what she promises it will (lift, sculpt and conceal, all with a natural glow), it's a steal at seventy-five euro.

PPS Asked Joe if he thought I looked different in any way.

'What do you mean?' he said suspiciously, looking up briefly from a pile of paperwork.

'Is there anything new about me?' I said, flicking my feather cut about and willing him to take me in his arms, say I looked just like I did when we first met and that he would never, under any circumstances, sleep with his new personal assistant.

'You're a bit pale?' he ventured doubtfully.

19 February

Tried in vain to replicate 'low-maintenance, easy-to-care-for' hairstyle to no avail. Subtle, age-reducing lowlights look suspiciously like purple granny rinse in the cold light of day. Also, scalp and hairline are both a lurid plum colour that screams, 'Middle-aged and trying to hide roots,' rather than giving a natural, sun-kissed effect. No wonder Joe's mother looked at me so strangely when I came back yesterday. My head looks like a giant blackberry.

Called Sandra (sorry, Zandra) to discuss matter urgently. 'Hi, Zandra,' I stuttered, trying to sound confident and businesslike. 'It's Susie Hunt here. There seems to be some sort of serious problem with my hair this morning.'

Silence.

'Susie who?'

'Susie Hunt. You did my hair yesterday?'

Silence. Followed by lots of loud chewing. 'Blonde streaks?'

It was becoming clear that Zandra had no recollection of me whatsoever. Quite shocking, considering she had confided some of her deepest, darkest secrets about her nether regions.

'No. Feather cut and lowlights,' I said, trying not to panic.

'Oh, yeah. Hiya, Zoe.'

Decided not to correct her, and soldiered on. 'The thing is, Zandra, the colour doesn't look the way it did in the salon yesterday.'

'Yes, the lights in here can be harsh, all right.'

No dispute there, then.

'And the thing is, there seems to be a lot of colour left on my scalp and hairline.'

Silence. Chewing.

Decided to throw the ball into her court. 'So, what do you think I should do, Zandra?'

'You should probably wash it, Zoe. It'll be fine after a wash.'

She hung up before I could argue that the reason I went to the salon in the first place was to get my hair professionally cut, coloured and blow-dried. May picket her poxy salon. Or even ring *The Gerry Ryan Show* on radio and start some kind of campaign. It's an absolute disgrace that you should have to part with eighty euro (not including tip) to have your hair ruined. In fact, it's a prime example of rip-off Ireland. I'm sure Gerry would be outraged.

PS Jack is traumatized from watching purple-hair-dye massacre in the shower. He refused his Ribena for the first time ever.

PPS Rang *Gerry Ryan Show* hotline and snotty-nosed radio producer said they were really trying to tackle more serious issues. 'What can be more serious than being the victim of daylight robbery?' I asked her. After a bit more haggling, she promised to put me on the list, right after the child-with-leukaemia story and the radon-seeping-into-schools exposé.

Spent nearly an hour getting ready for mother-and-toddler group this morning. Took ages to apply the new, natural-looking makeup I bought in the Centre. Discovered it takes approximately twice as long to look natural as it does to look tarty and made-up. In fact, it's almost impossible to cover the spots and wrinkles when you use the translucent, dewy stuff. Over-thirty model in the ad must definitely have had Botox or some other cosmetic treatment. Am now convinced that her startled expression is more thanks to surgery than shock at how good she looks wearing dewy makeup.

Finished off natural-effortless-beauty look with my favourite red top and the push-up bra I found at the bottom of the laundry basket (to lift and separate sagging granny boobs). Jack looked stunned to see me so groomed. He'll have to get used to the new me. If I'm going to be a tragic single mum, I'll have to start taking better care of myself. In fact, am quite looking forward to looking gaunt and skeletal when I stop eating with the shock and trauma of possible imminent marriage break-up. Not sure when it will kick in. Probably not until I find the cheating adulterer copulating with his lover and catch it all on videotape to seal his fate in a court of law.

Had two chocolate Hobnobs to perk myself up, then sauntered casually into the mother-and-toddler group, trying not to let my pain show. No one seemed to notice my distress, so am obviously an excellent actress, although I did sense glam-mummy Marita staring at me strangely as we all sang 'Incy Wincy Spider' in a circle. Tried to arrange brave, single-mother expression on my face.

'You look different today,' she said, when we had finished idiotic dancing and pretending to be spiders with our totally uninterested offspring.

'Do I?' I answered.

Finally someone was sensing my internal torment. Maybe I would have to fight back tears and the whole group would console me.

'Yeah, you definitely *glow*, doesn't she, Heidi?' She nudged her VBF meaningfully in the ribs. Heidi giggled.

'Glow?' Haggard and bereft, more like. Knew I should have applied less bloody Egypt Wonder.

'Yeah, definitely,' Marita replied. 'Do you have something to tell us, Susie?'

Was starting to suspect that the conversation was not going the way I'd intended.

'Yeah, come on, Susie, we're all dying to know.' Egged on by her partner in crime, Heidi decided to join in gamely. 'Those jeans are starting to look a bit tight. Is there another little bun in the oven?'

Mumbled something about Jack trying to escape and retreated to the far corner of the hall, sucking in my spare tyre and willing myself to stop blushing scarlet like a schoolgirl.

Spent the rest of the hour watching out of the corner of my eye as Marita flirted openly with Lone Father, flicking her peroxide hair and rubbing her acrylic nails up his arm every two seconds. The poor guy put on a brave face, but I caught his eye as we were singing 'Old MacDonald' and he mouthed, 'Help,' at me. Tried to hide my giggles behind a tub of Play-Doh. Marita and her acrylic nails are not to be trifled with.

PS Joe home early for once. Maybe the guilt of leading a double life is getting to him.

PPS May call Joe's mother to borrow Unislim belt.

21 February

It has been nine days since Louise blamed me for her break-up and implied that Joe is a two-timing rat. Cannot believe she still hasn't called me to apologize. Have decided to pursue friendships with other, more suitable women of my own ilk (i.e., anyone with sagging boobs and unwashed hair). Luckily, playschool mothers are ripe for the picking – it's a well-known fact that stay-at-home mothers will go anywhere to get out of the house. Will invite a little friend of Katie's over and the mother can come too. We're sure to hit it off and form a lifelong friendship that will continue through the years via our loving children.

PS Loads of good stuff in gossip magazines about Jen/Brad/Angelina love triangle. Want to call Louise and discuss, but must stick to my guns. Instead, spent ages reading *OK!* in corner shop until sixteen-year-old manager began hovering at my shoulder, coughing loudly and pointing to the sign that read 'If You Want to Read it, By [*sic*] It'. Proceeded to lecture him about bad spelling, but he ushered me out of the door as if I was a common criminal. Am convinced my new hair may have had something to do with this blatant discrimination.

PPS Joe has still not commented on my new feather cut, although he keeps throwing me sideways glances and I did catch him inspecting a picture of Michael Douglas in the paper a little too long for my liking.

22 *February*

Did stake-out of playschool mothers when I picked up Katie from school today. Struck off anyone who looked too arty, too well-groomed or too desperate (nothing worse than a cling-on).

List of Things to Look for in Prospective New VBF

- New VBF must be at least half a stone heavier than self.

- If new VBF is not fatter than self, she must possess large hook nose or some other unattractive facial feature.

- New VBF's child must not be prettier/smarter/cuter than Katie.

- New VBF must not drive BMW/Mercedes/Lexus.

- New VBF must not be vegan-type earth-mother who turns up nose at chewy Rice Krispie bars or Monster Munch crisps.

Eventually decided to invite Amy (Katie's VBF) and her mother Anya for an afternoon play-date tomorrow. Anya does drive a 4×4, but it's only a Land Rover, and her ears definitely protrude more than is strictly necessary. She is the perfect candidate for long, motherly chats over home-baked cookies (from deli) and freshly brewed coffee (if I can find the cafetière). Cannot remember why I never organized it before. Arranged the play-date as loudly as possible at the school gate – could see Eco-mother pretending not to listen as she finished off a row of knitting with one hand and breastfed her freakishly happy infant with the other. Ha!

23 February

Spent all morning cleaning the house and making the place look shabby chic (i.e., untidy in a Bohemian as opposed to half-finished-bowl-of-mouldy-cornflakes-in-the-living-room way). Strove to create atmosphere of carefree family home, where fun and games are order of day and cookies are baked at drop of a wide-brimmed sunhat. Hid all incriminating copies of *Hello!*, *Heat* and *Sunday World* under the stairs and scattered *Sunday Times* supplements about in haphazard, Bohemian manner. Don't want Anya to think I haven't got two brain cells to rub together. Spent ages looking for wedding-gift cafetière. Nescafé Gold Blend might not cut the mustard.

Was bit cross when they arrived twenty-five minutes late, but stuck on a welcome-to-our-happy-home smile before I answered the door.

'Sorry I'm late, Sonya,' Anya panted on the doorstep, while a whining Amy clung to her leg. 'We got stuck at the chemist. Amy has head lice again and I wanted to pick up some NitRid. We go through that stuff like nobody's business. Now, I'll be back to pick her up at four – unless I get stuck in traffic. Anyway, I'll text you.'

Then, before I had a chance to insist she come in for coffee, she was gone, leaving behind a wailing four-year-old, who was scratching woefully at her head, like an abandoned puppy with fleas. Was a bit dumbstruck that she would dump her child with a complete stranger. I could be a raving axe-murderer for all she knows!

Spent afternoon trying to entertain whining Amy and keep her ten feet away from Katie and Jack at all times. Head lice is the last thing I need.

Her negligent mother swanned back at four thirty. 'You're an angel, Sonya,' she panted, shoving Amy into the 4×4 and revving up the engine before I had a chance to correct her. 'Must organize for your little one to come back to mine some time.' Then she was off in a cloud of diesel and NitRid fumes.

PS Why are people finding it so difficult to remember my name, these days? Am obviously such a sad, nondescript housewife that no one can be bothered to commit it to memory. Am seriously considering starting to wear bright primary colours, or adopting some kind of cutesy eccentricities – like wearing sunglasses on my head, even when it's raining. May also start spelling my name with a Z instead of an S – if it works for Zandra it might for me.

PPS Am monitoring Joe for signs of infidelity. So far, have come up with nothing but he may be being very, very careful.

24 February

Got a missed call from Louise this morning! Ha! Knew she wouldn't be able to hold out. She didn't leave a message, but obviously she wants to say sorry in person. Have decided to be generous, loving friend and accept her apology with good grace.

PS Joe filled the dishwasher last night. *Without me asking him to.* Highly suspicious behaviour.

25 February

Didn't hear from Louise all afternoon, so called her back last night. Obviously she was having difficulty plucking up the courage to call again. Adopted gentle, conciliatory tone so she would know I was ready to forgive and forget.

'Hi, Louise,' I started off, doing my best to sound like Sister Mercy, my favourite nun at school.

Silence.

'Em, you called me earlier?'

Silence.

'I pressed your number by mistake, Susan. I certainly didn't want to speak to you, if that's what you think.' She sounded oddly cold and businesslike.

Decided to play along with the didn't-mean-to-call-you fantasy – admitting you've been wrong can be a difficult and rocky process, but making the first move is vital and she had already proven she wanted to reconcile by dialling my number. Louise has always had issues dealing with her true emotions, which has probably led to a lot of the romantic difficulties in her past. Now was not the time to bring *that* up.

'OK. Well, I was just wondering how you are,' I said.

'Fine.'

Was a bit bored by the frosty attitude so decided to play my trump card and turn things round as quickly as possible. 'Did you read all the new stuff about Brad and Jen and Angelina?' I said casually.

It worked immediately. Proceeded to have fab hour-long conversation about the trials and tribulations of celebrity marriages, and how fame and money don't guarantee happiness, etc., etc.

Louise confessed that she thought Jen was never good enough for Brad in the first place and that Angelina is much more his type. I was forced to agree – poor Jen's chin has always let her down, no matter how perfect her hair is.

Was fab to reconnect with my VBF, even if she still didn't say sorry for outrageous outburst re MOM (abject apology bound to come later). Am sure Brad and Jen would be glad that at least *something* good came out of their break-up. May write and tell them that their pain brought two lifelong friends back together again.

PS Louise thinks Joe's Valentine's Day bouquet was loving and thoughtful gesture, not sign he is shagging Barbie secretary.

'You're lucky to have him, Susie,' she said. (A bit sharply I thought.) 'Don't fuck it up.'

Didn't think there was any need for that kind of language, but decided to let it slide as we are still in the making-up stage.

PPS Katie and Jack took total advantage of important, in-depth conversation I was having and proceeded to draw stick people all over the walls. Was tempted to use the F-word myself.

26 February

After stern talking-to by Louise, brought Joe his breakfast in bed this morning. Tea, toast *and* a boiled egg. Was tempted to take photograph to prove to Joe's mother that I am exemplary wife but couldn't find an egg-cup to put egg in and had to balance it precariously on a plate, so decided against it.

'Thanks, love,' Joe mumbled, when I presented the breakfast in all its glory, 'but I've decided to cut out eggs. They're really bad for your cholesterol.'

PS Head really itchy. Will never darken Zandra's door again.

27 February

The most embarrassing day of my life. Ever. So traumatized I cannot write any more.

28 February

Can barely bring myself to describe yesterday's events. Went to mother-and-toddler group and was having perfectly acceptable (if slightly boring) time when Lone

Father appeared at my shoulder. 'You've got to help me.' He looked over his shoulder nervously. 'I can't endure another conversation with that woman. Please talk to me, I'm begging you. I'll pay you if you want.'

'It had better be big bucks,' I replied. 'I don't fancy being top of Marita's hit list. I hear she can take you down with one flick of her fake nails.' (Quite pleased that I thought of something witty to say right there and then, instead of two hours later.)

Anyway, turns out I was right: he is a writer (although not an award-winning war correspondent). He does reviews for various papers *and* he's writing a book! Ended up having a really fascinating, intellectual conversation while we watched the boys play. Felt very cultured and intelligent discussing contemporary fiction/*Sunday Times* hardback bestsellers, etc. Naturally he did most of the talking, while I nodded knowledgeably and tried not to scoff the free scones too quickly but, luckily, he didn't seem to notice.

Then, just when it was getting interesting and he was complimenting me on my knowledge of nineteenth-century women writers (could only remember George Eliot from useless arts degree back in the eighties, but I threw her in and he seemed impressed), Marita and her sidekick Heidi decided to gatecrash our conversation.

Marita started fawning all over Paul (nice, manly name as befits his toned, muscular physique), being all touchy and clingy and shoving her thirty-two DD cups in his face. (Those chicken-fillet fillers fool no one, but everyone's too terrified of her to admit it. Marita looks the type who wouldn't hesitate to whip one out and use it as a weapon.)

Meanwhile Heidi just stood there, grinning idiotically at her friend, who was putting on a peep-show for Lone Father and anyone else who cared to watch.

Then, out of the blue, Marita was screeching like a fishwife, roaring and pointing at my new feather cut. Was scandalized – knew my 'do' was not the biggest success story of the spring, but it wasn't that bad. Then, like something out of a horror movie, she fell against Lone Father, gasping and clutching at her huge chest (which looked like it was heaving extra hard for effect).

'Susie has head lice!'

'That's ridiculous,' I retorted, as the hall went deathly quiet. Even the *kids* shut up.

'Susie,' Marita announced with glee, 'there's one crawling on your *forehead*.' She paused for dramatic effect. There was a collective sharp intake of breath, and I waited for a fainting spell to overcome me. Then she said, 'I used to work in an old persons' home – I know a head louse when I see one.'

'That's right,' hateful Heidi chimed in. 'Marita had to work with really filthy old dears, who couldn't even wash their own *hair*. They were practically *crawling* with lice.'

That sealed it. There was a communal gasp of horror and everyone (including Lone Father) backed off. I was left to drag Jack screaming and roaring out of the hall and gallop straight to my friend the chemist, who took great pleasure in calling loudly to her assistant in the back, 'Do we have any NitRid left, Maureen? The *extra large* bottle?'

The humiliation was almost too much to bear, especially when all the grannies started shuffling backwards with their walkers to get away from me and my lice-infested head.

'Sorry, but we're out of bags,' the hateful chemist lied, as she deposited twenty euro in her till, smirking sanctimoniously.

Shuffled, shame-faced, out of the chemist, trying to hide the NitRid under my arm.

Spent hours massaging vile lotion into my head, then fine-tooth combing my feather cut over the bath, watching lice tumble down the plughole. Poured a bottle of extra-strength bleach down after them. Thankfully, Katie, Jack and Joe seem to be clear, but I don't want to take any chances.

Joe was quite concerned when he came home. 'Maybe you should boil-wash the bedding, Susie,' he suggested, scratching his head.

Was tempted to remind him that he was lucky I was still breathing and that I was in no fit condition to do heavy-duty housework. I might have been overcome by those NitRid fumes.

PS House engulfed in vile NitRid odour. Rose-scented aromatherapy candles (bought in ill-guided attempt at seduction about two years ago) do nothing to mask the revolting smell.

PPS Cannot find bloody washing-machine instruction manual to investigate boil-washing intricacies. Refuse to ask anal-retentive husband, who probably has it filed away in a folder marked 'Undone Chores'.

PPPS Am so ashamed I may never appear in public again. Am also so disheartened that the first proper intellectual conversation I have had in years had to end in complete and utter humiliation.

1 March

Dropped Katie off at playschool this morning, my slicked-back hair neatly disguised under one of Joe's baseball caps. (Why a thirty-five-year-old executive feels the need to collect baseball caps emblazoned with things like Chicago Bears and Seattle Dodgers is still beyond me but, for the first time ever, they came in handy.)

Thought I was getting away with concealing my head-lice infestation and that the gallon of Clinique Happy I had dumped over myself would mask the smell of NitRid, when Anya screeched up to the gates in her 4×4, shoved Amy out the door without bringing the car to a complete stop and yelled across the walkway, 'Nice baseball cap, Sonya! Not trying to hide the dreaded head lice, are you?' Then, with a gay laugh and a roar of her 1.8-litre engine, she was off. The gaggle of mothers gossiping on the path parted like the Red Sea as Katie skipped along it, singing, at the top of her voice, 'Mummy has gross bugs in her hair, Mummy has gross bugs in her hair,' to the tune of 'Pop Goes the Weasel'. Will the shame never end?

PS Mum called to tell me that head lice can also 'travel'. Spent ages trying to decipher what she was on about, until I heard Dad bellow in the background: 'They can get in your bits, Susie!'

Dropped phone in shock. He cannot be serious. There is no _way_ I am putting NitRid down there.

PPS Looked it up on-line. Mum is right – they _can_ 'travel'. Feel sick. And very itchy. All over.

PPPS After hours of trawling Internet sites devoted to head lice (accompanied by magnified images of their vile, hairy bodies and bloodsucking jaws), I have decided to explore alternative therapies. Will drive across town to random health-food store, where no one will recognize me and I will be spared more crushing humiliation.

2 March

Head lice can become immune to NitRid! Cannot believe that this kind of freaky, mutant behaviour is possible, but Blossom (alternative-therapy girl in health shop) assures me it's true and she should know: she once shaved her head when all else failed after she picked up nits in a squat.

Am at wit's end. Not a big fan of my new feather cut, but even less a fan of the horrible butch look that Demi Moore sported in that military movie (panned by the critics and public alike, if memory serves – *and* I think she split up with Bruce soon after, so it's not a good look to bring to an ailing marriage either).

Blossom's other recommendation was to douse my head (and any other 'Affected Areas,' ahem) with olive oil. 'That drowns the little bastards,' she whispered conspiratorially across the counter, her tongue stud glinting off the wind chimes and dazzling me.

Not totally convinced that this will work, but am willing to consider anything.

PS Spent more than an hour in rush-hour traffic battling way back across the city with Jack shouting,

'Bwastards, bwastards,' and Katie grilling me on the pros and cons of drowning.

PPS Letter arrived from Beth Howard of the Pure and Simple Store.

Dear Ms Hunt,

Thank you for your recent letter regarding 'Sleep Tight, Little Mite'. I am sorry you did not find the product to be satisfactory. We do invest a lot of time, effort and money on product development, using only the most natural ingredients, to try to create the best possible aromatherapy range in the world so I am sorry you feel it was not effective. 'Sleep Tight, Little Mite' underwent three years of intensive testing with eight different control groups before it was released on to the market and the feedback since its inception and release has been extremely positive. In fact, it was recently awarded Best New Product by many baby magazines.

However, there can be no denying that each and every child is different and what works for one may not work for another. I believe *Secrets of the Baby Whisperer for Toddlers* offers an effective sleep routine for a difficult baby – perhaps you should give it a try. In the meantime, please accept, with my compliments, a voucher to the value of fifty euro that you can use in your local Pure and Simple Store. I hope you enjoy it!

Best wishes,
Beth Howard

Am buoyed up by continued success of consumer activism. May consider running for a political career.

3 March

Instead of going to the mother-and-toddler group and reliving head-lice horror, I spent the morning planning satisfying, morally uplifting visit to Pure and Simple Store in the Centre to wave my voucher in consumer-activist fashion.

Practised angry activist expressions on Jack while I got dressed in my khaki combats and white T-shirt combo (tough-but-fashionable-activist look quite easy to pull off). My contortions seemed to have little effect but, then, he is probably used to me looking slightly deranged.

Stomped into the shop, ready for a dramatic show-down, my extra-special voucher and the personal letter from Beth Howard held aloft. But the snotty shop-girl who had refused to take back overpriced bubble bath in the first place was not there (Beth had evidently fired her for being so rude to a loyal customer). Had to try to explain to a Spanish student the importance of the letter and how I had struck a blow for consumers worldwide. Think it went over her head a bit – she kept saying, '*Si*, *si*', and pointing me in the direction of the henna hair dye. She was smiling (rather a lot, actually) when she said it, so Beth has obviously taken on board my comments about staff-hiring, and has refused to employ haughty, sullen types any more. Unfortunately, there weren't that many customers about so I couldn't make a dramatic scene while a crowd of onlookers applauded my efforts (although Jack did clap and yell a bit in his buggy).

Tried to strike up small-talk with an elderly lady so I could explain that I was doing my bit for mankind and the everyday consumer on the street, and wasn't just another yuppie overly concerned with material wealth and appearance, but she kept poking me with her walking-stick and shouting, 'Where is the haemorrhoid cream, dear?'

PS At least the lice seem to be gone. The extra-virgin olive oil worked a treat, and I'm sure I'll be able to get rid of the oily stains on the back of the sofa. And my best Marks & Sparks undies.

PPS Bit sad I missed the mother-and-toddler group, but unless I change my appearance so radically that no one recognizes me (could get Posh-type hair extensions and all over perma-tan?), I can never darken the doors of the parish centre again.

PPPS Quite missed intellectual chat with Lone Father/Paul. Flicked through *Middlemarch* in the book-shop, but decided to buy *Heat* instead. Celeb special on bikini bodies absolutely not to be missed.

4 March

Got strange text from unknown person this morning: 'Mssd u ytday. Hp u r OK.'

Spent ages racking my brain to try to remember if I had arranged to meet someone and then forgotten (unlikely, as am officially sad, lonely housewife with no friends or outside interests). Decided, from the appalling spelling, it was from one lovestruck teenager to another so I sent a kindly reply. Tried to use adolescent lingo, so they would understand: 'U snt this 2 de wrng homie.'

Got quite misty-eyed about innocent teenage love, and reminisced for ages about how Joe used to leave little love notes round the house when we were first together (in ancient pre-texting days back in the nineties). Was a bit tempted to tell texting lovestruck teenager to make the most of the romantic stage because in a few years' time the most romantic thing you will be doing is scrubbing your partner's underwear with a Vanish bar, but decided against it. Who am I to shatter love's young dream?

PS Panic! Text was not teenage love message gone astray, but sex text *à la* David Beckham and Rebecca Loos!

Was experimenting with the ancient sugar hair-removal system I'd bought with my voucher while Jack napped (mixing the sugar, then spreading it evenly on hairy bits with an orange stick is quite tricky – may have to write to Beth again) when my phone beeped: 'No mistake. This is Paul. R U OK?'

Got such a shock that Lone Father was texting me that my hand slipped and I stuck the orange stick in my eye instead of across my hairy upper lip. (Definitely inherited unsightly moustache effect from Dad's side. Great Aunt Nora looks like a man in some of those ancient black and white photos.)

Was washing sticky gloop out of my eye, before I was permanently blinded by all the natural, additive-free ingredients, when the phone beeped *again*: 'Hp u will cme bck 2 de group. Enjyed chat lst tme.'

Was so gob-smacked I abandoned the dehairing exercise. (Was quite glad to have an excuse, actually – ancient sugar system is highly barbaric. Glad our civilized society has discovered the joys of bleach, even if it does destroy the ozone layer.)

How did Lone Father even *get* my mobile number? Have no recollection of giving it to him. Counted backwards from twenty as fast as I could to make sure that the onset of premature Alzheimer's wasn't imminent and that I wasn't giving my phone number to strangers in the street without realizing it, then read it again: 'Hp u will cme bck 2 de group. Enjyed chat lst tme.'

It was definitely from him. He must have lifted my phone number from the sign-in sheet at the mother-and-toddler group.

Automatically punched Louise's number to have deep analytical discussion over vague sexual undertones of message before I realized that, as responsible wife and mother of two young children, I was morally obliged to ignore flirtatious text and never darken the door of the parish hall again. If I'd known my new feather cut, natural makeup and push-up bra were going to cause such a sensation I would never have worn them. Being a sexy yummy mummy definitely has its drawbacks. This must be how Liz Hurley feels all the time. Must be so draining.

Had cup of very sweet tea (three spoons of Sweet'n'Lo) and raided the secret stash of mini Mars Bars hidden in the garage for the shock (how poor Liz supposedly survives on one meal a day is beyond me, if this is the sort of stress she has to deal with), then decided I was overreacting. Spending time out of the workplace and isolated from the rest of normal society has made me totally socially inept. Text was not attempt to kindle extramarital affair, but kindly query as to state of my mental health after humiliating head-lice incident. This is the twenty-first century, and men and women can be friends and discuss high-brow literature without sexual tension – or ripping each other's clothes off over the free scones and coffee at the mother-and-toddler group. Anyway, it's high time I had a male friend just like *When Harry Met Sally*.

Spent ages composing off-the-cuff, witty text to send back. 'Thank u 4 ur concern. Nit alert was false alarm. Will be back next wk.' Did a smiley face to make sure he knew it was supposed to be funny.

No harm lying about the nits. Marita can't prove anything.

Got instant message back: 'Good.'

Ignored funny tingly feeling in my tummy. There's nothing to be uneasy about. Just have to get used to talking to a man who is not my husband, that's all. It's not as if I'm attracted to him in any physical way.

PPS Just in case, I decided not to tell Louise. Or Joe.

PPPS Just remembered. Harry and Sally did actually rip each other's clothes off in the end.

5 March

Decided to cook special Nigella meal for Joe to prove I am faithful, non-roving wife of saintly virtue. Spent ages chopping vegetables (real ones, not from a Marks & Spencer packet) and marinating chicken breasts so they would be mouthwatering and tender, just like it said on the jar. While I was basting and chopping, I practised sucking marinade off my fingers in a sensual, just-out-of-bed way like Nigella, but nearly gagged on the horrible taste of garlic on my fingernails (note: garlic press may be useful buy and not finicky marketing ploy). Don't know how Nigella manages to look so sexy and unruffled while knocking up a feast for hordes of people dropping by at all hours of day and night. Thank God I don't live a Bohemian lifestyle (gypsy skirts are *so* hard to wear). Caught sight of my reflection in the oven door and my face was bright red with the exertion of chopping, basting and trying to be sexy all at once. Most unflattering. Suspect Nigella has at least three nannies and probably someone to chop and baste as well.

Had to run the kids in loops round the garden to wear them out and persuade them to go to bed by eight (minor miracle of saintly Mother Teresa proportions). Had quick shower to get rid of nasty garlicky smells and was arranging low, flattering lighting (to hide half-moustache), scented candles and unchipped, almost-matching china on table when the phone rang.

It was Joe. 'Susie, don't bother doing anything for me,' he barked. 'They're ordering pizza here. Don't wait up – it's going to be a late one.'

Didn't get a chance to answer before the phone clattered in my ear and he was gone.

Scraped chicken and vegetables into bin, like bitter, lonely housewife on TV soap, and watched a re-run of

American Idol with tub of Chocolate Chip Cookie Dough. Should be shareholder in Ben and Jerry's – am practically keeping the company afloat single-handed.

6 March

Mum called to say she's had a brilliant idea for my birthday present this year – a full year's membership at the gym of my choice. 'It was your dad's idea, really, darling, so I can't take credit,' she said. (Could hear Dad chortling evilly in the background.) 'It will give you a chance to have some time to yourself,' she wittered on. 'Lots of gyms have crèches so Jack could play while you do some exercise.'

Told her I'd think about it. Am desperately trying to forget about dreaded upcoming birthday and, anyway, would be mortified to have to expose jelly belly, wobbly bum and bingo-wing arms in a public place. In Lycra.

PS Jack has a favourite new sentence: 'Daddy ish cool.' Spent nearly an hour trying to get him to say, 'Mummy is cooler', to no avail. He just kept clapping and saying, 'Daddy ish cool' over and over again. Feel utterly despondent. He barely sees his father and he *still* thinks he's cooler than me.

Katie tried to cheer me up. 'Mummy, I think you're the best mummy in the whole world,' she lisped, wrapping her grubby little arms round my neck.

'Do you, darling?' I smiled, glad that at least my daughter appreciated my efforts.

'Yes, I do. I like you *almost* as much as I like my teacher.'

PS Louise left me a message – something about another weekend away. She must have a new MOM.

PPS Joe left me a muddled message – something about dinner, blah, blah. Obviously he'll be late home *again*. May well apply for single-mother allowance.

PPPS Have decided to explore gym-membership options. It can't hurt. Well, it probably can, but it can't hurt to *look*. You never know, this might be the year I'll finally be able to wear a thong bikini. Or any bikini, for that matter.

7 *March*

Called a few gyms for the low-down on getting fit and sylph-like. The first 'fitness co-ordinator' was a bit scary. 'How active are you, madam?' he growled, in a fat-people-should-be-exterminated way.

'Fairly active?' I guessed. (Not officially a lie. Sprinting up and down the stairs to make sure Jack doesn't throw himself off the top step again is like boot camp every day.)

'Aha.'

He could totally tell I was lying. (Probably due to years of intensive SAS training.) 'And what sort of structured exercise routine do you follow at the moment?'

Was tempted to tell him that changing a dozen nappies every day, unloading the dishwasher and lugging mounds of dirty laundry around is enough to keep Rambo fit, but decided to keep quiet.

The next gym sounded much nicer. Cathy, the fitness

adviser ('We're here to guide not to intimidate') was sympathetic and gentle. 'It must be really tough for you to fit any exercise in, Susie, if you're at home all day,' she said, in a really soft I-will-look-after-you voice.

'Yes, it is, actually,' I agreed, delighted that someone was on my side for a change. 'But I do try my best.' (No need for her to know that that is a complete lie.)

'I'm sure you do, Susie, I'm sure you do,' she soothed, 'but, unfortunately, it may not be enough. It's women like you who drop dead of a heart-attack when they hit forty. Too much fatty food and too little exercise, that's the problem. It's the children I feel sorry for, really, poor little orphans. Now, when shall we pencil you in for a quick assessment?'

Signed up straight away. Felt a bit sniffly about poor orphan Katie and Jack, so had a chocolate muffin. May as well finish off the box – my new fitness regime starts next week.

8 March

One week to my thirty-fourth birthday and the cloud of black depression has descended right on cue. Spent the morning eating an entire packet of fig rolls.

What have I done with my life? My closest relationship is with the dishwasher. Confided in Mum that I may have wasted my youth and energy on two ungrateful children, one who thinks his 'daddy ish cool' and the other who loves her teacher more than she loves me. Not to talk of a husband who takes me totally for granted.

'Snap out of it, darling,' she chirped. 'Life begins at

forty. Look at your father and me. You should take a leaf from our book and get out more.'

Pointed out that was not approaching forty yet and rang off, feeling even worse.

PS Feel a bit nervous about mother-and-toddler group tomorrow, but have to go back for Jack's sake – he loves playing with all the other kids. Some sacrifices a mother just has to make.

9 March

Spent all morning practising false air of confidence in preparation for mother-and-toddler group. Chanted positive affirmations all the way there in the car (quite difficult to do with Jack roaring in the back seat, especially as could not close eyes and visualize lapping sea or field full of corn while driving). 'I am a confident, special person. I am a confident, special person.'

Was almost believing it until I spotted Marita and her thirty-two DDs wobbling across the car park to the parish hall, head to toe in canary yellow, dragging her toddler behind her. 'Oh, *hi*, Susie!' she roared, at the top of her voice to make sure all the other mothers could hear. '*Great* to see you back. Aren't you brave? I wouldn't be able to show my face in public so soon, I can tell you that much!' She leered at all the other mums within earshot, smirking and pointing knowingly to her head, just in case they were in any doubt as to what she meant.

All at once I could feel ten pairs of beady eyes on me. If I was ever going to hold my head up in the parish hall again, I had to think of something really cutting to say. 'Brave? Me? Not at all, Marita. *You're* the brave one. How *did* you cope when you were fired from that old persons' home? Was it cruelty to elders or incompetence they got you for in the end?'

Couldn't believe I'd come up with something so good so fast – no wonder all the celebs swear by chanting. It turns you into Joan Rivers!

Marita stopped dead in her tracks. 'I wasn't fired from that hell-hole. I resigned.' She fixed me with an evil stare.

'Funny – that's not what I heard,' I answered, holding her gaze.

'Well, you heard wrong.' She turned on her scuffed yellow stilettos and marched into the parish hall, hauling her toddler by the scruff of the neck. Caught a few of the other mothers winking at me conspiratorially. Hurrah! May well have toppled Marita's reign of terror.

PS No sign of Lone Father today – he's probably busy writing some high-brow book review. Pity. Had planned lots of literary things to say and witty off-the-cuff remarks to make, just in case. Feel a bit strange and empty. Probably delayed shock from nasty show-down with evil Marita.

10 *March*

Louise is whisking me away to a spa retreat for my birthday! 'Do you fancy a couple of nights away for your birthday, Susie?' she yelled down the phone. (She was somewhere foreign on business. Think I was supposed to know where she was already so didn't dare ask.)

'Yeah, suppose.' I picked Play-Doh remnants out from under my nails and wondered how I was meant to pull that off – drop the kids into town and tell them to find their own way home, perhaps.

'OK. Well, get packing cos I've booked us two nights in that new spa in Cork. I called Joe so he's going to sort out the kids to give you a break.' Crackle, crackle, crackle . . .

Couldn't hear the rest, but who cares? Had heard all I needed to!

Cannot wait to spend two nights of unadulterated luxury being pummelled to within an inch of my life. Will come back to Dublin cellulite- and wrinkle-free with rock-hard thighs and taut bum, looking no more than a girl of thirty.

Spent ages trawling the hotel website to see what kind of treatments I'm going to get. Healing massage looks great, and so does the floating therapy (although being all alone in a dark pool could be slightly scary – might stick to traditional beauty treatments that guarantee instant success).

Was a bit shocked to see the seaweed wrap was seventy euro, but you're guaranteed to lose four inches off your hip and thigh area and that's good enough for me. Will be back in pre-pregnancy Top Shop jeans in no time. Hurrah for kind, well-paid girlfriends!

PS Called Joe at work to hyperventilate about birthday treat, but got his voicemail so hung up. Sweet of him to keep it a secret, though. Definitely not the action of an adulterous love cheat.

PPS Hope I won't have to be naked in front of Louise. The last time she saw me without full body armour was years ago in Corfu, pre-babies and stretch-marks. Also, am a bit worried about removing body hair after last waxing fiasco. Maybe I can wear Lycra bicycling shorts the entire time.

11 March

Katie has a boyfriend! 'I'm getting married, Mummy,' she announced calmly, as she clambered into the car after playschool today.

'Are you, darling?' I asked, hiding a smile at her cuteness. 'Who are you going to marry?'

'Matthew,' she answered seriously. 'He pulled my hair at lunch, so I pinched him on the arm and I thought we should get married.'

Was aghast at Matthew's domestic-violence tenden-cies but didn't voice my concerns. Instead of wrenching couples apart, parental disapproval can drive young lovers closer together, just like Romeo and Juliet.

'Does Matthew know you're getting married?' I asked casually, trying to remember which snotty-nosed little terror he might be. (Hope he's the one whose mother drives the Beemer. Wealth may not be everything, but it helps.)

'No, not yet.' Her voice was steely with determi-nation.

Silence.

'Zoe was being a cry-baby at school today.'

'Was she?' I asked, secretly delighted that even Eco-mother couldn't morph her child into a tantrum-free cherub. 'Why was that?'

'She thinks Matthew's *her* boyfriend. But he's not. He's mine.'

Have to admire her grim determination. Zoe doesn't stand a chance.

Joe very snappy. Interrupted him as he waded through some paperwork at the kitchen table. 'Honestly, Joe,' I said, 'why don't you read a good book instead of burying yourself in work day and night?'

'A good book?' He looked blank.

'Yes. Reading is a stimulating and mentally challenging pastime,' I said, a picture of Lone Father flashing in my mind. 'You really should do it more.'

'Well, I'd love to,' he growled, glaring at me, 'but if I don't get through these reports on time I may as well resign right now.'

Retreated to watch *10 Years Younger* on Channel 4. Suspect Joe may be part of the new dumb-down culture. Don't think he's read a real book in years. *Men and Motors* definitely doesn't count.

PS Had vivid dream where I was sobbing mother of the bride in unflattering lavender hat and Katie was tripping up the aisle on her father's arm, dressed in her Barbie wedding dress. Then, when she got to the altar, her husband-to-be turned to face her and it was Lone Father! Wonder what that means. Must look it up on yourdreams.com.

Joe's mother rang this morning to wish me a happy birthday.

'Thanks, Mrs H,' I slurped (am drinking lots of pro-biotic yogurt in preparation for intensive detoxification process at spa retreat), 'but my birthday is actually the fifteenth.'

'Is it, dear?' she asked, sounding as if she couldn't care less when it was. 'Anyway, I hear you're gallivanting off to Cork for a week.'

Knew there was some ulterior motive for fake birth-day call. Will fillet Joe when I get my hands on him. 'Not for a week. For two nights.'

'Right, yes. And will poor Joe have to mind the children when you're gone?'

Was tempted to remind her that they are half his, but didn't. No point having huge family row just as I'm about to be de-stressed and de-cellulited. Toxic stress can contribute hugely to cellulite deposits (it said so on naturalhealth.com). (Just thought – Mrs H is probably directly responsible for every lump and bump to be found on my lardbum and thighs. And upper arms, for that matter. In fact, it's all her fault I cannot wear sleeveless strappy tops like Kate Moss and have to cover flabby bingo-wing arms with ridiculous-looking cardigans in the middle of summer.)

'I'm sure he'll manage,' I retorted (quite cheekily, I thought).

'Yes, well . . .' She didn't sound too convinced. 'I've told him to bring the children round for their dinner.

I'll do them a nice roast. All that pasta is well and good, but there are no nutrients in it. Children need building up. And Joe's looking a bit peaky. He needs a bit more meat on his bones. All those long hours can't be doing him any good. He needs a holiday himself . . .'

She droned on and on and on, so eventually I held the phone away from my ear. I let her ramble for a few minutes, then cut across her, faking panic. 'Oh dear, Mrs H. Got to go. Jack's just slipped and cut his knee. See you soon.'

Jack looked up at me and smiled. 'Mummy ish cool,' he lisped.

13 March

Drove to Cork in Louise's company BMW. Not a sexy convertible but still pretty cool. (Black, with black leather interior and darkened windows so you can make childish faces at truckers and not be detected. Bonus!) *And* it definitely beats a worn-out people-carrier hands down. Was a bit cross when Louise arrived to pick me up dressed to the nines in a fuchsia-pink velour Juicy Couture tracksuit (a *real* one, not one of the cheapo versions from M&S). So much for the empty promises that this was going to be a low-maintenance, glamour-free weekend, not a fashion extravaganza. Definitely should have splashed out on some new trackies. Have feeling of doom that washed-out grey bottoms with bleach stain on crotch will not pass muster. Hope there are lots of fluffy white robes about so will not have to wear own clothes for two days.

Felt a bit sniffly leaving the kids behind – they looked so angelic tucked up fast asleep in bed when I crept out at the crack of dawn. (Louise insisted on leaving at six a.m. – to make the most of the day, she said. Felt she was being a bit forceful about it, actually, but didn't like to say anything.)

Had stern talk with self on the motorway to make sure I didn't blub.

Reasons to Make Most of Mini-break and Not Blub
All the Way to Country Retreat

- I deserve a break from mundane, thankless tasks and life of sheer drudgery (such as cleaning toilets, emptying dishwashers and changing stinky nappies).

- The happier I am, the happier my children will be (although they seem pretty happy even when I feel completely downtrodden and miserable).

- The children need to learn to be without me, and can take the opportunity to spend some vital bonding time with their father.

- They will probably be better fed and cleaned by Joe's mother than by me.

- They may appreciate my lenient ways a bit more when they spend a bit of quality time with Joe's mother.

Was soon in a better place mentally and began to relax. It was fab not having to stop for toilet breaks, and not sing *Barney* songs all the way (or clean up vomit on the back seat). Instead, had leisurely journey listening to proper grown-up radio (well, before we decided an item on nuclear waste was deadly dull and switched to Sun FM's 1980s hits hour). Felt like a carefree teenager singing along to Duran Duran and Queen. It was great to be bonding with VBF again (although was teeny bit nervous about destroying delicate equilibrium by mentioning men. Or children).

Spa hotel very nice, although room a bit cramped (especially with Louise's luggage crammed in one corner. Think she may have been a bit selfish bringing such a vast assortment of designer bags on a mini-break, but decided not to tackle her on it. Was here to have fun, not bicker about morality of possessing real Louis Vuitton luggage when there are so many starving children in the world.)

There was a bit of a tussle over who got the bed by the window, but I won (fake attack of claustrophobia worked a treat) and we headed off for the first treatment of the day. I wanted to stop for coffee and cake in the bar in the foyer (who could last on the can of Coke and chocolate I had on the trip down?) but Louise raced along, pulling me past the muffins at full-speed (only wholewheat ones so was not too traumatized). Spent rest of the day being bashed about on a trolley (a.k.a. 'deep-tissue massage') and lying with my face covered with gloop (a.k.a. 'invigorating seaweed facial') to rejuvenate body and soul. Think it may have worked – definitely felt genuine spiritual calm descend over me in an I-am-at-one-with-the-universe fashion. Have decided that 'Don't sweat the small stuff' will be my mantra from now on.

6.30 a.m. On train back to Dublin. Life in tatters. VBF hates me. Worst birthday ever.

8.30 a.m. Cannot eat or sleep. Probably counts as detoxifying course (minus horrible green muck you're forced to drink). Can only face Lucozade and mini Mars Bars so know I'm seriously depressed.

'What on earth happened?' Joe asked, wide-eyed with shock when I arrived on the doorstep a full day ahead of schedule, red-eyed and face blotchy from crying.

'I don't want to talk about it.' I sniffed. (Tear ducts dry after buckets cried on cold and dingy train back from the country all by myself.)

'OK. I'll leave you alone.' He retreated back to the safety of the living room and the Premier League.

Felt like beating him round the kitchen with my fake Gucci handbag. Everyone knows that when a woman says she doesn't want to talk about it she means she wants you to make her a nice cup of tea, pull out the Jammie Dodgers and talk all about it. At length. For as long as possible. Or until the Jammie Dodgers are well and truly devoured.

Everything had been going so well. Felt like brand-new version of self after intensive rounds of scrubbing, exfoliating and massaging. Even managed to wedge myself into one of Louise's skimpy designer dresses for dinner (*and* it didn't burst open after huge three-course meal of real food – not gross vegetable juices).

We had fab girlie bonding session and slugged loads of the house white, just like the old days when we met after work and spent hours in the pub, even on a week night. Definitely felt we were back on track, all arguments forgotten, so decided the time was right to tackle the subject of her disastrous love life and give some wise old-married advice. Unfortunately it wasn't received all that well. Suspect the colonic irrigation (barbaric procedure of horrific proportions) might have disagreed with her.

'You're a fine one to give advice, Susie,' she snarled. 'It was all *your* fault that Steve and I broke up. If I'd never taken your stupid advice in the first place, we'd still be together. In fact, he'd be here with me now.'

'What are you talking about?' I stuttered, hoping too much cheap white wine was leading to a horrible mix-up and she didn't mean that.

'We had this weekend booked before we broke up,' she admitted, refusing to meet my eye.

'What do you mean?' I asked, still not getting it. 'You booked this trip for my birthday. You told me so.'

'No, Susie, I didn't. I only brought you because it was too late to cancel. I would have lost the entire deposit.'

'So, what are you saying? That you'd prefer to be here with Steve?' Suddenly I felt very tearful.

'If I'm totally honest, yes.' Louise looked away.

My chest constricted with pain (although might have been the skimpy designer dress, which was now digging fiercely into my ribcage).

Completely and utterly humiliated, I wobbled away from the table in the too-tight dress, spent a sleepless night tossing and turning on the specially designed orthopaedic mattress and snuck out of the hotel room first thing in the morning before Louise woke up.

I should have known that, deep down, she was still furious with me about the Steve break-up. It was exactly like that time when I accidentally kissed her first boyfriend when we were thirteen. (Is it my fault the Coke bottle pointed at me? She was the one who insisted on playing Spin the Bottle.) Back then, she'd pretended to forgive me, then deliberately snogged Garvan Ryan, my first love, at the end of a school disco three years later in a bitter act of revenge.

15 March: My Birthday

Mum and Dad rang at ungodly hour to sing 'Happy Birthday' down the phone to me as if I'd turned four, not thirty-four.

'Cheer up, darling,' Mum cooed, when I complained at being woken with silly song suitable for toddler, not grown woman with saddle-bags and serious spare tyre to rival any *Celebrity Fit Club* contestant. Then she launched into the I-remember-the-morning-you-were-born-like-it-was-only-yesterday story.

'Oh, God, Mum, I'm not in the mood,' I whined, burying my head under the duvet. Why, oh, why my parents insist on telling this sorry tale every year is beyond me. It's not as if Mum gave birth in the supermarket or at the side of a road or anywhere really exciting. Still, they seem to relish reliving it every year.

'Yes, I was nibbling some toast when I felt a very strange sensation and I said to your dad . . . What did I say, darling?'

'You said, "I think I'm in labour, Teddy,"' Dad chimed in, on the other phone.

'That's right!' Mum exclaimed triumphantly, as if Dad had just this minute remembered that very important detail.

'And then *I* said,' Dad's voice boomed, '*I* said, "Don't be silly, woman, you've got indigestion from the toast, that's all."'

'You didn't believe me, so you didn't, pet,' Mum said affectionately, and they chuckled together as if it was the first time they'd told the story, not the millionth. 'So, I said, "No, it's definitely not gas, Teddy."'

'And *I* said, "OK, let's get you in, then, Bernadette."'

'And then *you* were born, two hours later!' they finished in unison.

'Gosh, that takes me back. Does it take you back, Teddy?'

'Yes, it does, it really does,' Dad agreed.

Could almost see them nodding at each other, lost in time. Coughed to let them know I was still there.

'Anyway, darling,' Mum came to, 'sorry we can't be with you, but the golf tournament kicks off today and we can't miss that. Anyway, I'm sure Joe has something smashing lined up for you, pet.'

'Yeah, I'm sure,' I muttered doubtfully, eyeing him on the other side of the bed, where he snored on, oblivious.

'Now, buck up, Susie,' she coaxed. 'Didn't you have a lovely time away with Louise? You should be on top of the world. And you'll have a smashing romantic night tonight, I'm sure.'

Didn't like to tell her that Louise and I are officially

not speaking and that Joe has most definitely not booked a romantic meal for two: his parting shot to me before he collapsed into his nightly coma was 'Can we do the birthday thing next week, Suse? I'm up to my tonsils in work.' As if you can postpone a birthday like you can reschedule a meeting.

'OK, then, 'bye, love,' Mum chirped. 'We have to get on with the juicing before we go. Antioxidants are so good for your stamina.'

Rang off to Dad making lewd remarks about stamina and Mum giggling like a teenager.

Officially hate birthdays. They're just another depressing reminder that life is moving on and I'm stuck in rut of enormous dimensions. Spent day trying to put on brave face for sake of children, who were leaping around looking for birthday cake from crack of dawn. Was reduced to buying my own in corner shop and singing 'Happy Birthday' to myself with kids clapping along. Very bleak. This is what it will be like when I'm old and decrepit, with no husband, children who only visit when they want something, and friends who have concentrated on their careers and discarded me by the wayside.

Spent night trawling through stack of old diaries in fit of morose nostalgia, fuelled by raiding a bottle of very expensive Chablis that Joe had been saving for 'an extra special occasion'. Discovered one hilarious entry – well, it was hilarious after half a bottle of Chablis – when I was going through my if-you-can-see-it-you-can-be-it phase. It read:

I am 24 today. In ten years' time, I will be a communications director in a high-profile PR firm. I will have the following:

- *A Mercedes convertible (for weekends).*
- *A BMW (for school run, if I decide to have children).*

- *A wardrobe packed with designer clothes, accessories and luggage.*

- *An enormous mansion with guest wing and sprawling grounds.*

- *Staff (to include, at a minimum, housekeeper, cleaner and gardener).*

Instead, I have the following:

- An embarrassing people-carrier littered with sweet wrappers and crushed crisps.

- A fake Gucci handbag that doesn't fool anyone (fraying plastic handles dead give-away).

- A wardrobe stuffed full of well-washed fleeces and trackie bottoms (most with vomit/dried snot on shoulder).

- A four-bed semi-detached shack, with teeny garden that I still can't keep on top of (note: may have to write to *Gardeners' World* requesting total garden makeover).

- A general skivvy (me).

Add to the mix no career, a faltering relationship with husband and no relationship with ex-VBF and I think I'm bang on track, really. Ha! Ha!

PS Am bit concerned have started drinking alone. First step towards fully fledged alcoholism. Will probably have broken veins and large purple nose before very long.

PPS No call from Louise – the first time in years that I haven't spoken to her on my birthday.

16 March

Head thumping from Chablis, but dragged myself and Jack to mother-and-toddler group to fill another morning. Glad to see Lone Father there as was sure to have nice, comforting chat about life, art and literature. Perfect opportunity to show off brushed-up knowledge of famous Irish writers, such as Yeats, Joyce, etc. (Abridged study notes from bookshop really very good.)

But Lone Father cut straight to the chase in unsettling, psychic-like manner. 'You seem a bit blue today, Susie,' he asked, in a concerned new-man voice, his head tilted to one side in a very endearing way.

(Noticed he has lovely blue eyes that are all crinkly and smiley, just like Hugh Grant in *Love Actually*.)

'Yes, I am a bit down in the dumps, I suppose,' I admitted, weakening under his penetrating gaze. 'It was my birthday yesterday and it was all a bit of a disaster.'

'But surely your husband swept you off your feet and whisked you away somewhere romantic for the night?' he asked, his eyes roving across my face in an unsettling way (probably homing in on an enormous pimple pulsating on chin, unbeknown to me).

Didn't want to admit that, no, had spent evening

drinking alone, reading old diaries, watching *Nip/Tuck* and plotting which procedure I would get done if I won the lotto (entire face-lift, and boob job, I should think).

'Em, well, he's very busy at work, so we'll do something next week. Probably. Anyway, birthdays are so overrated at our age. I think it's best just to forget them.' (Was babbling quite a bit. Deep, penetrating gazes can be most off-putting.)

'Reeaally?' he drawled, eyes raking suggestively over my Gap T-shirt (wish had ironed it). 'Well, if I was your husband I'd sure as hell be whisking you away for a night of passion for no reason at all. He'd better watch out or someone might whip you away from right under his nose.'

Our eyes locked in a *Love Actually* way for what seemed like ages, before Jack started screaming because someone had stolen his truck and I had to rescue him. Thank goodness, because I could feel hot rash of embarrassment spreading up my neck like lovestruck teenager.

There was no denying it. Lone Father was *flirting* with me. Wonder what his wife would think. Maybe they have an open relationship. Oh, my God – maybe they're swingers and they want Joe and me to join in their sick sex games. Perverts.

PS Was quite nice, though.

17 March: St Patrick's Day

Hallelujah! Joe off work! Thank you, St Patrick, for banishing all the snakes from Ireland, etc., etc., and creating a much-needed national holiday in the process. Quite comforting that our little country is still able to eschew horrible blatant commercialism for one day to honour our cultural heritage. (And overworked employees get a chance to spend some quality time with their families – bonus!)

Paid dutiful visit to Mrs H so she could pin large amounts of fresh shamrock to the children's chests for the parade. 'Did you go to Mass, Katie dear?' she asked, as she tied a green satin bow to Katie's head in honour of the occasion.

'Mummy said if you asked that question I was to pretend not to hear you,' Katie said proudly, flashing me a smile.

'Did she now,' Mrs H said grimly, studiously ignoring me. 'Well, you tell your mummy that Our Lord and St Patrick are watching over our every move here on this earth.'

'Just like Santa?' Katie said, thrilled with this nugget of blackmail-worthy information.

'Oh, much worse than that,' Mrs H replied, brushing Jack's hair and jamming a green beret on his head. 'Much, much worse.'

Battled our way through mayhem traffic into the parade to soak up the cultural/carnival atmosphere but spent the afternoon trying to avoid drunken louts and gangs of teenagers throwing up on each other. Have good mind to ring *Gerry Ryan Show* to voice alarm at manner in which society is disintegrating into complete cultural hooliganism. In my day you were at least sixteen before you hit the cider. Tried not to let menacing lager louts ruin the first family outing we've had in months, but it was quite difficult, especially when we had to keep a firm grip on Jack to stop him running off with drunken teenagers. My God, in ten years' time that could be Katie, swigging from a cider bottle and getting her stomach pumped in A and E. Feel quite sick thinking about it (or it might be the remains of last night's bottle of Chablis – definitely should not have finished it by myself). Vow to start making most of these innocent years while kids are alcohol- and hormone-free, instead of moaning about the sheer monotony of it all.

Went for pizza after the parade (if people waving from slow-moving cars counts). In the restaurant, Joe reached across the table to hold my hand in unusual Public Display of Affection. 'You're a great mum, Susie,' he said, looking at me with a funny expression on his face.

'Am I?' I laughed, licking some tomato sauce off Jack's finger because I couldn't find a napkin and had given up trying to catch the sulky waitress's eye to ask for one.

'Yes, you are. I'm sorry I haven't been around much recently. I know it's tough on you. But once this year is over, and they make me a director, I won't have to do such long hours.'

Was so overcome with emotion that I didn't trust myself to answer so just nodded and tucked into Katie's leftover pizza. Am riddled with guilt. Poor Joe is working his heart out to get on in the world, thinking I am kind, overworked mother (well, that part is true, actually) when really I am entertaining flirtatious, lustful thoughts about Lone Father. There. I have admitted it to myself. I have a crush on Lone Father. Which is the first step to moving on. Perfectly natural for married people to flirt harmlessly with other married people and fantasize a bit about bodice-ripping, etc. All natural and above board, as long as bodice-ripping doesn't take place. Actually, fantasizing could spice up own love life. No, yuk. That's way too weird.

Sulky waitress kept raising perfectly arched eyebrows at me in I-won't-bring-you-extra-napkins-but-I-can-see-into-your-soul type way. Vow to be much better mother and wife from now on.

PS Had nookie for first time in ages. Quite nice, except Joe's breath stank of the garlic bread. Tried to block all images of Lone Father and his Hugh Grant eyes from my mind.

18 March

'Are you all set for next week, then, Susie?' Joe asked, as he left for work, munching the last toasted heel of stale bread. (NB Using freezer to store necessities like bread instead of just ice lollies and M&S ready meals may be good idea.)

'Why? Are you whisking me away for a few nights of passion?' I teased, delighted that my birthday treat was upon me at last.

Cue blank look of utter confusion. Then he said, 'Eh, no, I mean the dinner party, Susie. Don't tell me you forgot?'

'Dinner party? Who's having a dinner party?' I asked, mentally trying on and discarding all possible dinner-party outfits in my head. Cannot remember being invited anywhere suave and sophisticated recently.

'Eh, we are. Next week, for the directors and their wives. You *didn't* forget, did you, love?'

Felt so faint that Joe had to sit me down and put my head between my legs. Most ungainly. Apparently, a few weeks back, I agreed to host a sit-down dinner for three of Joe's work colleagues. Not just work colleagues, in fact, but senior directors and their wives. So that Joe can *impress them and be made a director too*. The pressure is way too much. Was I drunk? Chablis can't be that strong, surely. Am in severe state of shock that will now have to cook and serve a dinner for eight people, including Joe and me. How the hell am I going to pull this off? Rang Mum for advice.

'Give them melon to start and lamb chops for main, darling,' she suggested. 'Back-to-basics is all the rage. Ooooh! I know! Do sausages and mash. That Kate What's-her-name had it at her wedding and she's minted, darling, so if it's good enough for her they're sure to love it.'

'I dunno, Mum.' I doubted that all the Hollywood movie moguls at Kate Winslet's first wedding had been all that impressed with sausages. 'These people will be used to something a bit more *cordon bleu*.'

'How about a buffet? That's very European.'

Had images of the directors shuffling along in single file to collect their vol-au-vents in paper napkins. Not sure that's what Joe had in mind when he envisaged an intimate dinner for eight.

'Anyway, whatever you do will be gorgeous, I'm sure,' Mum continued, in a blatant attempt to boost my flagging confidence. (Along the lines of 'You're just as nice as that Claudia Schiffer. Nicer in fact.')

Have decided to get caterers in. Definitely the way forward.

19 March

Caterers off the table. Discovered that, like children's entertainers, they charge extortionate amounts of money for doing very little.

Now need Jamie Oliver-type geezer to turn up in my kitchen and whip something up with lots of 'awright, mate' and little fuss. Could be tricky as don't actually know any Cockneys and think Jamie is too busy changing the face of food in Britain today to make an appearance. Wish he could let malnourished schoolkids have their chickenless chicken nuggets and get round here to sort out my culinary crisis. (That's a good programme idea, actually – may write to BBC to suggest it.)

Right. Just have to concentrate and apply myself, and will be able to pull it off. Something simple but delicious. All about presentation and confidence. Also, Nigella-type flowing hair and flawless porcelain skin might help.

<u>List of Things to Do to Carry Off Corporate Dinner for Eight</u>.

• Purchase classy new crockery (chipped, mismatched cheapo plates no good).

• Purchase new cutlery (tarnished knives and forks and Bob the Builder plastic spoons also no good).

- Purchase unstained brilliant white tablecloth (keep away from children at all costs).

- Borrow four chairs from someone (Joe's mother?).

- Practise poised, I-am-the-wife-of-a-potential-director gait (NB Ditch Reeboks and practise walking in high heels).

- Read up on current events so have something to discuss other than tragic Brad/Jen/Ange love triangle.

20 *March*

Got cryptic text from Lone Father this morning: 'Wud u like to meet in de park? Px'

Obviously am not going. Most improper for a married man to be texting a married woman to arrange surreptitious meeting. He has a nerve. *And* he put a kiss after his name – very flirty and inappropriate. (And made me feel all hot and bothered). Of course, it *would* be in broad daylight, in the park, surrounded by loads of other people. Not as if he would drag me off to the bushes and rip my bodice apart before ravishing me in a brutal, yet tender fashion. If I wore a bodice, that is. Also, it would be very selfish of me to force Jack to play indoors on such a glorious morning because of a stupid paranoia that Lone Father wants to have his wicked, wicked way with me.

For all I know he's gay, and his marriage is one of convenience. In fact, that might explain a lot. Such as why

- He is into culture and literature.

- He goes to a mother-and-toddler group.

- He wears tight-fitting pastel-coloured V-necks that show off his lean, muscular body.

Quickly decided that all those artistic, trapped-in-a-loveless-marriage-of-convenience types probably put kisses after every text and that it's nothing to worry about. Spent ages composing my reply: 'OK. C u at 12x'. (Added the *x* as didn't want to seem rude and judgemental of his alternative lifestyle.)

Quite excited that I will now have new best friend just like Julia Roberts and Rupert Everett in *My Best Friend's Wedding*, or Madonna and Rupert Everett in that other movie. Or Rupert Everett in any movie, actually. Eat your heart out, Louise! I no longer need you and your MOM dramas draining my energy. I have a potentially new VBF.

PS Pity Hugh Grant never gets to play the gay guy.

PPS Tomorrow is Jack's birthday. Am riddled with guilt that I have not organized extravagant party event. I am to blame if he suffers from Second Child Syndrome in later life.

21 *March*

Had innocent, platonic play-date with Lone Father in the park. Not a smouldering look passed between us – must have imagined it last time. Spent ages feeding the ducks with the boys, throwing bread and generally larking about *à la* playful Gap ads. Confided in him about dinner-party débâcle.

'Bit inconsiderate of your hubby to land that on you, wasn't it?' he said, handing some more bread to the children so they could tease the ducks.

Felt a bit funny bitching about Joe to another man, even if he is just a totally platonic friend.

'Em, well, he says he told me ages ago. I must have forgotten.' (Funny how I still have no recollection of that conversation, though.)

'It's no wonder you forgot. You have so much on your plate already.'

'Aw, not really.' I blushed, concentrating very hard on tearing up the bread.

'Don't run yourself down, Susie,' he said. 'Staying at home with children full-time is a very noble choice. I wish my wife would do it.' He sounded wistful and sad.

'Has she a very successful career, then?' I tried not to sound too nosy but was desperate to find out.

'Oh, yes, Arabella loves her career.' He laughed bitterly, looking off into the middle distance, just like something out of a Jane Austen mini-movie. 'She certainly makes it her number-one priority, that's for sure.'

Deep mystery to be uncovered there. Was just about to probe a bit, when Rodney started screaming: 'Me no like ducks,' he wailed, as a fat little duckling waddled its way towards him (at alarmingly high speed, it must be admitted).

'It's only a duck, Rodney.' Lone Father threw his gorgeous Hugh Grant eyes to heaven in an aren't-kids-hilarious way.

'Me *no like*,' Rodney screeched, stamping his feet and turning blue.

'Oh, for God's sake, Rodney, don't be such a little poof. It's only a bloody duck, for Christ's sake,' Lone Father snapped.

Hmm. Lone Father obviously not gay, if he makes blatant homophobic remarks to his own child. Bit worrying.

'Sorry, Susie.' He smiled ruefully, running his fingers through his (seriously sexy – wonder if he uses Bedhead?) hair. Forgave him instantly for potential permanent psychological scar he may have inflicted on his child. 'I was up half the night working on my book. I think I have writers' block. I guess I'm a little irritable today.'

Wow. My new friend has writers' block. I am officially friends with a bona-fide arty, literary type. This is definitely more like it. Barely miss Louise any more.

PS Jack seemed very happy with his low-key birthday affair. He spent ages mushing his Barney birthday cake into the carpet. Thank God he is not high maintenance like his sister.

22 March

Right. Must focus. Posh dinner party less than a week away. Rang Joe's mother to borrow chairs. Huge mistake. 'Hang on a second, dear,' she bellowed. 'I'll just get the remote.' Could hear posh bloke from *Location, Location, Location* rabbiting on in the background. Quite sad, the way she has to watch daytime TV to fill her time. And where she thinks she's moving to is beyond me.

'Now, dear,' she said, 'I just turned the volume down. I do love that *Location, Location, Location*, don't you? *So* interesting. Do you know that Liverpool is very up-and-coming?' She whispered the last bit confidentially, as if about three million people hadn't just been told the same thing.

'Really?'

'Oh, yes, it used to be full of crack whores and illegal immigrants, but apparently they're quite trendy now.'

'That's lovely,' I said, digging my nails into my palms to stifle a scream. 'Em, anyway, Mrs H, I'm just calling to ask if I can borrow some chairs, please?'

'Chairs?' she asked. 'Why do you need chairs? Has one of the children hurt themselves, dear?'

Couldn't fathom the reasoning behind that one so had to give full and frank account of upcoming dinner party and need for chairs for senior directors and their wives, etc., etc.

'Oh. Very nice.' She was plainly put out that she wasn't at the top of the guest list. 'Isn't it a pity Joe never thinks to ask his mother to any of these little *soirées*? I could do with getting out of the house from time to time. Still, *Coronation Street* will keep me company. It's on almost every night now, you know. Just as well, I suppose.'

Cue grand silence, which I felt obliged to fill by asking her to join us in fit of supreme stupidity and patent self-sabotage.

Maybe it'll be better than expected. She'll probably help me with the meal so the pressure will be off a bit. She may be overbearing, but she *is* a good cook. Also, she'll be on hand to manhandle the children to bed, in case they get raucous and disorderly (very likely). Should have thought of it sooner. Will all work out swimmingly.

PS Won't break it to Joe just yet.

23 March

Mrs H rang at eight thirty a.m. to discuss the Dinner Party Menu. Instantly recognized the unmistakable woman-on-a-mission tone and felt a dread in the pit of my stomach.

'Now, I was thinking beef,' she said, launching straight into it. 'And what about a table plan, dear? That's very important. And do you want to do nametags? I have some very nice cream card.' She had barely drawn breath.

Could hear her sucking her sharpened pencil, notepad at the ready. Had horrible vision of senior directors and their wives (*all of whom know each other*) standing round with enormous nametags attached to their lapels and Joe's mother talking to them really slowly, using their names over and over again, as if they were out on day release: '*Maurice*, how are you, *Maurice*? It's lovely to see you, *Maurice*.'

'Em, can I call you back, Mrs H?' I tried, desperate to get her off the line ASAP. 'I'm just trying to give the kids their breakfast.'

'My goodness, are the poor mites not fed yet? Their tummies must think their throats have been cut.' (Nice turn of phrase for toddlers, I thought.) 'Why, I have half a day's work done already. It takes the early bird to catch the worm, you know – early to bed, early to rise, that's my motto.'

Was tempted to continue conversation to see how many more clichés she could cram in, but knew had to be brutal and cut her off quick before she sabotaged the entire posh dinner party.

'Listen, Mrs H,' I said, trying to sound conciliatory, 'thanks for your offer of help and everything, but I'm perfectly capable of handling a few people over for dinner. So, I'll see you then, OK?'

'Right.' She sniffed. 'I see. I'll go now, then.'

Hung up, filled with dread. Wonder if I could fake my own death. Will investigate.

PS Wish I could call Louise and ask her advice about the Dinner Party of Doom but I absolutely, under no circumstances, cannot be the first one to call. Obviously she is quite happy for us to go our separate ways, even if we have been VBFs since for ever.

PPS Hope she doesn't come looking for her thoughtful, perfectly wrapped presents back.

24 March

Got kind, well-meaning message from Cathy, the fitness adviser, on my mobile today: 'Hi, Susie. According to my records, you missed an assessment appointment with us. Can you please give me a call to rearrange?' Very impressed by efficiency and following-up approach. Will call her today.

Bang on track with dinner-party preparations. No word from Mrs H. She must have got the message and backed off.

Mrs H arrived on the doorstep (wearing what looked suspiciously like a Delia Smith apron under her raincoat) at eight fifteen. She had quite obviously hidden in the bushes until Joe's car had pulled out of the driveway. 'Now, Susie, no need to panic,' she said, seeing the utter horror on my face. 'I just thought this morning that there's only a day to go to Susie's little shin-dig so you might need my help with the last of the preparations.'

'Em, no, I think I'm all set,' I replied, rubbing my eyes to see her properly. (Note: special eye makeup remover in bathroom cabinet will not apply itself.)

'Let's see, shall we?' she replied, elbowing her way into the hall. 'Anyway, I may as well have a cup of tea and see my grandchildren while I'm here. Let me put the kettle on while you get yourself organized.'

Gave in and trundled upstairs to get dressed. Caught her polishing the kettle when I got back to the kitchen. 'Now, Susie,' she cajoled, 'please let me help. You can't be expected to do all this on your own. Sure I have nothing to do with my time. I'd love to give you a hand.'

Couldn't resist pathetic beseeching look of a sixty-five-year-old woman, so relented in fit of foolish weakness. 'Well, OK, then,' I muttered, annoyed with myself for caving so quickly.

'Good girl. Now, I've devised a little plan of action,' she announced, whipping what looked like a military-style operation from her handbag and laying it on the table with a flourish. 'First, we need to give the place a little clean,' she said, eyeing the kitchen countertops with distaste. Catching my eye, she backtracked quickly, in case I rallied the strength to chuck her, with her Jif Extra Strength, out on her ear. 'You can't be expected to do it all on your own and, besides, I'm only too happy to help. Sure what else would I be doing? My own place is like a new pin – there's nothing to do over there. Now, this would be a challenge, and challenges are good for a woman of my years.'

Then she was off, pulling on her Marigolds with precision, like a surgeon about to perform a life-saving operation.

'We'll start upstairs and work our way down,' she announced, with grim determination.

'But we're not having the dinner party upstairs, Mrs H,' I protested feebly, aghast that she was going to witness the pit that was my bedroom.

'That doesn't matter, Susie,' she said, as if a child of three would have understood the gravity of the situation. 'You never know what kind of emergency might happen. Someone may feel faint and have to lie down. Wouldn't it be terrible if you were caught out?' She looked positively turned on by the idea.

Never thought of that. Would be very embarrassing if a senior director or his wife had to shove all the dirty laundry off the bed before they could collapse into a semi-coma. Decided to step aside and let her get on with it. No point arguing with a professional.

Have new-found respect for mother-in-law. House
unbelievably clean. Bed linen is *ironed* (a first in my lifetime) and toilet water is blue (instead of usual murky
grey). Can now understand why cleaning may become
addictive: Mrs H was certainly on a high – her eyes
were glassy and she was nearly foaming at the mouth
with the excitement of tackling such filth. Was exhausted just watching her.

She spun round every room in a frenzy, whipping up
concoctions of borax and ammonia and singing show
tunes while she scrubbed ('I'm Gonna Wash That Man
Right Out Of My Hair' seemed to be a favourite).
Would be quite scary if it wasn't so impressive. Had to
dissuade her from making kids wear gloves for the
next twenty-four hours, but otherwise am smug about
gleaming domestic arrangements. Was able to spend
entire day reclining on dust-free sofa reading *Hello!*.
May get her to do it on a regular basis – who am I to
deny an old woman simple pleasures? The children are
a little confused by so much cleanliness and order.
Katie keeps complaining that she didn't want all her
Strawberry Shortcake clothes washed and ironed, and
Jack keeps sniffing his trucks suspiciously. (Mrs H said
the ammonia smell should wear off in a week or two.)

PS Joe casually announced at eleven fifteen p.m. that
his Barbie secretary is coming to the dinner party!

'What?' I screeched in dismay. 'I thought it was just
the old fuddy-duddies?'

'Well, she *is* the secretary for the department, Susie,'

Joe replied, flossing his teeth diligently in the bathroom mirror. 'It would be pretty rude not to ask her.'

'Right. She can sit beside your mother, then,' I retorted, stamping out of the bathroom before I could wrap the dental floss round his neck in a fit of blind rage.

'My *mother*?' he stuttered, his head snapping round so quickly so that the floss got stuck between his two front teeth. 'Ouch! Bloody hell!'

Serves him right. Can't believe he invited Barbie without telling me. What does he think I am? A complete mug? Prissy perfect-wife outfit of choice now completely unsuitable in light of new developments. Will have to find something glamorous yet understated at extremely short notice. Wish I could call Louise – her wardrobe is packed with fab sexy gear. Really miss her. But there is no way I'm calling her first – I have my pride.

27 March: Dinner Party

8.00 a.m. Very important day. Vital to impress Joe's work colleagues and pull off exquisite, tasteful dinner-party soirée. Am trying to ignore feelings of doom.

9.10 a.m. Just got really sweet text from Lone Father: 'Hp dinner party goes well Nigella!' So nice of him to remember. And so cute that he has a pet name for me.

9.12 a.m. Sent witty reply: 'Get me out of here Jamie!' (exclamation mark v. important so he knows I am full of fun and not downtrodden middle-aged housewife with no Sense of Humour.)

9.13 a.m. Just got his response: 'Any time . . .' Hmm . . . line of trailing dots seems very flirty, as if the intended message is 'to be continued . . .' However, will not read anything into it. All innocent banter.

11.30 a.m. Have prepared vegetables – just have to chop and cover with clingfilm, then pop into a hot oven an hour before the guests arrive. All very easy – should entertain more often really. Barbie secretary the only fly in the ointment, but will not be paranoid, jealous, possessive wife. She is innocent work colleague and just as boring as fuddy-duddy partners and wives.

1.00 p.m. Katie feels a bit under the weather. Have tucked her up on the sofa to watch *The Wiggles* DVD. Hope she is not coming down with anything.

1.15 p.m. Jack has thrown up all over the stairs. Can't remember what to do with vomit stains – borax? Ammonia? Suddenly wish I had accepted Mrs H's offer to compose a comprehensive list of how to tackle 101 Household Stains. Have dabbed it up as best as I can – think spraying Clinique's Happy perfume about has masked the vile smell. Am trying to swallow horrible, panicky feelings.

1.35 p.m. Katie just threw up all over the newly washed rug in the living room. Am slowly detecting a pattern. Vaguely remember something about a vomiting bug doing the rounds. Why does God do this to me? Why?

1.45 p.m. Children are taking turns to throw up every ten minutes. Tupperware bowls Mrs H gave me for birthday last year are coming in handy at last – have them scattered in a track from the living room to the kitchen to catch the vomit.

Katie in severe state of girlie distress about grossness

of it all and is spending lots of time wailing. Am doing best to console her that the worst will soon be over. Not right time to explain that a twenty-four-hour bug will last all day long. Especially when her concept of time is limited to half-hour *Dora the Explorer* stints.

Jack keeps finding new and ingenious places to throw up – like the back of the sofa and the fridge.

2.00 p.m. The diarrhoea has started. Jack's nappy has leaked into the feet of his all-in-one fleece pyjama suit. Katie is inconsolable that her new Barbie pants are ruined.

Will have to cancel dinner party. Cannot pull off posh three-course meal under these conditions.

5.00 p.m. Oh my God. Have just woken up. Vaguely remember collapsing into bed with two delirious children either side of me at about three o'clock. Must have fallen into (totally understandable) exhausted sleep. House stinks of vomit and poo, and guests due in less than *three* hours!

5.10 p.m. Joe says it is too late to cancel dinner party. Am trying not to hyperventilate with fear. (Blowing into a large Tesco carrier-bag proving useless.)

Joe maintains that people aren't expecting a five-course meal and a perfect home – it's meant to be a relaxed, casual get-together more than anything else. He also promises to be home in half an hour to help.

5.15 p.m. Decided I have actually experienced the End of the World. Wonder if I could include this as a Life Skill if I ever need to update my CV.

Still in state of shock after Dinner Party from Hell.

By six forty-five had managed to get relatively clean (baby wipes indispensable, multifunctional cleaning tool – good for faces, bums and kitchen tops. Note: possible new marketing ploy for baby-wipe company. Must investigate.)

Shoved beef and vegetables into oven and sprayed hall, kitchen and bathroom with Happy perfume again to mask revolting vomit/diarrhoea odour. (Note: purchase air-freshener ASAP. Also purchase new perfume – gone right off Happy.)

Had no time to find new sex-kitten wife outfit so had to make do with Amish-style frumpy black dress (its only nod to style was that it was sleeveless). Luckily, Mrs H-style Delia Smith apron (with flower appliqué and ruffle trim) covered most of it. Unluckily, had no time to shower or shave underarms so had to grip arms to sides all night in nutter-on-day-release manner.

Joe was dunking kids in the bath and I was trying to tame my unruly hair with Jack's tiny Bob the Builder hairbrush (adult brush mysteriously AWOL) when the first guests started banging on the door. At seven-forty-five! Don't they know when people say eight they mean at least eight thirty! Bloody senior citizens – wanting to eat their dinner and get home in time for the evening news.

Corralled them all in the living room with wine and cheese straws while I tried to put the final touches to the table (no time to wash new crockery, just tried to peel price stickers off the back of the plates and gave them a quick wipe with the tablecloth).

Could hear Jack and Katie, re-energized after their long nap and the (very) quick bath Joe gave them, bouncing round the room in their clean (and mercifully ironed, thanks to Mrs H) pyjamas, showing all the senior directors where they had puked.

Katie was particularly proud of her recovery. 'I was practically *dying*, you know,' she announced, to one of the wives. 'Mummy said she had never seen so much shit – ever!'

Hid in the kitchen, basting the beef and roasted vegetables and swigging Calvados to keep calm.

By five past eight there was still no sign of Mrs H – the first time in living memory she's been late for anything: she's usually panting on the doorstep at least thirty minutes ahead of schedule 'To factor in any mishaps, dear.' Never thought I would say this, but I'd been waiting for her to arrive and take over on the cooking front. (Suspected beef was erring on the side of charred rather than crisp and needed her expert opinion.)

Had horrible sense of foreboding that she had been knocked down by a bus or had collapsed dramatically after inhaling one too many cleaning products. Kept whispering to Joe to call her and check, but he was too busy pretending to be the perfect host/future director and making stupid chit-chat with dusty old folks to take any notice.

At eight-fifteen Becky the Barbie secretary swanned in, wearing a figure-hugging pinstripe suit and clutching a large bouquet of roses in one hand, with a Winnie the Pooh jigsaw and what looked like a box of chocolates in the other. Watched her air-kiss Joe in the hall, then throw back her head and give a throaty laugh in a totally fake way at something he said before she sashayed into the living room. Not quite as slutty as I remembered, although there didn't seem to be much under the pin-stripe jacket.

'These are for you, Susie,' she simpered, in a phoney I'm-so-sincere voice, handing me the flowers, while I struggled like a Stepford wife to get the oven glove off. 'I've heard so much about you, I feel I know you already,' she cooed, flashing dazzling white teeth. 'Now, where are the little darlings? I can't wait to meet them – they look so cute in the photos on Joe's desk.'

Right on cue, Jack sprang from nowhere and threw himself at her lean, toned thighs in glee, wrapping himself round them in a vice grip.

Ha! I thought. Now your fake 'I love kids' routine will be laid bare – Jack's kamikaze stunt has floored grown men.

To my horror, Barbie/Becky was unperturbed, grinning down at him and ruffling his hair. 'You big boy!' she purred. 'Will we play with this?' With a flourish and a wriggle of her ample charms she produced the jigsaw and Jack was putty in her hands, immediately trying to crawl on to her lap.

Then Katie appeared from nowhere. 'Who are you?' She eyed Becky from the doorway, her chubby little hands on her hips and her eyes slits of suspicion.

Atagirl, Katie, I thought joyfully. Do your mother proud and humiliate the wagon.

'You must be Katie,' Becky breathed, and squatted at her level.

Nice touch, I thought. Been practising your seduction technique.

'I love your Barbie pyjamas – is pink your favourite colour?'

Had to hand it to her – the woman was a pro: 'pink' and 'Barbie' in one sentence.

'I can see your boobies,' Katie gasped, as Becky's fitted jacket fell open and revealed a lacy pink bra.

'Uh-oh.' She giggled, making no attempt to cover herself. 'Silly Becky! Come on, let's open these Barbie chocolates – if it's OK with your mum?'

'Oh, don't mind Mummy,' Katie announced, linking her new VBF as if she'd known her years. 'She can't eat chocolate – she says it makes her fatter.' And off they sauntered, chatting about Disney princesses and the pros and cons of plaits versus curls, Jack trailing in their wake, mouth hanging open in awe.

By eight forty-five Joe's mother still hadn't turned up so was forced to serve the beef before it was completely cremated. All was going quite well until the doorbell rang at nine. There stood Mrs H, swaying, eyes glassy, undeniably pissed. 'Evening, all,' she slurred. 'Everyone having a fabulous time?'

Joe managed to shove her into the kitchen before any fuddy-duddies spotted her. 'Mother,' he hissed, 'have you been drinking?'

'Only a little drop, darling.' She flapped him away. 'Don't be such a fusspot.'

'How much is a little drop?' Joe was furious.

'A bottle?' Her eyes crossed and uncrossed with the effort of talking and sitting up straight at the same time.

'Oh, my God.' Joe collapsed into a kitchen chair,

cradling his head in his hands. 'This is a total nightmare – you know you can't drink.'

'I'm absolutely fine, Joseph,' she slurred. 'Stop being so dramatic. Now, what can I do to help? Will I go in and chat to everyone? I've been listening to *Newsnight* all week so I'm all brushed up on current affairs. I have some great stories about sleazy politicians shagging their tarts. Do you know at least thirty per cent of men use brothels?' She tried to struggle up from the kitchen table but, luckily, her legs gave way beneath her before she could get anywhere.

Joe looked as if he was going to faint.

Felt a bit weird myself. Don't think I've ever heard Mrs H use the T-word before – unless it was of the apple or rhubarb kind. Also, didn't think she even *knew* the word 'shagging'. Very shocking. But then it got worse.

'Did you know, Susie,' she said, 'that Joe's father once shagged a tart?'

She hiccuped.

All the colour drained from Joe's face.

Stood dumbfounded in horrified fascination – was like watching a dysfunctional family episode of *Dr. Phil*, right in my steamy kitchen.

'Susie,' Joe appealed to me, his face grim and white, 'will you put Mum to bed? I have to go back in to our guests.'

Was a bit disappointed – there were probably loads of family secrets to be revealed, but Joe was so distraught that I had to spring into action and save the day. Had to lure Mrs H up the stairs with the promise of a Bailey's nightcap. Made great progress, tiptoeing and stage-whispering our way across the landing, until the bathroom door opened and Becky emerged, rubbing her nose. (Diarrhoea smell still noticeable, it has to be said.)

'Who are *you*?' Mrs H bellowed, looking her up and down with disdain.

'I'm Becky,' Barbie answered, producing her best mega-watt smile and proffering a manicured, moisturized hand.

'Well, Becky,' Mrs H countered, 'you might think about putting your breasts away. You look like a high-class hooker.'

Tried to turn my snort of laughter into a cough before pirouetting Mrs H into our bedroom, leaving an open-mouthed Becky behind.

'You'd want to watch that slag with Joe, dear,' Mrs H whispered. 'Men can't resist boobies on show – and I should know.' Then she fell into a drunken stupor on our bed, singing some indecipherable show tune.

29 *March*

Joe is in a serious state of decline. He keeps muttering about lost promotion chances, life over, etc., etc., with a very wild look in his eye.

Tried to convince him that no one saw his drunken, out-of-control mother (except Barbie/Becky, who doesn't count). And even if any senior directors did see anything, he had handled the situation with poise and professionalism, which only goes to show what a worthwhile asset he would be to the firm. (Thought that might have been pushing it a bit, but felt I had to concoct positive spin for mental health and well-being of spouse.)

'She was hilarious, actually.' I tried to get him to see the funny side. 'Imagine her thinking your dad had been with another woman.' I chuckled again, trying to imagine Mr H doing anything more strenuous than playing Scrabble when he was alive.

'He had an affair years ago, when I was a child,' Joe said wearily, a haunted look crossing his face. 'My mother never really forgave him.'

PS Am completely gob-smacked by Joe's shocking family revelations. Joe's dad was the least likely Lothario I've ever seen.

PPS Very disturbing that Joe has kept this dark secret to himself for so many years. What else is he keeping from me?

PPPS Mrs H's words about Becky and her breasts keep ringing in my ears – what if Joe turns out to be a chip off the old block?

30 March

Lots of post today

- Handmade thank-you card from Becky/Barbie slut.
  Dear Susie, thank you so much for a delicious dinner and your kind hospitality. Your children are adorable! Hope to see you all again soon,
  Best wishes, Becky.

- Reminder notice from the gym

    Susie! You missed your assessment appointment!
    Call me to reschedule!
    Engage to achieve!
    Cathy.

  Cathy very persistent. Going off the idea of the gym a
  little bit. Don't want to join boot camp.

- Rude postcard from old friend on holiday in Las
  Vegas

    Having a ball here in Vegas! Fab to get out of
    London for a while. Will be in Dublin next month
    – can you put me up? Nxxx

  Hell. Haven't heard from Nikki in years. Definitely
  not a good time for long-lost friends to come out of
  the woodwork, even if we *were* really close booze
  buddies when we worked together in London years
  ago. Will have to call and put her off.

  No word from Mrs H.

  Joe is officially not speaking to his drunkard mother.
  His father was apparently a wild rover in his heyday.
  And Joe has hidden all this from me for years. Oprah
  could devote a whole special to us.

31 March

Louise's birthday today. Trying to ignore nagging feeling that should call her and make up, but just can't
bring myself to do it. Even *Oprah* special on lifelong

friends would not persuade me. Am officially hard-hearted, bitter crone.

Went to mother-and-toddler group to cheer myself up. Lone Father/Paul was really sympathetic about my plight. 'She sounds like a proper bitch, Susie,' he said, rubbing my arm in a comforting way. 'You just don't need toxic people like that in your life, draining you of energy.' Felt a bit funny that he was calling my oldest friend a bitch, but forced myself not to be so stupidly loyal and agree with him.

Also felt a bit funny when he was rubbing my arm but it did take my mind right off my worries. That is, until I caught glam-mummy Marita mouthing something at me that I couldn't quite make out. It looked like 'slapper', but that can't be right.

Dragged myself back to what Paul was saying about negative energy and draining personalities, etc., etc. He really is a fount of information – he told me all about a similar experience he'd had when his best friend got really uptight about some news scoop so he just cut him from his life.

Sounded a little harsh, but he probably has a point. Louise has been funny with me ever since I had the kids. Maybe he's right and our relationship has run its course and it's time to move on.

PS Mrs H has gone underground. Tried calling her this morning but got no reply, and I know she was definitely in because a *Location, Location, Location* double bill was on and there is no possible way she would leave the house.

Really want to check she's OK after horrible, humiliating display she made of herself the other night. More importantly, want juicy details of Mr H's wandering hands and extramarital affairs from years ago. May be able to cancel Sky subscription and just listen to her tales of secret sex sessions instead.

PPS Katie came home with cute little bunny drawings and mini papier-mâché eggs from playschool – have decided to plan old-fashioned Easter-egg hunt.

1 April

Busy organizing Easter festivities. Am planning home-made Easter extravaganza like the ones I had as a child. Have bought loads of eggs to hard-boil, then hand-paint with Katie and Jack. Can download cute little bunnies and chicks from craftsrus.com, then trace them on.

'Nonsense, darling,' Mum tinkled down the phone, when I filled her in on my grand idea. 'You never had anything but Cadbury's eggs when you were little. You used to take the foil wrapper off, eat the chocolates inside, then wrap it back up again.'

Hmm . . . Nostalgic childhood memory must have been from *Blue Peter* or some other show. Definitely remember seeing eggs being painted somewhere. Any-way, am determined to give Katie and Jack great memories of happy times together, despite family secrets of lurid sex and alcoholism.

PS Joe called to say the company is having an Easter-egg hunt and picnic for employees' children on Sunday. Glad to see they're taking their family responsibilities seriously for once. Will write a letter of commendation to applaud them on their efforts.

PPS Wonder if there will be free wine for the adults.

Decided drastic times call for drastic measures so made a dawn raid on Mrs H this morning. (Well, at eleven thirty, but had to make sure she'd be there so waited for *Antiques Roadshow* to start before I rang the bell.)

Was expecting downtrodden, humiliated version of mother-in-law to greet me on steps so was unpleasantly surprised when a dapper Mrs H appeared, looking as if she'd just been dry-cleaned from head to toe. 'Hello, Susie dear,' she chirped, as if nothing untoward had happened and I had not put her to bed and wiped drool from her mouth a few nights earlier.

'Hello, Mrs H.' I patted her arm sympathetically. (Obviously she was doing her best to remain composed after her shattering experience. Was determined to break through that ASAP and get to the good stuff.) 'How. *Are*. You?' I said, slowly and deliberately, so she would know to what I was referring.

'I'm fine, Susie dear,' she said, as if she hadn't a care in the world. 'How are you? Won't you come in? I'm just waxing the floors.' She wasn't batting an eyelid. This wasn't going to be as easy as I'd thought. Still, would persevere.

'No,' I battled on, getting a bit frustrated. 'What I meant was – are you OK?' I eyeballed her, but she didn't flinch.

'Of course. Why wouldn't I be?' she said, prising open her tin of homemade lemon sponge and taking out the Royal Doulton china.

'Well, I just thought, after the other night . . .' I trailed off, leaving her to fill in the blanks.

She had the good grace to pause for a split second before she answered. 'Oh, *that*. Well, you see, Dr Tynan gave me antibiotics for my ingrown toenail and I made the mistake of having half a glass of sherry before I came over to you – it made me a little tipsy, all right. Thank you for looking after me. Now, one lump or two, dear?'

'So, Joe was wrong – his dad never had an affair?' I changed tack, in an attempt to catch her off-guard and unearth a few graphic details at the very least.

She froze, a Royal Doulton cup in mid-air. 'What nonsense. Joe has always been such an imaginative boy.' She continued to slice the lemon sponge into small, even pieces, a funny look on her face.

Not sure what to believe and am afraid to broach the subject with Joe. He attacked the hedges in the garden with the extra powerful electric clippers yesterday so I know he's still in a foul temper.

3 April: Easter Saturday

Did dress rehearsal for tomorrow to make sure kids look clean and respectable for company picnic. Extremely difficult to get all Play-Doh out from underneath Jack's nails but I managed it eventually (teeny comb from Strawberry Shortcake set very useful in case of emergency).

Had bit of a to-do with Katie, who was very unhappy with my outfit of choice – gorgeous blue sundress with matching bonnet and basket bought for extortionate amount of money at the Centre on a whim. 'I look stupid.' She stamped as I tried to tie her hair into two pigtails of exactly matching length.

'You look gorgeous, darling,' I said, out of the corner of my mouth, trying not to inhale the hair-slides and talk at the same time. (Need three hands to do pigtails – may well consider getting her a GI Jane crew-cut soon.)

'I don't look like Barbie,' she moaned. 'I look like a little girl.'

Refrained from explaining that she *is* a little girl, not a ridiculous fantasy figure that makes ordinary women feel dumpy and inadequate. Knew I should have put my foot down and banned those stupid Barbies – they give an idealized version of femalehood that is just not natural. Was about to explain that minuscule waist and huge boobs are not realistic interpretation of the female figure (although probably unlikely Mattel will manufacture doll with saddle-bags, cellulite and stretchmarks) when she hit me for six.

'Becky looks like Barbie,' she announced stubbornly. 'She has the exact same hair and everything.' (Yes, peroxided to within an inch of its life.) '*And* she has really cool clothes, like Bratz.' She eyed me up and down with distaste, taking in the crumpled linen ensemble that no Bratz worth her salt would be caught dead wearing.

Jack was easier to dress, the only battle being to get the clothes *on* him. Picnic better be good.

4 April: Easter Sunday

Woke to drizzling rain and felt quite cheerful. Company BBQ would now have to be moved indoors and would be a much more civilized occasion.

Was horrified to discover when we arrived that, instead of moving the whole escapade to a plush Italian eaterie with on-site crèche, they whipped out enormous yellow windcheaters with the company logo emblazoned across the front and urged everyone to 'get in the spirit'!

Spent about half an hour trying to get in the spirit, but failing miserably. Shoes ruined from traipsing across wet, muddy field, trying to look cheerful and searching for cheap Easter eggs that had been bought in bulk from the Co-op. (They had obviously been made with cocoa powder instead of milk chocolate, and contained dangerous plastic toys made in Taiwan that posed a serious health and choking risk to young children. Had to wrestle them from Katie and Jack's hands for fear of their lives being cut short.)

Two senior directors seemed to go out of their way to avoid me – couldn't figure out why, until a third approached me as I crouched in the people-carrier, trying to warm my feet on the blow-fan. He tapped on the fogged-up window to get my attention. 'How are you, Susan?' He peered through the window, as I scrambled to pull my linen skirt down to cover my hairy ankles.

'Grand, great, Maurice,' I answered, as cheerfully as humanly possible. 'Isn't today great? The children are just loving it. It's so . . . *great.*' I finished lamely. (Was babbling and self-conscious under intense gaze of important senior director with the ability to make or break spouse's career with a flick of his Mont Blanc pen. Also very aware was telling lots of lies about greatness of the day, considering it was an awful day of nightmarish proportions and Katie was still sulking about blue sundress and bonnet ensemble.)

'And how *is* your poor mother, Susan?' he continued, ignoring my attempts to chat.

'My mother? She's fine, thanks,' I said, wondering why he was asking about her.

'Yes,' he answered, sticking his head through the window to whisper confidentially, 'my own mother was an alcoholic so I know only too well what you're going through.' He nodded sympathetically, fixing me with a watery gaze. 'It's a terrible thing. A disease. Unfortunately, it's genetic.'

He scoured my face intently, obviously searching for traces of any alcoholic-related signs. (Have lots of broken veins and a big red nose, but from the cold not gin.) Then he sniffed, pulled a monogrammed cotton handkerchief from his yellow windcheater and blew his nose loudly. 'Anyway, we all have our cross to bear, my dear. Must get back – I believe the Easter bunny is making an appearance at any minute now. Dear Becky has volunteered to do it this year. She was *so* brave to step in at the last moment because Hugh had that nasty heart-attack. It's just the type of can-do attitude we appreciate here at Pyramid. That girl is going places, mark my words.'

Rolled up the window in shock. Leery Maurice

thought drunken Mrs H was *my* mother, not Joe's! Worse, he thought I was a secret drinker too. How on earth had he jumped to that conclusion?

Mulled it over for a bit while I tried to get warm, but decided to deal with it later. Absolutely could not, under any circumstances, miss Becky humiliating herself in moth-eaten rabbit costume with extra large teeth and ears.

5 April: Easter Monday

11 a.m. In bed with horrible, probably life-threatening flu or some other superbug that will be resistant to antibiotics or any other medical intervention. No wonder, after being soaked to the skin during yesterday's egg-hunt fiasco. Will probably die in a pool of sweat, unloved and uncared-for by vile husband and oblivious children. Wonder if Joe's firm will be held responsible for my tragic untimely death after it forced me to stand in torrential rain for most of Easter Sunday. He will probably get a huge payout and buy the three-storey townhouse in Dublin 4 that I have lusted after for years. Then he'll marry some young trollop who will hate the kids and send them to boarding-school. No one will visit my grave.

2.00 p.m. Am quite obviously delirious as keep having disturbing hallucinations about Becky in a skin-tight Playboy-bunny outfit, fishnet stockings and six-inch stilettos, handing Easter eggs to bewildered children. May be suffering from meningitis. At very least need more painkillers. And some homemade soup. Or Lucozade and a Twix. Nobody has been to check on me for hours. In fact, house suspiciously quiet and child-free. May well have been abandoned altogether.

4 p.m. Dreamt Lone Father/Paul snuck into my bedroom wearing breeches and white frilly shirt open to the navel, hair slicked back in very sexy way.

'Would you like me to give you a rub-down, Susie?' he whispered seductively, nuzzling my earlobe and brandishing a bottle of Vick's expectorant.

'Mmm, yes, please,' I moaned, throwing my head back in Becky-esque fashion and clasping him to my bosom. Feel bit better, actually.

6.00 p.m. Managed to eat the Pick'n'Mix that Katie brought me from the cinema. (Liquorice Allsorts definitely undervalued in the confectionery world.) 'It was fab, Mum,' she enthused, bouncing up and down on the bed. 'We went to the movies *and* McDonald's! Can you be sick again next week?'

'Thought you might like a bit of peace and quiet so you could get some rest,' Joe said, hovering at the end of the bed, looking haggard. 'Are you ready to get up yet?'

11 p.m. It's all coming back to me. Dreams of Becky in skin-tight Playboy-bunny outfit were not hallucinations brought on by superbug symptoms! Can vividly remember her sashaying down the field, boobs spilling out over the top of her black satin corset, dispensing eggs to the kids while the men stood drooling, mouths agape.

'Thank you, Hugh! Having that heart-attack was the best thing you ever did,' one guy muttered, under his breath. (Wife duly bashed him over the head with her Easter basket.)

'Do you like it?' Becky stopped directly in front of Joe and leery Maurice and did a twirl, twitching her nose (cute and button-like, no broken veins in sight) and wiggling her bottom (pert and cellulite-free), bunny-style. 'That mouldy old bunny outfit was just so *gross* I decided to take the matter into my own hands. I made it myself. What do you think?' She batted her lashes at Joe. Quite blatantly, in fact.

'Very, em, inventive,' Joe stuttered, looking hot and bothered while I tried to battle my way through the throng to stand at his side. Was beaten back by every lusty male there, all of whom seemed to have a renewed interest in chocolate confectionery.

Have decided that Becky is officially a slapper operating at the highest and most dangerous level – a slapper who pretends she's professional and business-like, but wears lacy bras under her fitted suit, then appeals to every man's fantasy by dressing up in a bunny outfit. Even worse, she's a slapper who appeals to children. Thought this type of woman was only an urban legend. Could be in serious danger. Especially as she seems to lust after my husband.

6 April

Sat in crusty old PJs all day, feeling weak and feeble. (Still, managed to force-feed myself large tube of Pringles Sour Cream and Onion and some strawberry Pop-Tarts. Obviously have to keep my strength up for the kids.)

Couldn't bring myself to take a shower, as was afraid

might faint and bash head on tiles and lie undiscovered for hours. So, lay on sofa, trying to ignore the faint smell of BO, and took time to catch up on some serious channel-surfing while Katie and Jack ran in circles round the room. Lots of Nurofen Plus seemed to dull the noise a bit. (And the tube of Pringles they munched between them stopped them gouging each other's eyes out.)

At three thirty there was a knock at the door so shuffled to answer it, hoping it might be the postman with a mystery package for me (never happened before, but I still live in hope). Wrenched door open (took superhuman effort as am so feeble from horrific dose of superbug) and there, standing on the step, Rodney swinging from his hip, was Lone Father.

'Hi!' he said brightly, while I blinked up at him stupidly. (Even pathetic excuse for Irish sunlight caused already unattractive bloodshot eyes to water.)

'Oh, Paul,' I managed to squeak, aghast that he was seeing me at my very smelliest. (Note for future reference: security peephole, installed at great cost, there for a reason.)

'Em, I'm sick today . . .' I babbled, pointing (unnecessarily) at my stained pyjamas (blast those gooey Pop-Tarts) and pasty, unmade-up face in case he thought I usually looked as if I'd been dragged through a bush and had stopped on the way to make sure I looked as terrible as possible.

'You poor thing.' He seemed appalled by my plight. 'That must be why you never answered my texts. Will I come in and make you a nice cup of tea? The kids can have a play and we can chat.'

Texts? What texts? Wish I'd turned my phone on now.

Wordlessly, waved him through to the kitchen, trying to figure out how I could bolt upstairs and straighten myself out before I died of embarrassment.

Note: next time fashion-conscious mother calls to say she has seen the blonde one from breakfast TV having a simply marvellous makeover with the Bobbi Brown multipurpose blusher/eye-shadow/highlighter/shader/concealer I will not laugh like a hyena and tell her she has lost the plot and that expensive designer makeup is a waste of time and money. Instead I will thank her for valuable fashion titbit and make way to designer store post-haste. Because if I had bought said product I could then have transformed myself with a few masterful strokes in the downstairs toilet.

'I'm sorry to drop in on you, Susie,' he called, over his shoulder, as he stalked purposefully to the kettle, prising little Rodney off his leg as he went. 'I just needed to talk to someone, and you're such a good friend.'

'I am?' I choked, trying to do up the buttons of my fleecy pyjamas before he noticed the acres of flabby flesh creeping over the waistband.

'Yes, you are,' he answered meaningfully, his dark eyes boring into mine across the kitchen island. (Scattered boxes of cereal and remnants of burned toast did nothing to dim the moment.)

'Em, there's some Jaffa Cakes in the top press,' I said, to break the loaded silence. 'I put them there to stop the kids getting at them.'

'That was a good idea,' he said quietly, smiling a heart-melting lop-sided smile. 'Always wise to keep the goodies *just* out of reach, don't you think?'

Spent next hour listening as Paul confided in me how

(a) His book is going nowhere.

(b) He feels like chucking the whole thing in and getting a proper nine-to-five job.

(c) His wife doesn't understand him and is completely unsupportive.

Persuaded him, over a full packet of Jaffa Cakes, that

(a) His Booker Prize novel will not only top the *Sunday Times* bestseller list but will also earn rave reviews from serious literary critics who slam chick-lit endeavours as work of the devil.

(b) He will never have to do any proper work ever again once the royalties start flooding in (except for guest appearances on chat shows and Radio 4).

(c) He probably should confide in his wife (even if she is a hopeless, self-centred person who cannot even take time out from her hectic scale up the career ladder to attend to her husband and child).

'Thank you so much, Susie,' he gushed, as he herded Rodney out the door an hour later. 'You have no idea how much better I feel. No idea.'

He clasped me to his bosom in a massive bear-hug before he took off after Rodney, who was racing down the pavement, swinging his nappy-bag viciously against every car on the road.

Feel very virtuous. May well have a top-notch career in counselling ahead of me.

PS He smelled really yummy – definitely some

designer aftershave and, quite possibly, matching shower gel.

PPS Joe came home late and wanted to regale me with boring office politics, blah, blah, blah – what does he think I am? Some kind of dumb listening device?

7 April

Mrs H called to say that we're going to the live recording of *Doyle Tonight* chat-show this Friday night. Had completely blanked it from my mind.

'Yes, dear! Don't you remember you got those tickets way back and invited me to go along with you?' she trilled. 'Well, it's this Friday! I really should get you a diary, dear, you do seem to have a habit of forgetting things. Delia does a lovely one – with recipes for every day of the year, so you'd never run out of ideas! Anyway, pick me up at six thirty. We need to give ourselves plenty of time to get to the TV studios. You never know who we might see!'

Can think of nothing worse. She will probably try to accost one of the celebrity guests and bombard them with Irish-mammy recipes stuffed full of carbohydrates and full-fat milk.

Called Joe to devise cunning plan to try to get out of it.

Busty Barbie answered the phone. 'Oh, hi, Susie. How are you, you poor thing? Joe told me you'd been really sick.'

'I'm fine now, thanks, Becky,' I said, making a face down the phone. 'Is Joe there?'

'No, sorry, Susie, he just had to pop out of the office.'

She sighed, as if she missed him desperately. 'Will I tell him you called?'

Of course tell him I called, you stupid moron, I wanted to yell.

Suddenly feel morally obliged to take mother-in-law out. Poor woman deserves a night out. (Also, may be able to prise out of her some details of dead husband's alleged infidelity.) What harm can it do? Joe will just have to get home early to give the children their tea and put them to bed. About time he rowed in for a change.

PS Trying not to dwell on fact that had planned to take Louise to *Doyle Tonight*. Hope there will be some serious celebs there – that will show her. Ha!

PPS Have just weighed myself and have lost four pounds! Without even trying! Quite glad got that superbug now – am practically fading away.

PPPS Must decide what to wear – no stripes, dots or garish colours: don't want to look like an umpah-lumpah on national television. Black probably best bet.

PPPPS Mum confessed that Dad had told everyone in the golf club that I'm going to be on TV. He's setting the DVD player to record the show, just in case they can catch a glimpse of me.

8 April

Thought I saw Louise whiz by in a new Mercedes convertible when I was lugging mounds of shopping into the people-carrier in the car park at the Centre today. Hard to tell, behind the massive designer sunglasses, but almost sure it was her. Was instantly tearful and felt a real, physical pang of loss. Then realized the jumbo packet of nappies had strained my shoulder. But still. Very upsetting to see former friend carrying on with life in a devil-may-care-drive-at-forty-m.p.h.-through-the-car-park-and-endanger-young-children's-lives manner. Especially in a new Mercedes soft-top. May well have to call confidential police hotline and make official complaint about dangerous driving. And it wasn't even sunny so have no idea why she was wearing ridiculous oversized Gucci glasses. Real ones. Quite possibly dangerous to wear sunnies when there is no sun. Will add that to the complaint.

PS Nice policeman said if I don't have the car reg, he cannot file a report. Told him I had the person's name but he says that won't do. 'Sure then we'd have every Tom, Dick and Harry ringing us up to rat on people.' He snorted (rather unprofessionally, I thought). Will have to take this up with the Garda commissioner. Obviously children's safety is not a priority for the force.

PPS Will have to make sure to get a seat right at the back for TV show tomorrow night. Couldn't bear for glamorous ex-friend to see me out with mother-in-law.

PPPS Am quite anxious about *Doyle Tonight*. Ricky Doyle is quite sweet (even though he has had to endure all those vicious rumours about his sexuality all these years), but Mona is scary. The tabloids *hate* her. They call her Moaning Mona and are always photographing her looking rough with no bra on. She was meant to have gone mad when they did those before-and-after shots. Hope I don't accidentally get in her eye line.

9 April

Was in queue outside studios, Mrs H clutching my hand and gasping with the excitement of it all, when I spotted Jennifer Goode with a clipboard in her hand. Instantly recognized her from her photo on the website (glad to see she'd ditched the bad perm – it really did nothing for her round face). Decided it would be positively rude if I didn't say hello – after all, she and I are probably responsible for the development of a new women's show in the afternoons.

She looked a bit blank when I introduced myself – poor woman is completely overworked – but once she realized who I was she reacted with lightning speed. 'Kevin!' she yelled, shoving Mrs H and me at a skinny guy wearing a baseball cap back to front (very nineties but didn't want to say). 'These are friends of mine – make sure they get good seats, won't you?'

Was still glowing that Jennifer considers me a friend (knew we had connected) when skinny boy started shoving us through the throngs of people waiting to get into the studios. Tried to tell Jennifer that would catch her later to discuss programming issues, but she had disappeared into the crowd. Probably some high-level emergency. Thought Mrs H was about to have a panic-attack with unrestrained glee when skinny boy stuck large VIP passes in our hands (for free booze, he winked) and plonked us right in the front row. In the dead centre, right under the eagle eye of Mona Doyle.

'Isn't this fabulous?' Mrs H guzzled her second glass

of complimentary champagne. 'Everyone will be able to see us!'

Felt sick at the thought so let her have my champagne too.

Tried to compose face into I-am-unaware-of-the-cameras expression as best I could, and all went well until Mona announced that the next guest was going to be Samantha Brennan, presenter of hot new makeover show, *Duckling to Swan*. Everyone in the audience craned their necks to catch a glimpse of Samantha – former air hostess turned It girl (and possibly the new Amanda Byram according to last week's *Gazette*).

'Now, we need a volunteer,' Mona said sweetly. 'Samantha is going to give us a little demonstration of how the selection process for the *Duckling to Swan* works.'

'Susie, Susie, Susie!!' Mrs H propelled me out of my seat with the strength of a Titan.

Before I knew it, Mona was poking me in the bosoms with her microphone and asking Samantha Brennan if she thought a boob job would make them less droopy.

'Em, well, self-improvement starts with the inside – it's not so much the physical that's important, it's all about being happy with yourself.' Samantha threw me a kind look. (Comforting that she has the common touch, just like Amanda. Maybe she too will make it in America and earn a squillion dollars a year.)

'Interesting point, interesting point,' Mona continued. 'So, what you're saying is, she needs some therapy?'

'Em, not necessarily.' Samantha looked horrified. 'I mean, I've never met this lady before, so I couldn't say.'

'Yes, but she does look very downtrodden, wouldn't you say?' Mona continued, undeterred, rubbing my arm as I stood motionless, blinded by the lights, like some sort of halfwit. 'Of course, you'd have to get her out of that awful black as well – it's so ageing.' Mona smoothed her turquoise silk wrap top round her and tried to look concerned for my welfare.

'Well, the studio lights can be very draining . . .' Samantha trailed off, mortified. Out of the corner of my eye, could see skinny boy waving stick arms energetically to signal time was almost up.

'Ohhhkaaay,' Mona started to wrap it up. 'So, to sum up, you'd give her intensive therapy sessions to sort out her miserable personal life, then a full face-lift and boob job to sort out her miserable body. Fabulous. We'll put all the details on the website. Now, everybody, we'll be back after the break when Ricky will be interviewing Mr Gay Universe. Don't go away.'

10 April

Am still in complete and utter shock at total humiliation in front of an audience of millions. Am trying to console myself with the following:

• Did not speak so maybe people will not recognize me.
  Note: fact that 'Susie Hunt *Duckling to Swan*
  wannabe' kept flashing across the screen underneath
  my pallid face might have given the game away (have
  watched tape Dad made, and couriered to me,
  approximately twenty-five times). Also, the
  not-speaking did make me look like a complete nutter.

- Most people will have hectic social lives and will have missed the show (including Louise, hopefully).

  Note: unfortunately it is repeated on Sunday afternoons, when the people with the hectic social lives are usually lying on the sofa recovering from hangovers and eating Pringles.

- Mona came across as a complete and utter cow and was quite obviously humiliating me for her own devious purposes – i.e., that she is old and decrepit and has a gay husband.

  Note: unfortunately, this was quite entertaining for the uneducated man on the street. (My father seemed to find that bit particularly hilarious.)

The only up-side is, Mrs II made an even bigger fool of herself. You could plainly hear her shouting, 'You could do with a boob job yerself, Mona!' from the front row. Am quite comforted that mother-in-law was trying to defend my honour.

PS Joe is not talking to me. He is furious that

(a) I was totally humiliated on national TV, and that his fuddy-duddy senior directors were probably watching and marking his scorecard; and

(b) I allowed his mother to drink alcohol and shout abuse at the nation's best-known chat-show hostess.

Tried to explain that his mother is a force to be reckoned with, especially when there is free booze to be had, but it fell on deaf ears.

PPS Samantha Brennan is a lovely girl – not at all

uppity. She gave me a hug afterwards and said she was terribly sorry about it all. She even gave me her business card in case I ever want to have a chat about 'ageing with confidence'. I'm sure she meant well.

PPPS Really, really hope that Lone Father didn't see it. Think am quite safe – he's bound to hate anything as culturally trivial as *Doyle Tonight*.

11 April

In an effort to distract myself from crushing national humiliation have decided to throw myself into toilet-training Jack. Katie was well out of nappies at his age. Second time round, it should be easy-peasy.

PS Lone Father texted me. 'Saw u on TV!! That Mona is a btch . . . Think your boobs are perfect just the way they are.' Damn, damn, damn. What the hell was he doing watching that tripe? Surely he should have been creating some bestselling masterpiece, not watching useless Friday-night chat-show.

PPS Felt quite funny and flushed at boobs comment. He can be very flirty sometimes. Decided to play it cool and not reply.

PPPS Sent him a quick text, just so didn't come across as rude. Said, 'Thank you kind sir' – perfect I'm-not-bothered-by-crushing-national-humiliation tone.

12 April

Jack thinks toilet-training is a game and keeps prancing round the house with the potty on his head, yelling, 'Poo! Poo!' Am letting him do it – very important for him to be comfortable with his body and its functions.

PS Have changed him five times already as he keeps weeing on everything. He is now wearing a bright pink pair of leggings belonging to Katie as all his other clothes are wet. Forgot how draining toilet-training can be, but will persevere. Don't want him to have weird Freudian hang-ups about it.

PPS Just thought – wearing pink may give Jack a whole other set of Freudian hang-ups. Parenting is so tricky.

13 April

Just back from the children's hospital. Turned my back for five minutes (ten, tops) to catch up on celeb gossip (exclusive, shocking revelations about secret feuds between Lindsay Lohan and Paris Hilton absolutely riveting) and somehow, Jack managed to get the potty wedged on his head. Had to drive to A and E like a lunatic, Jack strapped into back seat, potty stuck on his head and wee dripping on to his shoulders. (Apparently, he managed to do one in it beforehand.) Katie's nose was firmly out of joint that she was not at the centre of the drama – am sure she tried to catch her fingers in the car door when we got there to even things up a bit.

The hospital staff took the situation dead seriously (once they'd stopped laughing, that is). They spent ages trying to figure out a way to get the blasted thing off, without taking Jack's head with it.

Was forced to give my brave little soldier lots of e-additives and colourants to comfort him during the trauma. Doctor types tried to tell me that all the crisps and fruity chews would only make him more hyper – but what would they know? Yes, they might have had years of medical training, but do they have any *children*? Ones they take home, that is. Sometimes, in these life-or-death emergencies, a mother knows best.

In the end, the A and E consultant was called. Was quite looking forward to having a George Clooney type smoulder at me over the bedpans but was very disappointed. Consultant had rank BO and was very fierce-looking – not a bit like George when he was on *ER* and at the height of his gorgeousness. He threw me dagger looks, as if I was some kind of deadbeat mum who didn't deserve to have kids, then beeped someone on his pager to join us. Was terrified they would have to admit Jack to Intensive Care, or fly him to Great Ormond Street, so was quite surprised when grungy-looking guy in smelly overalls arrived, wielding giant pliers in his unusually large hands.

'Who's that?' I squeaked, feeling faint.

'That's Eddie the handyman,' one of the male nurses whispered, in awe. 'He's only called for the really serious cases.'

Had to sit down, felt so woozy and light-headed. When I came to, Jack was bouncing round the day ward, potty-free, screaming, '*Can we fix it*? Yes, we can!'

at the top of his lungs. Eddie had apparently cut the potty off his head with the massive pliers while pretending to be Bob the Builder.

Was quizzing consultant on the risk of Jack having suffered serious, long-term brain damage, or irreversible skull deformity, when I spotted Katie in a huddle with some of the nurses. 'Yes, I've fallen down the stairs *loads* of times,' she announced, in a sad little voice, looking at me accusingly across A and E while the nursing staff huddled in the corner, nodding and whispering. Felt faint when two angry-looking ones approached me. Would be just like *Law and Order: Special Victims Unit* if Katie and Jack were hauled off by social workers and put in care because of unjust criminal system. Was gearing up to defend my good-mother status when the first spoke.

'Were you on *Doyle Tonight?*' she asked.

'Em, yes,' I said, kind of chuffed that my first official fan was going to ask me for an autograph.

'I *knew* it!' she whooped, while the other looked downcast. 'Maggie said it wasn't you, cos you looked a lot fatter on the telly, but I knew it was you. You owe me a pint, Maggie!'

'Yeah, OK, Sharon, it is her,' the other admitted, ignoring me. 'But her boobs looked a lot worse on TV. Maybe it was the lighting or something.'

And off they trundled, openly discussing my bits in broad daylight. At the tops of their voices. Celebs are always saying how Joe Public treats them like they're not real people. Now I know what they mean. Finally, I have something in common with Lindsay Lohan.

PS Dad says that if a mother knows best, how come

I let Jack get the potty stuck on his head in the first place? Mum says to ignore him. Honestly, he has no idea of how active toddlers can be.

PPS Have not told Joe about the potty fiasco. He is still very cross with me about *Doyle Tonight* and am a bit nervous he will accuse me of not watching Jack properly. Amazingly, kids haven't uttered a word about it so my secret might be safe.

PPPS Just thought. Maybe kids so traumatized by hospital experience that they have blocked it from their minds and it will only come to the surface thirty years from now when they go on a psycho killing spree. Am riddled with guilt.

14 April

Another humiliating morning at mother-and-toddler group – am getting used to it now. Marita and her cronies kept sniggering and shouting about Samantha Brennan and cosmetic surgery. Does everyone watch that blasted show? Was sure I'd read somewhere that its ratings were down.

Took the higher ground and decided not to comment. Lone Father seemed oblivious to it all. He is worried about his book – apparently his editor says it lacks oomph, whatever that means. He was distraught. Found myself thinking I'd like to cradle him to my bosom and take away his pain. Instead asked him back for coffee and Rich Tea biscuits. Threw my haughtiest look in Marita's direction as we left, but she was busy hauling her bra straps higher to stop the chicken fillets escaping.

PS Joe still in a huff. Honestly, you'd think it was him who'd been violated on national television.

15 April

Am in total flap. Nikki, booze buddy from London, arrived on my doorstep this evening with two identical (and rather chubby) little girls in tow. Thought she was a Jehovah's Witness at first so smiled in a kindly way and waited patiently for her to deliver her patter before I explained that I was perfectly happy with my own faith, thank you very much. Suddenly she launched into a very bad rendition of the Spice Girls' 'If You Wanna Be My Lover', pouting and pointing her finger *à la* Posh pre-fake-tan. Was about to congratulate her on taking a new and different approach to spreading the Good News when I realized who she was. We used to play the Spice Girls album on a loop in the London office and Nikki always baggsed being Posh. (I had to be Ginger Spice cos my boobs were the biggest.)

'Hope you have the champers on ice, Susie!' she bellowed, enveloping me in her skinny arms. 'I'm parched!'

Off she trotted to the fridge, teetering on her four-inch heels, the twins trailing sulkily behind her. Vaguely recall her having them with her Spanish shoe-importer millionaire husband, but in the photos she sent a few years back they were so cute – all smiles, curls and frilly matching frocks, not miniature scowling shot-putters.

Nikki seems to think she's staying with us. Have

sinking feeling I may have forgotten to call her and put her off. Joe is fuming – he never could stand her and he doesn't seem to have taken to her two kids either. They do seem particularly sullen for eight. Maybe they hate being identical twins. They seem to speak some weird language – can't understand a word they say. Katie's freaked because she can't tell them apart and because they refuse to talk to her and just glare at her balefully when she tries to engage them in Barbie chat. Even the dog is acting strangely and has taken to cowering behind me. Jack is the only one who doesn't seem to mind the new house guests. He keeps pulling his pants down and showing them his willy. Not sure they're impressed.

PS Haven't the heart to ask Nikki how long she plans to stay. Can't be for more than a few days. Hopefully, she'll be put off by having to share the spare room with the twins.

16 April

Absolutely exhausted. Nikki persuaded me to stay up drinking wine half the night 'just like the old days'. Couldn't be rude so drank a bottle and a half of Chablis to keep her company. Spent ages reliving hilarious memories of drunken nights and hung-over days in the London office. Can't imagine how we used to drink so much and turn up for work the next day. Funny how, in the olden days, you didn't feel like you were going to die the morning after. Nikki wanted to 'hit the town' but managed to put her off. Fell into bed after two a.m., head and stomach spinning, Joe grumbling about the noise keeping him awake.

All the wine seemed to have no effect on her. Stumbled downstairs to find her chain-smoking at the kitchen table, in full warpaint at eight a.m. Was congratulating her on her amazing stamina when she admitted she hadn't gone to bed.

Spent rest of day traipsing round Dublin, head throbbing, to show Nikki and her sulky twins all the tourist hot-spots. Discovered that Dublin really doesn't have that many.

Sulky twins moaned all the way that Dublin was crap. Natural-history museum was especially crap – all the dinosaurs were too small. In an effort to cheer them up, joked that all the biggest dinosaurs obviously liked the UK better and that maybe the Irish ones were smaller, distant cousins. Katie loved this idea and spent ages trying to explain the theory to passing Japanese tourists ('who are teeny-tiny too, Mummy!'), but sulky twins just blinked at me through slitted, suspicious eyes.

Nikki seemed oblivious to it all and drifted aimlessly, chain-smoking her way through dozens of Marlboro Lights. Tried to explain that smoking in all public places is now banned in Ireland, but she refused to believe me. 'Ha! Ha! Susie, you are a scream!' she guffawed, her Marlboro Light dangling dangerously close to a Tyrannosaurus Rex. 'Imagine! No smoking in Ireland! That's a good one, it really is.'

She was not so amused when the eighty-year-old security guard informed her that she would probably be arrested if she lit up indoors one more time, and spent the rest of the afternoon muttering darkly about

Big Brother, civil liberties and a Stalinist state. Feel I may take up drinking in a serious way.

17 April

Bloody Irish weather. How are you supposed to entertain demon visitors when it refuses to stop drizzling, even for five minutes? I can't work under these conditions. May well consider moving to France, buying a ramshackle old barn and becoming an award-winning wine producer.

Nikki and her sulky twins spent most of the day in front of the TV watching *Big Brother* highlights reruns. Tried to interest twins in a game of Monopoly but got blank stares. Meanwhile Nikki lay chain-smoking on the settee.

'I'm not sure this is suitable for the girls, Nikki,' I ventured, as two housemates frolicked naked in the *Big Brother* swimming-pool.

'They're fine,' she muttered, waving me away. 'You always were a bit of a fusser, Susie. They just want to chill out.'

Restrained myself from telling her that they looked like they need lots of fresh air and some serious exercise – best not to get involved in other people's idea of child-rearing. Each to her own and all that. May just leave a copy of *How to Raise a Happy Child* lying about, just in case.

'How's that friend of yours, Susie?' Nikki fired, obviously peeved about the insinuation that she was not Mother of the Year. 'What'shername . . . Laura?'

'Louise.' Nikki always accidentally-on-purpose forgot Louise's name – it used to drive Louise mad.

'That's right. *Louise*. Do you see much of her now?' Her steely gaze was unnerving, like that of some ruthless war-crimes interrogator.

'Not really. She's very busy – you know how it is . . .' I trailed off, at a loss to explain how a bitter, life-changing feud had turned us practically into sworn enemies.

'Oh, yes, I *know* . . .' Nikki stretched her arms over her head, almost setting light to the lampshade. 'She was always a stuck-up cow, anyway.'

Retreated to the kitchen to make more tea and sandwiches and reflect on that last comment, when Katie cornered me. 'Mummy, why are they so *weird*?' she stage-whispered loudly.

'They're not, darling.' I wearily buttered another loaf of sliced white for the twins. 'Not all girls like to play with Barbies.'

'All normal ones do.'

Decided not to tackle the Barbie-rules-the-world agenda.

'Daddy says they're *really* weird,' Katie continued, twirling her curls round a finger. '*And* he said that Auntie Nikki's a slob.'

'Well, let's not share that with Auntie Nikki, OK, pet?' I answered, resolving to have a serious discussion with Joe about age-appropriate dissemination of information. 'Daddy didn't mean it.'

'Well, no good will come of it, I can tell you that much,' Katie announced solemnly, then took her best Barbie upstairs for a haircut. (Quite worrying that she is using Mrs H quips at such a young age. Must tackle Joe about his mother's overbearing influence ASAP.)

Was finishing off buttering another sliced loaf when had to rescue Jack from sitting room – twin number one had dissolved into tears because he had squawked, 'Willy,' in her ear once too often.

PS Mum says I should try to reconnect with Nikki in a meaningful way. 'Good friends are hard to come by, Susie,' she proclaimed darkly, in a thinly veiled reference to Louise. 'You had lots in common with her once. Try to recapture it.'

Didn't want to tell her that unless I took up serious binge-drinking, smoking and snogging unsuitable men I wouldn't be able to reconnect with Nikki ever again.

PPS Consulted thesickkid.com about twins' weight issues and general behavioural problems – am convinced they're physically and emotionally fraught due to Nikki's *laissez-faire* attitude to parenting. Twin number two almost had total meltdown when Jack took a running jump at her this afternoon. As I suspected, it advised that eight-year-olds should be playing physically interactive games that fuel their imaginations instead of watching totally inappropriate adult shows that might warp their developing young minds. Am racking brain for things to play with them. Jenga, maybe?

18 April

Have decided Mum is right and am determined to rekindle old friendship with Nikki. We used to be really close in London – weeing-in-the-same-cubicle close –

and cannot just throw all that away. In attempt to reconnect and remember why I used to be friends with her in the first place, spent ages making what had been her favourite meal in London – pasta with king prawns and cream sauce.

'Thanks, Susie, that's sweet,' she said, when I presented it to her, with a flourish, on the best unchipped plate at lunchtime, 'but I don't do carbs any more. They really clog your heart.' Cue deep drag on Marlboro Light. 'I'll just stick to my Chablis.'

Don't think I've seen her eating since she got here – which is odd because the twins seem to consume enough to feed a small country. I'm buying sliced bread to beat the band, but it disappears faster than I can replace it. Nikki wanted to have another old-times session, but I pretended to have really bad period cramp so I could go to bed early.

'You should get the whole lot whipped out, Susie.' She waved her Marlboro Light with authority. 'I did, years ago. Gives you so much more sexual freedom.' Didn't want to ask why she needs sexual freedom when she's happily married to the Spanish millionaire. Seemed a bit inappropriate.

PS Keep having whispered arguments with Joe when everyone is tucked up in bed. He is demanding to know when Nikki and the twins will be leaving. 'We're spending a bloody fortune on wine, not to talk of all the food for those little monsters,' he fumed, tapping on his calculator to figure out how much cash it was taking to keep them fed and watered.

'Don't exaggerate,' I hissed. 'The twins don't eat *that* much, and Nikki doesn't eat at all.'

'Yes, but she could keep a small winery going,' he hissed back. 'She's obviously a raging alcoholic and those twins are complete loonies. What are they even doing here? They should be in school.'

'Maybe they're on their Easter holidays?' I ventured weakly.

'Easter, Susie,' he hissed, spit forming on his top lip, 'is well over. Something is up, and you'll have to find out what. I'm not putting up with this much longer.'

Am quaking. Cannot think of anything worse than asking her outright to vacate the premises.

PPS Plagued by Nikki's comment – am I a fusser?

PPPS Found excellent article on house guest from hell in the Sunday papers. It did not make pretty reading. Hid the supplement from Joe.

19 April

House of Horrors. Joe not speaking to me (again) because Nikki spent over an hour in the bathroom this morning and he wanted a shower. Tried to explain to him that she has never been seen in public without full camouflage makeup, and that applying three coats of foundation, plus blusher, false eyelashes and drawn-in eyebrows takes quite a bit of time, but he refused to listen and spent ages popping his head in and out of the bedroom door every time he heard a squeak on the landing.

Had to make another emergency run to the shop for bread supplies and arrived home, loaded with more sliced white loaves, to find Lone Father sitting at the kitchen table with Nikki, sipping wine and chatting cosily.

'Susie, you naughty girl,' Nikki tinkled. 'You never told me you had such a gorgeous friend. Where *have* you been hiding him?'

'Hi, Susie!' Paul called, looking delighted with himself. 'Nikki's been filling me in on your wild years in London – I know all your darkest secrets now!'

'Great,' I answered lamely, furious that Nikki had lured him to the dark side.

'Oh, I haven't told you the best one yet, Paul!' Nikki screamed, clasping his biceps totally unnecessarily. 'One time, she was so drunk she puked into someone's lap on the tube on the way home!'

More screeches of laughter.

Stomped off in annoyance to find the kids, whom I had entrusted to Nikki's care for all of twenty minutes. Found the twins, Katie, Jack and Rodney sitting in front of the TV open-mouthed watching two housemates on *Big Brother* scream abuse at each other.

'Mummy, what does "smelly whore" mean?' Katie asked.

'Why don't you ask your auntie Nikki?' I snapped, turning off the TV to howls of protest.

Spent rest of afternoon glaring at Nikki across kitchen table as she got more and more flirty with Paul. And he lapped it up. When he left, she fell on me, practically foaming at the mouth. 'He is *gorgeous*, Susie,' she panted. 'Are you shagging him?'

'Don't be ridiculous,' I snapped, terrified one of the children would hear. 'I'm a married woman and he's a married man. We're friends – that's all.'

'Yeah, right. That's why he lusts after you.'

'He does not,' I said, secretly a bit pleased that she thought he did.

'Oh, yes, he does – and you should do something about it. Let's face it, Joe's no Casanova, is he? When was the last time you had amazing sex with him? I'll bet Paul's dynamite in bed. He can certainly flirt for Ireland. You'd better be careful or someone else will snap him up.'

She tapped her Marlboro Light on the edge of the ashtray and gave me a meaningful stare. 'You seemed a bit put out that I was flirting with him. You wouldn't care if you had no feelings for him.'

'Were you? I really didn't notice, Nikki,' I answered, as casually as I could although my heart was pounding in my chest because I knew she was right.

'Yes, I was, but unfortunately he only has eyes for you, so I've no chance.'

Went beetroot with mortification and tried to hide by sticking my head in the fridge to find something for dinner. Am furious. And a bit intrigued. What if she's right and Paul really does lust after me? Bit exciting. Not that anything can ever come of it, of course.

PS Have decided that Joe is right – Nikki has to go. Will tackle her about her future travel plans/general arrangements regarding accommodation tomorrow. Will butter her up with a few stiff drinks first.

Nikki has confessed, over a bottle of duty-free blue-label vodka and a jumbo packet of Marlboro Lights, which she had hidden in her suitcase, that her marriage to the rich Spanish shoe-importer has fallen apart. Apparently in no small part because he found her in bed with their off-shore tax consultant. And they were not going over the figures, if you catch my drift. 'It was awful, Susie,' she sobbed, her defences weakened by four vodkas with cranberry juice. 'Juan just stood there, picking his teeth, and said he'd cut me off without a penny. I've thrown it all away for a quick romp between the sheets – and it wasn't even that *good*. How am I going to live?' More sobbing and wailing.

Was a bit flummoxed by revelation that Nikki has, in fact, been thrown out by her husband and is presently of no fixed abode. Thought she was ecstatically happy with him, but by all accounts he only cared about shoes and paid her no attention whatsoever.

'The really sad thing is, I still love him,' she hiccuped drunkenly, a few hours later. 'We used to have so much fun together before those fucking shoes took over his life.'

Am quite shaken by the sudden turn in events. First Brad and Jen, now Nikki and the shoe-importer. Who's next? Posh and Becks?

Admittedly, Nikki was always a bit flirty (distinctly remember a carry-on between her and a cocktail waiter in London), but never thought she'd actually engage in a full-blown affair. With sex. With a tax consultant.

'He was a boring little fart,' she confessed, cranberry juice trickling forlornly down her chin, 'and he hadn't a clue about sex, but he did pay me lots of attention. Don't you ever crave that, Susie, someone who thinks you're fabulous?'

Had nagging feeling she was on to something, but ignored it. Instead launched into really good speech about sanctity of marriage, how trust and commitment are key, not shagging off-shore tax consultants for a bit of attention.

'What if the guy is really sexy, though? Like your Paul? Is it OK, then?'

'He is *not* my Paul,' I answered firmly. 'And, no, that is not OK. Adultery is wrong in all circumstances.' Threw in lots of facts and figures about children of broken homes and how they can end up on drugs and in prison in an effort to impress upon her the vital importance of reconciling with the shoe-importer. Felt I was making headway when she fell into a reverential silence. In fact, spent ages pontificating about commitment and trust in an effort to persuade her to call her hubby and work things out. She was still silent and respectful. Eventually I realized she had passed out on the kitchen table. Tucked a blanket round her and left her snoring. Crawled into bed and had vivid erotic dreams about Lone Father feeding me grapes and telling me how gorgeous I am. Seemed to have had hair extensions in the dream – quite suited me.

21 April

Emerged from bedroom this morning after another fitful night's sleep to find Nikki and the sulky twins standing on the landing, suitcases at their feet. 'We're off, Susie.' Nikki beamed. 'I rang Juan last night and we had a heart-to-heart. We're getting back together!'

Flung my arms round her in sheer relief and bounded downstairs to start buttering the twins some bread for their homeward journey. Within ten minutes a grumpy taxi driver was banging down the door and they were gone, the twins clinging to their tinfoiled sandwiches as if they were lifejackets in a storm.

Was quite sad to see them go. Must be traumatic for the twins to be hauled halfway round the world with their parents at each other's throats – no wonder they're so sullen and silent. Am lucky that Jack and Katie are such happy, well-adjusted children.

PS Found mounds of uneaten bread under one of the beds in the spare room, most of it covered in green mould. Will wring those twins' necks if I get a chance.

22 April

Joe so delighted that the house guests from hell have departed that he took the kids to a movie and McDonald's for a treat. Decided to stay at home and have some well-earned Time to Myself. Was soaking in delicious bubble bath with a Boots extra-strength deep-conditioning treatment for seriously deranged locks slathered in my hair when the doorbell went. Decided to ignore it – probably window salesman or some other such annoying person. But it went again so emerged, fuming and dripping wet, to answer it.

It was Lone Father, brandishing a bottle of Chardonnay in one hand and a bunch of lilies in the other. 'Hi, Susie,' he muttered, looking rather sheepish, as I struggled to wrap the threadbare towel round me.

'Nikki's gone, Paul,' I answered, as icily as I could, heart thumping to see him so soon after my lust-filled dreams. Thank God, had just shaved legs in bath.

'Yes, I know – she texted me earlier.' He handed over the flowers. 'These are for you.'

Was even more furious to hear they swapped phone numbers – they'll probably engage in sensational sex-texting all the time. Nikki is officially off my Christmas-card list.

'Why are you giving me flowers and wine?' I asked, trying hard to remain dignified, aloof and focus on the facts at hand – i.e., he had flirted outrageously with Nikki in my house. Was quite difficult to avoid his lovely crinkly blue eyes, though.

'Because I was probably a bit tipsy the other day and I don't think you were too pleased with me. And it would kill me if you were annoyed. With me. Ever.' He stared at me in a funny way, and I felt a red blush creeping up my neck as if I was a hormonal teenager.

'Where's Rodney?' I asked, craning my neck round the door jamb to see if he was ready to pounce with his toy automatic rifle and scare me half to death.

'He's with Arabella.' He sniffed. 'She's going to look

after him for the afternoon.' He gave a small, bitter laugh. 'Where are your two?'

'Joe's taken them to the cinema.'

There was a silence and we realized we were alone for the first time. Ever. And there we were, staring at each other, like two lovestruck fools, and all I could think of was that I was naked under my towel and hadn't had a chance to pluck out the hair that always grows on my left nipple.

Then, as if he was moving in slow motion like something out of a Hugh Grant movie (well, any movie except *Notting Hill* – definitely casting cock-up: there was no chemistry whatsoever between him and Julia Roberts), he stepped into the hall, closing the door determinedly behind him, his eyes boring deep into mine. Without saying a word, he wrapped his arms round me and kissed me full on the lips before I had a chance to stop him.

23 *April*

Am practically fully fledged adulterer. Feel sick and excited all at once.

Reasons Not to Panic About Adultery

- Kiss was fairly short – approximately ten–fifteen seconds. However, am not completely sure about this because, just like in corny romance saga, time really did seem to stand still.

- Kissing a friend is not all that bad – celebs snog each other all the time and no one bats an eyelid. Angelina

Jolie even snogs her own *brother* and it's perfectly acceptable.

- There was no fondling of other body parts.

- Managed to extricate myself and ask him to leave before things got too heated and we threw ourselves on to the hall floor and had mind-blowing sex.

Reasons to Panic About Adultery

- Kiss was incredibly passionate – lots of sighing and gripping of hair just like proper movie kiss.

- Everyone knows that, in the sordid game of adultery, a kiss can be just as bad as a rampant ten-hour marathon sex session.

- Desperately wanted other body parts to be fondled.

- Feel I may only have asked him to leave because had not had chance to pluck Bearded Lady nipple hair, shave under arms or do bikini area (or vacuum dust bunnies on hall floor where possible mind-blowing sex would have taken place).

Cannot look Joe in the eye. Am decamping to Mum and Dad's ASAP to rethink whole sordid direction my life is taking.

24 April

Katie not impressed with sudden and unexplained removal from playschool for mid-week visit to grandparents. 'We're making ladybirds today!' she squealed, stamping her foot with rage that she was going to miss out. Jack joined in, flinging himself off the wall for effect. Calmed her down by making empty promise to find living, breathing ladybird in the country instead.

Joe seemed nonplussed that I was leaving. 'Have a nice time, love,' he called, not looking up from the file he was working on at the breakfast table.

'Thanks,' I yelled, shoving the kids into the car, relieved for once that he was preoccupied and I didn't have to speak to him. Felt pressing urge to blurt out whole horrible kissing episode, but sense Joe could turn us all on to the streets *à la* Nikki's shoe-importer so daren't. Must keep one stupid mistake to myself and live with the guilt for the rest of my days. Maybe I can confess on my deathbed. Just to get it off my chest. Drove off under a cloud of guilt and shame, old Mrs Kenny's curtains twitching next door as she monitored my every movement. Restrained myself from making an obscene gesture at her.

PS Was halfway down the motorway when I realized I really wanted to discuss disastrous, life-changing events with Louise. She would tell me what to do. However, in an impressive act of self-control, which involved a quick stop at a Maxol petrol station to purchase emergency supplies of chocolate and Pringles, I managed not to call her. She's obviously getting on quite nicely without me, so I'll have to do the same.

So much for being comforted in the bosom of my family. Mum and Dad are too busy talking about fund-raising for some charity or other to notice that I'm in dire need of serious counselling and that they should probably be calling in a professional as a matter of urgency.

'What's wrong darling?' Mum quizzed, as I blatantly ate the fourth Wagon Wheel in a row in front of her in a desperate cry for help.

'Just a bit down in the dumps, I suppose,' I said, reluctant to tell her the truth. Although I would have spilled my guts if she'd probed a bit.

'Well, gaining another five pounds isn't going to cheer you up,' she said (quite harshly I thought). She took the Wagon Wheel from my clammy hand and tossed it delicately into the bin, as if it were some sort of con-taminant. 'Now, you can come fund-raising with us this afternoon. It will help take your mind off things – there are always people a lot worse off than you.'

Spent afternoon shaking a tin in front of passers-by on the street corner; Mum reminding me every five minutes to smile, and Dad making jovial remarks to strangers about my teenage puppy fat hanging on in there. Katie and Jack collected almost a hundred and fifty euro between them. Feel a bit better that have collected some money for charity at least.

PS Have discovered that have not been collecting for charity, as previously thought, but for garish extension to the new golf club. Am total fraud. Katie and Jack have been declared the club's official mascots.

PPS Mum keeps prodding me to apply some makeup ('Look your best and you'll feel your best!'). Can't admit that to apply makeup would mean looking myself in the eye in a mirror.

PPPS No word from Lone Father. Perhaps he's feeling as guilty as I am.

PPPPS Still, he might have sent a quick text, to make sure I'm all right.

26 April

Finally Mum and Dad seem concerned for my health and well-being. Perhaps seeing me watch endless repeats of *The Osbournes* on MTV has alerted them to the fact that something is seriously awry. Have caught them whispering to each other in the hall a few times today – Dad seemed quite agitated and was flailing his arms round, saying something about 'golf tournament' and 'if you don't do something about it, I will' in a strange, strangled voice. Sweet of him to think a round of golf would improve my mood, but not sure it would work. Don't think I could bat away the guilt of an adulterous affair with a four-iron. If only they knew why I'm in such turmoil. Maybe I should pull myself together – don't want him having a heart-attack on my account.

PS Drawing lots of comfort from Sharon and Ozzy's seriously dysfunctional family. Maybe I should get a camera crew in and make millions from my misery and confusion. Wonder if Jennifer Goode at RTÉ would be interested.

PPS Thank goodness Joe is too busy being a captain of industry, blah, blah, to call.

27 April

Have decided that once-off kiss with Lone Father can be excused on the ground of insanity. Sleep deprivation can do serious damage to a woman's mental health – it's a well-documented fact. Anyway, one kiss is practically nothing compared to the stuff some mothers do when driven demented by demanding children and lack of shut-eye. At least I don't shoot up drugs in the utility room or hide vodka under the kitchen sink. Vow to forgive myself for one solitary error and absolve self of all unnecessary guilt. It will never happen again, so will wipe whole sorry episode from my consciousness.

PS Dad in great mood – spending lots of time watching some golf tournament on Sky Sports.

PPS Joe called, wanting to know when we're coming back. He must be running out of clean shirts and ironed underwear. 'By the way,' he said, 'I opened a bottle of Chardonnay you had in the fridge – it was delicious. We must get some more.'

Felt stab of guilt in my black heart. Little does he know he has been drinking the bottle of wine his love rival brought to seduce me.

28 April

Have been practising innocent one-kiss-does-not-mean-
I-have-committed-adultery expressions in the mirror.
Think I am doing OK, although a bit hard to tell as is
quite tricky to *do* the normal-nothing-untoward-here
expression and critique it at the same time. May need
Polaroid instant camera to gauge effect. Not sure they're
still manufactured, though, what with new digital inven-
tions – bloody technical progress isn't all it's cracked
up to be.

Dad caught me doing it in the bathroom mirror this
morning. 'Are you a bit constipated, love?' he bellowed.
'Fig juice'll sort you out – I'll make you a smoothie
right away.'

29 April

Katie is insisting that we find a ladybird to bring back for
playschool. 'Zoe's always bringing stuff in for the nature
table,' she announced, in front of Mum and Dad so they
would be sure to know how hopeless a mother I am.

Didn't want to be outdone by Eco-mother again so
spent all afternoon trudging round the field behind the
house searching for ladybirds. Managed to find a few
slugs, some earwigs and a snail, all of which Katie is
insisting on taking home in a shoebox that Dad gave
her. She and Jack now have dirt so engrained under their
nails that I fear they'll have to be surgically removed to
be clean again.

PS Mum and Dad dropping heavy hints that they're off to luxury country-house hotel in Cork for the weekend so we will be forced to leave. 'Joe's probably missing the children dreadfully, Susie,' Mum ventured, ironing a see-through lacy nightie carefully. 'Perhaps you should head back to the city – do something nice and cheerful together for the weekend.'

Didn't commit – am dreading going home.

PPS Still no word from Lone Father. He must have decided to wipe the whole sorry incident from his mind, too. Which is a good thing. Obviously.

30 April

Must grab bull by horns and go back to the city. Need to confront mistakes of the past before I can move on and all that. (Also, Mum and Dad blatantly packing their suitcases for luxury weekend away in full view in the living room. In front of the TV.)

Wish had taped the *Dr. Phil* special on forgiving yourself – can only remember bits and pieces. May write off for the tape.

PS Jack and Katie packing with gusto for return home (under Dad's direct supervision). Jack emptied an entire packet of corn flakes into his Bob the Builder rucksack. Meanwhile Katie refuses to be parted from her creepy-crawlies shoebox and has resolved to sleep with it beside her pillow. Don't want to refuse her – feel she may be acting out some deep-rooted fear about her parents separating. Children can be perceptive about that sort of thing.

1 May

Have discovered I'm a gifted actress. Did Academy Award-worthy performance greeting Joe home from work today. Quite difficult to do when standing at the scene of the crime – i.e., the front door. Luckily, he seems more distracted than usual – he droned on and on about some important deal being in danger of falling through, etc., etc. Tried hard to look as if I was listening to what he was saying as I tossed some sausages into the deep-fat fryer, but an image of Lone Father and me wrestling each other in passion kept flashing into my mind.

PS Tried to analyse Joe objectively as he sat snoring on the couch after dinner, dribble running unattractively down his chin. We used to be blissfully happy, so it's baffling that I'm developing this dangerous obsession with another man. Maybe all the preservatives in modern food are unhinging me.

PPS Katie and Jack are delighted to be home – they re-created the Amazon trail by spreading corn flakes up the stairs and into Katie's bedroom, then tried to bribe the creepy-crawlies along it.

2 May

Must get a grip. Mrs H dropped by today and am sure she suspects something. 'Are you all right, Susie dear?' she said, peering at me strangely.

'Yes, of course. Why wouldn't I be?' I answered,

panicking that she would see the guilt written all over my face and haul me off to the archbishop to be exorcized of my demons.

'You seem a little distracted,' she said, sipping her tea. 'Are you worried about anything?'

'Not really,' I answered, trying to fight back the tears. Am desperate to confide in someone, but don't think Mrs H would take kindly to the news that I have been unfaithful to her precious son. Even if no bodily fluids were exchanged (well, except saliva).

'Maybe we should organize another night out,' she said brightly. 'That would cheer you up.'

3 May

Nikki called from Cancún where she and the Spanish shoe-importer have gone to 'reconnect' (without the sulky twins in tow). 'It's like we're on a second honeymoon, Susie,' she babbled. 'In fact, I can't recommend infidelity highly enough – it's brought us so much closer together. You should definitely give it a go!'

Didn't want to rain on her parade by reminding her that less than a week ago she was bitterly regretting her fling. Nikki always had a short memory. May have something to do with all the hair-straightening solutions she used in London to look more like Posh in pre-GHD days.

4 May

There are posters of Mona Doyle, Samantha Brennan and me plastered all over Dublin. Was driving to the supermarket today when I spotted an enormous bill-board straight ahead and almost ran over a little old lady and her German shepherd. It's obviously a still from the show because Mona is poking me in the boobs, while Samantha watches and I look dazed and confused in the centre. Under the picture, in neon-pink lettering, is the slogan '*Get it off your chest with* Doyle Tonight!'

Feel seriously violated. Am considering suing. Surely they have to ask my permission before they launch big-budget publicity campaign?

Mum rang to say there are posters of me in Cork too. There is one right on the road outside the luxury country-house hotel. My God – they're conducting a nationwide campaign.

Burst into tears when I heard her voice. Think it may have something to do with the strain of near-adultery coupled with crushing national humiliation.

'Don't cry, darling,' she soothed. 'You look lovely and natural – not like that Mona Doyle. She looks like a dog's dinner. You always took a lovely photo.'

'It's not lovely, Mum,' I gulped, unable to stop crying. 'One of my eyes is half shut *and* it looks like I have no chin!'

'That's only because Samantha Brennan has such wonderful bone structure, darling. Honestly, you look so pretty. Very homely, in fact.'

Could hear Dad laughing and shouting a lot in the background – something to do with three chins.

Decided to pull myself together and send Jennifer Goode at the network a stiffly worded email to get to the bottom of it. Just because we're friends it doesn't mean she can take advantage of me – must put her in her place. Don't like doing it, but have to take a stand some time.

> Hi Jennifer, Hope all is fine with you. [(Had decided to get straight to the point.)] I am writing to you to express my shock and horror at seeing my image all over posters in the city advertising *Doyle Tonight*. I almost crashed the car, causing myself and my two defenceless young children serious harm and injury, when I spied one today. My mother informs me that the campaign has now gone nationwide. Surely I should have been notified before my image was brandished about willy-nilly? I must say that I am very disappointed on a personal level that you should do this. I would appreciate it if you could get back to me soonest. Best regards, Susie

Got almost instant reply – very gratifying.

> Dear Susie, Thank you for your email. As sales and marketing co-ordinator, I am not actually responsible for the advertising campaigns as we use an outside agency. However, I can understand your concern and I did contact the legal department about your predicament. Unfortunately, there is very little that can be done in this instance as the disclaimer form

that all the studio audience guests signed before the show is very comprehensive and covers the use of your image by the company for promotional purposes. In fact, the phrase John in Legal used was 'watertight'. Sorry if this comes as a shock, but look on the bright side – you'll be almost famous!
Best wishes,
Jennifer Goode

Can vaguely remember signing something before I went into the studio. How was I to know it would lead to this? No one ever reads the fine print.

PS Hopefully, Joe is so distracted by work he won't notice the forty-foot images of me all across town. Don't think he would be very understanding.

5 May

Joe called to say he has to go to Los Angeles for a few weeks! Was delighted – work/holiday break bound to do us all the world of good, especially with all the adultery and so forth. Lots of sun and serious designer shopping bound to wipe all traces of guilt from my mind quick as a flash. Spent the afternoon fantasizing about a few weeks' R&R in top-notch hotel with three pools and on-site spa. Called him back to ask what child-care facilities his company will be providing for the children in LA. Should be easy to organize – Katie will be thrilled to prance round in a Barbie bikini for a few weeks and Jack will be happy as long as there is lots of physical activity, such as windsurfing for toddlers.

Joe seemed a bit stumped by my question. 'What are you talking about, Susie? The children aren't coming,' he snapped.

'Well, who's going to look after them when we're away?' I asked, a bit put out that full-time child-care was not included in the work/holiday deal.

Joe then spent the next five minutes explaining to me, as if I were a five-year-old child, that he was travelling alone to LA – i.e., without the excess baggage that he seemingly considers his wife and two children to be. Spent afternoon surfing job websites. Obviously he will have to leave present blood-sucking company and take a job elsewhere.

6 May

In defiant act of putting career before family, Joe is not resigning. He is, in fact, going to LA for an undefined amount of time, leaving me to cope with two hysterical children and one overwrought mother-in-law, who keeps ringing every five minutes to sob that she doesn't know how she'll manage without him. Especially if her washing-machine blows up again.

PS Katie has announced that she wants Joe to buy her a pair of cut-off shorts, a crop top and some rollerblades in LA so she can look like Malibu Barbie.

PPS Am officially not speaking to Joe. His disregard for the family unit and willingness to abandon us all on a whim is most disturbing.

Bumped into Lone Father in the frozen-food section of the supermarket. Tried in vain to hide behind a super-jumbo pack of chicken nuggets, but he saw me instantly. He looked adorable, all hollow-eyed and distraught. Has probably spent endless nights agonizing over our stolen kiss and wondering how he will live without me. He has definitely lost weight. Tried to suck in my ample jelly belly, which has become even more ample since I've munched my way through approximately a million packets of custard creams since our adulterous snog.

'Hi, Susie,' he said quietly, giving me his gorgeous, heart-stopping, lop-sided grin. 'I wouldn't have taken you for a chicken-nugget kind of girl.'

'Hi, Paul,' I rasped, my tongue suddenly twice its normal size. 'Gosh, no, never eat them – full of eyeballs and testicles, did you know that?' Mortified that I'd mentioned part of the male genitalia, I continued yammering at several knots per hour until, mercifully, Jack and Rodney started belting each other with abandon and we had to prise them apart with Jelly Tots.

Thank goodness first awkward meeting after furtive kiss is over and done with. Can now move on with rest of sad, empty life as practical single parent. Have decided to start eating fig rolls again – custard creams do not hold all the answers.

PS Got text from Lone Father on way home: 'I miss u.' Extremely heart-wrenching *à la* Cathy and Heathcliff. Did not reply.

8 May

Had weird erotic dream that Lone Father and I were out on the moors, entangled in each other's arms, kissing passionately, when suddenly Joe was striding across the bracken in plus-fours, wielding a birch stick. We tried to escape, but all the heather on the misty, romantic moors got knotted in our hair and we were left powerless. Then, out of nowhere, Samantha Brennan galloped up on a big white stallion and whisked me away, leaving Joe and Lone Father to beat each other senseless. Does this mean am really closet lesbian? Very confusing.

9 May

Epiphany. In some sort of cosmic message directed specifically at me, Oprah has come to my rescue. The woman deserves another Emmy at the very least. In a special edition all about men and women being best friends, Sam and Molly from Arkansas were interviewed. They have been best friends since their mid-thirties, when they discovered they had a shared interest in flower-arranging.

'Were you ever sexually attracted to each other?' Oprah asked, squinting and looking intense.

'Oh, yes, we went through that phase!' Molly laughed gaily. 'We kissed once, but then we realized we cared more for each other as brother and sister than lovers.'

'And how did your spouses feel about your friendship?' Oprah asked. 'Weren't they jealous?'

'Oh, no.' Sam smirked. 'They know they have nothing to worry about – men and women can be friends without sex entering the equation.'

They giggled happily, delighted with themselves.

The camera panned to the two spouses in the front row, who were scowling and didn't look altogether thrilled with the arrangement.

But a weight has lifted from my shoulders! Had one slight blip in friendship with Lone Father, but that's not to say we can't move on, develop lifelong friendship and start flower-arranging classes together. Thank God for Oprah. Immediately sent him a cheerful 'Let's do coffee,' text. Will meet him next week. When Joe goes away. Although could meet him when Joe is still in the country. Have nothing to hide. In fact, will introduce Lone Father to Joe. As soon as he gets back from LA. We'll probably end up going on double dates together and laughing about any silly misunderstandings.

PS Have sneaking suspicion that Dr. Phil would have ripped Sam and Molly apart like a savage bulldog, but am trying to put that from my mind.

PPS Lone Father says he would love to meet for coffee and will call over on Thursday at two. Luckily there is no need to engage in any major exfoliation, defuzzing or beautifying extravaganza as we are now on the road to innocent, asexual friendship, like Molly and Sam, and it will be of no consequence if froth from my latte gets stuck in my moustache.

10 May

Joe flew to LA this morning. Had planned tearful good-bye in Departures, with both kids hanging off his legs sobbing uncontrollably, just to remind him of how he is abandoning his family, etc., etc., but for first time known to man, both kids slept until past eight so he had already crept out. Suspect he may have slipped them both some sort of tranquillizer.

Katie and Jack thrilled with little notes he left on their pillows to tell them he loved them and would see them soon. (Very touching, but with no specific return date outlined.)

'Mine says he's going to buy me an iPod,' Katie announced, elbowing Jack in the ribs.

'IPod, iPod!' Jack screeched.

'You are too little to get an iPod, stupid,' she replied witheringly. 'You have to be at least four and a half, don't you, Mummy?'

Felt momentarily guilty to see that Joe had left me a note as well, propped up beside the kettle. Guilt vanished when saw note had handwritten instructions to leave the bins out on Wednesdays, pay the electricity bill and double-lock the doors at night. This is what we have come to. No wonder I fell prey to the seductive charms of Lone Father and his come-to-bed eyes.

Mrs H called in, looking mournful and downtrodden. 'Poor Joe,' she said sadly, stirring a third spoonful of sugar into her tea. 'All that travel isn't good for you, you know. It can make you very irregular.'

'Really?' I wondered how long she was planning to stay and if I should suggest some light cleaning to take her mind off her son and his bowel movements.

'Oh, yes, you can get quite bunged up. Do you think we should post him some laxatives?' She looked a bit brighter at the prospect.

'Why don't you do that?' I suggested, eager to get rid of her once I'd grasped she was not going to tackle the ironing.

'Thanks, Susie,' she said, a lot more cheerful. 'It's very hard on me, what with having two emigrant sons. Us girls will have to stick together.'

PS It *is* a bit strange now Joe has gone. Am on alert for children pining and reacting with serious antisocial destructive behaviour. Jack bit less boisterous than usual – he let me wash his face this morning. Feel his spirit may be broken.

12 May: Our Wedding Anniversary

Eight years ago today I swept down the aisle to 'Islands in the Stream', positive that my life would be one big romantic fairytale of warm croissants and freshly squeezed orange juice in bed, interspersed with long, romantic walks and cuddling by the fireside with a jumbo tube of Pringles to share. In fact, I was so positive that Joe was my soulmate I almost clocked Louise when she asked me if I was sure I wanted to go through with it. 'Don't be ridiculous,' I hissed, through gritted teeth, conscious of the sweaty cameraman recording every blessed minute. 'Joe is the *love of my life*. He *completes* me.' (This was back in the days when someone completing you was a good thing, way before Oprah decided that, actually, you should be financially and emotionally self-sufficient before you commit yourself to your life partner. Seems a bit pointless to get married at all, really, if you're that sorted.)

Perhaps I should have taken Louise more seriously. Then maybe my marriage wouldn't be a shambles. Really miss her sometimes. Wonder how she is.

PS Joe didn't even call to wish me a happy anniversary.

13 May

First stab at best-friends-with-no-sexual-tension scenario went appallingly. Lone Father arrived at two on the dot. Spent first five minutes pretending everything was fine and chatting inanely like two pensioners about how freakishly cold it was for the time of year. Then, the minute the kids went outside, we pounced on each other and snogged again over the kitchen sink while Jack and Rodney played Spiderman in the garden, oblivious to their parents' wickedness.

'I think I love you, Susie,' Paul whispered, raining

butterfly kisses down my neck and across my shoulder-blades — the sexiest part of a woman, according to this month's *Prima*. Luckily had worn my boat-neck M&S T-shirt in freakish act of destiny.

'No, you don't,' I said, half thrilled and half appalled.

'Yes, I do,' he murmured. 'You're so sexy, and you don't even know it, which makes you even hotter.'

'No, I'm not.' I giggled breathlessly, hoping he would elaborate and thanking the Lord I'd changed my mind about not de-fuzzing the hairy lip.

'Oh, yeah,' he growled. 'The way you look at me is *sooo* sexy. And the way your bum wiggles when you walk drives me crazy.'

Were interrupted when boys came galloping back into kitchen, screeching for juice and mini KitKats. Spent rest of afternoon throwing smouldering looks at each other over Bob the Builder jigsaws.

For first time in life, felt like a siren. Quite liked it. Except for bum-jiggling comment.

2 a.m. Cannot sleep. What am I doing? May be officially embarking on affair with a married man, like something out of *True Confessions Weekly*. Before you know it, our former partners will get together and do a tell-all interview detailing our deceit and betrayal. With close-up unflattering photos of Paul and me scurrying into our rented caravan somewhere in exile. Am worried that lives will be ruined and children scarred for life. Am also panicked by his declaration of love. He will probably want us to set up home together with Katie, Jack and Rodney, just like the Brady Bunch. Except, of course, our other halves wouldn't be dead: they would be bitter divorcees intent on revenge. It all seems so surreal.

14 May

Spent all day sending hot and heavy texts to Lone Father and receiving same in return. Can now understand why Becks and Rebecca Loos allegedly got so hot and bothered by it. You can say all sorts of smutty things to each other you never would usually. Was mortified by first few, but got hang of it eventually.

Paul: 'Want to kiss you all over.'

Me: 'Sounds nice . . .' (Lame, but sex-texting can take a bit of getting used to.)

Paul: 'What do you want to do to me?'

Me: 'Kiss your earlobes?' (Second sexiest part of a woman according to *Prima*, so probably applies to men as well.)

Paul: 'You tease . . .'

Can't believe I engaged in proper sex-texting session. Totally neglected children and allowed them to sit, trance-like, in front of Nick Jr. all afternoon. Am like robot on automatic pilot. All can think about is Paul. We're making feverish plans to meet again, alone this time, and 'talk about things'. Am really jittery and flushed. May never need to use Clarins Beauty Flash Balm again, ever.

15 May

Sex-texting continuing unabated. Only problem is, am sort of running out of kinky things to say. Bought *Cosmopolitan* in corner shop this morning to get a few ideas. Was outraged by racy content. My God, this is what Katie will be reading in a few years' time! Am seriously considering writing to Ombudsman or Advertising Standards Authority or some such. Surely this type of stuff should not be freely available on corner-shop shelves. Am also looking into private convent education for Katie and a total ban on all adult-related material until she is at least twenty-five.

Meanwhile, in freaky Mothers-are-Intuitive-Beings-who-know-when-you're-Up-To-Something fashion, Mum has cottoned on that something is amiss. 'Your dad and I are thinking about coming to visit you and the children, darling,' she announced firmly, when she rang. 'I'm sure you must be dreadfully lonely without Joe.'

'I'm fine, Mum, honestly,' I said, aghast that she was planning an impromptu visit. 'The kids are keeping me busy and I've lots to do.' How can I indulge in another full day of sex-texting if Mum and Dad are on the premises, watching my every move with their beady hawk eyes and 20–20 vision thanks to all the carrot and orange smoothies?

But Mum wouldn't take no for an answer. 'We insist, darling – we'll be on the three o'clock train tomorrow. See you then!'

Damn, damn, damn. Must practise looking less like excited schoolgirl and more like pining wife.

PS Joe called from LA. 'So, what's it like?' I asked, trying to sound innocent. 'All blondes with false boobs whizzing round on rollerskates I suppose.'

'Dunno. Haven't seen any of it. I've been in meetings all day.'

There was an awkward silence so I passed the phone

to Katie to say hello. This is the nub of the problem: there are five thousand miles between us emotionally as well as physically. Very depressing.

16 May

Paul thinks parents descending in unexpected ambush (well, on the three o'clock train, but still) might work in our favour.

Had spent ages plucking up courage to dial his number to discuss catastrophe that is impending visit of eagle-eyed relatives.

'Hi, babes,' he purred, when he answered. 'Have you called to talk dirty to me?'

Was absolutely mortified at thought of saying intimate things *out loud* so laughed that off, explained the situation and that we wouldn't be able to talk to or see each other until pesky parents had gone home.

'Couldn't you get them to babysit and tell them you're meeting a girlfriend?' he wheedled. 'It's the perfect opportunity for us.'

'Em, yes, I suppose,' I said, not keen on lying to Mum and Dad, but desperate to see him again, have a proper conversation and discuss Our Situation.

'Great,' he breezed. (A bit businesslike, I thought.) 'Arabella's off tomorrow morning so I'll tell her I have a meeting with my editor and she'll take Rodney. I'll meet you at the Holiday Inn on Cobbler Street at eleven.'

Then he was gone. Was a bit annoyed he'd been so short with me. Also feel a bit funny about all this blatant plotting. Wish he hadn't mentioned Arabella and Rodney. Obviously have never met Arabella and am sure she is a selfish, unsupportive cow, but am quite fond of Rodney, even if he is a bit rough with Jack. Just as well, really – he'll probably be my stepchild any day now.

PS Got text from Paul: 'Sorry couldn't really talk babe. Can't wait 2 c u. Ur txts driving me insane. If don't c u soon, will explode.'

Giggled girlishly at that, but was a bit alarmed. What if he was referring to real, honest-to-goodness sex? Oh, God, I may have to go to bed with someone other than Joe. Not sure I'll remember where to put what. And suppose he wants me to talk dirty to him? Will quite definitely die of embarrassment. Bad enough he'll see my stretchmarks, varicose veins and cellulite bottom.

PS Wonder why he wants to meet at the Holiday Inn – that's a bit out of the way.

PPS Have hand-washed silk négligée.

PPPS Have decided against bringing silk négligée. Way too old-fashioned and contrived. Also, will probably be so overcome with passion that will just rip each other's clothes off and get to it against the wall or somewhere equally outrageous.

PPPPS Feel teeny bit sick.

17 May

Bloody hell and damnation. Didn't make it to Holiday Inn. Dad tripped and fell over Jack's Tinky Winky Teletubby on the stairs so had to bring him to A and E. Was convinced he was faking it and tried to persuade him to put his leg up and watch Sky Sports for a bit, but Mum insisted. Of all the times for her to become a fusspot she had to go and do it when I was off to seal my fate and possible future happiness with Lone Father. Was livid.

'But, Mum,' I pleaded, 'I have to meet a friend. It's Very Important.' Voice was trembling with anxiety (and possibly a bit of suppressed lust).

'You're not saying, Susie,' she enunciated, very slowly and carefully, 'that meeting this friend is more important than bringing your father to be attended to at the hospital?'

Stomped off to hospital very cross. Am sure Dad deliberately sabotaged my meeting with Paul. Not sure how, but seems too much of a coincidence.

Even doctor was in on the conspiracy. 'You've sustained a very nasty sprain there.' He shook his head as if he'd not seen such a serious injury in years. 'In fact, you're very lucky you didn't break anything.'

'Yeah, like his neck,' I grumbled, still fuming that my tryst had been thwarted and that Paul might have been trailing his fingers down my spine *at that very second* if I wasn't stuck in A and E.

'Actually, toys left on stairs are one of the primary factors related to household accidents.' The doctor stared at me intently, as if he was trying to place me. 'In fact, I've had people in here with extremely serious neck and back injuries because of children's toys.'

Then he paused, scanning my face. 'Don't I know you from somewhere?'

'No, I don't think so,' I said, suddenly developing a riveting interest in Dad's ankle area.

'Hmm . . . You look very familiar.'

Bluffed my way out of it. Couldn't admit he was the same doctor who'd treated Jack when he'd had the potty stuck on his head. Don't want to be hauled before the courts for infant *and* geriatric abuse.

All went over Dad's head. He was too busy adopting his cheerful-under-fire, lived-through-a-war-and-nothing-can-be-as-bad-as-that persona. 'Good thing I'm so physically fit and active, eh?' He winked at the junior nurse who was briskly bandaging his ankle. 'Guess what age I am?'

'I have no idea,' the nurse deadpanned back, well used to old-timers trying to impress her.

'Go on, have a guess.' Dad grinned at me knowingly over her head.

'Seventy?' the nurse said, rolling her eyes to heaven.

Had to take Dad for stiff drink to stave off shock of someone thinking he was anything over fifty-five.

Locked myself in the pub toilets to text Paul and explain why I couldn't meet him. Got terse one-word text back: 'OK.'

Was in serious mental anguish. What did it mean? Was he furious I had to stand him up? Would he ever want to see me again? Could have cried with frustration. Agony perpetuated when arrived back to house and found Mum teaching Katie and Jack the dog position in the front room. All was quiet, calm, serene with not a TV in sight.

'I'm going to show all my friends how to do yogi tomorrow,' Katie said, through her legs. 'Granny says it's very good for your posing.'

'Posture, darling,' Mum corrected, peeling herself off

the carpet and stretching nimbly, then giving Dad a quick peck.

'What have you done to your father, Susie?' She frowned as Dad swayed in the doorway, muttering about hair thinning and Botox.

'The doctor said to give him a few brandies,' I lied. 'For the shock.'

'Hmm.' Mum wasn't too convinced. 'Some chamomile tea would have been a lot better, but never mind, let's get him off to bed. I need to have a chat with you.'

And, with an ominous glance, she steered Dad upstairs, weaving him gingerly through a path of Lego, Jack's cars and various Barbie-related accessories.

18 May

Desperate to see Paul, but have to get rid of Mum and Dad first. Unfortunately, Mum is hovering round every corner like some sort of omnipresent being. She thinks I need to take up a hobby. 'You seem so stressed, darling,' she hummed, handing me another cup of elderflower tea and a pile of brochures for *t'ai-chi* classes in the parish hall as Jack ate his way through a box of finger-paints. 'It's not good for the children to be around so much anxiety. I'm sure that's why Jack's hyperactive. If you're not careful, he'll be on Ritalin next.'

Almost confided in her about Lone Father/brink of full-blown affair scenario but was put off when she started lecturing me about Joe having enough stress on his plate, trying to create a sustainable career, without me adding to it, blah, blah, blah. Don't know where she gets these nineteenth-century ideas of marriage from. Wouldn't surprise me if she had me shuffling along behind Joe in a subservient manner like a surrendering wife next.

Feel like popping a few Ritalin myself – sure they're miles better than elderflower tea for calming, soothing and generally blocking out all thought. 'This tastes like cat's wee, Mum,' I said, suddenly bone weary and desperate to get away. 'I'm going to lie down. I have a headache.'

'How do you know what cat's wee tastes like, Mummy?' Katie piped up from behind the door.

PS Picture of *t'ai-chi* instructor on front of brochure looks suspiciously like glam-mummy Marita from mother-and-toddler group! The at-one-with-the-universe look is marred by acrylic nail extensions and chicken fillets straining out of leotard, though.

PPS No news from Paul. Am tearing out my thinning hair.

19 May

Jack has taken to limping round the house, pretending he's an invalid like his grandad. Meanwhile, Dad has taken over the front room and is watching Sky Sports round the clock, Mum is whipping up organic smoothies to fight ageing free radicals, and Katie is bandaging every-thing in sight, from bananas to table legs.

In an effort to distract myself from lustful thoughts, initiated discussion with other housewives at school gate about whether Nick and Jessica will ever get back together and if making *Newlyweds* was their downfall. Suddenly, out of nowhere, Eco-mother strode purposefully up to the gate, shoving the buggy with one hand and waving flyers with the other. Everyone fell silent, terrified she would discover that not only do we all own at least two TVs but that we watch reality shows at random and do not choose one educational, culturally diverse show from the Discovery Channel or National Geographic every week. Am positive she has never even heard of *Newlyweds*, what with all the knitting and baking and teaching four-year-olds to read freakishly early.

'Now, ladies,' she bellowed, 'I'm recruiting volunteers to help the aged in the community. If any of you have a few spare hours on your hands, I could use some help.' We looked at each other guiltily, mumbling about being snowed under with other commitments. Let's face it, working with old dears isn't exactly sexy, is it? Would prefer to host some charity ball, *à la* Elton John and David Furnish, instead of having to deliver meals on wheels.

'I'll give you a cheque,' I volunteered, rummaging in my bag, delighted with myself for having thought of it. Am definitely a generous, giving person who happens to be over-committed in other areas of life. Also, donating to worthy cause will help quash feelings of adulterer's guilt, and suspicion that I will now never be nominated for the sainthood for services to children.

'*Actually*, Susie, an hour of your time would be a lot more use to me,' Eco-mother said pointedly, her kaftan flapping round her hairy ankles.

Felt hot rage bubbling to the surface. Most out of

character, so am definitely under horrendous stress and strain of the type to make you lose your marbles and shoot strangers in the street.

'*Actually*,' I snapped, in retaliation, 'I already have my invalid parents living with me so I feel I'm doing my fair share. Now, you either accept my generous donation or you don't. It's all the same to me.'

There was silence as we stared at each other, all the other mums looking on agog. Then Eco-mother dropped her eyes and backed away, mumbling something under her breath about social responsibility to no one in particular. Feel enormously self-satisfied with victory. No wonder politicians wear those smug grins – it's very gratifying to be powerful and in control. Also, a lot of the other mothers were looking at me with new respect.

PS However, do feel bit guilty for lying about invalid parents. Hope have not wished ill-health on them now, in some sort of bad, lying karma. Although was not technically lying. Dad is practically disabled right now, and Mum may well get that way if she continues with all those ridiculous yoga contortions.

20 *May*

Buzz from humiliating Eco-mother has vanished. Now feel strangely empty and as if I'm yearning for something. Think it may be Lone Father.

Mum dragged me along to *t'ai-chi* in the parish hall this morning. Tried in vain to get out of it, but could hardly explain that the hall held too many painful memories related to Lone Father and our doomed, tragic love affair so had to go along. Luckily, did not have to change as was already wearing regular uniform of trackie bottoms and trainers. Pulled up outside hall to see stream of *t'ai-chi* devotees on their way home, looking absurdly pleased with themselves and glowing with inner peace.

'Oh, no,' Mum wailed. 'I must have got the time wrong.'

Was delighted. *T'ai-chi* is definitely not my cup of tea. But Mum insisted on going into the hall to ask the instructor time of next class. And there, clad in a neon-pink G-string leotard, more suited to an eighties aerobics class than touchy-feely *t'ai-chi*, was glam-mummy Marita, her arms wrapped round some poor guy and her acrylic nails (sporting the star-spangled banner) tangled in his dark curly hair. We stood, watching uneasily and waiting for them to finish their tonsil tennis for what seemed like ages, until Mum did a few loud coughs. They came up for air and turned to face us.

Felt blood draining from my face when I saw him. Marita's latest victim was Lone Father – in a sweaty Adidas T-shirt and bicycling shorts.

22 May

Still in shock. Lone Father was never in love with me. In fact, he is low-life love-rat worthy of an entire *Cheaters* special. Now I know what it feels like to go weak at the knees as felt them buckling with shock when Lone Father disentangled himself from Marita and looked at me. Luckily the wads of cellulite that protect my knee-caps came into their own.

'Oh, hi, Susie,' Marita drawled. 'Sorry about that. Paul is always so *keen*.' Then she pushed him playfully, while he readjusted his sweatbands and had the good grace to be shamefaced.

'Did you want to sign up for *t'ai-chi*?' Marita looked from my mother to me quizzically.

'Yes, I thought we did,' Mum said, glancing at me strangely, 'but I don't think this is exactly what we're looking for, is it, darling?'

'No, I guess not,' I stuttered, and let her lead me blindly from the hall, eyes stinging.

Feel totally and utterly betrayed. And a complete fool. Almost sliced my little finger off in a blur of tears while chopping carrots for Dad's smoothie. Not that anyone would care if I became an invalid and had to live in an assisted-care facility.

'Will I bandage it for you, Mummy?' Katie asked, leaping into action with her box of Barbie plasters. 'I'm Supernurse, you know. I can mend anything.'

Didn't want to burst her bubble and tell her a broken heart can't be mended.

Had horrible dreams all night – Marita chasing me round the parish hall in neon pink, followed by Joe, Lone Father and the Dalai Lama. Am such a fool. In fact, feel worse now than I did when horrible sagging face was plastered on forty-foot posters all over Dublin city and regions. And that's saying something.

Got grovelling text from Lone Father: 'Sorry, Susie, you are so special to me.'

Will not, under any circumstances, text him back. He is a weak, spineless toad, not cultured New Man, as previously thought. Can't believe I ever fell for him. Thank God only shared a few kisses and nothing more.

Keeping busy with kids – made entire Play-Doh village this afternoon, then spent ages mushing all the people into the floor. Quite comforting.

PS Oh, my God. Am at wit's end. After bottle of Pinot Grigio, sent Lone Father text: 'You are a weak, spineless toad, not cultured New Man as previously thought. Can't believe I ever fell for you. Thank God we only shared a few kisses and nothing more.'

Got text back from Joe in LA, asking what the hell was going on. In drunken haze, had sent text to him by mistake. He is ringing in next hour when he 'gets out of very important meeting'. Whole world is caving in.

11.30 p.m. Have unplugged phone and turned off mobile. Need more time to concoct web of lies.

Confessed whole sordid tale to Mum. She was furious with me.

'You are a complete fool, Susie,' she barked – most out of character, so I knew things were Very Serious. 'Joe may be boring, but he adores you and the children. How could you have put all that at risk for a fling with that greasy cretin?'

Tried to explain that Lone Father hadn't seemed like greasy cretin at the time. He seemed intelligent, cultured and well-read. More importantly, he thought I was 'hot'.

At this, Mum sighed a lot and went on about fulfilling yourself before finding fulfilment with someone else, blah, blah.

She says I must fly to LA to explain situation to Joe and get him to forgive me. On bended knees, if necessary. I must outline in rational way that nothing untoward happened, really, and that it was just a little blip in otherwise blemish-free marriage.

Not sure about this. OK, so Joe is upstanding family man who can always be relied upon, unlike Lotharios who apparently just want to have rampant sex with as many women as possible. But, surely, if he had been lavishing me with enough love and attention, none of this would have happened.

'And when you come back you must take up a hobby,' she said. 'It will keep you out of trouble.'

Obviously, *t'ai-chi* is out.

PS Joe has left three angry voicemails on my mobile, demanding an explanation. Feel it will be better to explain face to face so am not calling back. Also, am secretly hoping I will be struck by freak bolt of lightning any time soon and will never have to face him.

PPS Have horrible, panicky feeling in pit of my stomach. How could I have been such a fool to think that Lone Father was ever interested in me or my disfiguring stretchmarks? Even worse, what if Joe decides he never wants anything more to do with me – ever again?

25 May

Endured hellish night of tossing, turning and grappling with conscience. Have decided that

(a) Lone Father is a predatory alpha male who sensed I was vulnerable victim so decided to toy with my feelings for sick kicks.

(b) My subconscious child-self may have sent the text to Joe accidentally on purpose in a desperate cry for help. I have this inner child to thank that we are forced to discuss his lack of involvement in the relationship and, quite frankly, his neglect of both me and the children.

(c) I may need serious psychological counselling and/or a rebirthing session to discover the real reason I behaved so out of character.

(d) My parents are probably to blame for the entire episode.

Feel a bit better now that it is all clear in my mind.

26 May

On flight to LA. Quite exciting and glamorous. Except for tragic circumstances of marriage on rocks, of course. Also, air hostess quite snappy. Timidly asked for extra pillows and rug, but might as well have asked for Cristal champagne and a private jet.

'I'll get to you in due course, madam,' the old crone snapped, the trowelled-on layers of makeup cracking round her cheeks and mouth, and her green eye-shadow flashing dangerously.

Tried to remember that angry people have their own issues and that she might have had tragic news just that morning and be struggling to hold it together professionally under trying circumstances.

Twenty minutes later, again asked if a blanket would be too much trouble.

'I will get to you when I *can*, madam,' she snarled, as if she was dealing with a genuine air-rage incident. 'Now, please, *calm down.*'

Lots of other passengers looked back nervously, as if I was going to jump up and start brandishing an Uzi. Cowered in seat at once and put my dark sunglasses back on. Will definitely compose letter to CEO of airline. Could have chosen any carrier to LA, didn't have to take this flight. (Well, did, actually, as booked at such short notice, but that's not the point.)

Airlines must be made to realize that consumers now have choice, what with market competition and all that. We do not have to put up with behavioural problems of cabin crew, even if they do have to deal with air rage on an everyday basis. In fact, feel strongly that air hostesses who are past their prime should be put out to pasture. If they have to wear more than one layer of foundation to look remotely human, they are quite obviously too old to deal with the day-to-day difficulties of the job.

11 a.m. In bit of a pickle. After repeated attempts to catch air hostess's eye, tried to sneak into first-class cabin to get extra blanket. Was immediately apprehended by burly American in tight-fitting suit and too-short trousers. 'Please return to your seat, madam,' he drawled, swaying over me in a very intimidating manner.

Quite bravely, after two glasses of in-flight wine selection, proceeded to tell him he couldn't tell me what to do and it was a free world, etc., etc. Unfortunately, this seemed to antagonize him.

'Actually, madam,' he said, in a creepy I-am-calm-but-may-assassinate-you-at-any-second-with-a-flick-of-my-wrist voice, 'I *can* tell you what to do. I am a US marshal and if you don't go to your seat I will be forced to take you into custody.'

Naturally went and sat down, but felt like asking him where exactly he was going to take me into custody – in the cockpit? Typical of bullying American attitude *à la* Bush and whole war-for-oil thing. Was going to say that but US marshal looked as if he might be one of those nerds who had facts and figures about war at his fingertips so decided to let it go. Must remember that my children are depending on me so cannot get gunned down in mid-air on a point of principle. Although would probably be considered a war hero if that did happen. Might even get own postage stamp and feast day. Anyway, can't understand what all the fuss is about – they have cashmere blankets going begging in first class.

PS Smug air hostess keeps throwing smirks in my direction. Notice she is refilling marshal's coffee cup every five minutes. Suspect collusion. May have to notify American authorities when I disembark.

PPS Smug air hostess has turned air-conditioning on to super-high – vent right over my head. Afraid to say anything in case I'm arrested. Neck in spasm.

PPPS Just thought – disability may work in my favour and get sympathy vote from Joe.

27 May

12.00 noon local time. Joy, oh, joy! Airline has lost my luggage and will have to furnish me with a blank cheque so I can go shopping on Rodeo Drive and buy brand-new wardrobe packed to hilt with designer gear, just like Julia Roberts in *Pretty Woman.* Can't wait to give some snooty shop assistant her comeuppance! Big mistake. *Huge!* Ha! May sneak in discreet rejuvenating cosmetic procedure while I'm at it. In-flight magazine had fabulous article on micro-dermabrasion. Not too keen on having face blasted with fine sand and lava rock, but am keen to look ten years younger in less than an hour so may consider it. Stress of adultery situation, coupled with US marshal incident and bad airline food, seems to have aged me terribly.

Am really looking forward to forming lasting friend-ship with bearded hotel concierge who will take me under his wing and think it's cute and appealing when

I do something ungainly, such as use the wrong cutlery at dinner, etc.

1.00 p.m. local time. Hate America and all things American. Stupid, incompetent airline is 'unsure' when my luggage will be located. Also, they do not issue blank cheques to buy new wardrobe, even if they have lost your bag through no fault of your own.

Will never watch *Friends* reruns again. May also boycott *Oprah* and *Dr. Phil.* Will have to keep this anti-American sentiment to self, in case am hauled away to Guantánamo Bay or elsewhere for conspiracy to treason or incitement to hatred or some other such fabricated reason.

'Did you have nametags on your luggage, ma'am?' the customer representative drawled when I marched up to the desk to explain my predicament and collect my cheque.

'Not exactly,' I replied. (Surely, it being the twenty-first century and all, everything is logged electronically now. Bit worrying she was not aware of this.)

Admit I was getting quite snappy, but had just endured ghastly Immigration and Customs, where was frisked like common criminal by scowling sweaty Immigration officers. Then had waited for ages at baggage carousel while every other moron from the flight picked up their cases, but mine never appeared. *Then* had to explain to anyone in earshot that, no, the lone bag still circling the carousel, with the *I Love Jesus* stickers plastered all over it, was definitely not mine.

'Do you have travel insurance, ma'am?' The customer-services rep's pink bubble-gum snapped between her unusually white teeth.

Hesitated a fraction of a second too long for Miss Colgate's liking. Not sure if took out insurance or not. Is that covered in price of ticket?

'Fill out this form and we'll contact you if we locate your baggage.' Chew, chew, snap.

Am furious. Quite obvious that the marshal and snooty air hostess engineered this whole thing to make me pay for subversive activity on board. Useless to put forward my theory about the air hostess and her marshal lover. They're probably all in on it.

3.00 p.m. local time. Am feeling very sorry for self. And not without good reason. Was quite cheery when I reached Joe's hotel, as was very *Pretty Woman* type establishment, with marble floors and water displays everywhere. However, good mood vanished quickly when had to spend ages trying to convince receptionist at front desk that was bona-fide wife, not some terrorist nutter about to blow the entire Beverly Hills Hilton to kingdom come with my fake Gucci handbag.

'I'm afraid I cannot possibly give you guest information, madam,' she snapped, eyeing me up and down with distaste when I asked for Joe's room number. (Admit may not have looked 100 per cent my best, but what can you expect after long-haul flight, coupled with serious emotional trauma, near-arrest and internment by US marshal?). Attempted megawatt Julia Roberts smile but receptionist stayed stony-faced. *And* there was no sign of kindly hotel manager to take me under his wing and whisk me up to the penthouse, pronto. Apparently you actually have to *be* a prostitute with a heart of gold before you can get anywhere in this town.

In face of serious adversity, decided to play best card.

'I did a really bad thing,' I confessed, suddenly tearful and very, very tired. Could see her perking up immediately so sexed up adulterous activities, remorse, probable divorce, etc.

'It sounds just like an episode of *The Bold and the Beautiful*,' Honey said, when I finished, swallowing genuine tears of remorse and shame about my hedonistic shenanigans. (Honey's real name is Joan, but Honey sounds much better for making it in Hollywood.)

Was quite pleased that someone thinks I have a dangerous lifestyle. Decided against confiding in her that am actually boring, stay-at-home housewife and not international jet-setter with penchant for fast living.

She scribbled Joe's room number on the back of her actor's stage card and checked me into Room 101 so I could freshen up before I threw myself on his mercy. 'A little warpaint never did any harm,' she whispered conspiratorially, squeezing my hand kindly before I trundled away. And she should know.

6.00 p.m. local time. Feel much better. Spent ages in massive shower using all gorgeous free beauty products to wash away disaster of journey. Unfortunately have no clean clothes to change into so have wrapped myself in thick towelling robe. Hopefully, when Joe sees me, I will look all cute and vulnerable and he will call room service immediately and forget all about that silly text I sent him by accident. Have used extra strong mouthwash in anticipation of reunion kiss.

Reasons Should Not End Life in Dramatic Drink and Drugs Binge à la Hollywood Star

- My two children would be motherless (although have sneaking suspicion Katie would quite enjoy the drama factor involved in that scenario).

- My parents would be bereft (once they noticed I was gone).

- Marita, the yoga crone, would probably invent a new *t'ai-chi* position with delight.

- Would probably end up back on TV, thus further embarrassing entire family.

- Do not know where to get any Class A drugs. Concierge seems unlikely to help.

Reasons Should End Life in Dramatic Drink and Drugs Binge à la Hollywood Star

- Have made total and complete fool of myself with sleazy berk a.k.a. Lone Father.

- Have lost VBF Louise. Probably for ever.

- Have lost suitcase with new top from Principles that actually made me look at least two pounds thinner than usual.

- Found Barbie/Becky cavorting in husband's LA

hotel room wearing skimpy outfit and a smile. Husband seemed to be AWOL. Probably scoring some Class A drugs for orgy-type activities.

29 May

Very bleak. Sobbed into my luxury goosedown pillow all night, so face swollen to twice its normal size. Am almost Elephant Woman. Cannot bear even to open the curtains, so am lying in bed in the dark, watching American TV and wondering how my life went so tragically wrong. (Excellent new episodes of *Desperate Housewives* showing, but pointless as can barely even see TV through the tears and the swelling. Very annoying.)

The smug expression on Becky's face when she opened the door to Joe's room will be stamped for ever on my subconscious. Not to mention the image of her inexplicably perky breasts pouring out of her Wonderbra. Luckily I didn't give her the chance to say anything, so at least do not have to erase the memory of her squeaky voice and feeble attempts to explain her half-naked presence in my husband's hotel room. Have barricaded myself in Room 101 and given Honey strict instructions to let no one disturb me under any circumstances. (Obviously Joe will go begging on hands and knees to be given my room number so he can then beg (on hands and knees again) for my forgiveness. But, there is no way I'm talking to him. Possibly ever again.)

'Oh. My. *God*,' Honey gasped, when I called her on the fabulous retro cream phone to fill her in on Joe's shenanigans with the office harlot.

'And with that *slut*, too. Men just can't look beyond great breasts.' (Tried to ignore that remark. Who can tell if the girl actually has great boobs? You have to take a Wonderbra off to find that out. Then felt sick at the thought that Joe probably knew for sure one way or the other.)

'Sweetie,' Honey went on, 'I'm going to send up our deluxe detoxifying pack straight away. The lemon and lime balm will give you positive energy and revive your spirit. It's totally awesome. And try the green tea. It's just fabulous!'

Would have preferred jumbo bar of Galaxy or even a low-fat Flyte to revive my spirits (not usually big fan of low-fat chocolate but it was an emotional emergency). However, didn't want to seem rude so mumbled my thanks and hung up.

Feel I am in serious shock and may lapse into unconsciousness at any second. Am definitely cold and shaky, but that may be down to chocolate withdrawal. Wish I had Internet access so I could check the symptoms and be sure.

Am aghast that Joe has been capable of such deception. He is not the strong dependable type (a.k.a. boring type) I thought he was. Find it impossible to comprehend that:

(a) Joe has committed real, honest-to-goodness adultery, involving push-up bras and plush hotel suites.

(b) He has committed said adultery with someone practically half his age (and definitely half my weight).

(c) He has set aside his wife and two children with no thought of the pain and misery (and years of expensive therapy) he may be inflicting.

(d) He had the audacity to send me on an enormous guilt trip about Lone Father when all along he was shagging his Barbie secretary.

Now I know how Posh must have felt when Becks (allegedly) strayed away from home. Thank God I don't have to go out and about, posing for any lurking *paparazzi* on the ski slopes and pretending to be ecstatically happy. Will definitely write to Posh when I get home and tell her how much I admire her strength of character. How she managed to look glam in a skin-tight Chanel snowsuit while undergoing such heartbreak is beyond me. I may never get dressed again. In fact, I may never recover from the humiliation and pain. OK, I may have had an innocent flirtation with Lone Father, but at least he never paraded around my hotel bedroom in a Wonderbra (or male equivalent).

PS Now have crippling migraine pounding in my temples. As well as suffering from serious shock, may have developed life-threatening brain tumour that has come upon me because of appalling discovery of husband's double identity.

PPS Just remembered that Joe's father had a sordid liaison years ago. Obviously the adulterous gene runs in the family.

PPPS Am also very worried that Honey will remember very soon that I was only supposed to be using Room 101 as a place to tidy myself up. Who knows?

Could be thrown on to the street in my dressing-gown at any moment. My only consolation is that things cannot get any worse.

PPPPS Am also missing regular Barry's Gold Blend teabags. They're really good in a crisis such as husbands committing adultery. Green tea looks and smells positively revolting.

5.00 p.m. Just woke up. Obviously fell into some sort of semi-diabetic coma. Realized have not eaten anything for days (well, not since the woeful plane meal, which everyone knows doesn't count as real food). Luckily, still have fake Gucci bag to hand, with Joe's credit cards in my purse. Have decided, in unprecedented bout of shopping-rage, to indulge in some retail therapy, then eat something very fatty and laden with calories. Honey, gem that she is, said she would send her friend Renata from the hotel boutique to my room with a few outfit choices as there was still no sign of my luggage.

'She's European,' Honey said, when I explained my clothing dilemma, 'so she, like, totally gets fashion.'

Sounded very promising so cheered up a bit. Would choose gorgeous new outfit, eat three Big Macs, then decide on my next step. Must be sensible and clear-headed. No point trying to decide what to do with rest of sad existence on an empty stomach. That would be like going grocery-shopping hungry – which, everyone knows, is a serious no-no as it can lead to impulse buys such as 24-packs of cheese and onion crisps and three-for-one offers of Pringles.

Seemed to take Renata for ever to arrive, but she eventually wheeled a rack of clothes through the door as I was polishing off the no-fat corn snacks from the mini-bar. 'Hmm . . .' She eyed me critically, as I tried to pull the hotel dressing-gown round me even tighter. 'What star sign are you, honey?'

'Er, Pisces,' I answered, not sure what that had to do with anything, but too hungry to argue.

'Yes, I thought so. Pisces.' Renata sucked in her pinched little cheeks, 'I'm not sure we have anything suitable. These are more Aquarius, Cancer, even.' She raked her perfectly manicured nail along the clothes rack she had wheeled into the room, shaking her head in an alarming way.

'Well, maybe my moon rises in Cancer.' I was terrified that she and her clothes rack would disappear and I would have to wear the dressing-gown to Starbucks.

The pinched little face lit up. 'I thought so!' She beamed, hauling what looked like a giant tea-towel off the rack. 'You definitely seem more like a Cancer to me. This is perfect for you!'

'Em, I'm not sure,' I said, appalled by her outlandish choice. I wanted to blend in, not wear a garish, multi-coloured dress that screamed, 'Look at me,' and would barely cover my bum. 'Maybe I'll just try the pale blue T-shirt.' Tried to inject my voice with a thank-you-very-much-for-your-kindness-but-I-am-much-meeker-than-you-may-think tone, but Renata and her fiery European temperament were having none of it. (Am suspicious of the 'European' tag – her accent sounded very dodgy at times.)

She slapped my hand away. 'No. Blue is no good for you. You need colour. Punch.'

Too feeble to protest, struggled into the tea-towel and tried to look enthusiastic.

'It's perfect,' Renata trilled, slipping some shocking-pink wedges on my feet. 'You are ready to go.'

6.00 p.m. Skulked across hotel foyer, struggling to keep tea-towel outfit down round my thighs and bum and wobbling precariously in the neon wedges. (Note: must get unsightly bunions seen to ASAP. Also, must make appointment to have ingrown toenail removed as spotted Renata gagging when she tried to give me a genuine LA pedicure.) Luckily, still had my sunglasses so did not have to make eye-contact with anyone. Was fumbling my way against the wall, trying to find the revolving doors to the outside world, when I heard an Irish voice behind me: 'Susie, is that *you*?'

Tried to ignore it and kept going, cursing Renata and her ridiculous astrology fashion sense, which meant all eyes in the hotel lobby were firmly fixed on me. Now was not the time to have a showdown with Becky/Barbie. Maybe in a few weeks when I'd lost serious weight and was looking gaunt and wistful. Not now when I looked like something the cat threw up after raiding a box of Lucky Charms.

'Susie Hunt!' the voice said again, and I felt a hand on my shoulder.

Apparently, Becky was not in the least bit fazed by my unexpected arrival. Maybe she wanted us to be friends and share Joe in some warped wife-swap scenario. It was never going to happen. Was suddenly engulfed with rage. 'Look here, you little slapper,' I hissed, whipping my head round to glare at her. 'Why don't you just piss off and leave me alone? Haven't you done enough damage?'

'Wow, Susie, I just wanted to say hello,' the figure replied.

It wasn't Becky. Mercifully I realized this before my hand connected with her face. It was *Duckling to Swan* presenter Samantha Brennan, looking more than a little bewildered at my psycho outburst.

'What are you doing here?' I gasped, sure I was hallucinating and that all the stress of Joe's secret life had finally sent me over the edge.

'I'm here to meet some Hollywood producers,' she said, looking round nervously, 'but you mustn't tell anyone, it's top secret.'

Once I realized she was not Becky, I promptly fell apart and collapsed sobbing into her arms – I was so relieved to see a friendly face. Professional that she is, she seemed to recover her composure pretty quickly and whisked me away in her VW Beetle *tout de suite*. (Was bit disappointed she didn't have stretch limo waiting to chauffeur her hither and thither, but suppose you don't have a limo until you're earning squillions of dollars and are world famous. Really hope she breaks the States soon and becomes VBFs with some A-listers. Can't wait to hobnob with Sharon Stone and Reese Witherspoon, etc.

'You poor thing,' she sympathized, when I explained the whole sorry tale over a bucket of curly fries and a Diet Coke at In and Out Burger (obviously *the* in place to see and be seen in LA).

'I never thought our marriage would be another statistic, Samantha,' I lamented, feeling very, very sorry for myself even though I was eating with a would-be celeb and I could see people were staring at us and probably wondering if I was a celeb too. (Sunglasses dead giveaway.)

'Maybe it's just a little blip.' Samantha took a long drink of her Diet Coke and gave a little burp (obviously on purpose to reassure me that even though she's on the way to being mega-rich and famous she can still be a normal, gross person, which I thought was very thoughtful of her). 'Maybe Joe is having some sort of mid-life crisis and this Becky person is just a passing phase.'

'Well, she's welcome to him,' I said, deciding not to confide in Samantha about Lone Father, in case she thought less of me and it affected our newly found friendship.

'Hmmm.' Samantha didn't seem too convinced. 'Why don't you talk to him about it, have it out and then think about what to do next? Loads of couples go through issues – you do have the kids to think about too.'

That started me off again and Samantha had to order another cheeseburger to calm me down. How am I going to explain this to Katie and Jack, to Mum and Dad? Will need all my *Dr. Phil* expertise to cope. Wonder if any of Samantha's Hollywood connections know Dr. Phil. Maybe she could arrange an emergency one-to-one session. I may even be willing to let her record it for *Entertainment Tonight*.

'Have you called your mum?' Samantha asked, taking my greasy hand in hers and cocking her head sympathetically to one side.

'No – why? Is she OK?'

'I'm sure she is.' Samantha looked puzzled. 'I mean, have you called her to tell her what happened? Family are important in a crisis.'

Didn't want to admit that have only texted Mum to

say I landed safely – and, in fact, am too scared to call her in case she goes ballistic and starts blaming me unfairly for this whole sordid state of affairs.

Anyway, she probably thinks Joe and I are acting like love's young dream and having a second honeymoon in sunny LA, and who am I to shatter her illusions?

Concentrated on eating the rest of the cheeseburger and not dribbling the secret-recipe sauce all over the tea-towel outfit.

'Listen, I'm really sorry about *Doyle Tonight*,' Samantha continued, looking embarrassed. 'Mona Doyle was way out of line. I really hope you didn't take offence.'

'No, of course not,' I said, wondering if Samantha was going to finish her fries.

'A lot of people don't really get *Duckling to Swan*. It's not so much about physical appearance, it's more to do with how you feel inside – you know?' She seemed genuinely concerned.

Nodded in agreement and thought of saying that I felt really, really terrible inside, so could she hook me up with a top-notch surgeon to carve fifteen years off me ASAP?

Samantha dropped me back at the hotel at nine. Was teeny bit disappointed she didn't suggest hooking up with some other celebs, but kept that to myself. Don't want her to think I'm some kind of stalker.

The streets were eerily deserted, but I crept upstairs to my room in case I happened to bump into Joe and Becky. He's probably been camping outside my room all day to try and talk to me.

9.00 a.m. Dumb hotel receptionist (Honey gone to an audition for a new Spielberg movie) claims there are no messages for me. Neither, apparently, has a man deranged with grief and remorse been pacing the hotel, searching every nook and cranny for me.

'I think you must be mistaken,' I said, outraged that so many messages could have gone missing in such a short time. 'Can you look again, please?'

'I have looked, ma'am,' dumb receptionist replied. 'There are no messages. No one has been looking for you. Can I interest you in a deep-tissue massage?'

Slammed retro phone down in foul temper. Am very put out. How dare Joe not be banging down my door with remorse? Have decided to fly straight home and change the locks on the house. May also cut up all his ties and rip his suits to shreds before pouring a bucket of paint over his car.

That will teach him.

11.00 a.m. Think I may have broken very expensive retro phone. There seems to be a dial tone, but Joe still hasn't called so it's obviously out of order.

12.00 noon Am distraught that he hasn't battered down the door to find me. In fact, even though I keep checking that the phone is working and have craned my head round the door several times in case he's pacing the hallway outside, there's no sign of him. How can he throw away our marriage for that slut in a cheap push-up bra? No texts either. Not a single, solitary one, not even from Lone Father. Am bewildered as to how my life turned out this way.

Finally plucked up the courage to call Mum to confide in her how badly everything's going and tell her I'm flying back straight away to be comforted in the bosom of my family.

'Sorry, darling, can't talk now,' she huffed down the line. 'We're taking the kids for a run round the park and we have to keep the heart-rates up otherwise the whole thing is a total waste. Hope you're having a great time!'

Could hear Katie and Jack squealing with excitement in the background. It's so tragic. Little do they know that, within months, they will be at the centre of a bitter custody battle.

PS Have just thought. Neither Katie nor Jack even asked to speak to me. They don't miss me one bit. In fact, they'll quite possibly choose to live with their father and his near-teenage lover when push comes to shove.

PPS Having very painful flashbacks to Katie admiring Becky's long blonde hair and Barbie physique. Have ominous feeling she will definitely choose to cohabit with a Barbie lookalike instead of a frumpy housewife.

12.30 p.m. Hurrah! Called Samantha to say goodbye and she said she'll put a call through to one of her air-hostess buddies and get me upgraded on the flight home. Being pals with a mega-star in the making (and former air hostess) is already paying dividends.

'Make sure to keep in touch, Susie,' Samantha said, 'and try to sort it out with Joe, won't you?'

Agreed I would, but privately think Samantha needs

to get a grip on reality. It's not like I'm looking for a new nose and some liposuction to transform my life. Unfortunately, adultery cannot be fixed by a team of top surgeons, a life coach and a stylist.

1.00 p.m. Luggage finally turned up so was able to get rid of horrible tea-towel dress at last. Decided, in kindly act of charity karma, to give it to the Hispanic maid, who knocked on my door asking if I needed extra towels. She didn't look altogether impressed, but she took it anyway and gave me some extra mints.

Took ages applying and reapplying full makeup in case I bumped into Joe and Becky, then changed into my most flattering jeans and a T-shirt and went to leave goodbye note for Honey at the front desk. Tried to look casual and fixed a fake smile on my face, just in case I walked straight into them or they were observing me from behind the potted plants. However, fake smile was quickly wiped off my perfectly done face when the receptionist on duty presented me with a bill for three thousand dollars! Not including taxes and service charges! The tea-towel dress cost six hundred alone.

'Em, there must be some kind of misunderstanding,' I gabbled, panicking. 'Honey just let me use the room to freshen up.'

'For three days?' The receptionist smiled brightly, pushing the bill firmly in my direction.

Felt faint and very, very sick at first, then decided not to panic and simply handed Joe's credit card across the desk. It was his fault I had to spend vast amounts of money – he can deal with it.

PS Looked everywhere for the Hispanic maid to get the six-hundred-dollar tea-towel back, but she's nowhere to be found. She's probably using it to clean toilets by now.

3.00 p.m. On flight back to bosom of my family. But, more importantly, have been upgraded to first class! Samantha is officially my VBF for ever. Even better, snooty air hostess who traumatized me on the way over is back on duty. Have already asked for extra pillows and rugs and have sent my drinks back twice for being too warm. May even try clicking my fingers later. Revenge is sweet! Ha!

Added bonus: am surrounded by very wealthy male corporate types who may be in need of a second or third wife. They are a tad portly, but can easily get over that if they're willing to keep me in the manner I have become accustomed to in the last few days. After all, no one's perfect. Am weirdly content, considering life is in ruins. Was quite obviously born to travel first class. Trying hard not to seem too impressed by facilities, but cannot believe they give you personal DVD players and warm cookies *whenever you want*. Don't know how I'll bear to go back to cattle class.

PS Have just remembered that when planes crash, it is usually first class and business passengers who eat dust first. Have decided not to mind. If I go down, at least it will be in style, snuggled up under a cashmere rug and happily watching two movies at once.

31 May

Never so glad to see dreary, rain-drenched Dublin. First class was amazing, but it's quite a relief to be surrounded by ordinary, ugly Irish people again and not be bumping into the perfect noses and enormous inflatable boobs of LA.

'Go on through.' The guy at Passport Control sighed with boredom when I waved my Irish passport proudly at him. Didn't take umbrage but instead smiled fondly at his grumpiness and held myself back from kissing him with relief. Great to see honest-to-goodness bad humour for a change and not fake bonhomie.

In taxi on way home, braced myself for serious discussion re divorce, etc., with Mum and Dad, but the house was empty when I let myself in, laden with bags of goodies from Duty Free.

'Oh, hi, darling, are you home already?' Mum sounded surprised to hear from me when I called her to explain I was back and ask her why the hell she wasn't there, waiting for me with a cup of Barry's tea in one hand and a Galaxy bar in the other. 'We got the train home to give the kiddies a taste of the country air,' she said, sounding a little defensive. 'I'm sure those nasty city toxins are a health hazard. They're positively blooming down here.'

Not altogether happy that parents have absconded with their grandchildren, without prior consent from me, but felt I was not in a position to argue.

Instead, found myself agreeing to drive down and collect Katie and Jack, even though am traumatized and exhausted from overseas trip. Sometimes Mum can be terribly selfish. Taking the children to the country without my permission is one thing. Expecting me to traipse down and collect them is quite another.

1 June

It's official. The whole world has gone mad. Mum and Dad have put the family home up for sale and are moving abroad. Have taken to my bed.

2 June

Had horrible jetlag nightmare that Mum and Dad were selling the family home and buying a villa in a plush golf resort in Portugal with the funds. Woke up in my old room and realized the horrible nightmare was true and that the estate agent's sign was winking at me through the bedroom curtains.

Mum tried to haul me out of bed to meditate at the crack of dawn.

'You obviously have unresolved issues about abandonment, Susie,' she soothed. 'A salute to the sun is exactly what you need to align all the positive energy in your body.'

Restrained myself from hitting her over her new-age head with my bedside clock. 'I don't want to,' I wailed. 'How can you do this to me? Just go away and leave me alone.' Felt like I was fourteen again and they were refusing to let me go to the youth-club disco. Except this time they're moving overseas, abandoning me and my children to the unknown. No one has even asked how the LA trip went.

Could hear whispered discussions in the hallway, something to do with jetlag, emotional trauma and green tea, but pulled my pillow over my head to muffle the conversation. Eventually Dad threw the two kids in at me and left, banging the door behind him, muttering something about selfish and immature behaviour and wanting to give me a good slap. Which really takes the biscuit, considering he's selling my inheritance out from under me, just when I need it most.

Tried to pretend to be asleep, but gave in when Jack kept prising open my eyelids and sticking his Action Man up my nose. Katie, meanwhile, had no interest in me *per se*, but stood tapping her feet impatiently and demanding to know where her presents were. Once they had been ripped open and inspected thoroughly, she perched on the end of my bed, grilling me about LA and wanting to know did I meet any real Bratz.

'No, I didn't, darling,' I admitted, too exhausted to fabricate a tale of rollerblading down Rodeo Drive with Barbie on one side and a Bratz on the other.

'Your trip must have been really *boring*, Mummy,' she said, rubbing my hand in sympathy and I felt myself choke up.

'Anyway,' she continued, trying to console me, 'Daddy will probably meet some real Bratz, so when he comes back, he can tell us all about it.' And off she marched, dragging Jack behind her.

Her innocent confidence tore at my heartstrings so much that had to muffle a sob in my treasured Bon Jovi pillow. Little does she know that Daddy may not meet any real Bratz but he has definitely come across real Tartz.

PS Confided the whole sorry tale to Mum over a pot of tea and some giant duty-free Toblerone. Could see her twitching as I stuffed piece after piece into my mouth, but I eyeballed her fiercely so she didn't say anything. Was definitely in no mood for lecture on caffeine and saturated fat.

'So, all the time I was flirting innocently with Paul,' I finished, 'Joe has been having an affair with Becky.'

It seemed very sad and final when I said it out loud like that.

'Do you love Joe, Susie?' Mum asked, her face soft and understanding.

Was a bit taken aback. Had been hoping Mum would threaten to kill him and his extended family once I'd told her what had happened. Hadn't spared her any of the gory details so she would realize how awful he had been and how much he had betrayed me. 'Well, do you?'

Suddenly saw that, even though Joe and I have grown apart and he insists on using the toilet with the bathroom door open, I do love him. But it's too late now, he has set me aside like a *First Wives Club* reject and I must harden my heart.

'Sometimes we can forget how much we love someone,' Mum went on. 'Life gets in the way and you can grow apart without knowing it. But if you can recapture that first flush of love, it can carry you through the rest of your days together. All marriages have their ups and downs – it's how you deal with the downs that counts.'

Sniffed into my tea, considering what she had said. Suspect she may be right (she has read heaps of self-help books), but think too much has gone on for us to recapture anything. For one thing, how would I ever let Joe see my droopy boobs again, knowing he has frolicked with Becky's perfect specimens?

PPS Have switched my mobile back on. Six missed

calls: three from Mrs H wanting to know how poor Joe is and should she post him some King crisps. Three from Joe, wanting to know where I am and why I haven't contacted him. What does he call flying all the way to LA and knocking on his door doing? The pre-divorce mind games are starting already.

3 June

Have decided to throw myself on my parents' mercy and beg them to reconsider their ill-advised stunt of selling up and moving to foreign soil. What with a broken marriage and no career prospects, I'll probably have to move back in with them. And even if I don't, they're far too old to make life-changing decisions. Am bit worried they're both suffering from early onset of Alzheimer's or some other brain-wasting disease. Where else would these foolish notions of five-star golf resorts and year-round sun have come from? They should be spending lots of time in their slippers, taking it easy, not strutting about a brand-new golf course, even if it was designed by Nick Faldo. Who knows what will become of them in a foreign country, surrounded by people who can't even speak their own language? They could find themselves in all sorts of trouble. Just like that couple who ended up in a rat-infested jail cell because they used their pidgin Spanish to ask a policeman for directions. Turned out they were prop-ositioning him to do something lewd and unlawful. Will do some research on the Internet and throw some facts and figures at them. Needs must and all that.

PS Mrs H rang again. Accidentally answered the call when I was trying to reject it. (Hands very jittery what with all the stress and extra coffee.) 'How are you, Susie?' she crooned. 'Have you heard from poor Joe? He must be exhausted, working in that terrible heat. I've been keeping an eye on the weather. He burns so easily, being fair like myself. It's a blessing, really, that the children got your more leathery skin.'

Something inside snapped. Decided to give her piece of my mind for first time in my life. After all, she would be an ex-mother-in-law soon, and even though I would miss her homemade scones and Trojan cleaning abilities, she needed to know the truth.

'Mrs H,' I started, deciding to break it to her gently, 'you know the way you kind of admitted once that Mr H played away from home?'

There was a deadly silence.

'What on earth do you mean, Susan?' Her voice was cold.

I ploughed on regardless: 'You know, bonking, shagging, having naughties with another woman?'

Could hear a strangled gurgle on the line.

'Well, the apple doesn't fall far from the tree, if you know what I mean.' Felt that was the kind way to break it to her that her son was a cheating, two-timing rat, without going into graphic detail.

'I have no idea what you're talking about, Susie. What do you mean "apple"?' She sounded genuinely confused.

'I'm sorry to tell you this, Mrs H . . .' With a jolt of surprise, I realized I *was* sorry. This wasn't giving me as much pleasure as I thought it would. In fact, I felt terrible. 'Joe has been having an affair. I found his secretary in his hotel room in Los Angeles. In her bra.'

There was a gasp. 'It can't be true.'

'I'm afraid it is.' This was torture. 'I'm in my parents' house, trying to sort a few things out, but obviously we'll be splitting up.'

'Susie, I'll have to call you back,' she croaked, 'I feel a bit peculiar.'

4 June

The throwing-myself-on-my-parents'-mercy tack is not going according to plan. 'Nonsense, darling,' Mum breezed, when I told her that lots of older people have been taken advantage of when buying into these foreign-property deals.

'What if you end up living on a building site for years?' I said, as ominously as I could. 'Or, even worse, what if the development doesn't exist and some chancer runs off with all your money?'

Was delighted with myself for thinking that one up on the spur of the moment.

'Don't be silly. John Doran and his second wife moved out there last month.' Mum giggled. 'They even emailed us some photos of their villa. It looks amazing.'

Cursed my parents and their unnatural computer savvy.

'Well, what about Katie and Jack?' I said, grabbing Katie by the arm and shoving her in front of her granny. 'They'll be inconsolable if you move away.'

'I won't be colourable.' Katie pouted. 'Granny said

I can have my own room, with pink walls and everything. *And* there's a pool, but Jack can't go in it until he starts using a potty properly.' Katie shot a superior look at Jack, who retaliated by beating her with his plastic Power Rangers sword.

'No potty! No potty!' he roared.

Mum raised her eyebrows at me. 'No one else seems to have a problem with us trying to make the most of our golden years, Susie,' she went on. 'I think you'll have to try to come to terms with it, too.' She began to slice fruit calmly, as if I was making a big deal of nothing at all.

PS Jack seems to have developed an unhealthy obsession with the Power Rangers. Suspect Mum and Dad may have been teaching him some karate moves in my absence.

5 June

The nightmare is a reality. Prospective buyers are coming to view the house. Planned to hang about and mutter about asbestos and damp problems but Dad shooed me and the kids out of the front door and into the glaring sunshine in a most impersonal way. 'Who are these so-called buyers?' I asked warily, alarmed that the estate agent seemed to be actively trying to sell the house. Had always heard Joe say that all estate agents are lazy, good-for-nothing scroungers. Seemed most odd that they were getting viewings so quickly. 'They could be professional thieves, for all you know, just coming to case the place,' I threw in for good measure.

Dad looked at me witheringly. 'They are a wealthy Dublin couple who want a country retreat, actually. Now, go for a long walk on the beach,' he ordered sternly. 'Those children could do with some sun on their bones.'

Sulkily loaded Katie and Jack into the car, very annoyed that Dad seemed to be suggesting they were practically neglected. They do look a little pale, but only because I smother them in sun-block for their own protection. 'Sun worship is highly dangerous, Dad, although you obviously don't care about that or you wouldn't be moving to a country where you'll probably develop skin cancer in six to twelve months.'

'Off you go! Enjoy yourselves!' Dad yelled from the step.

'It's probably only neighbours coming to have a good snoop,' I shouted over my shoulder. 'Everyone knows that's what happens. You shouldn't be so naïve.' Unfortunately don't think Dad heard me as he'd already shut the solid mahogany door behind him. Skulked about a bit up the road to see who crawled out of the woodwork to tramp through Mum and Dad's house.

'What are you doing, Mummy?' Katie complained, from the back seat, furious she hadn't been beamed to the beach immediately. 'I want to go to the beach *now*.'

'Beach, beach, beach,' Jack chanted, banging his fist on his car seat.

'OK, OK,' I said, satisfied that it looked like no one was turning up. Now surely Mum and Dad would get discouraged and forget the whole thing. Only then spotted large silver Mercedes pull up and well-dressed couple step out to look around with interest.

'Oh, look, Mummy,' Katie squeaked. 'Those are the rich people who are going to buy Granny's house.'

'Over my dead body.' I gritted my teeth and gripped the steering-wheel, cursing rich people and their fanciful holiday-home notions.

'Dead, dead, dead,' Jack chanted happily.

6 June

Drove back to Dublin in very bad temper. Answer-phone crammed full of messages from Joe, but erased them all. Nothing he can say will make it any better.

'I want to talk to Daddy.' Katie pouted when she heard his voice. 'When is he coming home anyway? He's been gone for *months*.'

She started to cry, great heaving sobs that could only be stopped with a packet of chocolate buttons and her *Mary Poppins* DVD.

Meanwhile, piles of what look suspiciously like bills have gathered inside the hall door. Have decided to hide them behind the bread bin. Have no clue who is paid how much or when. Had stab of regret that Joe won't be here to sort it out, but will have to get to grips with all the finances and horrifically boring household administrative stuff. How hard can it be? Will just have to focus and bring all my former PR skills to bear. Will probably be satisfying and liberating in pseudo-feminist way.

Turned on my mobile to check latest onslaught of messages, but only one text popped up. Had to check the number about three times, but there was no mistaking it: it was from Louise, former VBF who had cut me from her life in cold and heartless manner: 'Susie, need to talk to you, can we meet, please?'

Was flabbergasted. Joe had evidently tried to get former VBF to talk to me on his behalf. Was furious she has agreed. Decided to ignore it.

Still, it was intriguing.

Texted back after a few minutes: 'Who is this?' She has a nerve, thinking I'd still have her number in my phone after all this time. For all she knew I deleted it months ago.

She replied straight away: 'It's me – Louise. Need to speak to you ASAP.'

I bet you do, I thought grimly. Resisted urge to answer, 'Louise who?'

Just sent one quick message back: 'OK, but am v. busy so will have to be quick.'

'Tanx. MoMos tmw at 7pm?'

PS Typical of Louise to assume I have no plans and she can summon me at such short notice. I could have had a dozen different outlandish engagements tomorrow and be unable to squeeze her in. Will go along to get to bottom of it, but will remain aloof and distant at all times. Vital to remember that she betrayed my trust and humiliated me beyond measure. Pretending she'd booked a five-star spa trip for my birthday when in fact she had intended to bring her MOM all along was unforgivable. Even if the massages were heavenly.

PPS Will offload Katie and Jack on Mrs H. Feel good to be able to do her a favour – their active night-time routine is bound to take her mind off her wayward son.

361

7 June

Did not have to spend as long as usual trying to look thin. Did not even have to wedge self into mammy pants as fit into skinny jeans first time for ages. Would have been thrilled if had not been so nervous due to meeting with long-lost friend after months of icy silence.

'You look *gorgeous*, Mummy,' Katie gasped, in admiration, when I came downstairs. 'Did your tummy go on a holiday?'

'Have a nice night, dear.' Mrs H hugged me tightly as I was leaving. Could have sworn I saw a glint of a tear in her eye. 'Don't rush home now. You deserve a little break.'

For once felt she meant it and wasn't just saying it so she could get extra snooping time in my bedside locker.

Was stunned when I saw Louise, sitting waiting for me. She seemed to have got quite pudgy and looked so rattled and pale. Her clothes were rumpled and her nails were actually *chipped*. Knew something serious was up, even before she spotted me weaving through the tables and fell on me, heaving and gulping great big sobs. 'Oh, Susie,' she wailed, 'I've missed you so much.'

Felt my heart soften a bit, but tried to remain cool and suitably aloof.

'What's up?' I said. Was very impressed by my cool tone, even though I was shaking with nerves inside.

Louise collapsed into the low velvet sofa and put her head into her hands. 'I'm pregnant,' she wailed, 'and that bastard Steve doesn't want to know.'

Spent next two hours being filled in on all goings-on

since our enormous bust-up. 'I've been such a fool,' she hiccuped, eyeing with lust the brandy I had ordered for myself to combat shock. 'You're a great friend and I was so jealous of you.'

'Jealous? Why?' I was astounded.

'Because you have it all, Susie. The perfect marriage, two fantastic kids. You're so happy and I'm so m-m-miserable.' She wailed again and I could see other customers staring at her in alarm.

'I'm not *that* happy, Louise,' I said, patting her swollen hand (water retention kicking in) and feeling uncomfortable.

'You are,' she insisted. 'You're so lucky to have Joe. Steve's such a bastard. He's even questioning whether the baby's actually his. Can you believe that?'

Could have believed anything at that stage, but felt it would be the wrong thing to say, so just nodded in sympathy.

'I'm so sorry about the spa retreat, Susie,' she whispered sorrowfully. 'It's just that I would have done anything to make my relationship with Steve work. I wanted to get married and have a baby so badly, but I shouldn't have blamed you when it went wrong. And I shouldn't have told you I'd have preferred to be there with him. I'll never forgive myself. Even if it was true.' Louise cradled her Diet Coke and shook her head in shame.

'Well, at least you have the baby, eh?' I said, unsure whether now was the right time to confide that my perfect life had been a sham and that it was all in tatters. 'Katie and Jack will be thrilled to have a new little playmate.'

Was desperate to cheer her up. Obviously don't hate her as much as I thought I did. In fact, it felt like the most natural thing in the world to be back together again. Also, was quite enjoying having the moral upper hand.

Louise brightened a bit. 'I suppose so.'

Spent rest of night discussing serious matters such as Britney's shocking weight gain and pimply skin. Almost forgot my problems for a while.

8 June

Had strange vivid dreams where Louise's baby popped out with Jennifer Aniston's head and started lecturing me about the importance of being honest before asking where she could lay her hands on a *Tomb Raider* DVD.

Spent ages thumping the pillows trying to get comfortable, but still tossed and turned all night. Should be thrilled that under the duvet is now a fart-free zone but, in ironic twist of fate, the bed seems enormous and very empty now that I have it all to myself.

Am thrilled Louise and I are reconciled, but am also racked with guilt that I didn't divulge my sordid secret life to her. Even if it is a bit tempting, it would be very unfair (and morally deplorable) to let her go on thinking that Joe and I have perfect Posh-and-Becks life. Called her at 8.04 a.m. to discuss.

'I can't believe it,' she gasped, when I regaled the whole sorry tale to her. 'You had an affair, now Joe's having an affair and you're splitting up?'

'Well, I never actually had an *affair* with Paul,' I

corrected her, anxious we get the finer details ironed out.

'Yes, but you would have done if your father hadn't almost broken his neck and Paul hadn't hooked up with the local slapper first.' Louise was impressively aggressive, despite having to take breaks every five minutes during the conversation to retch into the bathroom basin with morning sickness.

'Well, maybe,' I said, thoroughly ashamed of myself.

'And you haven't spoken to Joe because . . . ?'

'Because he slept with Becky,' I said, in a small voice, suspecting this sounded a bit weak. Kind of regretted spilling my innermost secrets now.

'Well, Susie, you're going to have to sort it out, for Katie and Jack's sake,' Louise went on, between bouts of retching, 'although how the hell you're going to explain all this to them is beyond me.'

Felt like telling her she had no right to take the moral high ground, seeing as she was up the duff and the father didn't want to know, but resisted. Those pregnancy hormones can be pretty fierce.

PS Joe hasn't called in days. Really, his lack of interest in his children's welfare is disturbing. Am sure the judge will be interested to hear all about it when we commence the bitter custody battle.

9 June

Am marginally cheered by the news that the wealthy Dublin couple have decided not to buy Mum and Dad's house.

'They decided it wasn't for them,' Mum said, when I

called for my hourly update on how the selling-my-inheritance-out-from-under-me plan was progressing.

'Yes, well, you can hardly blame them, Mum,' I said, thrilled the sale had fallen through. 'The house isn't exactly desirable, is it? *The House Doctor* would have a field day with it.'

'Well, that all depends on your point of view,' she said. 'Anyway, we have had other interest. Serious interest, in fact.'

'Really?' I said, trying to sound casual.

'Yes,' she went on. 'He's an overseas investor who wants a country retreat for his family.'

'Wants to bulldoze the whole lot and build an apartment block, more like,' I grunted, furious some wealthy bucko would steal the family home and destroy all my childhood memories.

'Oh, no, he's most definitely a family man,' Mum went on. 'He seems very devoted, in fact.'

Mumbled some reply, then hung up to fantasize about how I could sabotage the house sale – something with rats or ghosts might work.

10 *June*

Evil Anna, former work colleague and Official Office Gossip, called unexpectedly. Was terrified she had somehow found out what had happened and wanted to gloat, but she sounded most odd on the phone. 'Susie,' she stammered, 'I'm calling to apologize.'

'Apologize?' I almost gagged on my tea. Anna apologizing for anything was unheard-of.

'Yes,' she went on, in a small, tinny voice, as if she was reading an autocue. 'I've been having counselling sessions of late and my therapist suggested that before I could move on I had to let go the demons of my past.'

Was bit alarmed to hear myself classed as demon, but didn't interrupt. This was fascinating stuff. 'Counselling sessions?' I asked, thrusting a full packet of Jaffa Cakes under Jack's nose so he'd be quiet.

'Well, I . . . ah . . . chose to address some of my . . . ah . . . personal issues, I suppose.' Silence. 'Actually, that's not entirely true.' More silence. 'There was an incident at work and HR said if I didn't do some counselling I'd be fired.'

Spat a mouthful of tea down my T-shirt. This was getting better and better. 'An incident?'

'Yes, it was all blown out of proportion – you know what HR's like. I didn't *mean* to slam the photocopier on Noel's hand.' Then she coughed as if to focus. 'Anyway, in conclusion, I'm sorry if I ever verbally or physically bullied you in any way, OK?'

Had to bite my lip hard to stop myself exploding with laughter. This was priceless.

'Now I have to go. That slut Janet in Accounts is next on my list.'

PS Can't wait to tell Joe. He always hated Anna.

PPS Oh. Just remembered that Joe and I are separated and I can never again share a funny story with him. Feel most odd.

Mum called to say that the mysterious overseas investor definitely wants to buy the house. Could hear Dad whooping with joy in the background.

'That was quick,' I said, expecting to be devastated but instead feeling numb and empty inside.

'Yes, it was,' Mum said kindly, obviously expecting me to burst into uncontrollable tears. 'Why don't you pop down at the weekend and we can sort through all your things and have a little chat?'

Agreed, but privately think there's no point. Will most likely lose the Dublin house in the divorce settlement so will have no room for extra boxes crammed with Enid Blyton books and other childhood paraphernalia. Hear those women's shelters are crowded enough as it is.

PS Mrs H arrived with a fresh batch of homemade scones. 'Joe called me last night,' she said, spreading half a pound of butter on a scone for me.

'He did?' I was aghast. He's stopped calling me in the past few days. Not that I care, of course.

'Yes, but I told him I was refusing to speak to him.'

I nearly choked on a mouthful of scone.

Mrs H looked at me calmly, then wiped away the crumbs with the J-cloth she had produced from her handbag. 'There is something I must confess, Susie,' she went on. 'Joe's father, God rest him, did have a little dalliance in the early years. I always regret that I never really forgave him.' Her eyes glistened with tears. 'So, if you can find it in your heart to forgive Joe, you should.' I nodded, unable to speak. 'Of course, adultery is a mortal sin so if he doesn't get to confession quick smart he'll burn with the hounds of hell for all eternity.' She looked dead pleased with herself.

PPS Feel quite misty-eyed and emotional. Am so touched Mrs H has taken my side. Of course, she doesn't know about Lone Father and the sex-texting thing. Will keep that quiet for a while or the scone home-delivery service may grind to a halt.

12 June

Said tearful goodbyes to all the playschool mums today.

'Do you think it's wise to pull Katie from school so early?' Eco-mother inquired. 'Term doesn't end for another two weeks.'

'It's only playschool,' I said loftily, hoping she'd spontaneously combust any second. 'I don't think it'll do her any lasting damage.'

'Yes, but she *has* missed rather a lot of days already, hasn't she?' Eco-mother eyed me civilly. 'But I'm sure you'll do lots of intensive one-to-one over the summer to make up for it.'

Drove away in a rage, revving the engine on purpose so she'd choke on the toxic fumes. Hopefully she'll decide to home-school Zoe next year and I'll never have to clap eyes on her or her hairy ankles again.

Arrived at Mum and Dad's, exhausted after three hours of playing I Spy with Jack and Katie on the journey down. Was appalled to see dozens of huge brown boxes scattered all over the front lawn. A few bored-looking removal men were milling about, and Dad was directing the packing with a clipboard in one hand and a walkie-talkie in the other. 'Hello, darling!' he roared, as I pulled up. 'Another pair of hands to lighten the load – fantastic!'

Scowled at him and his boorish, insensitive ways. I'm in the middle of a traumatic marriage breakdown, but it's all he can do to stop himself dancing an Irish jig in the garden with delight at the prospect of moving to a warm climate a million miles away. Would serve him right if the development in Portugal isn't finished. In fact, I hope it takes years to complete and he's forced to hobble through a building site on a walking frame, trying to avoid cement-mixers, and builders with their bums hanging out.

Found Mum surrounded by old photographs in the living room.

'Who's that?' Katie asked, snatching a wedding photo of Joe and me from her hands.

'That's your mum and dad, of course,' she answered, giving me a smile of solidarity. 'Doesn't Mummy look beautiful?'

'Yeah . . .' Katie breathed. 'You look even better than Becky, Mum,' she said, in astonishment.

Had to leave the room before I started wailing, gnashing my teeth and pulling my hair out.

Dad insisted on having a last family BBQ before moving day.

Gathered mournfully round the stump of the oak tree (which has become the actual BBQ – was too weary to protest) and tried to force the kids to eat inedible organic sausages.

'I want *real* sausages,' Katie sulked.

'Sausages, sausages!' Jack roared.

'Now, children, you have to be on your best behaviour,' Mum intervened. 'The new owner is coming to view the house in a few minutes so I want happy, smiling faces.'

Kicked the ground in disgust. 'I thought the new owner lives overseas?' I said, furious that the last family meal in my childhood home would be ruined by the unexpected arrival of a greedy property tycoon, who would probably level the house and build an ugly (but highly profitable) apartment block in its place.

Suddenly Katie leaped to her feet and screamed hysterically. Had half agreed with her about the organic sausages, but did feel she was being slightly over-dramatic now. Was trying to summon up the energy to have serious words with her, when she roared, 'DADDY!'

Turned to see Joe walking carefully up the drive, stepping gingerly over the enormous brown boxes on the way.

6.00 p.m. Am in serious state of shock. Have discovered in last few hours that

(a) Joe is the mystery property investor/devoted family man.

(b) He has bought Mum and Dad's house as a holiday home/country retreat for us.

(c) He never had an affair with Becky/Barbie slut.

'But she was in your room!' I shouted, once Mum and Dad had dragged Katie and Jack off to seal the boxes with a jumbo roll of tape.

'Yes, Becky was in my room,' Joe agreed (somewhat surprisingly, I thought). 'And she *was* having an affair. But not with me – with Maurice. They asked if they could use my room because it was the only one with a Jacuzzi. Tacky, I know.' He loosened his tie and smiled wearily.

I suddenly thought how sexy and dishevelled he looked. 'Maurice? Your boss Maurice?' Felt a bit faint.

'That's right.'

'But why didn't you come after me?' I squeaked. 'I was in the hotel for three full days.' It was dawning on me slowly that I might have been badly mistaken about Joe and his alleged adultery.

'Becky and Maurice didn't surface from their room in all that time,' he said. 'I had no idea you'd been there and by the time I found out you were long gone. And I kept phoning but you wouldn't answer my calls, so I decided to fly back and talk to you properly.' He was looking at me in a very intense and erotic way. 'I have to know, Susie, is there someone else?'

Felt my heart stop in my chest as I looked into his troubled eyes and knew I would have to tell the truth.

Not an *OK!* version or a *Heat* version, but the real, unvarnished, honest-to-goodness truth, warts and all.

15 June

Am so happy I could burst. Joe has forgiven me for whole sex-texting/adultery débâcle. Added bonus is that he is accepting full blame for everything and does not seem to want to inflict any serious injury on Lone Father.

Once the shock of seeing him had abated, we spent hours having an excellent heart-to-heart and resolving many deep-rooted issues at the core of our marital difficulties. It turns out that many nights alone in an LA hotel room, with only the Living Channel for company, has matured him immeasurably – he is now a true devotee of emotional mapping.

Once I explained that my flirtation with infidelity was a direct consequence of his disregard for my emotional welfare, we were able to establish a true and deep connection, just as we had when we were teenagers and couldn't keep our hands off each other. Can no longer remember why I found Lone Father even remotely attractive.

'But how did you know Mum and Dad were selling the house?' I asked, wondering if he had spent nights watching the Psychic Channel as well.

'When you confided in Louise, she emailed me and explained the situation,' he confessed, 'so then I called your mum and dad and squared it all away with them.'

(Have made mental note to treat Louise to slap-up

meal once she stops puking. Have also made mental note to have serious words with Mum and Dad about their deception ASAP.)

'I'm sorry for neglecting you, Susie,' he whispered later, stroking my face tenderly as we curled together happily in my old single bed, kissing under my Bon Jovi duvet. (Full-blown making-up bonk out of question as Katie and Jack were snoring happily in sleeping bags beside us.) 'I put work first, above you and the children. Is it any wonder you became so friendly with that Paul guy?'

'It's OK,' I said, remembering why I love him so much, even if he does trim his nose hair in front of me. 'We both let things slide. Let's really make an effort to connect with each other from now on.'

Am overwhelmed by the sheer romance of it all. Am also overwhelmed by revelation that Joe has made a lot of money by pulling off a great deal in LA – which means we are now the proud owners of a second home in the country. With two en-suites and manicured gardens (except for butchered oak).

Will now spend school holidays and every weekend lounging in said country residence, pottering in the garden, baking homemade bread and sipping iced lemonade. Mum says the garden can be quite a lot of work but think she may be transferring her anxiety about relocating to Portugal on to me. Will invest in quaint wicker basket and Cath Kidson gardening gloves ASAP.

PS Joe has promised not to tell his mother about the whole sex-texting thing. Am very relieved as suspect she would excommunicate me from the family in the flash of a J-cloth.

PPS Do feel teeniest bit guilty about Joe blaming himself for everything but am trying to push it to the back of my mind.

16 June

Must be careful not to take new-found delirious state of happiness for granted. May renew our vows in Holly-wood-type extravaganza ASAP. At the very least, will book expensive, romantic weekend away to reconnect with Joe and cement our commitment. Joe is a bit vague about dates (some minor hiccup with the LA deal apparently) but has promised to pencil me in soon. Bless him. In the meantime, have composed the following guidelines for success:

Resolutions to Build a Stronger Marriage and Create a
Deliriously Happy Family who Treat Each Other
with Respect and Never Raise their Voices (unless in
an extreme emotional emergency)

• Will never take spouse for granted ever again. Even if he teaches children to belch their alphabet and chops onions on the bread board.

• Will never again be sucked into inappropriate relationship with another man, even if he has Hugh Grant eyes. In fact, even if he *is* Hugh Grant.

• Will cherish my children every day – even if they leave the tap running, the fridge door open and torture the dog on a regular basis.

- Will devote more time to developing inner spiritual self so will no longer have to rely on others' approval to fulfil my happiness.

- Will be Contented Wife and Mother in no time.

One week later

Met Lone Father in Tesco today. In surprising soul-baring session in the middle of aisle three, he informed me that

(a) He has left wife Arabella and moved in with Marita and her acrylic nails.

(b) Marita is now officially his muse (do not know what that entails exactly, but suspect it may involve a polyester leotard and a vulgar yoga position).

(c) He is working on a fabulous new book based on the sordid secret life of a thirtysomething housewife (sounds outlandish and positively unmarketable).

'My agent thinks it's going to be *huge*.' He smirked, as I wondered what I had ever seen in him and his freakishly blue eyes.

Luckily, before I had to answer, Jack scaled a promotional stack of Dreft and caused a mini security alert so was able to make hasty escape.

Called Louise to inform her that am completely over Lone Father and had been seriously demented ever to be remotely attracted to him in the first place.

'That's great, Susie,' she said, sounding bored. 'Did you know that my foetus is the size of a small orange now? Do you think it's too early to enrol him at Gonzaga?'

Hope Louise is not going to be one of those intense mothers who obsess about their children all the time. There really is nothing worse.

Acknowledgements

Warmest thanks to my editor Patricia Deevy, Michael McLoughlin, Cliona Lewis, Brian Walker, Patricia McVeigh and everyone else at Penguin Ireland. Sincere thanks also to Tom Weldon, Naomi Wheeler and the sales team, Sophie Mitchell, Hazel Orme, Ann Cooke and all at Penguin UK.

A big thank you to my agent Simon Trewin, Claire Gill and all at PFD.

Very special thanks to Mam and Dad for all your love, support and encouragement from the very start. This one's for you!

Huge thanks to Martina and Eoghan for the endless advice, laughter and long, long phone calls!

Big thanks to all my great friends for their enthusiasm.

Finally, thank you to Caoimhe and Rory for lighting up my life and bringing me enormous joy every day, and to Oliver for cheering me on every step of the way and for always believing in me – I couldn't have done it without you.